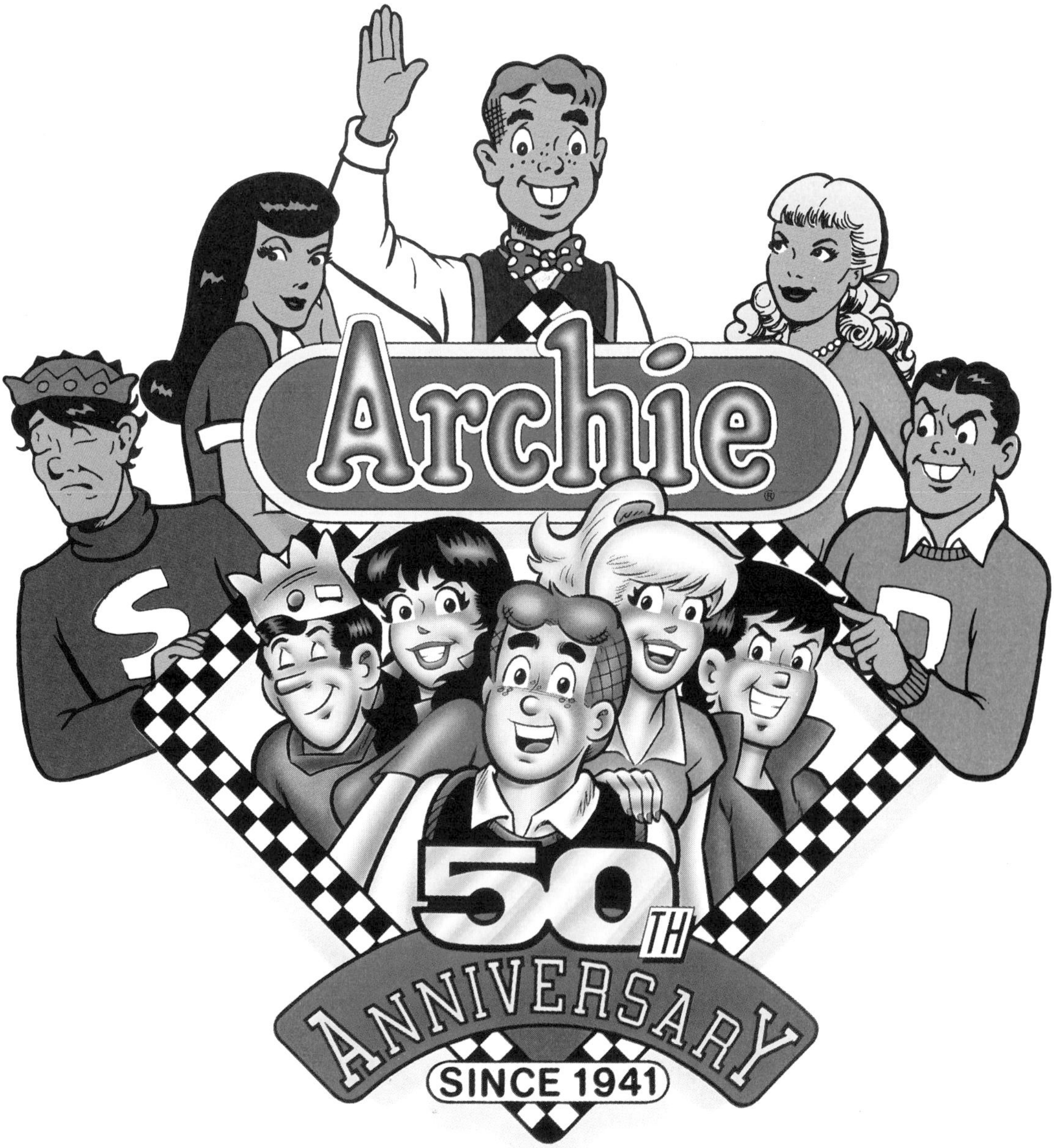
Archie
50TH
ANNIVERSARY
SINCE 1941

ARCHIE COMIC PUBLICATIONS, INC.

MICHAEL I. SILBERKLEIT
Chairman and Co-Publisher

RICHARD H. GOLDWATER
President and Co-Publisher

VICTOR GORELICK
Vice President /Managing Editor

FRED MAUSSER
Vice President /Director of Circulation

Archie characters created by
JOHN L. GOLDWATER

The likeness of the original
Archie characters were created by
BOB MONTANA

Americana Series Editor: **SCOTT D. FULOP**

Editorial Assistant: **PAUL CASTIGLIA**

Americana Series Art Director: **JOSEPH PEPITONE**

Front Cover Illustration: **REX W. LINDSEY**

Back Cover Illustration: **DAN PARENT**

Inside Cover Photography: **STEPHEN CIUCCOLI**

www.archiecomics.com

Archie

AMERICANA SERIES

BEST OF THE FORTIES

TABLE OF CONTENTS

THE IMPORTANCE OF BEING ARCHIE
BY STEPHEN KING

FOREWORDS, even when they're as short as this one, rarely touch the reader's heart unless the writer sends them out from that same location. That gives me at least a fighting chance, because I've spent a lot of hours in the company of Archie Andrews, Riverdale's premiere teenager, and I still count him one of my good fictional friends.

Literature—and even the comics are literature of a sort, I think—is meant to be pleasant and enjoyable, but I think it's also supposed to be useful, and Archie fulfilled a small but vital function in my life. In those painful, nerdy pre-teen years between eight and twelve, he and his friends (along with Dobie Gillis and **his** friends on the magic box), taught me how to live The Good Life as a teenager…if, that was, you were a fairly ordinary kid from small-town America. Well, I **was** a fairly ordinary kid from small-town America, so I took each lesson to heart.

I had a lot of fun along the way, and I also learned some useful lessons. Archie's adventures were amusing, but they were also unfailingly moral. I learned about the consequences of greed from Jughead, the consequences of being a gotta-win know-it-all from Reggie, and the **dire** consequences of having one too many girlfriends from Archie himself. I also learned one lesson which every high school-bound kid should know by heart: if you're acquainted with a kid as big as Moose, never-never-**never** try to make time with his girl.

And Archie took me **away**, both then and later, and that was sometimes a trip I badly needed to take. Adolescence isn't always the happiest time of life, a fact anyone who's ever been one knows very well. Raging hormones put a teenager's emotions on a roller coaster and sometimes turn his/her face into a war-zone. Relationships with parents are often strained and sometimes acrimonious. Old buddies change; new boyfriends and girlfriends leave, sometimes with little or no warning. All the same old tigers—everything from booze to that miserable adolescent fear of rejection —still prowl the high-school jungles, and a few new ones, like AIDS and drugs, have been added.

Against a background like that, Archie's world and Archie's friends look better than ever, and is there anything wrong with that? I think not. Riverdale was never an **escape** from reality for me, but it **was** a great place where I took many welcome **vacations** from reality. It was a place where the life of a teenager became simultaneously sunny and funny, a place where the misunderstandings were always amusing and everyone always ended up friends.

Archie's Pals and Gals were **my** pals and gals, and his standard attitude— "Well, I messed up again, but I know things will turn out okay because fate is kind"—became my attitude. There are worse ones to have during the storms of adolescence, believe me. And, as a slightly overweight high school freshman who was always puffing before the phys ed calisthenics were even half over, Jughead Jones was a beacon of hope. If **he** could eat that much and stay thin, I figured, maybe someday so could I (that day never came, alas).

And, of course, I fell in love with one of the two females in Archie's life; do you know any guy who didn't? I have a theory that a good psychiatrist could probably write a valid masculine psychological profile based on the answer to a single question: **Which one really did it for you— Veronica or Betty**? For me it was Betty. I couldn't believe—just could not **believe**—that Archie could go on ignoring her in favor of that spoiled little rich girl, Veronica. Betty was a **blonde**! And that figure! Va-va-**VOOM**!

The truth is that I had a serious crush on Betty, and while that was at least thirty years ago and I have been married for twenty of those intervening years, my guess is I'd still be mightily attracted if she came walking back into my life and wiggled her pretty little fingers…boy, I'd teach that Archie Andrews a thing or two…

Well, it's a sweet dream, but that's all it is; I'm forty-three now, not thirteen, but Betty hasn't aged a day. She wouldn't want anything to do with a dirty old man like me. But that brings me to the biggest attraction of Archie, his friends, the idyllic town of Riverdale, and Riverdale High, every kid's dream school. **None** of them have aged a day; they have drunk at the fountain of youth (or maybe there's something **really** special in those ice cream sodas Pop's always making them) and are enjoying a wonderful, happy immortality the rest of us can only envy…and enjoy.

So take it away, Archie; I think it's time you jumped into your jalopy and headed out. You've got a date (unfortunately for you, both Betty and Veronica think it's with **her**), and you're running behind schedule. Just say hi to Moose, Midge, Reggie, and all the rest for me, would you? Oh, and by the way—if you see Jughead, ask him where he got that hat. I've always sort of wanted one.

Stephen King is one of America's most popular writers, and his novels are worldwide best-sellers. Movie adaptations of his stories have entertained young and old alike for years.

ARCHIE ~~WAS~~ IS HERE

BY SCOTT D. FULOP

1941-

It was a time when you could buy a "glass" bottle of Coca-Cola for a nickel, President Franklin D. Roosevelt was in the White House, the world was at war. Humphrey Bogart and Clark Gable were on the big screen. A new form of entertainment, comic books, provided a medium for super-heroes to battle the Axis powers. As 1941 drew to a close, comic readers were about to receive a powerful "how do you do" from a certain freckle-faced, red-headed kid.

Comic books first appeared in the 1930s as reprint compilations of newspaper comic strips. It didn't take long before the early publishers of comic books realized that if reprints of newspaper strips were popular, comic books containing all **new** stories and characters would be more popular. During the late '30s and into the '40s comic books flourished in what was to be known later as the industry's "Golden Age". "Golden Age" comic books offered many awesome creations to a fantasy thirsty public. Many of these creations were of the super-hero genre since America sorely needed larger-than-life champions as freedom inspiring symbols to help combat Adolf Hitler's Third Reich menace. Many comic book titles proudly displayed numerous heroes thoroughly trouncing (much to the applause of the reader) the Axis forces. However, during these problematic times, Americans needed to laugh too, and new humorous titles appeared mostly dealing with funny animals.

In 1939, a new comic book publishing company was formed—a company that would later be the birthplace of a unique comic character that would last for more than 50 years. This new comic book publishing company, founded in November, 1939, was called **MLJ Magazines** (named after its three partners and founders—Maurice Coyne, Louis Silberkleit and John Goldwater). Their first title was **Blue Ribbon Comics.** One month later, they introduced their second title, **Top-Notch Comics.** In January, 1940, they launched their third publication, **Pep Comics,** and continued introducing a variety of adventure magazines throughout the rest of that year and beyond. MLJ's comics contained its own colorful battalion of costumed mystery-men within their adventure-based titles. To this day, Pep Comics #1 still stands out in the minds of most comic book aficionados as it introduced the industry's first "patriotic" super-hero, a super-hero whose costume depicts the colors and design of the American flag. This character was called the **Shield.** What better American character than a "G-man" who dons a flag costume to fight the Axis powers?

While MLJ continued to publish adventure comics to compete with the likes of Superman, masked marvels and glorified G-men, its founders soon realized that in order to continue to entertain the younger reader, and in particular the female reader, they needed to pursue a new avenue of expression. What the comic reader was missing was a taste of reality—a reality that demonstrated the ofttimes funny side of everyday life. If there was a Superman, why not an "everyman"? An "everyman" that readers young and old could relate to.

John L. Goldwater, co-publisher of MLJ, was inspired by the popular Andy Hardy movies of that era which starred a young Mickey Rooney. Goldwater was determined to develop an "everyman", a "normal man" the reader could identify with. John related his ideas to his partner and co-publisher, Louis Silberkleit, who managed the circulation, printing and other business aspects of MLJ. He and Maurice Coyne, the third partner of MLJ, gave Goldwater an overwhelming seal of approval and encouraged him to bring his concept to fruition.

In December, 1941, MLJ Magazines, utilizing the talents of writer Vic Bloom and artist Bob Montana, published a small, untitled six-page story. Sandwiched in the middle of the hero-laden pages of Pep Comics #22, this story introduced "America's newest boyfriend." Christened "Archibald Andrews" and requesting that you call him "Chick," Archie, his girl-hating, unusually named friend, "Jughead," and the new "girl next door," Betty Cooper, embarked upon a series of adventures that marked the dawn of an American institution. Shortly, following his inception in Pep Comics, Archie was also introduced as a regular, supporting feature in MLJ's **Jackpot Comics** #4. Soon after, new "Archie" characters were introduced in both Pep and Jackpot, including rich and gorgeous "sub-debutante" Veronica Lodge, archrival Reggie Mantle, and a whole host of characters and locations that provided the backdrop for Archie's antics. The combination of these characters' unique and varied personalities, their classic relationships to one another, their teachers and their parents and the locales they frequented lead to the world of **Riverdale**, USA.

In the winter of 1942, **Archie Comics** #1 was released and was the first MLJ title primarily dedicated to the adventures of America's "typical teenager," "The Mirth of a Nation," Archie. As Archie's visibility grew, so did his popularity. Readers were demanding to see more and more of the redheaded youth's exploits and MLJ was ready to satisfy those demands. The company started by increasing Archie's presence in Pep Comics. Pep #36, 1943, proudly displayed Archie's first Pep **cover appearance** along with the title's starring characters the **Shield**, and the **Hangman** (up until that issue there was no artwork or mention of Archie on any Pep cover). Pep Comics #49, 1944, unveiled the next increase in Archie's status as MLJ decided to give him the lead story position within the magazine. Pep Comics #51, 1944, showed Archie and his friends completely dominating the cover (no super-heroes)—a change that was reflected on every Pep Cover thereafter. MLJ and their new "wonder boy" were moving ahead at top speed.

In May, 1946, the company adopted the name of its flagship character and the letters MLJ gave way to the newly christened Archie Comic Publications. The new name coincided with a modification of the company's editorial direction which then concentrated primarily on the adventures of Archie and his buddies and less on superhero tales.

Following suit, in the Fall of 1946, Archie Comic Publications released **Laugh Comics**, the second title specifically created to feature Archie and other humorous characters. Finally, the publishers released one more Archie dominated title before the decade was over—**Archie's Pal Jughead.**

As the '40s yielded to the '50s, Archie and his pals continued to appeal to the young reader. Archie Andrews and the kids from Riverdale flourished into America's, and indeed the world's, most popular teenage humor comic book characters. In part, Archie's popularity and uniqueness stems from the fact that although the times changed, Archie changed with them. Archie and his peers have always remained contemporary to the times in which their stories were published, always sporting the latest fashions, verbalizing with the most current teenage slang, and participating in the trendiest pastimes. And although Archie did indeed change, his hilarious misadventures always contained the essence of the original concept—the situations and problems he and his pals faced were those that the reader could identify with, those adversities of adolescence that Archie had to meet and conquer. Those eternal high school juniors always lived up to their names—they were and still are "America's typical teenagers."

Fifty years after their inception, the perennial love triangle between Archie, Veronica, and Betty still exists, the meaning of the "S" on Jughead's shirt still remains a secret, and Archie is still running afoul of Mr. Lodge, much to the heart-warming delight of a new generation of grateful readers and their parents, and **their** parents. The current Archie management are the sons and grandchildren of original publishers Louis Silberkleit and John Goldwater. They continue to move forward with this American institution. Archie is the third-largest comic book company in the country. Archie Comic Publications publishes over 40 different titles each year which translates into sales of 16 million copies annually. Archie Comics are distributed worldwide in the English language and are also printed in 7 other languages, in 7 different countries. Archie is the largest selling English language comic in the country of India. Archie merchandise, everything from dolls to watches, to T-shirts, to games, grace the shelves of stores every-where. A radio show running from the '40s through the '50s, numerous live-action and highly-rated animated television productions from the '60s to the present, a studio band with two Gold Records (is there anyone out there who doesn't remember "Sugar, Sugar" and "Jingle, Jangle"?), and a nationally syndicated newspaper strip running continuously for the past 40 years are just some of the reasons why Archie remains a household name.

All of this brings us to the volume you now hold in your hands—the **Archie Americana Series, Best of the Forties.** Contained in this volume is a most comprehensive compilation of 1940's Archie comic book stories. Most of these stories have not seen publication in almost half a century. We have taken steps to bring you the very best stories from the first decade of Archie's "life." Each story has been carefully selected to give you a true meaning, and a true understanding of what the wonder of Archie Comics is all about.

First and foremost, the selected stories reveal the origins and first appearances of the major characters from Riverdale. It is interesting to note that while doing research on these first appearances, we witnessed (as will you upon reading the stories in this volume) the evolution of all the Archie characters. For example, in the second story in this volume Archie meets up with an unnamed man who turns out to be Riverdale High's new principal. Could this be the famous Mr. Weatherbee? The fact that he is indeed unnamed, and bears no resemblance to his "descendant" (although bald, he seems to be missing about 200 lbs!) undoubtedly illustrates the fact that he was an early Weatherbee prototype, used until a more well defined character was created. Another case in point was found in the fourth story in this edition. You will notice that a mischievous character called "Scotty" bares a striking resemblance to (as we know him today) Archie's nemesis, Reggie Mantle. When Reggie himself formally appears in a later story in this volume, he bares little resemblance to his modern day counterpart. Also of interest is the fact that two stories, one from Pep Comics #26 and the other from Archie Comics #1 (both included in this volume), showcase the first appearance of Veronica in Riverdale—and **contradict** each other. It is clear to everyone at

Archic Comics, and it will be clear to you, that in the early '40s, the formative years of Archie, the writers, artists, and editors manipulated various characterizations, artistic designs, and story concepts before finalizing on the version that we know of Archie Comics today.

In any event, we have taken pains to deliver the definitive first appearances of the Archie cast. When we say "first appearance" in our table of contents, we refer to the story that we accept as the first time the characters appeared by proper name, in the role they have clearly been identified with—the role that enables them to take their proper place in the Archie scheme of things. Other stories included with characters that bare some resemblance or similarity to their well known counterparts have been included not to confuse, but because they have some extreme merit such as the first appearance of Archie's Jalopy in Pep #25 along with Mr. Weatherbee's "skinny" predecessor.

Also included in this book are stories which show the magic of Archie's fabled hometown. For it is not only the characters themselves that make a story unique, but their surroundings, the world they live in and their frame of reference that set the tone and pace for the entertainment that will unfold. Finally, no retrospective publication would be complete without those stories that reflect the times in which they were published—stories that reflect culturally and historically significant values, trends, and fads of a bygone era.

Now, its time to enjoy these nostalgic and classic tales of yesteryear. Thrill to the adventures of John Goldwater's creations as they **originally** appeared when their antics were written and drawn by the likes of Bob Montana, Vic Bloom, Harry Shorten, Harry Sahle, Bill Vigoda, Ed Goggin, Ginger, Ray Gill, and more. Journey down the road to a small town that holds special memories and transform yourself into a spectator of a legendary time. Pull up a chair, put up your feet, and fix your lamp—your journey back to Riverdale, 1941, is about to begin.

Scott D. Fulop is the Editorial Director of New Product Development for Archie Comics.

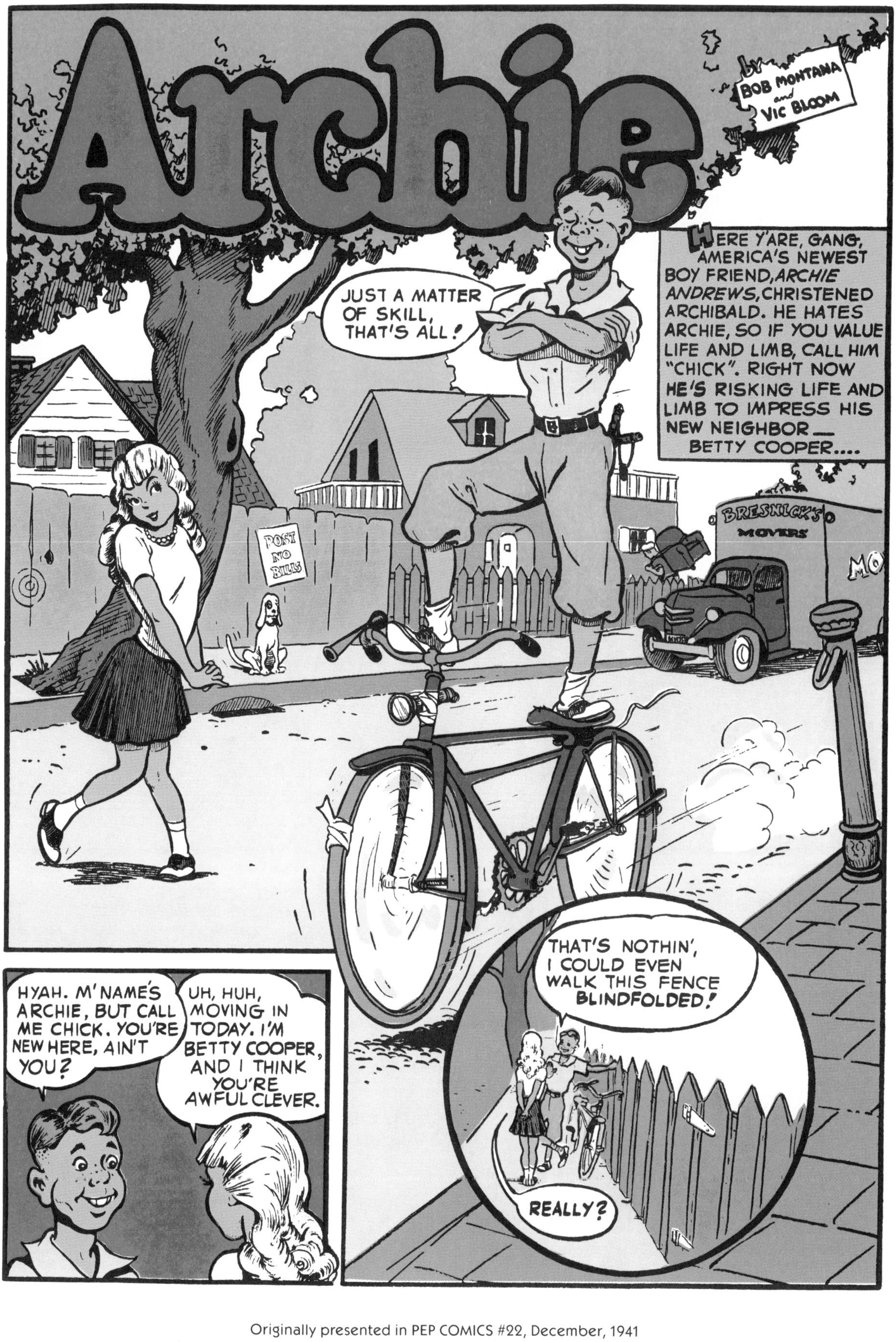
Archie
by BOB MONTANA and VIC BLOOM
HERE Y'ARE, GANG, AMERICA'S NEWEST BOY FRIEND, ARCHIE ANDREWS, CHRISTENED ARCHIBALD. HE HATES ARCHIE, SO IF YOU VALUE LIFE AND LIMB, CALL HIM "CHICK". RIGHT NOW HE'S RISKING LIFE AND LIMB TO IMPRESS HIS NEW NEIGHBOR — BETTY COOPER....
JUST A MATTER OF SKILL, THAT'S ALL!
POST NO BILLS
BRESNICK'S MOVERS
HYAH. M'NAME'S ARCHIE, BUT CALL ME CHICK. YOU'RE NEW HERE, AIN'T YOU?
UH, HUH, MOVING IN TODAY. I'M BETTY COOPER, AND I THINK YOU'RE AWFUL CLEVER.
THAT'S NOTHIN', I COULD EVEN WALK THIS FENCE BLINDFOLDED!
REALLY?

Originally presented in PEP COMICS #22, December, 1941

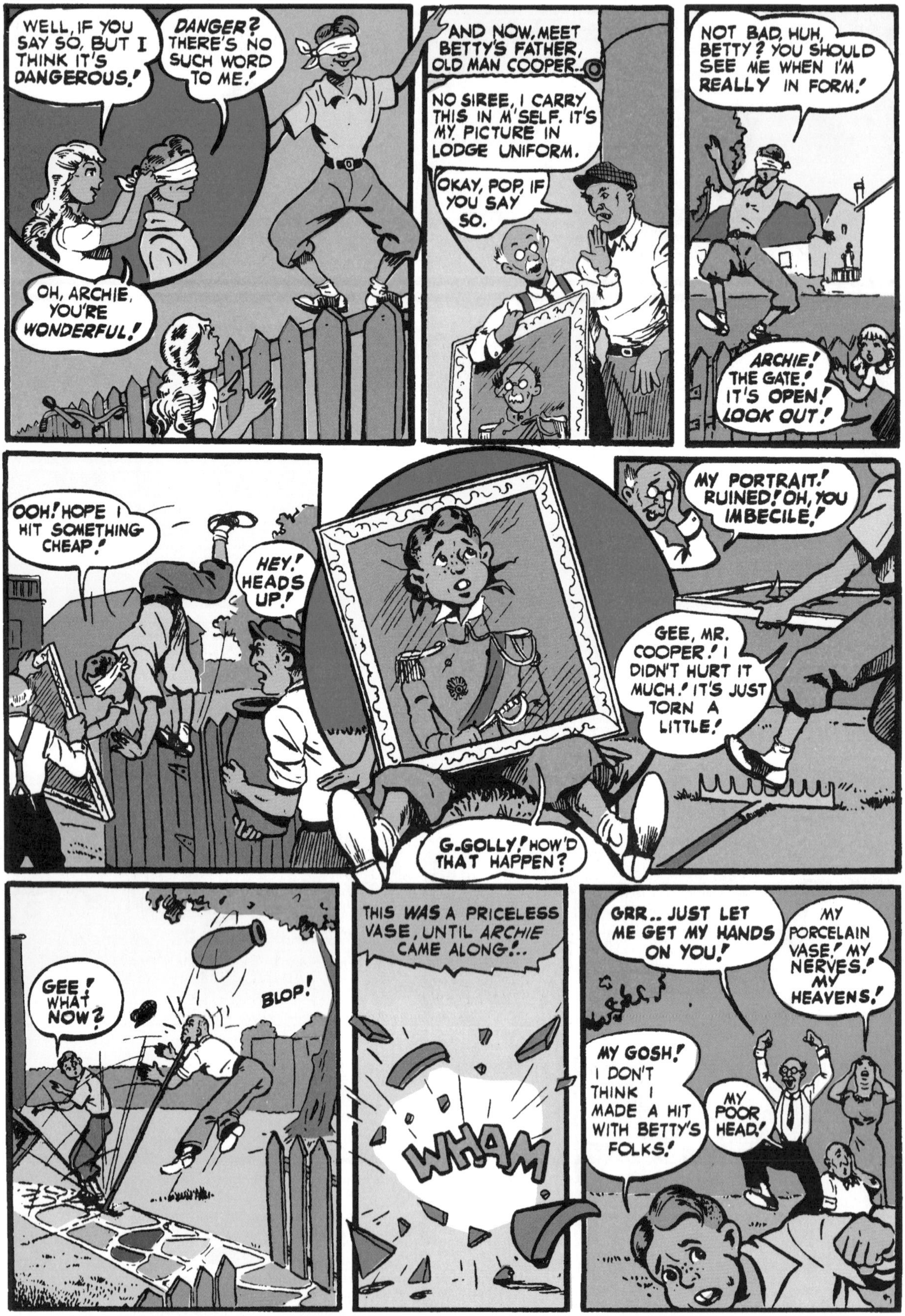
WELL, IF YOU SAY SO, BUT I THINK IT'S DANGEROUS!
DANGER? THERE'S NO SUCH WORD TO ME!
OH, ARCHIE, YOU'RE WONDERFUL!
AND NOW, MEET BETTY'S FATHER, OLD MAN COOPER..
NO SIREE, I CARRY THIS IN M'SELF. IT'S MY PICTURE IN LODGE UNIFORM.
OKAY, POP, IF YOU SAY SO.
NOT BAD, HUH, BETTY? YOU SHOULD SEE ME WHEN I'M REALLY IN FORM!
ARCHIE! THE GATE! IT'S OPEN! LOOK OUT!
OOH! HOPE I HIT SOMETHING CHEAP!
HEY! HEADS UP!
MY PORTRAIT! RUINED! OH, YOU IMBECILE!
GEE, MR. COOPER! I DIDN'T HURT IT MUCH! IT'S JUST TORN A LITTLE!
G-GOLLY! HOW'D THAT HAPPEN?
GEE! WHAT NOW?
BLOP!
THIS WAS A PRICELESS VASE, UNTIL ARCHIE CAME ALONG!..
WHAM
GRR.. JUST LET ME GET MY HANDS ON YOU!
MY PORCELAIN VASE! MY NERVES! MY HEAVENS!
MY GOSH! I DON'T THINK I MADE A HIT WITH BETTY'S FOLKS!
MY POOR HEAD!

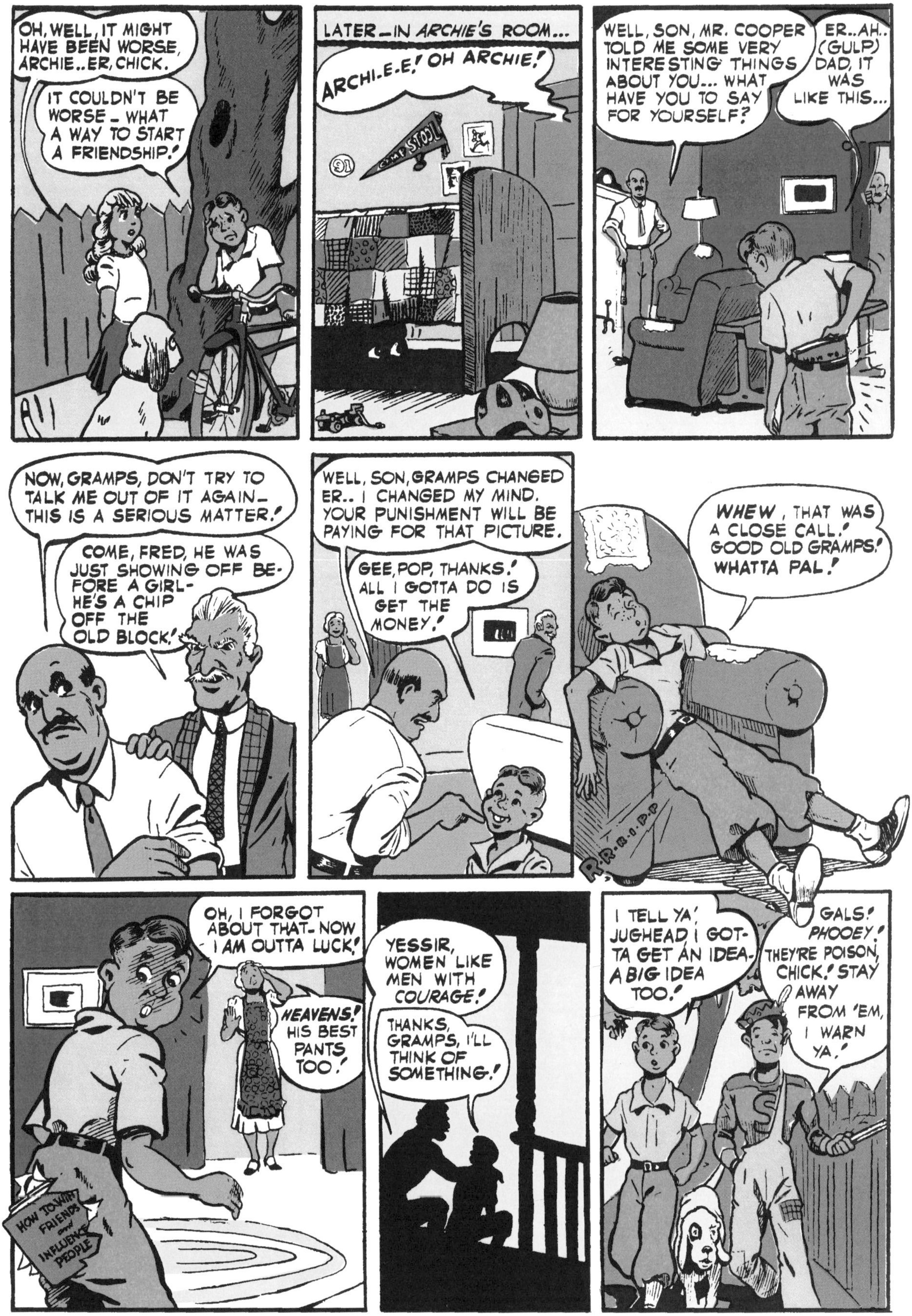
OH, WELL, IT MIGHT HAVE BEEN WORSE, ARCHIE..ER, CHICK.
IT COULDN'T BE WORSE - WHAT A WAY TO START A FRIENDSHIP!
LATER - IN ARCHIE'S ROOM...
ARCHI-E-E! OH ARCHIE!
WELL, SON, MR. COOPER TOLD ME SOME VERY INTERESTING THINGS ABOUT YOU... WHAT HAVE YOU TO SAY FOR YOURSELF?
ER..AH.. (GULP) DAD, IT WAS LIKE THIS...
NOW, GRAMPS, DON'T TRY TO TALK ME OUT OF IT AGAIN - THIS IS A SERIOUS MATTER!
COME, FRED, HE WAS JUST SHOWING OFF BEFORE A GIRL - HE'S A CHIP OFF THE OLD BLOCK!
WELL, SON, GRAMPS CHANGED ER.. I CHANGED MY MIND. YOUR PUNISHMENT WILL BE PAYING FOR THAT PICTURE.
GEE, POP, THANKS! ALL I GOTTA DO IS GET THE MONEY!
WHEW, THAT WAS A CLOSE CALL! GOOD OLD GRAMPS! WHATTA PAL!
R-R-R-I-P-P
OH, I FORGOT ABOUT THAT - NOW I AM OUTTA LUCK!
HEAVENS! HIS BEST PANTS TOO!
HOW TO WIN FRIENDS and INFLUENCE PEOPLE
YESSIR, WOMEN LIKE MEN WITH COURAGE!
THANKS, GRAMPS, I'LL THINK OF SOMETHING!
I TELL YA', JUGHEAD I GOTTA GET AN IDEA - A BIG IDEA TOO!
GALS! PHOOEY! THEY'RE POISON, CHICK! STAY AWAY FROM 'EM, I WARN YA'!

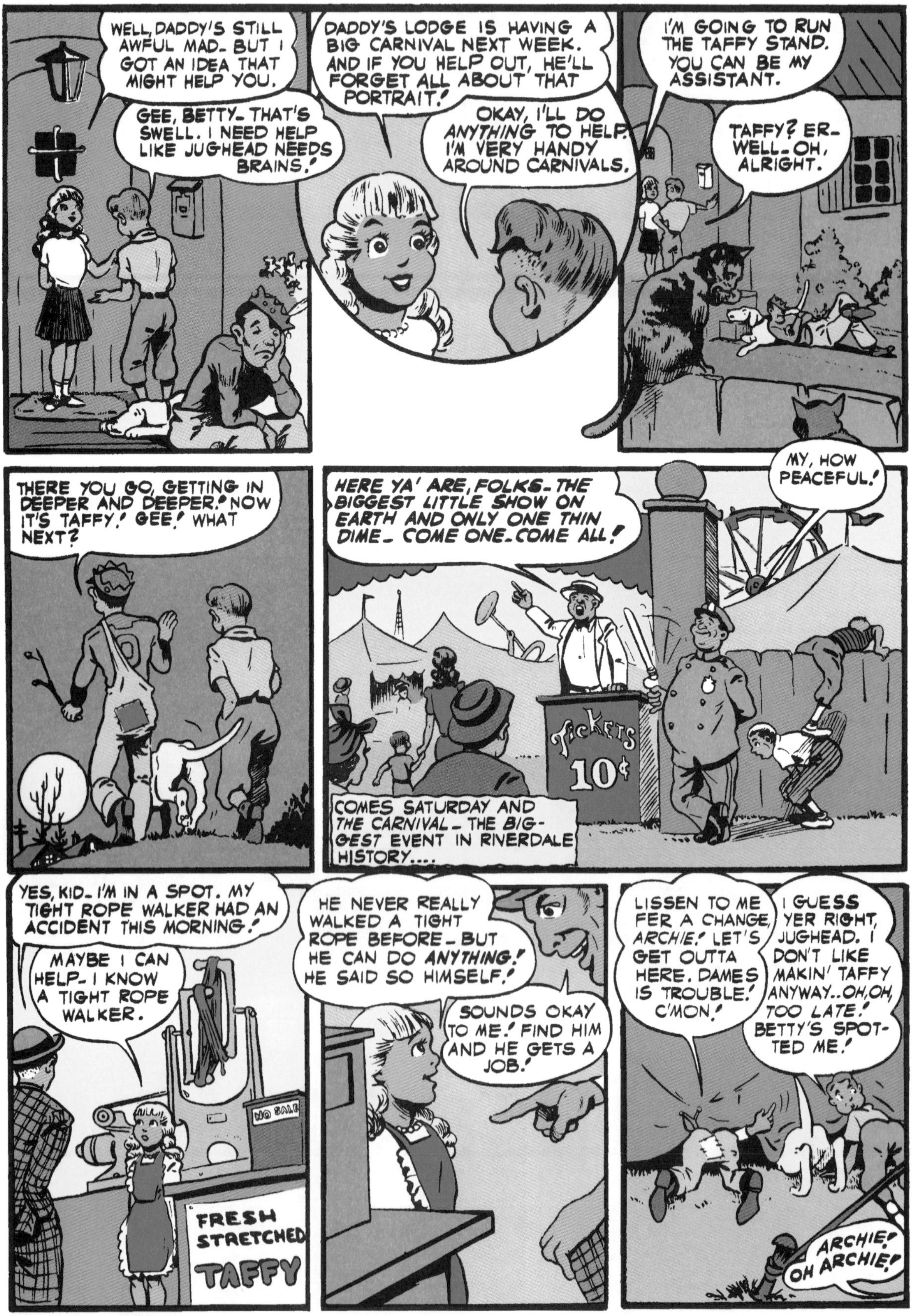
WELL, DADDY'S STILL AWFUL MAD- BUT I GOT AN IDEA THAT MIGHT HELP YOU.
GEE, BETTY- THAT'S SWELL. I NEED HELP LIKE JUGHEAD NEEDS BRAINS!
DADDY'S LODGE IS HAVING A BIG CARNIVAL NEXT WEEK. AND IF YOU HELP OUT, HE'LL FORGET ALL ABOUT THAT PORTRAIT!
OKAY, I'LL DO ANYTHING TO HELP. I'M VERY HANDY AROUND CARNIVALS.
I'M GOING TO RUN THE TAFFY STAND. YOU CAN BE MY ASSISTANT.
TAFFY? ER- WELL- OH, ALRIGHT.
THERE YOU GO, GETTING IN DEEPER AND DEEPER! NOW IT'S TAFFY! GEE! WHAT NEXT?
HERE YA' ARE, FOLKS- THE BIGGEST LITTLE SHOW ON EARTH AND ONLY ONE THIN DIME- COME ONE- COME ALL!
MY, HOW PEACEFUL!
TICKETS 10¢
COMES SATURDAY AND THE CARNIVAL- THE BIGGEST EVENT IN RIVERDALE HISTORY....
YES, KID- I'M IN A SPOT. MY TIGHT ROPE WALKER HAD AN ACCIDENT THIS MORNING!
MAYBE I CAN HELP- I KNOW A TIGHT ROPE WALKER.
NO SALE
FRESH STRETCHED TAFFY
HE NEVER REALLY WALKED A TIGHT ROPE BEFORE- BUT HE CAN DO ANYTHING! HE SAID SO HIMSELF!
SOUNDS OKAY TO ME! FIND HIM AND HE GETS A JOB!
LISSEN TO ME FER A CHANGE, ARCHIE! LET'S GET OUTTA HERE. DAMES IS TROUBLE! C'MON!
I GUESS YER RIGHT, JUGHEAD. I DON'T LIKE MAKIN' TAFFY ANYWAY.. OH, OH, TOO LATE! BETTY'S SPOTTED ME!
ARCHIE! OH ARCHIE!

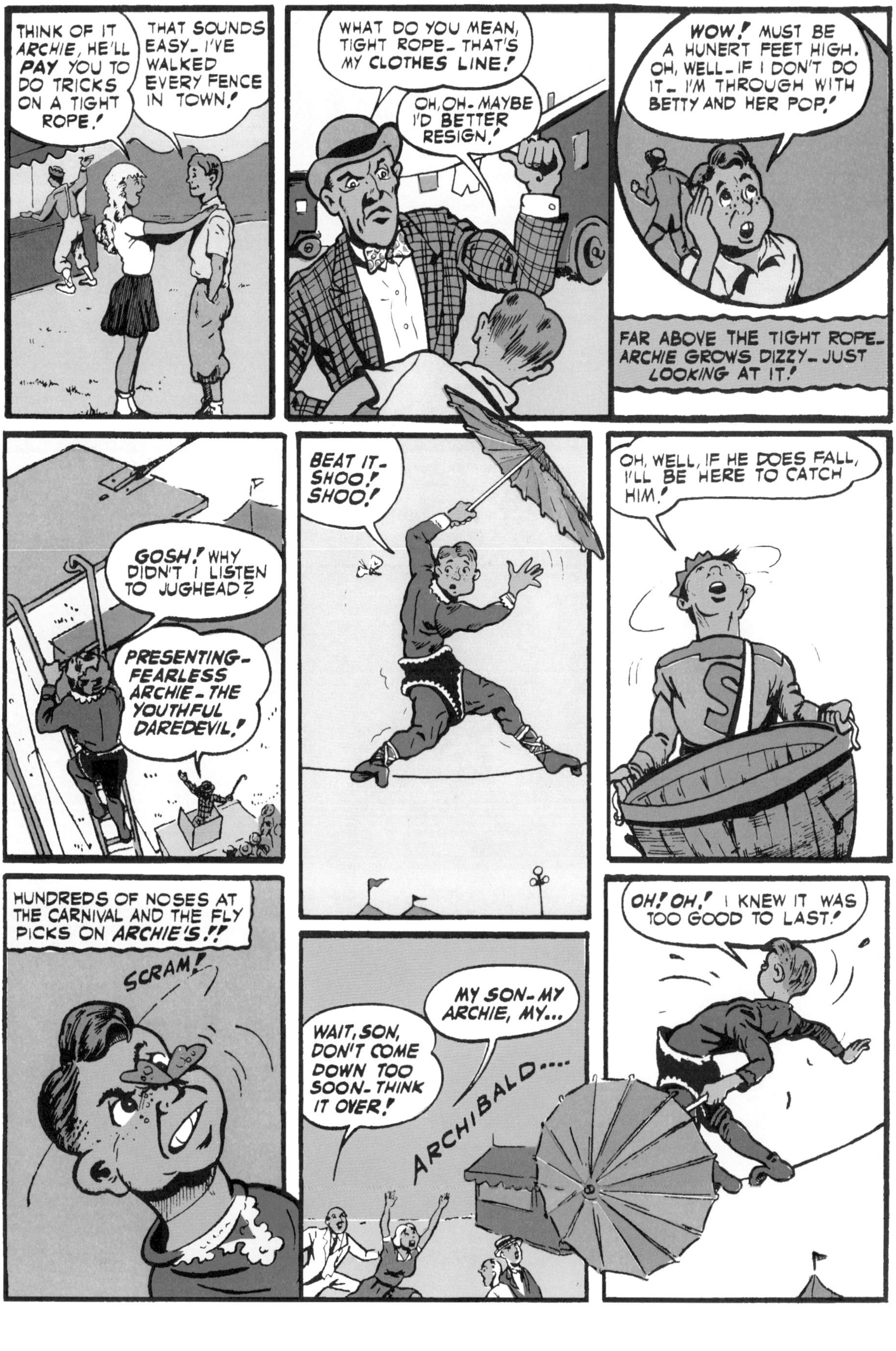
THINK OF IT ARCHIE, HE'LL PAY YOU TO DO TRICKS ON A TIGHT ROPE!
THAT SOUNDS EASY- I'VE WALKED EVERY FENCE IN TOWN!
WHAT DO YOU MEAN, TIGHT ROPE- THAT'S MY CLOTHES LINE!
OH, OH- MAYBE I'D BETTER RESIGN!
WOW! MUST BE A HUNERT FEET HIGH. OH, WELL- IF I DON'T DO IT- I'M THROUGH WITH BETTY AND HER POP!
FAR ABOVE THE TIGHT ROPE- ARCHIE GROWS DIZZY- JUST LOOKING AT IT!
GOSH! WHY DIDN'T I LISTEN TO JUGHEAD?
PRESENTING- FEARLESS ARCHIE- THE YOUTHFUL DAREDEVIL!
BEAT IT- SHOO! SHOO!
OH, WELL, IF HE DOES FALL, I'LL BE HERE TO CATCH HIM!
HUNDREDS OF NOSES AT THE CARNIVAL AND THE FLY PICKS ON ARCHIE'S!!
SCRAM!
MY SON- MY ARCHIE, MY...
WAIT, SON, DON'T COME DOWN TOO SOON- THINK IT OVER!
ARCHIBALD....
OH! OH! I KNEW IT WAS TOO GOOD TO LAST!

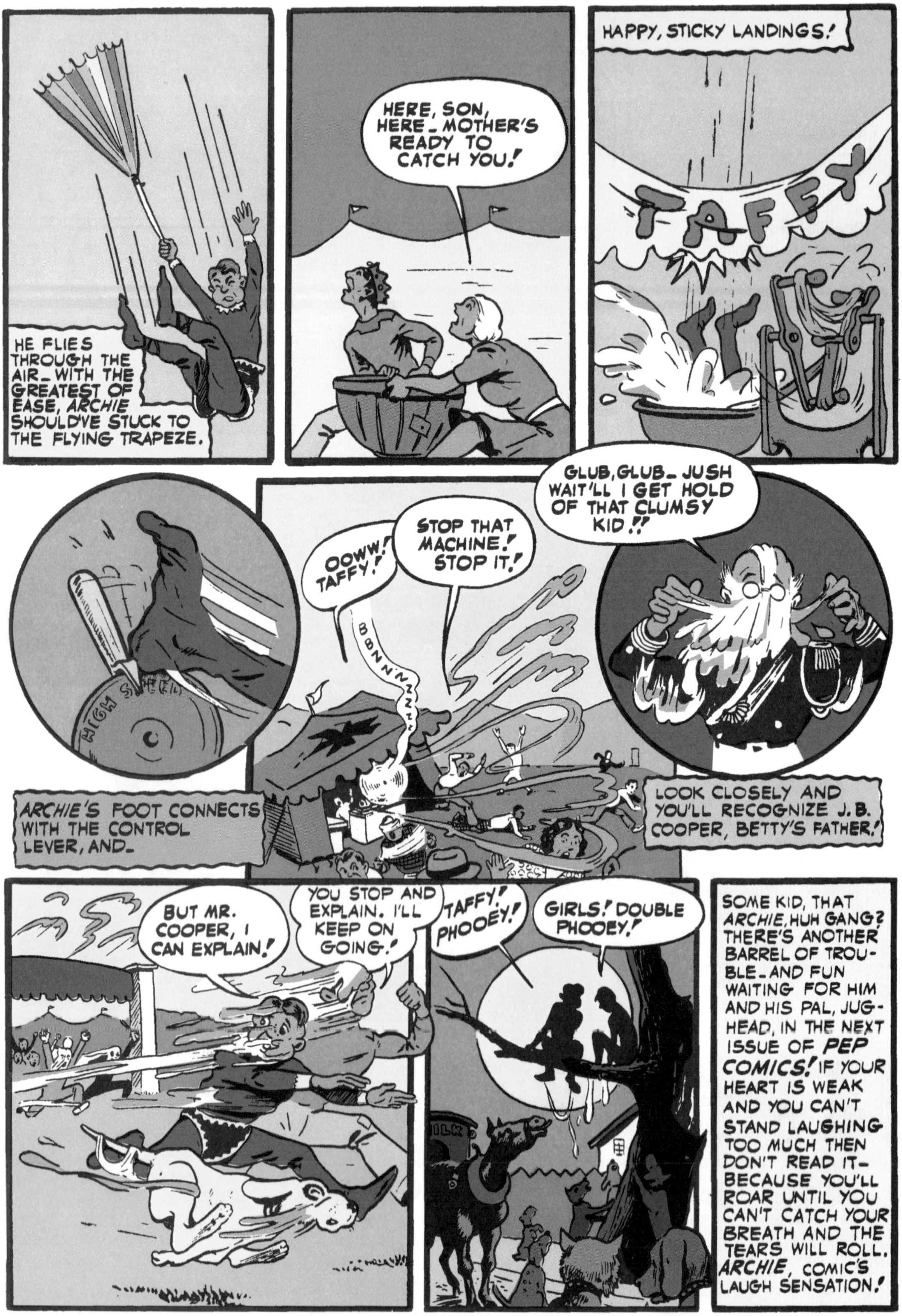
HE FLIES THROUGH THE AIR_ WITH THE GREATEST OF EASE, ARCHIE SHOULD'VE STUCK TO THE FLYING TRAPEZE.
HERE, SON, HERE_ MOTHER'S READY TO CATCH YOU!
HAPPY, STICKY LANDINGS!
TAFFY
ARCHIE'S FOOT CONNECTS WITH THE CONTROL LEVER, AND_
HIGH STEEL
OOWW! TAFFY!
STOP THAT MACHINE! STOP IT!
BBNNNNZZZ
GLUB, GLUB_ JUSH WAIT'LL I GET HOLD OF THAT CLUMSY KID!!
LOOK CLOSELY AND YOU'LL RECOGNIZE J. B. COOPER, BETTY'S FATHER!
BUT MR. COOPER, I CAN EXPLAIN!
YOU STOP AND EXPLAIN. I'LL KEEP ON GOING!
TAFFY! PHOOEY!
GIRLS! DOUBLE PHOOEY!
SOME KID, THAT ARCHIE, HUH GANG? THERE'S ANOTHER BARREL OF TROUBLE_ AND FUN WAITING FOR HIM AND HIS PAL, JUGHEAD, IN THE NEXT ISSUE OF PEP COMICS! IF YOUR HEART IS WEAK AND YOU CAN'T STAND LAUGHING TOO MUCH THEN DON'T READ IT_ BECAUSE YOU'LL ROAR UNTIL YOU CAN'T CATCH YOUR BREATH AND THE TEARS WILL ROLL. ARCHIE, COMIC'S LAUGH SENSATION!

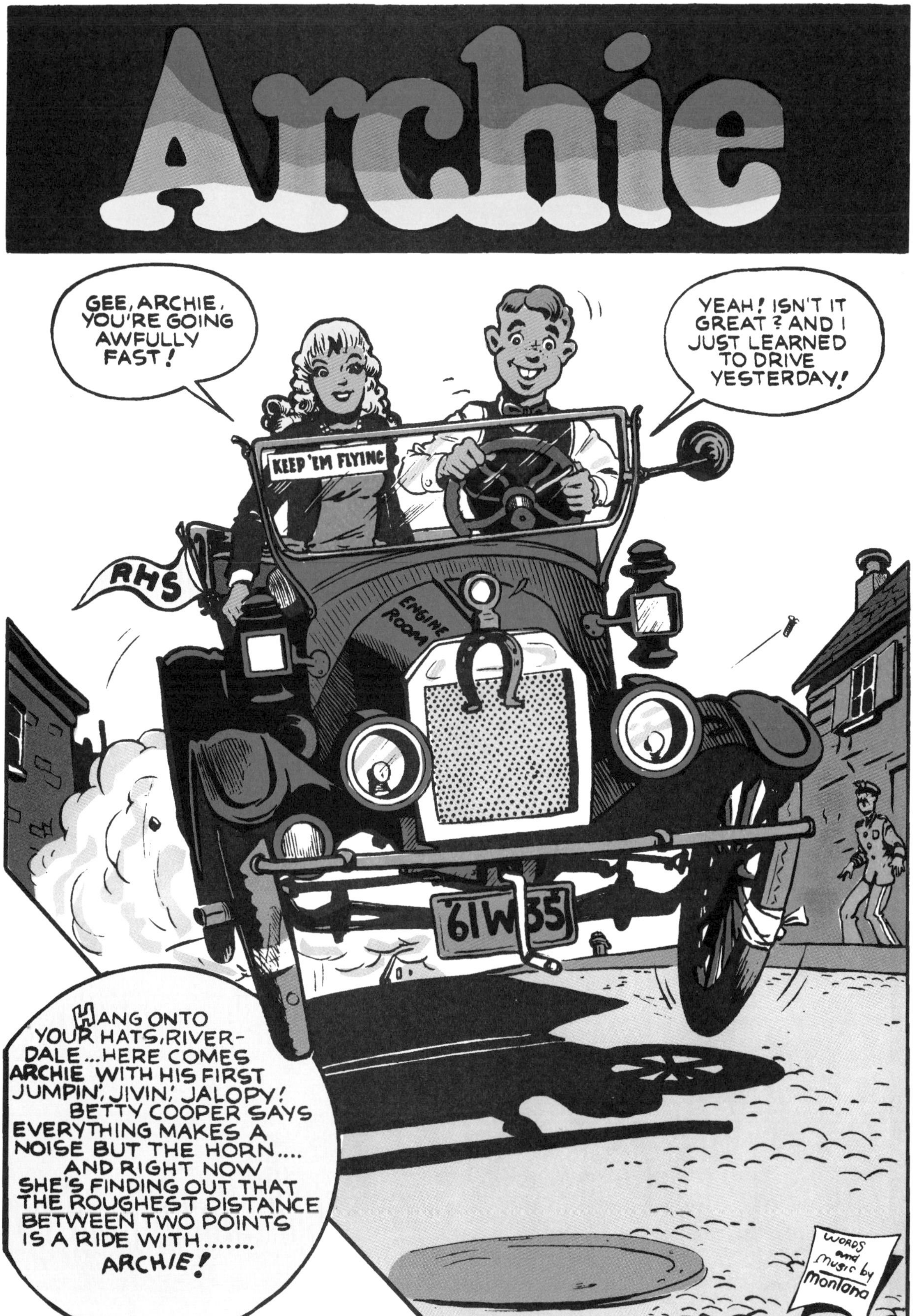
Archie
GEE, ARCHIE, YOU'RE GOING AWFULLY FAST!
YEAH! ISN'T IT GREAT? AND I JUST LEARNED TO DRIVE YESTERDAY!
KEEP 'EM FLYING
RHS
ENGINE ROOM
61W35
HANG ONTO YOUR HATS, RIVER-DALE...HERE COMES ARCHIE WITH HIS FIRST JUMPIN', JIVIN', JALOPY! BETTY COOPER SAYS EVERYTHING MAKES A NOISE BUT THE HORN.... AND RIGHT NOW SHE'S FINDING OUT THAT THE ROUGHEST DISTANCE BETWEEN TWO POINTS IS A RIDE WITH....... ARCHIE!
WORDS and Music by Montana

Originally presented in PEP COMICS #25, March, 1942

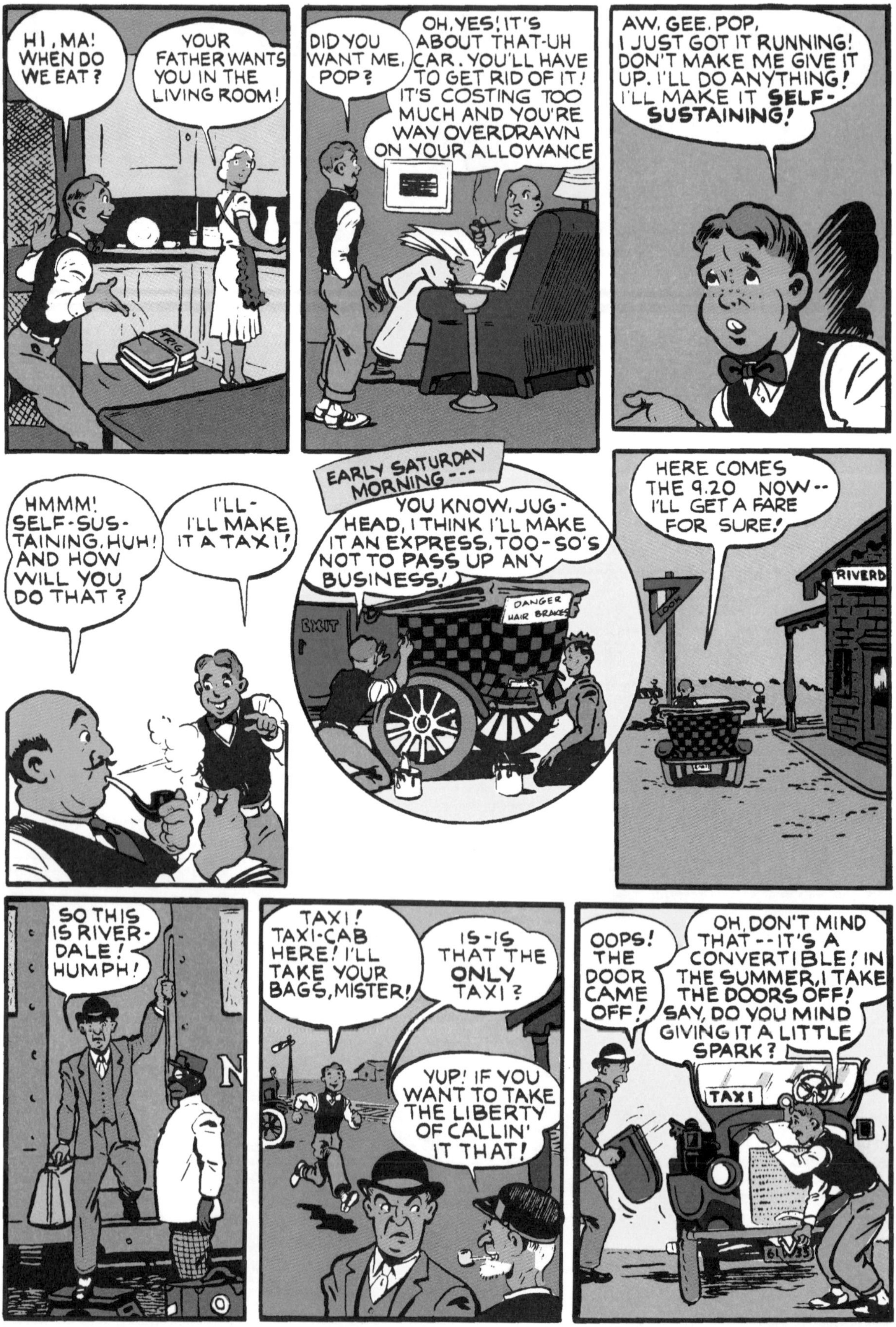
HI, MA! WHEN DO WE EAT?
YOUR FATHER WANTS YOU IN THE LIVING ROOM!
TRIG
DID YOU WANT ME, POP?
OH, YES! IT'S ABOUT THAT-UH CAR. YOU'LL HAVE TO GET RID OF IT! IT'S COSTING TOO MUCH AND YOU'RE WAY OVERDRAWN ON YOUR ALLOWANCE
AW, GEE, POP, I JUST GOT IT RUNNING! DON'T MAKE ME GIVE IT UP. I'LL DO ANYTHING! I'LL MAKE IT SELF-SUSTAINING!
HMMM! SELF-SUS-TAINING, HUH! AND HOW WILL YOU DO THAT?
I'LL- I'LL MAKE IT A TAXI!
EARLY SATURDAY MORNING---
YOU KNOW, JUG-HEAD, I THINK I'LL MAKE IT AN EXPRESS, TOO-SO'S NOT TO PASS UP ANY BUSINESS!
EXIT
DANGER HAIR BRAKES
HERE COMES THE 9.20 NOW-- I'LL GET A FARE FOR SURE!
LOOK
RIVERD
SO THIS IS RIVER-DALE! HUMPH!
TAXI! TAXI-CAB HERE! I'LL TAKE YOUR BAGS, MISTER!
IS-IS THAT THE ONLY TAXI?
YUP! IF YOU WANT TO TAKE THE LIBERTY OF CALLIN' IT THAT!
OOPS! THE DOOR CAME OFF!
OH, DON'T MIND THAT--IT'S A CONVERTIBLE! IN THE SUMMER, I TAKE THE DOORS OFF! SAY, DO YOU MIND GIVING IT A LITTLE SPARK?
TAXI

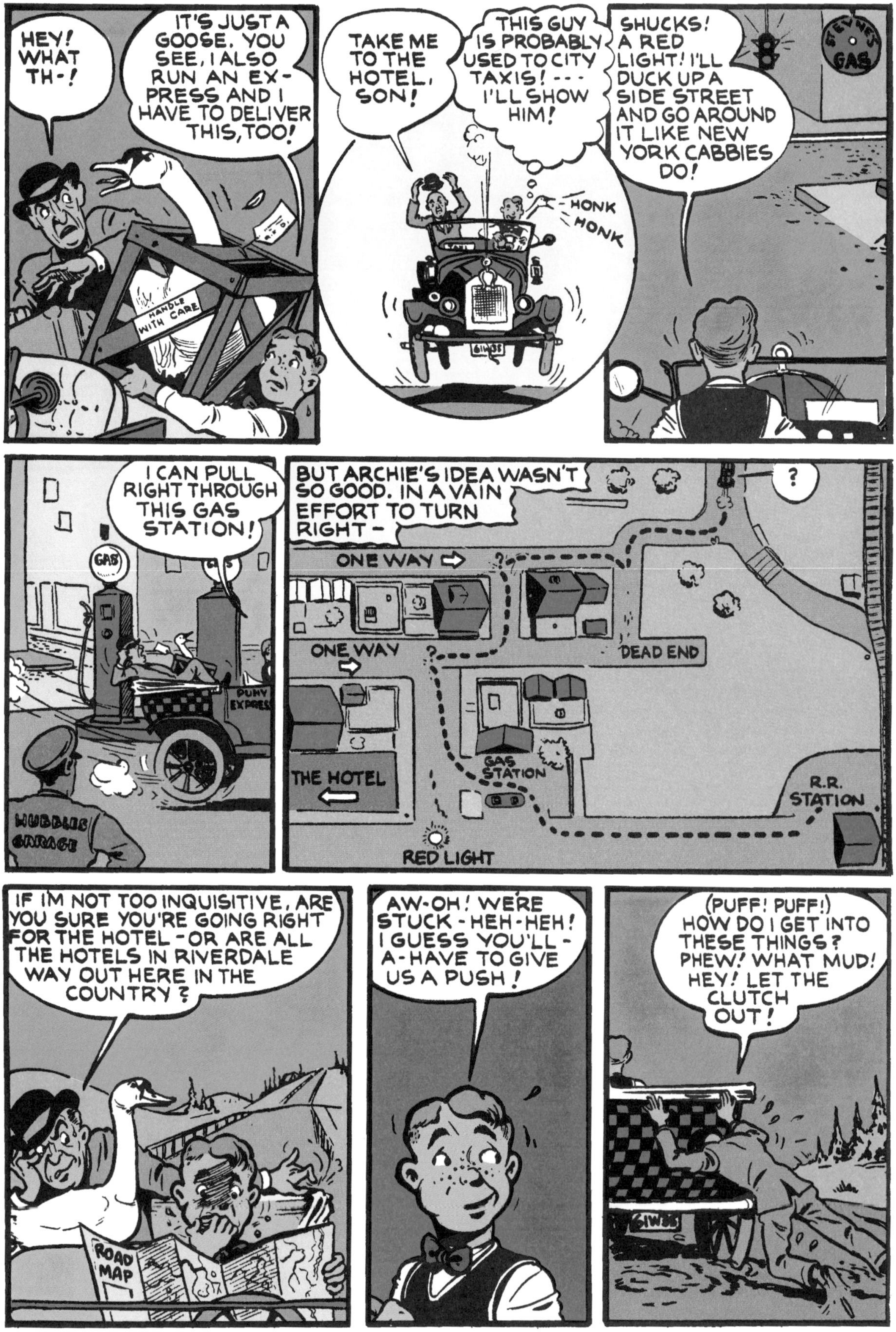
HEY! WHAT TH-!
IT'S JUST A GOOSE. YOU SEE, I ALSO RUN AN EX-PRESS AND I HAVE TO DELIVER THIS, TOO!
HANDLE WITH CARE
TAKE ME TO THE HOTEL, SON!
THIS GUY IS PROBABLY USED TO CITY TAXIS! --- I'LL SHOW HIM!
HONK
HONK
SHUCKS! A RED LIGHT! I'LL DUCK UP A SIDE STREET AND GO AROUND IT LIKE NEW YORK CABBIES DO!
GAS
I CAN PULL RIGHT THROUGH THIS GAS STATION!
GAS
PONY EXPRESS
HUBBLES GARAGE
BUT ARCHIE'S IDEA WASN'T SO GOOD. IN A VAIN EFFORT TO TURN RIGHT -
?
ONE WAY
ONE WAY
DEAD END
THE HOTEL
GAS STATION
R.R. STATION
RED LIGHT
IF I'M NOT TOO INQUISITIVE, ARE YOU SURE YOU'RE GOING RIGHT FOR THE HOTEL - OR ARE ALL THE HOTELS IN RIVERDALE WAY OUT HERE IN THE COUNTRY?
ROAD MAP
AW-OH! WE'RE STUCK - HEH-HEH! I GUESS YOU'LL - A-HAVE TO GIVE US A PUSH!
(PUFF! PUFF!) HOW DO I GET INTO THESE THINGS? PHEW! WHAT MUD! HEY! LET THE CLUTCH OUT!

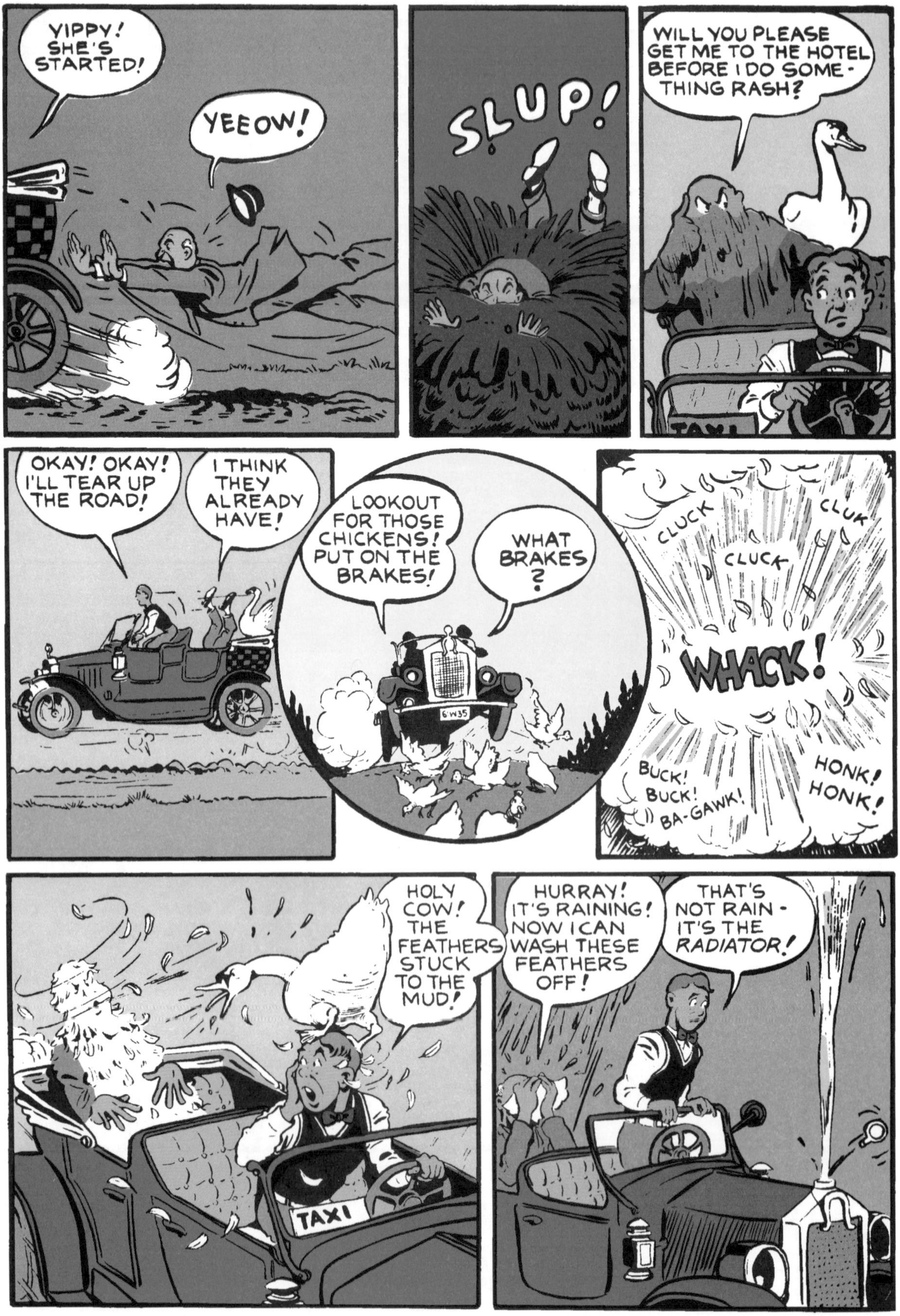
YIPPY! SHE'S STARTED!
YEEOW!
SLUP!
WILL YOU PLEASE GET ME TO THE HOTEL BEFORE I DO SOME-THING RASH?
TAXI
OKAY! OKAY! I'LL TEAR UP THE ROAD!
I THINK THEY ALREADY HAVE!
LOOKOUT FOR THOSE CHICKENS! PUT ON THE BRAKES!
WHAT BRAKES?
6-W35
CLUCK
CLUK
CLUCK
WHACK!
BUCK! BUCK! BA-GAWK!
HONK! HONK!
HOLY COW! THE FEATHERS STUCK TO THE MUD!
TAXI
HURRAY! IT'S RAINING! NOW I CAN WASH THESE FEATHERS OFF!
THAT'S NOT RAIN - IT'S THE *RADIATOR*!

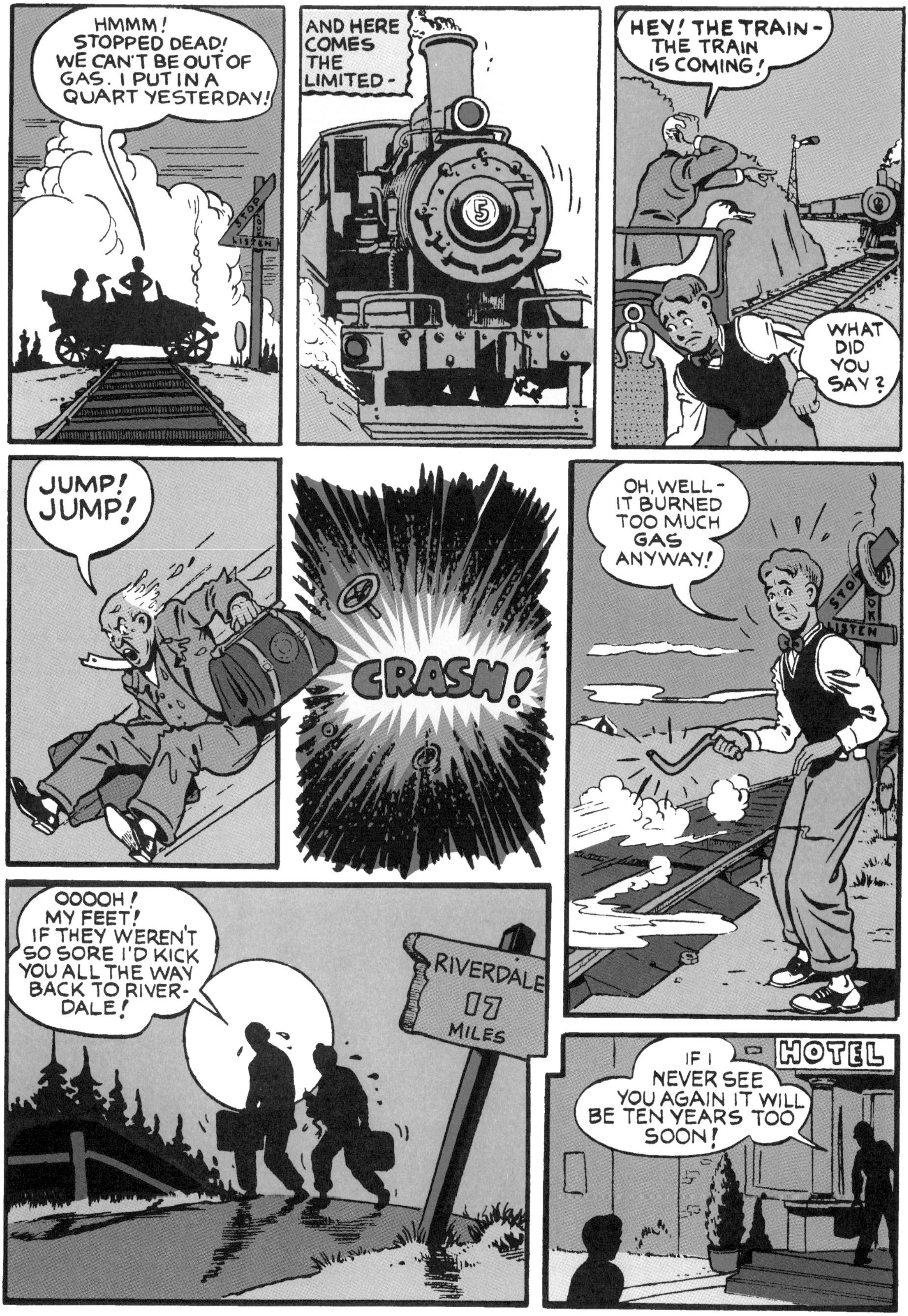
HMMM! STOPPED DEAD! WE CAN'T BE OUT OF GAS. I PUT IN A QUART YESTERDAY!
STOP LOOK LISTEN
AND HERE COMES THE LIMITED-
5
HEY! THE TRAIN- THE TRAIN IS COMING!
WHAT DID YOU SAY?
JUMP! JUMP!
CRASH!
OH, WELL- IT BURNED TOO MUCH GAS ANYWAY!
LISTEN
OOOOH! MY FEET! IF THEY WEREN'T SO SORE I'D KICK YOU ALL THE WAY BACK TO RIVER-DALE!
RIVERDALE 17 MILES
IF I NEVER SEE YOU AGAIN IT WILL BE TEN YEARS TOO SOON!
HOTEL

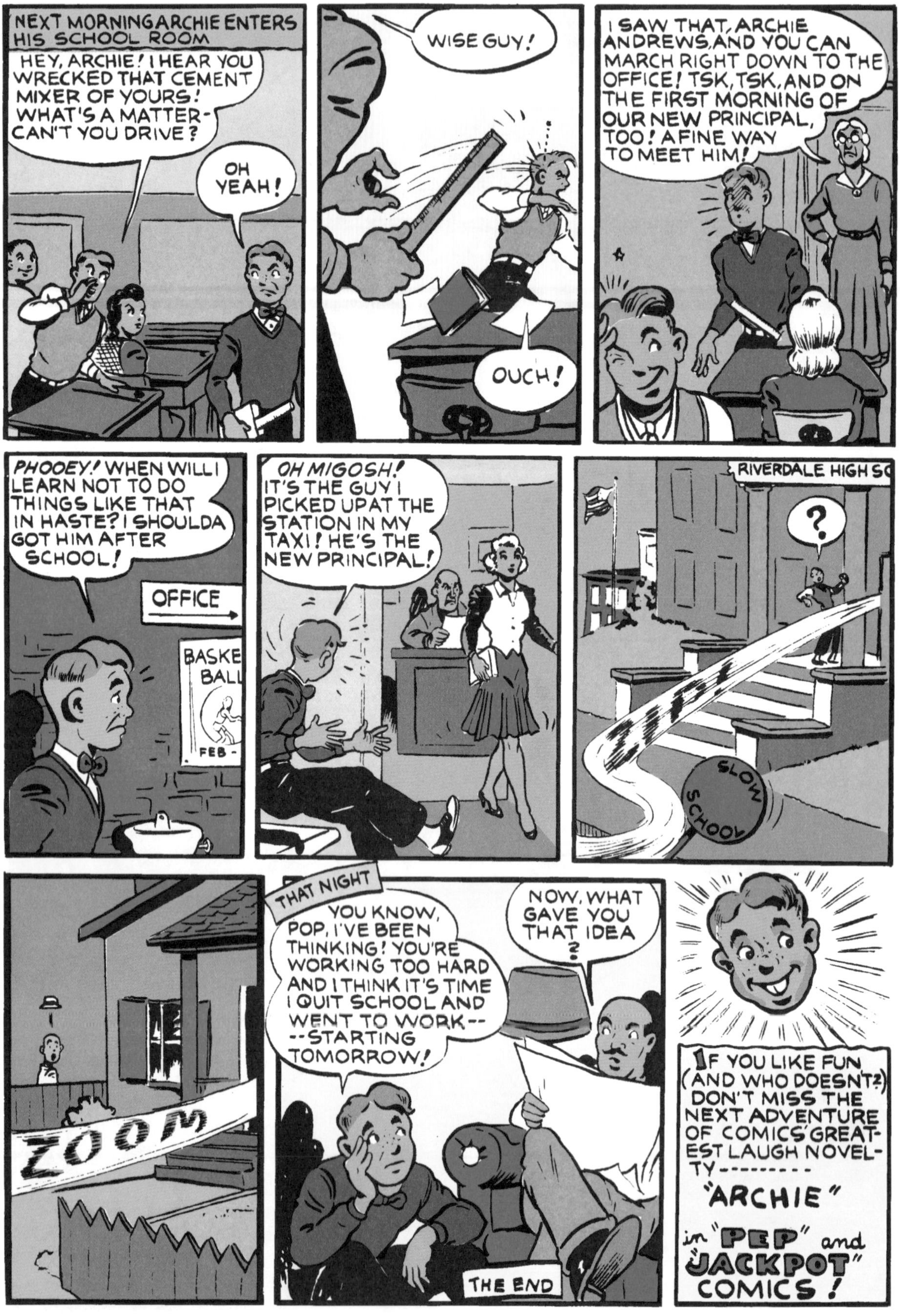
NEXT MORNING ARCHIE ENTERS HIS SCHOOL ROOM
HEY, ARCHIE! I HEAR YOU WRECKED THAT CEMENT MIXER OF YOURS! WHAT'S A MATTER- CAN'T YOU DRIVE?
OH YEAH!
WISE GUY!
OUCH!
I SAW THAT, ARCHIE ANDREWS, AND YOU CAN MARCH RIGHT DOWN TO THE OFFICE! TSK, TSK, AND ON THE FIRST MORNING OF OUR NEW PRINCIPAL, TOO! A FINE WAY TO MEET HIM!
PHOOEY! WHEN WILL I LEARN NOT TO DO THINGS LIKE THAT IN HASTE? I SHOULDA GOT HIM AFTER SCHOOL!
OFFICE
BASKE BALL
FEB -
OH MIGOSH! IT'S THE GUY I PICKED UP AT THE STATION IN MY TAXI! HE'S THE NEW PRINCIPAL!
RIVERDALE HIGH SC
?
SLOW SCHOOL
ZOOM
THAT NIGHT
YOU KNOW, POP, I'VE BEEN THINKING! YOU'RE WORKING TOO HARD AND I THINK IT'S TIME I QUIT SCHOOL AND WENT TO WORK-- --STARTING TOMORROW!
NOW, WHAT GAVE YOU THAT IDEA?
THE END
IF YOU LIKE FUN (AND WHO DOESN'T?) DON'T MISS THE NEXT ADVENTURE OF COMICS' GREATEST LAUGH NOVELTY---------
"ARCHIE"
in "PEP" and "JACKPOT" COMICS!

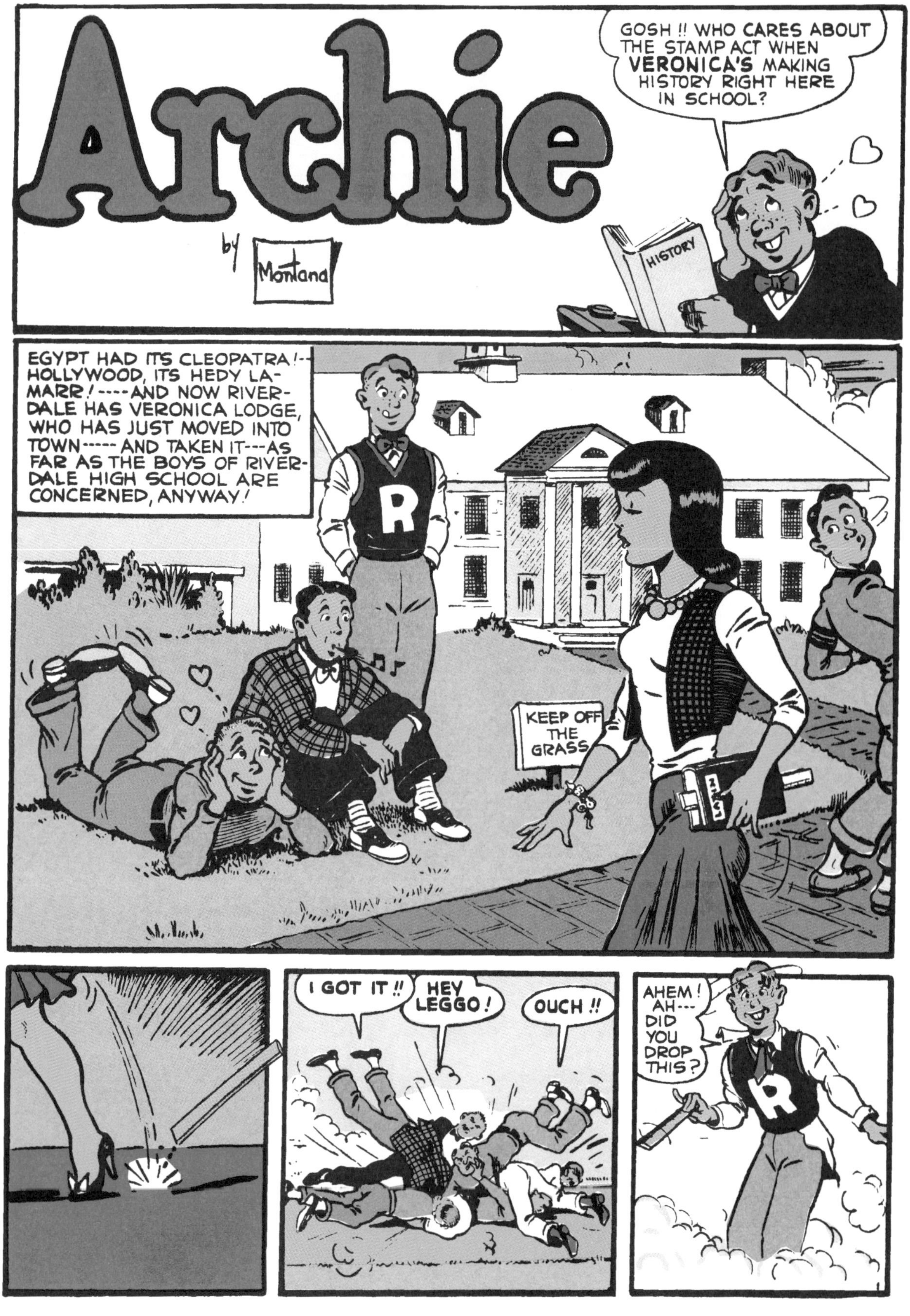
Archie
by Montana
GOSH !! WHO CARES ABOUT THE STAMP ACT WHEN VERONICA'S MAKING HISTORY RIGHT HERE IN SCHOOL?
HISTORY
EGYPT HAD ITS CLEOPATRA!-- HOLLYWOOD, ITS HEDY LAMARR!----AND NOW RIVERDALE HAS VERONICA LODGE, WHO HAS JUST MOVED INTO TOWN-----AND TAKEN IT---AS FAR AS THE BOYS OF RIVERDALE HIGH SCHOOL ARE CONCERNED, ANYWAY!
R
KEEP OFF THE GRASS
I GOT IT !!
HEY LEGGO!
OUCH !!
AHEM! AH--- DID YOU DROP THIS?
R

Originally presented in PEP COMICS #26, April, 1942

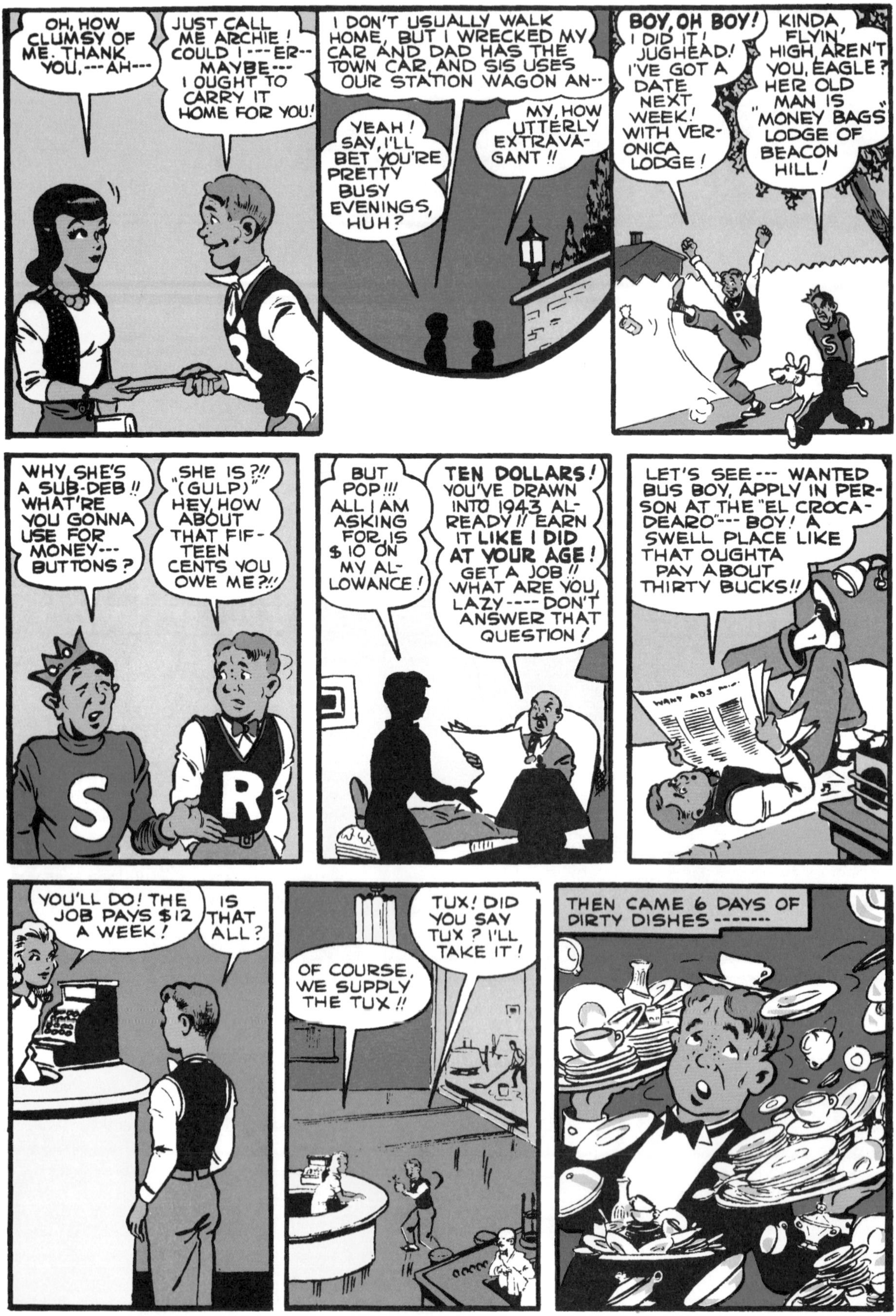
OH, HOW CLUMSY OF ME. THANK YOU,---AH---
JUST CALL ME ARCHIE! COULD I---ER-- MAYBE--- I OUGHT TO CARRY IT HOME FOR YOU!
I DON'T USUALLY WALK HOME, BUT I WRECKED MY CAR AND DAD HAS THE TOWN CAR, AND SIS USES OUR STATION WAGON AN--
YEAH! SAY, I'LL BET YOU'RE PRETTY BUSY EVENINGS, HUH?
MY, HOW UTTERLY EXTRAVAGANT!!
BOY, OH BOY! I DID IT! JUGHEAD! I'VE GOT A DATE NEXT WEEK! WITH VERONICA LODGE!
KINDA FLYIN' HIGH, AREN'T YOU, EAGLE? HER OLD MAN IS "MONEY BAGS" LODGE OF BEACON HILL!
WHY, SHE'S A SUB-DEB!! WHAT'RE YOU GONNA USE FOR MONEY--- BUTTONS?
"SHE IS?!! (GULP)" HEY, HOW ABOUT THAT FIFTEEN CENTS YOU OWE ME?!!
BUT POP!!! ALL I AM ASKING FOR IS $10 ON MY ALLOWANCE!
TEN DOLLARS! YOU'VE DRAWN INTO 1943 ALREADY!! EARN IT LIKE I DID AT YOUR AGE! GET A JOB!! WHAT ARE YOU, LAZY---- DON'T ANSWER THAT QUESTION!
LET'S SEE--- WANTED BUS BOY, APPLY IN PERSON AT THE "EL CROCADEARO"--- BOY! A SWELL PLACE LIKE THAT OUGHTA PAY ABOUT THIRTY BUCKS!!
WANT ADS
YOU'LL DO! THE JOB PAYS $12 A WEEK!
IS THAT ALL?
OF COURSE, WE SUPPLY THE TUX!!
TUX! DID YOU SAY TUX? I'LL TAKE IT!
THEN CAME 6 DAYS OF DIRTY DISHES -------

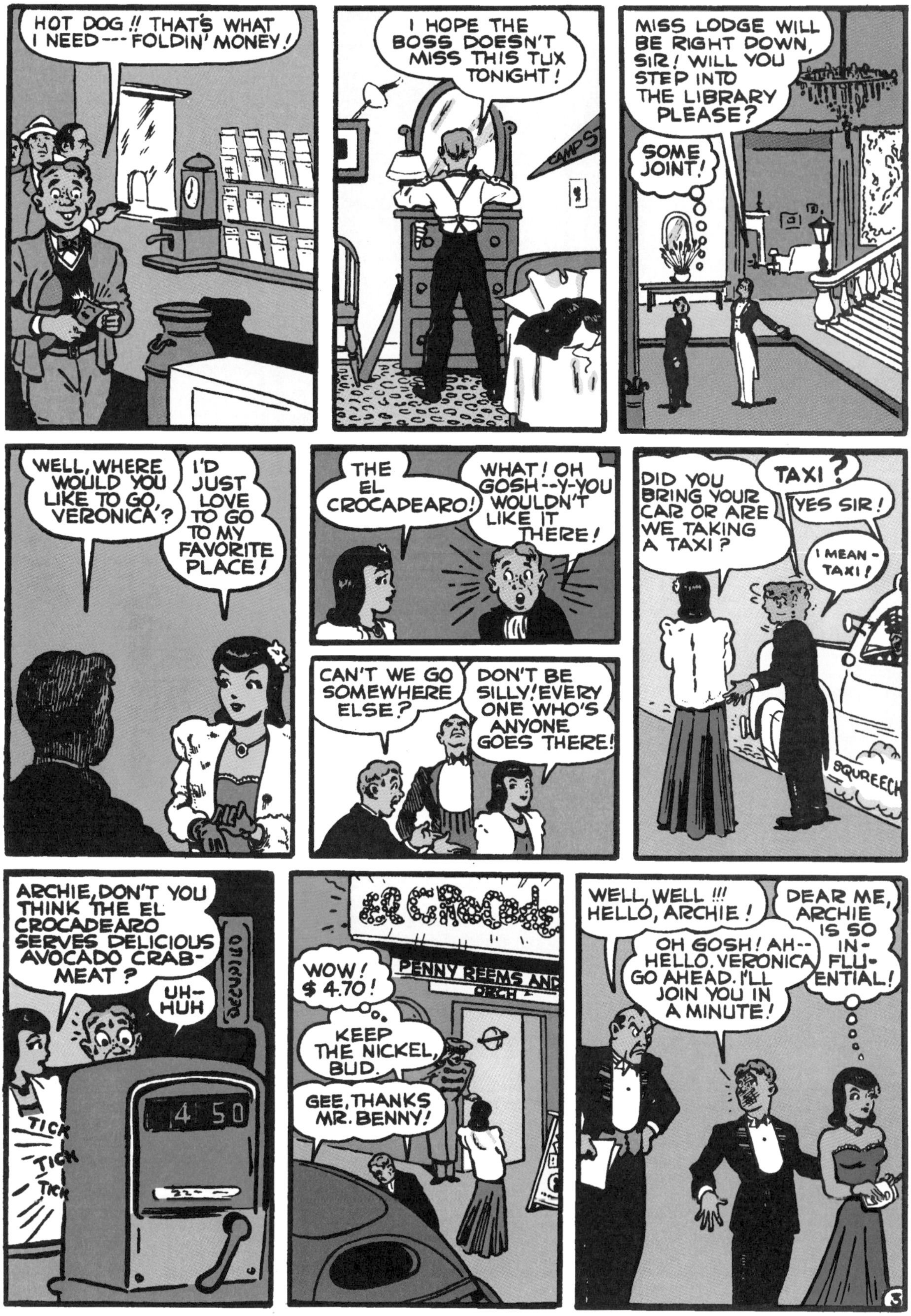
HOT DOG !! THAT'S WHAT I NEED --- FOLDIN' MONEY !
I HOPE THE BOSS DOESN'T MISS THIS TUX TONIGHT !
MISS LODGE WILL BE RIGHT DOWN, SIR ! WILL YOU STEP INTO THE LIBRARY PLEASE ?
SOME JOINT !
WELL, WHERE WOULD YOU LIKE TO GO, VERONICA ?
I'D JUST LOVE TO GO TO MY FAVORITE PLACE !
THE EL CROCADEARO !
WHAT ! OH GOSH -- Y-YOU WOULDN'T LIKE IT THERE !
CAN'T WE GO SOMEWHERE ELSE ?
DON'T BE SILLY ! EVERY ONE WHO'S ANYONE GOES THERE !
DID YOU BRING YOUR CAR OR ARE WE TAKING A TAXI ?
TAXI ?
YES SIR !
I MEAN - TAXI !
SQUREECH
ARCHIE, DON'T YOU THINK THE EL CROCADEARO SERVES DELICIOUS AVOCADO CRAB-MEAT ?
UH-HUH
4 50
TICK
TICK
TICK
PENNY REEMS AND ORCH.
WOW ! $ 4.70 !
KEEP THE NICKEL, BUD.
GEE, THANKS MR. BENNY !
WELL, WELL !!! HELLO, ARCHIE !
OH GOSH ! AH -- HELLO, VERONICA GO AHEAD. I'LL JOIN YOU IN A MINUTE !
DEAR ME, ARCHIE IS SO IN-FLU-ENTIAL !
3

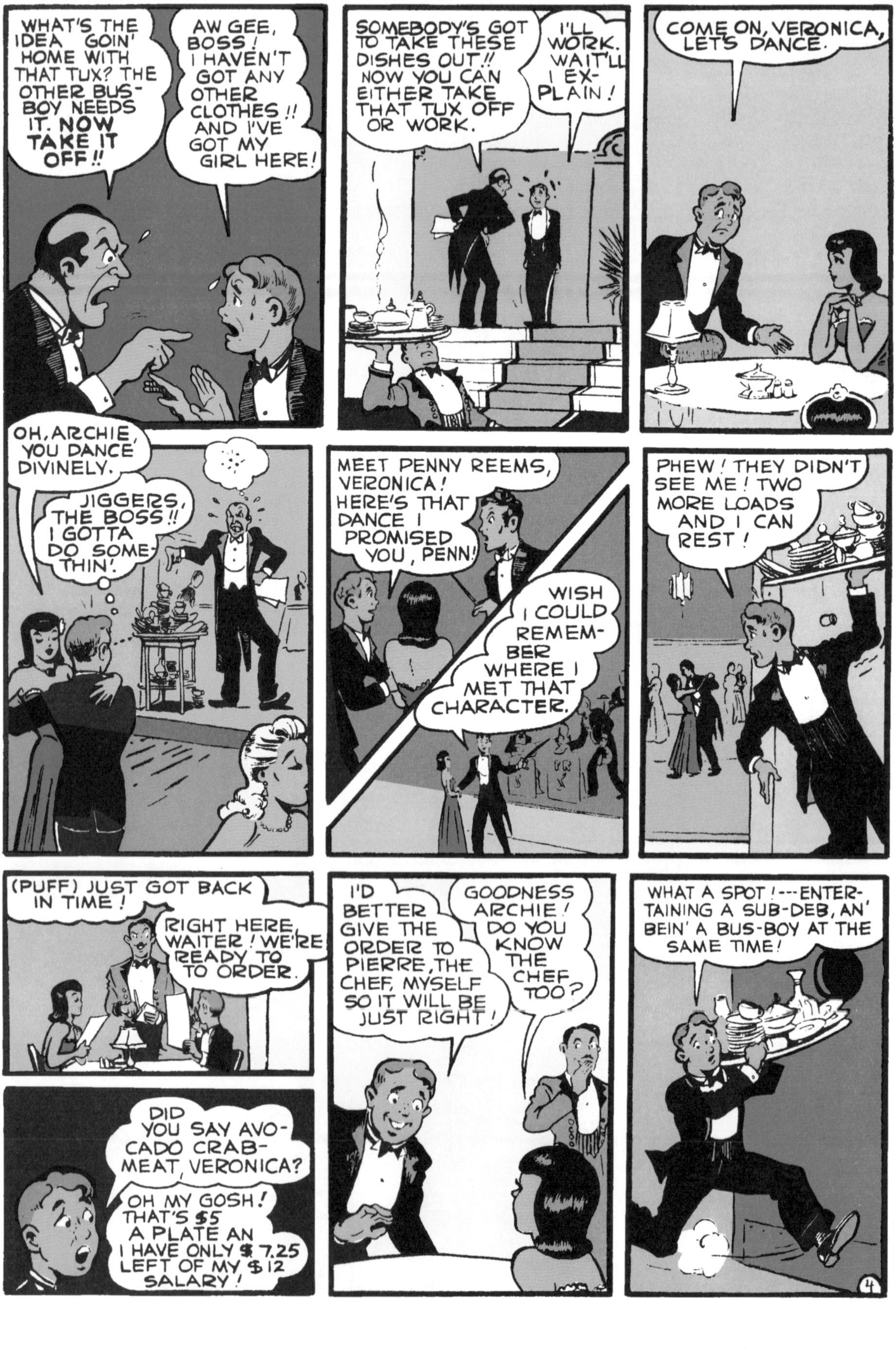
WHAT'S THE IDEA GOIN' HOME WITH THAT TUX? THE OTHER BUS-BOY NEEDS IT. NOW TAKE IT OFF!!
AW GEE, BOSS! I HAVEN'T GOT ANY OTHER CLOTHES!! AND I'VE GOT MY GIRL HERE!
SOMEBODY'S GOT TO TAKE THESE DISHES OUT!! NOW YOU CAN EITHER TAKE THAT TUX OFF OR WORK.
I'LL WORK. WAIT'LL I EX-PLAIN!
COME ON, VERONICA, LET'S DANCE.
OH, ARCHIE, YOU DANCE DIVINELY.
JIGGERS, THE BOSS!! I GOTTA DO SOME-THIN'.
MEET PENNY REEMS, VERONICA! HERE'S THAT DANCE I PROMISED YOU, PENN!
WISH I COULD REMEM-BER WHERE I MET THAT CHARACTER.
PHEW! THEY DIDN'T SEE ME! TWO MORE LOADS AND I CAN REST!
(PUFF) JUST GOT BACK IN TIME!
RIGHT HERE, WAITER! WE'RE READY TO TO ORDER.
DID YOU SAY AVO-CADO CRAB-MEAT, VERONICA?
OH MY GOSH! THAT'S $5 A PLATE AN I HAVE ONLY $ 7.25 LEFT OF MY $12 SALARY!
I'D BETTER GIVE THE ORDER TO PIERRE, THE CHEF, MYSELF SO IT WILL BE JUST RIGHT!
GOODNESS ARCHIE! DO YOU KNOW THE CHEF TOO?
WHAT A SPOT! --- ENTER-TAINING A SUB-DEB, AN' BEIN' A BUS-BOY AT THE SAME TIME!
4

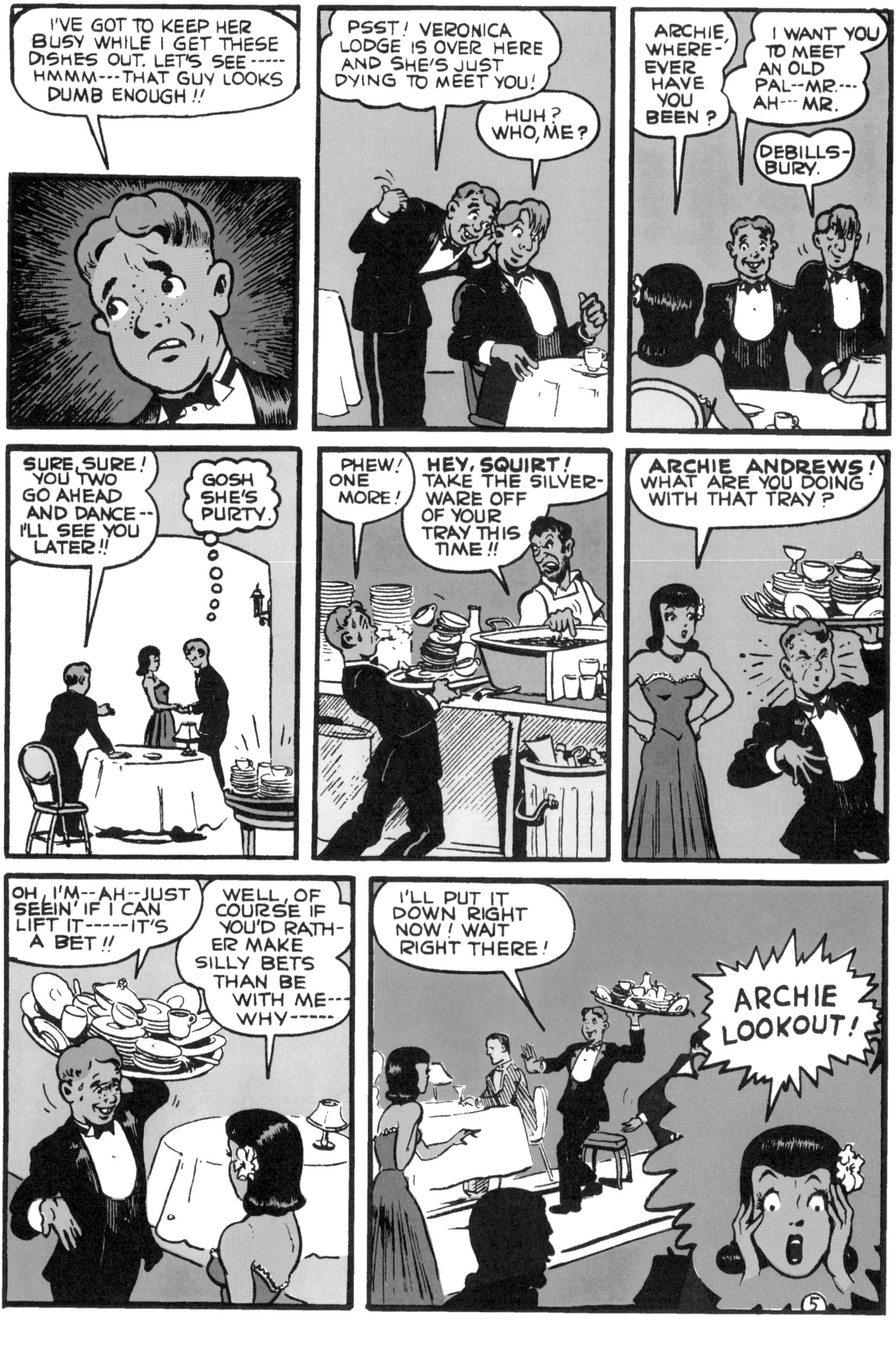
I'VE GOT TO KEEP HER BUSY WHILE I GET THESE DISHES OUT. LET'S SEE----- HMMM---THAT GUY LOOKS DUMB ENOUGH !!
PSST! VERONICA LODGE IS OVER HERE AND SHE'S JUST DYING TO MEET YOU!
HUH? WHO, ME?
ARCHIE, WHERE-EVER HAVE YOU BEEN ?
I WANT YOU TO MEET AN OLD PAL--MR.--- AH--- MR.
DEBILLS-BURY.
SURE, SURE! YOU TWO GO AHEAD AND DANCE-- I'LL SEE YOU LATER!!
GOSH SHE'S PURTY.
PHEW! ONE MORE!
HEY, SQUIRT! TAKE THE SILVER-WARE OFF OF YOUR TRAY THIS TIME!!
ARCHIE ANDREWS! WHAT ARE YOU DOING WITH THAT TRAY ?
OH, I'M--AH--JUST SEEIN' IF I CAN LIFT IT-----IT'S A BET!!
WELL, OF COURSE IF YOU'D RATH-ER MAKE SILLY BETS THAN BE WITH ME--- WHY-----
I'LL PUT IT DOWN RIGHT NOW! WAIT RIGHT THERE!
ARCHIE LOOKOUT!
5

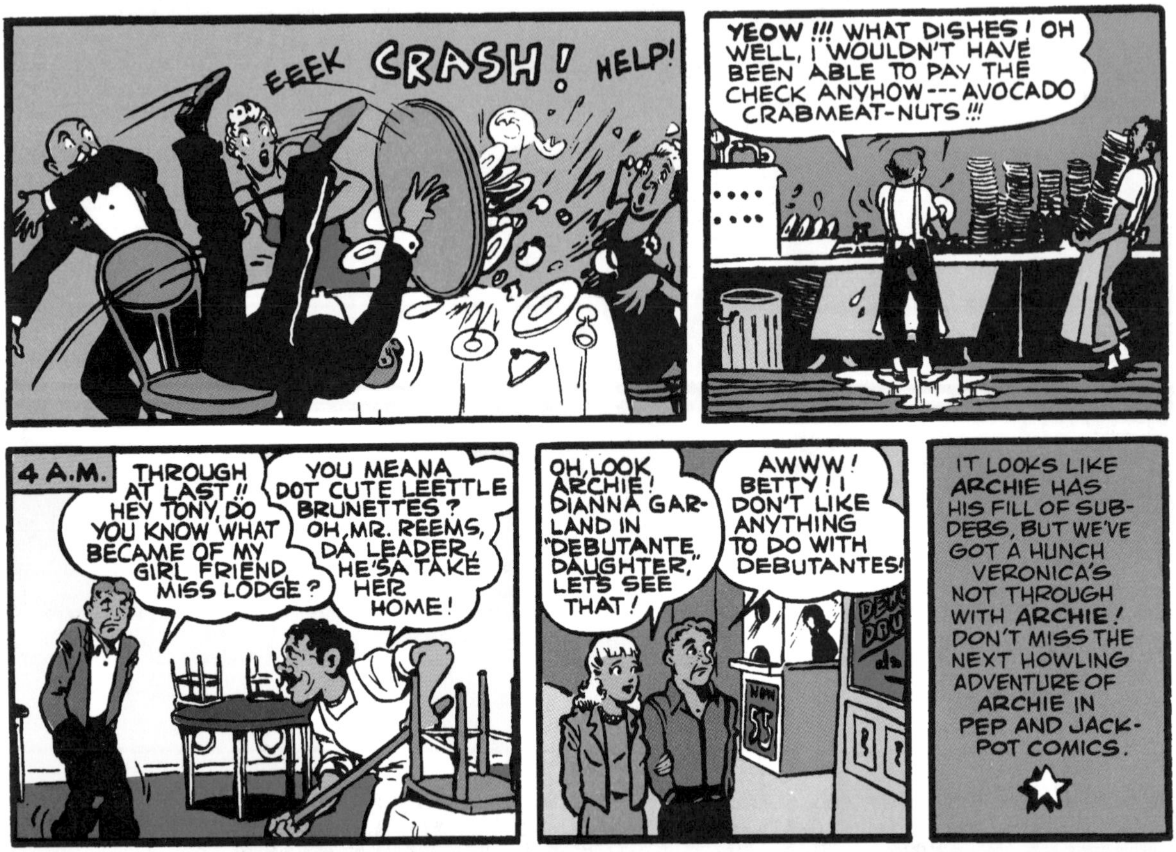
EEEK
CRASH!
HELP!
YEOW !!! WHAT DISHES! OH WELL, I WOULDN'T HAVE BEEN ABLE TO PAY THE CHECK ANYHOW --- AVOCADO CRABMEAT-NUTS !!!
4 A.M.
THROUGH AT LAST !! HEY TONY, DO YOU KNOW WHAT BECAME OF MY GIRL FRIEND MISS LODGE?
YOU MEANA DOT CUTE LEETTLE BRUNETTES? OH, MR. REEMS, DA LEADER, HE'SA TAKE HER HOME!
OH, LOOK ARCHIE! DIANNA GARLAND IN "DEBUTANTE DAUGHTER," LETS SEE THAT!
AWWW! BETTY! I DON'T LIKE ANYTHING TO DO WITH DEBUTANTES!
IT LOOKS LIKE ARCHIE HAS HIS FILL OF SUB-DEBS, BUT WE'VE GOT A HUNCH VERONICA'S NOT THROUGH WITH ARCHIE! DON'T MISS THE NEXT HOWLING ADVENTURE OF ARCHIE IN PEP AND JACK-POT COMICS.

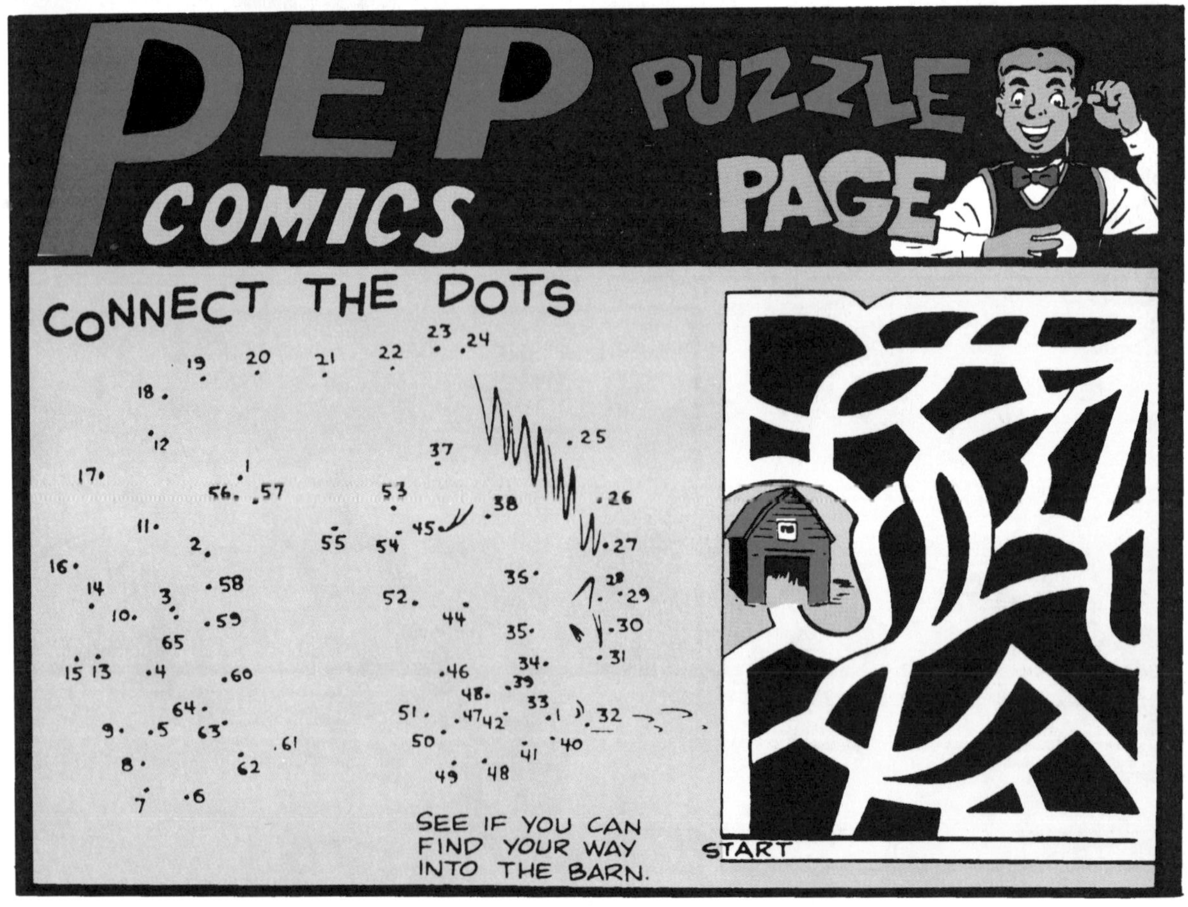
PEP COMICS
PUZZLE PAGE
CONNECT THE DOTS
SEE IF YOU CAN FIND YOUR WAY INTO THE BARN.
START

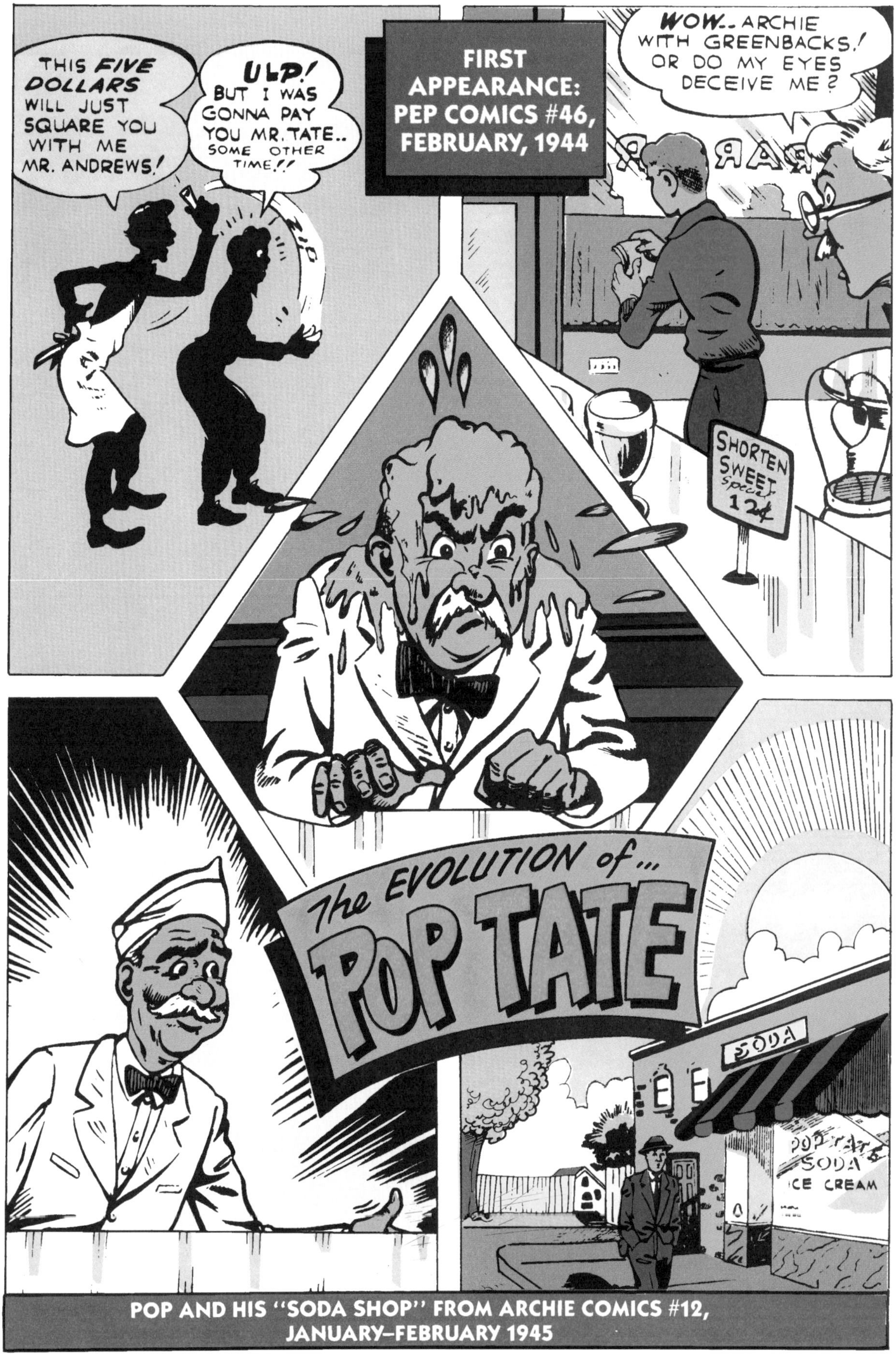
THIS FIVE DOLLARS WILL JUST SQUARE YOU WITH ME MR. ANDREWS!
ULP! BUT I WAS GONNA PAY YOU MR. TATE.. SOME OTHER TIME!!
WOW.. ARCHIE WITH GREENBACKS! OR DO MY EYES DECEIVE ME?
SHORTEN SWEET Special 12¢
The EVOLUTION of... POP TATE
SODA
POP TATE'S SODA ICE CREAM

FIRST APPEARANCE: PEP COMICS #46, FEBRUARY, 1944

POP AND HIS "SODA SHOP" FROM ARCHIE COMICS #12, JANUARY–FEBRUARY 1945

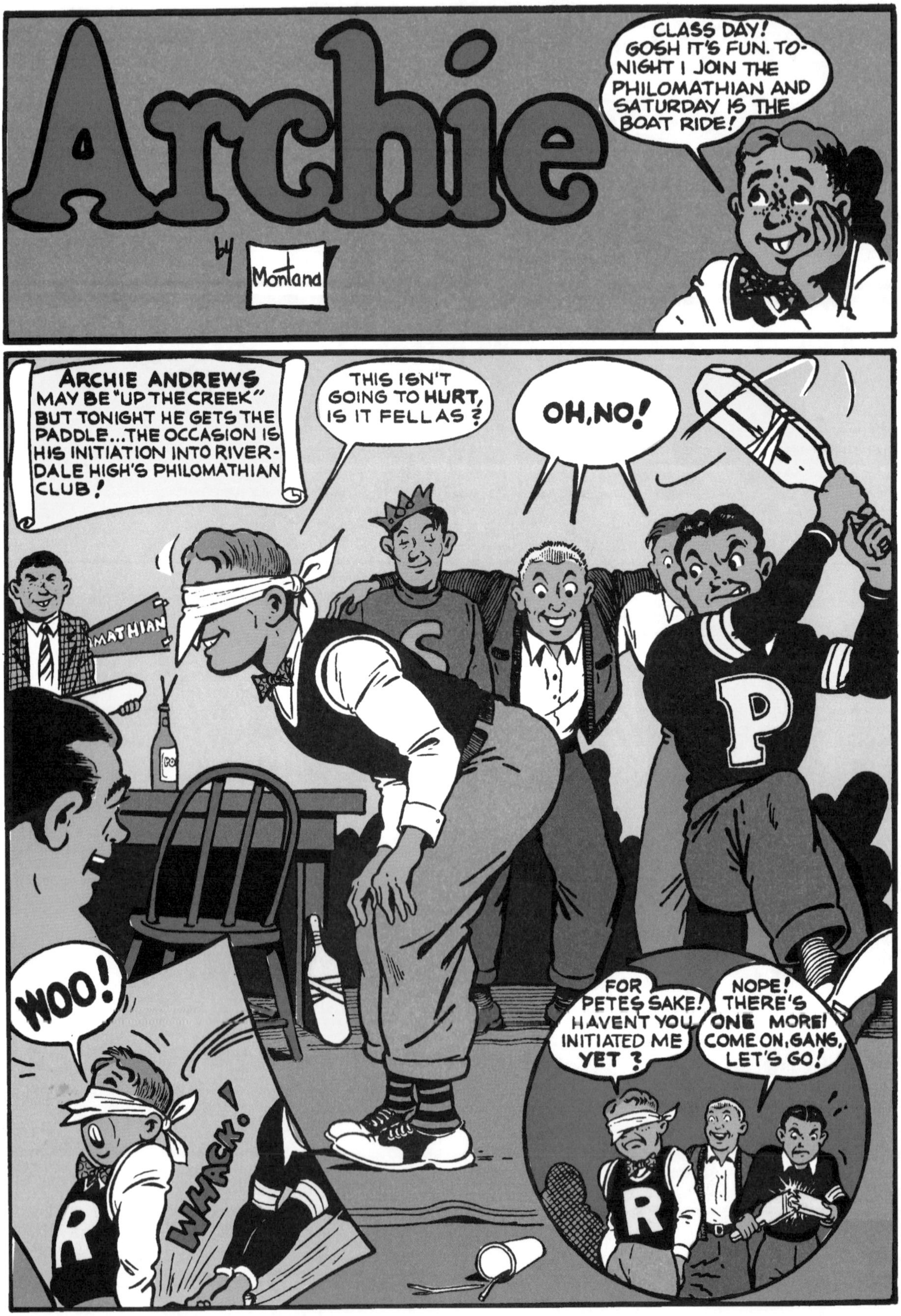
Archie
by Montana
CLASS DAY! GOSH IT'S FUN. TONIGHT I JOIN THE PHILOMATHIAN AND SATURDAY IS THE BOAT RIDE!
ARCHIE ANDREWS MAY BE "UP THE CREEK" BUT TONIGHT HE GETS THE PADDLE...THE OCCASION IS HIS INITIATION INTO RIVERDALE HIGH'S PHILOMATHIAN CLUB!
THIS ISN'T GOING TO HURT, IS IT FELLAS?
OH, NO!
MATHIAN
WOO!
WHACK!
FOR PETES SAKE! HAVENT YOU INITIATED ME YET?
NOPE! THERE'S ONE MORE! COME ON, GANG, LET'S GO!

Originally presented in JACKPOT COMICS #5, Spring, 1942

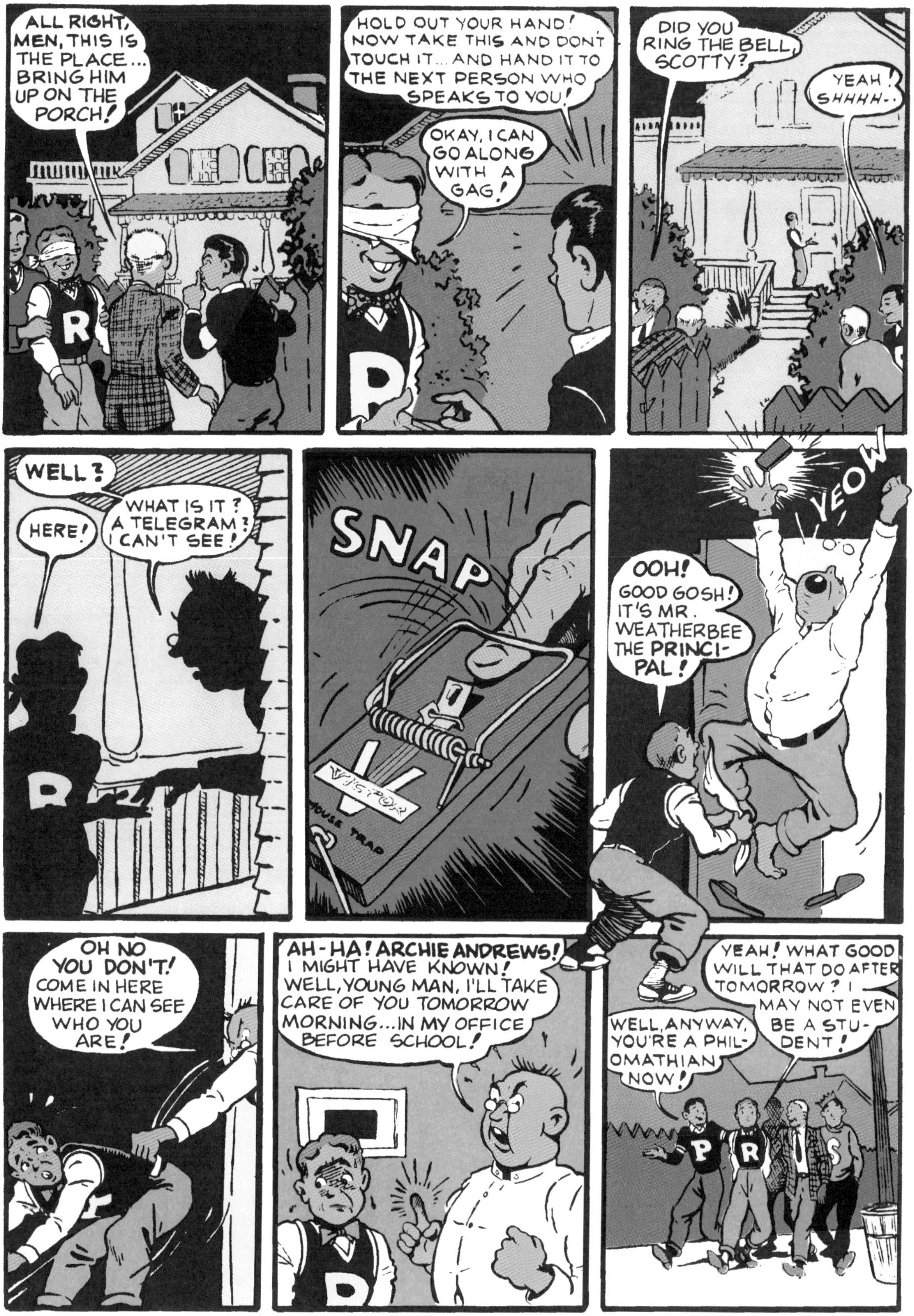
ALL RIGHT, MEN, THIS IS THE PLACE... BRING HIM UP ON THE PORCH!
HOLD OUT YOUR HAND! NOW TAKE THIS AND DON'T TOUCH IT... AND HAND IT TO THE NEXT PERSON WHO SPEAKS TO YOU!
OKAY, I CAN GO ALONG WITH A GAG!
DID YOU RING THE BELL, SCOTTY?
YEAH! SHHHH-.
WELL?
HERE!
WHAT IS IT? A TELEGRAM? I CAN'T SEE!
SNAP
YEOW
OOH! GOOD GOSH! IT'S MR. WEATHERBEE THE PRINCIPAL!
OH NO YOU DON'T! COME IN HERE WHERE I CAN SEE WHO YOU ARE!
AH-HA! ARCHIE ANDREWS! I MIGHT HAVE KNOWN! WELL, YOUNG MAN, I'LL TAKE CARE OF YOU TOMORROW MORNING... IN MY OFFICE BEFORE SCHOOL!
YEAH! WHAT GOOD WILL THAT DO AFTER TOMORROW? I MAY NOT EVEN BE A STUDENT!
WELL, ANYWAY, YOU'RE A PHILOMATHIAN NOW!

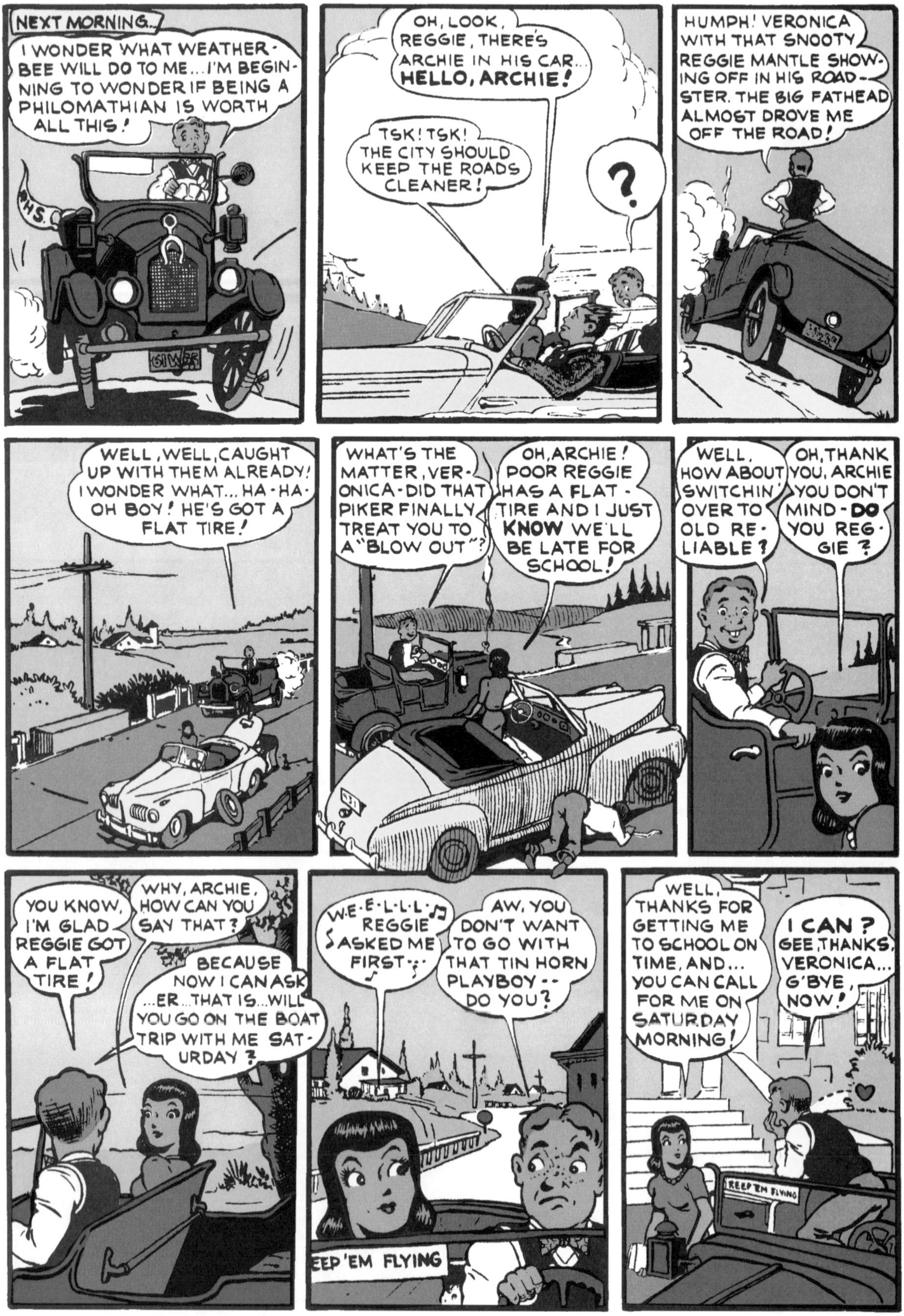
NEXT MORNING...
I WONDER WHAT WEATHERBEE WILL DO TO ME... I'M BEGINNING TO WONDER IF BEING A PHILOMATHIAN IS WORTH ALL THIS!
R.H.S.
OH, LOOK, REGGIE, THERE'S ARCHIE IN HIS CAR... HELLO, ARCHIE!
TSK! TSK! THE CITY SHOULD KEEP THE ROADS CLEANER!
?
HUMPH! VERONICA WITH THAT SNOOTY REGGIE MANTLE SHOWING OFF IN HIS ROADSTER. THE BIG FATHEAD ALMOST DROVE ME OFF THE ROAD!
WELL, WELL, CAUGHT UP WITH THEM ALREADY! I WONDER WHAT... HA-HA- OH BOY! HE'S GOT A FLAT TIRE!
WHAT'S THE MATTER, VERONICA- DID THAT PIKER FINALLY TREAT YOU TO A "BLOW OUT"?
OH, ARCHIE! POOR REGGIE HAS A FLAT TIRE AND I JUST KNOW WE'LL BE LATE FOR SCHOOL!
WELL, HOW ABOUT SWITCHIN' OVER TO OLD RELIABLE?
OH, THANK YOU, ARCHIE. YOU DON'T MIND - DO YOU REGGIE?
YOU KNOW, I'M GLAD REGGIE GOT A FLAT TIRE!
WHY, ARCHIE, HOW CAN YOU SAY THAT?
BECAUSE NOW I CAN ASK ...ER...THAT IS...WILL YOU GO ON THE BOAT TRIP WITH ME SATURDAY?
W-E-E-L-L-L REGGIE ASKED ME FIRST...
AW, YOU DON'T WANT TO GO WITH THAT TIN HORN PLAYBOY -- DO YOU?
EEP 'EM FLYING
WELL, THANKS FOR GETTING ME TO SCHOOL ON TIME, AND... YOU CAN CALL FOR ME ON SATURDAY MORNING!
I CAN? GEE, THANKS, VERONICA... G'BYE, NOW!
KEEP 'EM FLYING

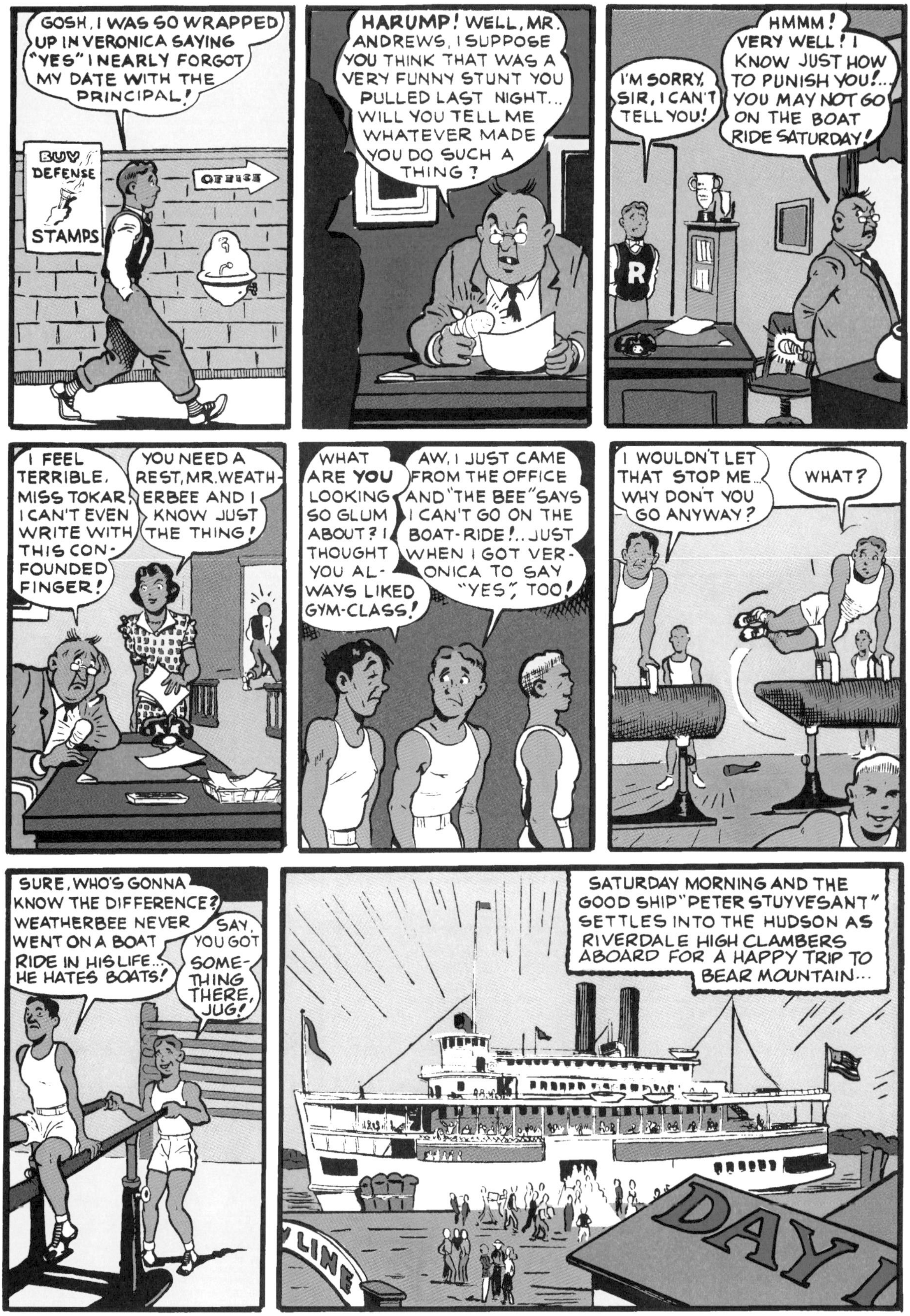
GOSH, I WAS SO WRAPPED UP IN VERONICA SAYING "YES" I NEARLY FORGOT MY DATE WITH THE PRINCIPAL!
BUY DEFENSE STAMPS
OFFICE
HARUMP! WELL, MR. ANDREWS, I SUPPOSE YOU THINK THAT WAS A VERY FUNNY STUNT YOU PULLED LAST NIGHT... WILL YOU TELL ME WHATEVER MADE YOU DO SUCH A THING?
I'M SORRY, SIR, I CAN'T TELL YOU!
HMMM! VERY WELL! I KNOW JUST HOW TO PUNISH YOU!... YOU MAY NOT GO ON THE BOAT RIDE SATURDAY!
I FEEL TERRIBLE, MISS TOKAR, I CAN'T EVEN WRITE WITH THIS CONFOUNDED FINGER!
YOU NEED A REST, MR. WEATHERBEE AND I KNOW JUST THE THING!
WHAT ARE YOU LOOKING SO GLUM ABOUT? I THOUGHT YOU ALWAYS LIKED GYM-CLASS!
AW, I JUST CAME FROM THE OFFICE AND "THE BEE" SAYS I CAN'T GO ON THE BOAT-RIDE!.. JUST WHEN I GOT VERONICA TO SAY "YES", TOO!
I WOULDN'T LET THAT STOP ME.. WHY DON'T YOU GO ANYWAY?
WHAT?
SURE, WHO'S GONNA KNOW THE DIFFERENCE? WEATHERBEE NEVER WENT ON A BOAT RIDE IN HIS LIFE... HE HATES BOATS!
SAY, YOU GOT SOMETHING THERE, JUG!
SATURDAY MORNING AND THE GOOD SHIP "PETER STUYVESANT" SETTLES INTO THE HUDSON AS RIVERDALE HIGH CLAMBERS ABOARD FOR A HAPPY TRIP TO BEAR MOUNTAIN...
DAY
LINE

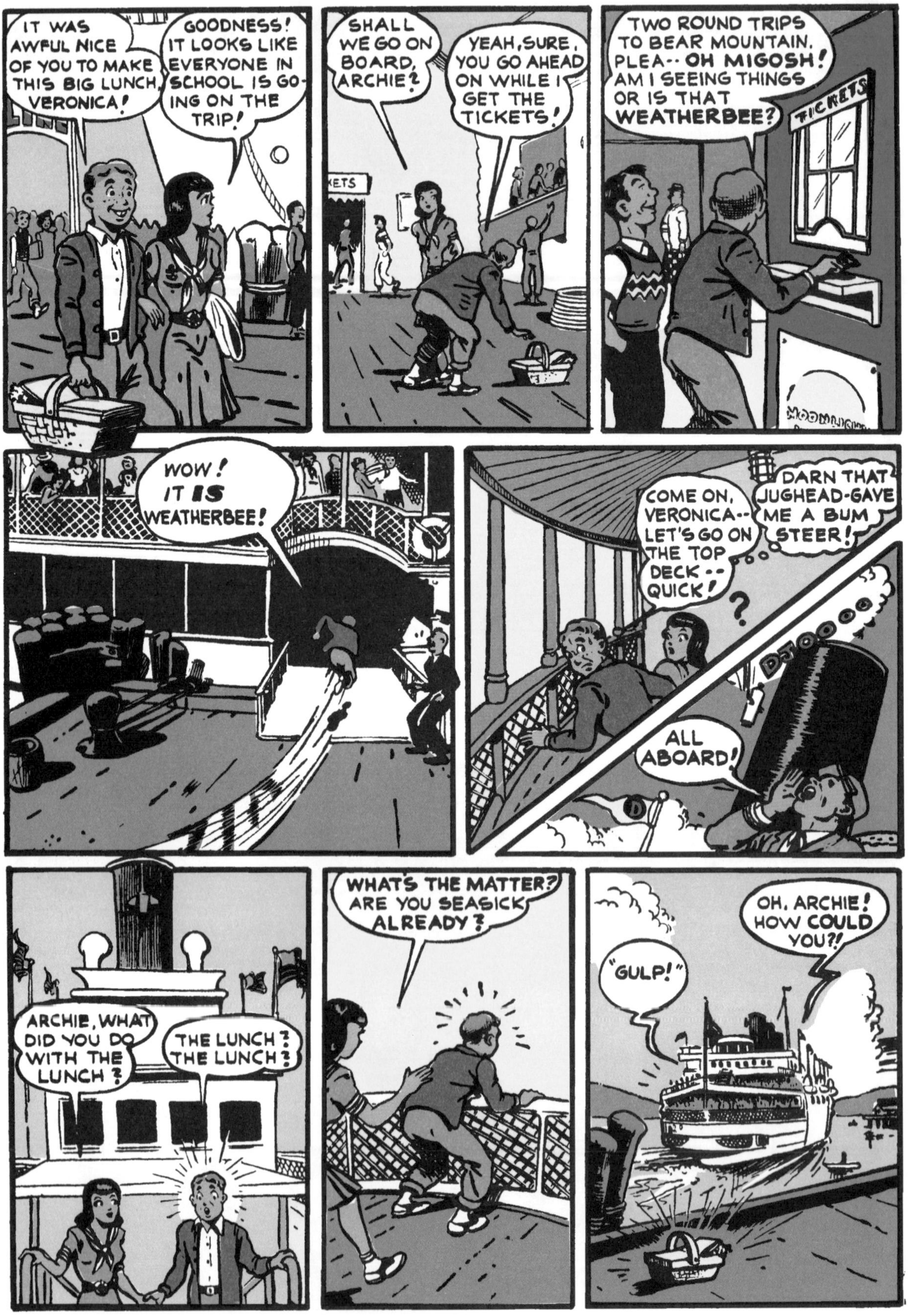
IT WAS AWFUL NICE OF YOU TO MAKE THIS BIG LUNCH, VERONICA!
GOODNESS! IT LOOKS LIKE EVERYONE IN SCHOOL IS GOING ON THE TRIP!
SHALL WE GO ON BOARD, ARCHIE?
YEAH, SURE, YOU GO AHEAD ON WHILE I GET THE TICKETS!
TWO ROUND TRIPS TO BEAR MOUNTAIN. PLEA-- OH MIGOSH! AM I SEEING THINGS OR IS THAT WEATHERBEE?
TICKETS
WOW! IT IS WEATHERBEE!
COME ON, VERONICA-- LET'S GO ON THE TOP DECK -- QUICK!
DARN THAT JUGHEAD-GAVE ME A BUM STEER!
?
DJOOOOO
ALL ABOARD!
ARCHIE, WHAT DID YOU DO WITH THE LUNCH?
THE LUNCH? THE LUNCH?
WHAT'S THE MATTER? ARE YOU SEASICK ALREADY?
"GULP!"
OH, ARCHIE! HOW COULD YOU?!

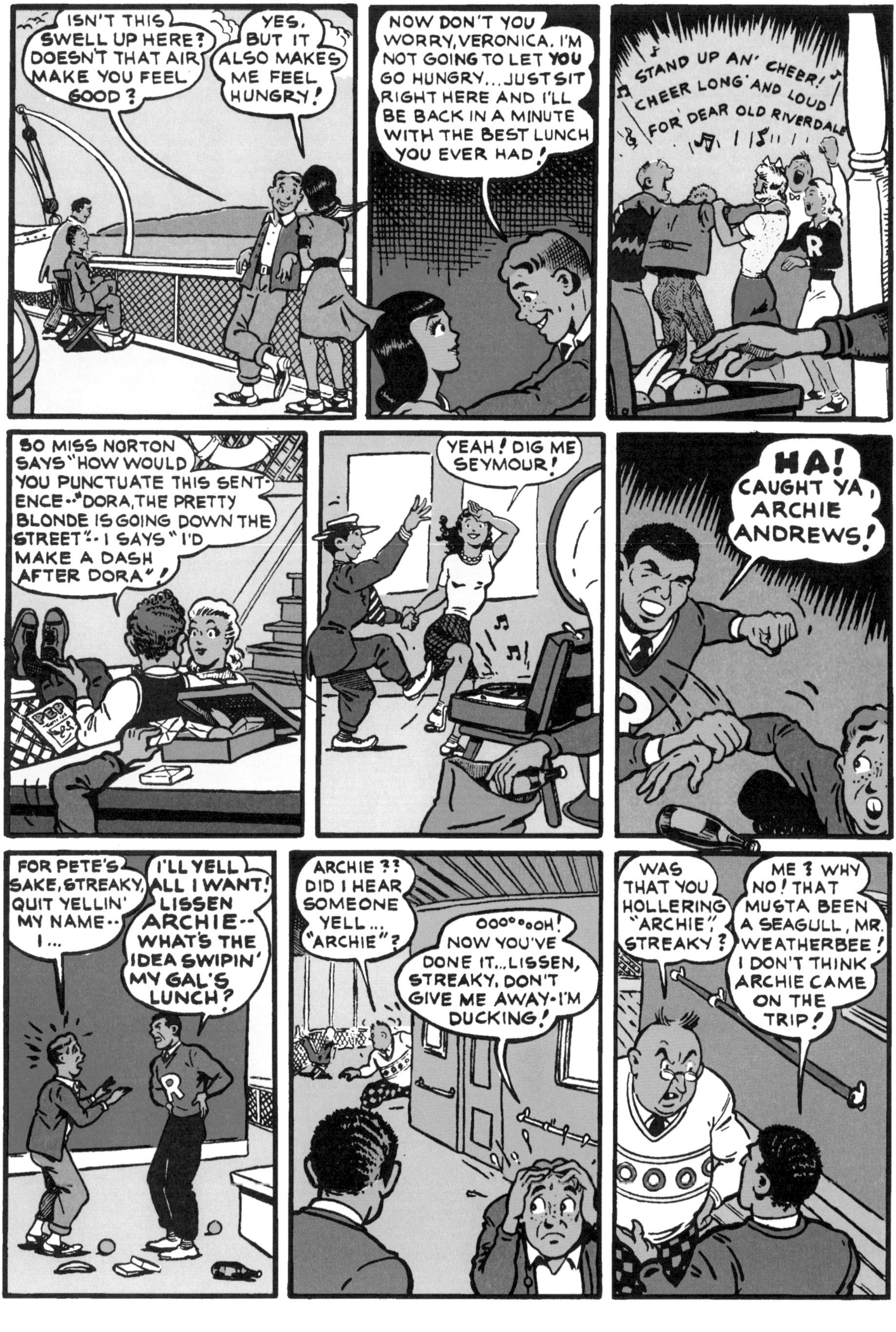
ISN'T THIS SWELL UP HERE? DOESN'T THAT AIR MAKE YOU FEEL GOOD?
YES, BUT IT ALSO MAKES ME FEEL HUNGRY!
NOW DON'T YOU WORRY, VERONICA. I'M NOT GOING TO LET YOU GO HUNGRY... JUST SIT RIGHT HERE AND I'LL BE BACK IN A MINUTE WITH THE BEST LUNCH YOU EVER HAD!
STAND UP AN' CHEER! CHEER LONG AND LOUD FOR DEAR OLD RIVERDALE
SO MISS NORTON SAYS "HOW WOULD YOU PUNCTUATE THIS SENTENCE--"DORA, THE PRETTY BLONDE IS GOING DOWN THE STREET"--I SAYS "I'D MAKE A DASH AFTER DORA"!
YEAH! DIG ME SEYMOUR!
HA! CAUGHT YA, ARCHIE ANDREWS!
FOR PETE'S SAKE, STREAKY, QUIT YELLIN' MY NAME-- I...
I'LL YELL ALL I WANT! LISSEN ARCHIE-- WHAT'S THE IDEA SWIPIN' MY GAL'S LUNCH?
ARCHIE?? DID I HEAR SOMEONE YELL... "ARCHIE"?
OOOOOOOH! NOW YOU'VE DONE IT... LISSEN, STREAKY, DON'T GIVE ME AWAY-I'M DUCKING!
WAS THAT YOU HOLLERING "ARCHIE", STREAKY?
ME? WHY NO! THAT MUSTA BEEN A SEAGULL, MR. WEATHERBEE! I DON'T THINK ARCHIE CAME ON THE TRIP!

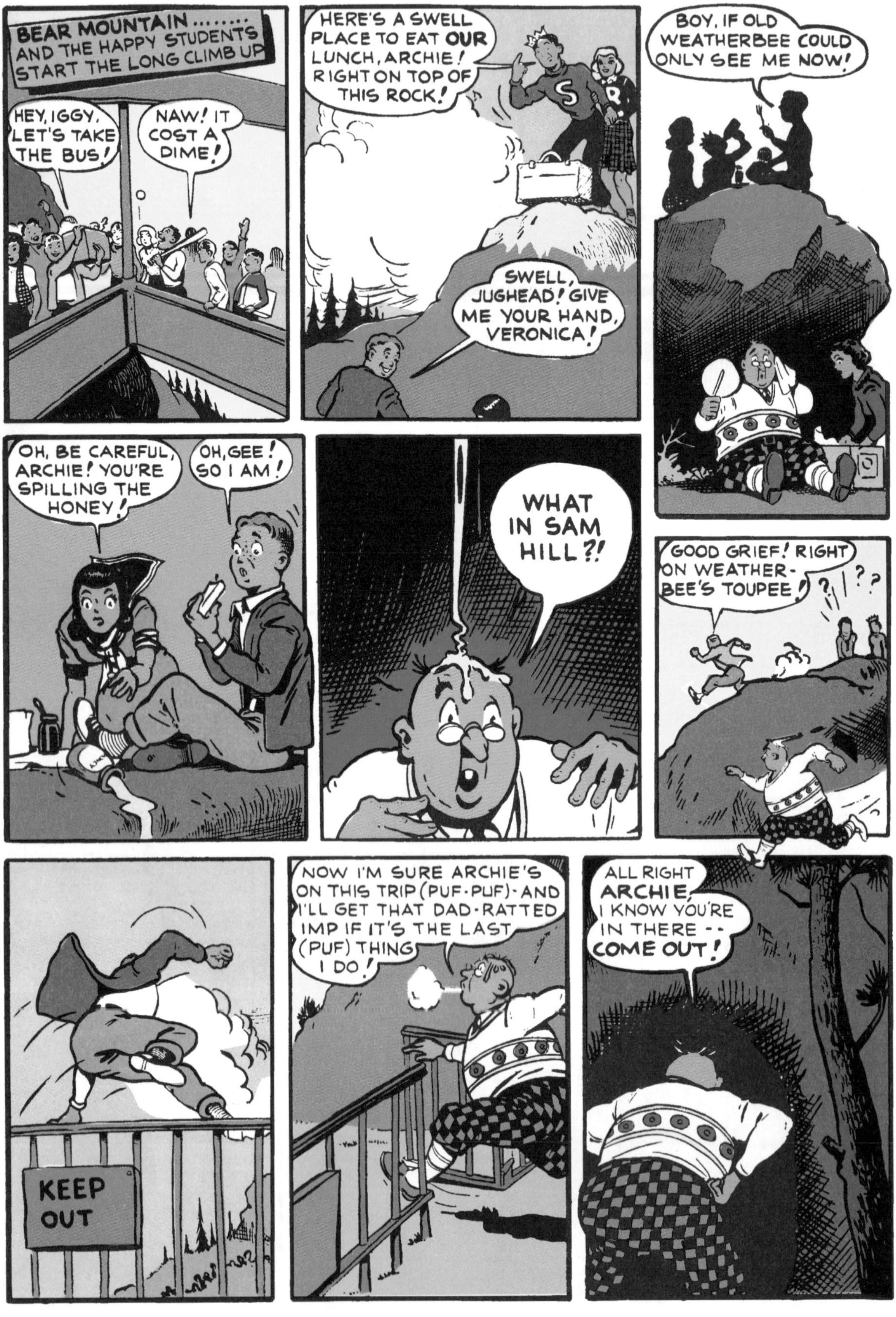
BEAR MOUNTAIN........ AND THE HAPPY STUDENTS START THE LONG CLIMB UP
HEY, IGGY, LET'S TAKE THE BUS!
NAW! IT COST A DIME!
HERE'S A SWELL PLACE TO EAT OUR LUNCH, ARCHIE! RIGHT ON TOP OF THIS ROCK!
SWELL, JUGHEAD! GIVE ME YOUR HAND, VERONICA!
BOY, IF OLD WEATHERBEE COULD ONLY SEE ME NOW!
OH, BE CAREFUL, ARCHIE! YOU'RE SPILLING THE HONEY!
OH, GEE! SO I AM!
WHAT IN SAM HILL?!
GOOD GRIEF! RIGHT ON WEATHER-BEE'S TOUPEE!
KEEP OUT
NOW I'M SURE ARCHIE'S ON THIS TRIP (PUF-PUF)- AND I'LL GET THAT DAD-RATTED IMP IF IT'S THE LAST (PUF) THING I DO!
ALL RIGHT ARCHIE, I KNOW YOU'RE IN THERE -- COME OUT!

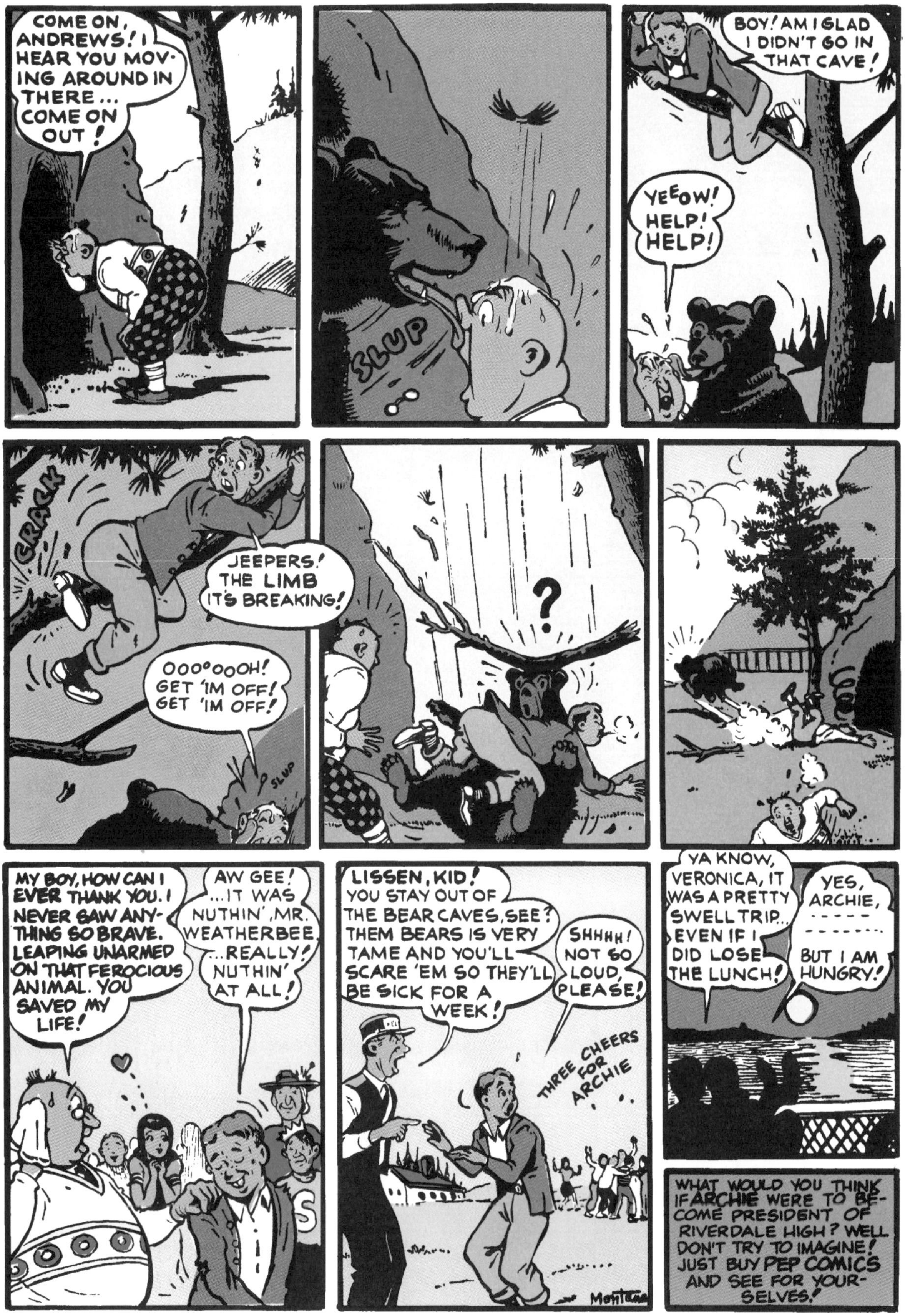
COME ON, ANDREWS! I HEAR YOU MOVING AROUND IN THERE... COME ON OUT!
SLUP
BOY! AM I GLAD I DIDN'T GO IN THAT CAVE!
YEEOW! HELP! HELP!
CRACK
JEEPERS! THE LIMB IT'S BREAKING!
OOOOOOH! GET 'IM OFF! GET 'IM OFF!
SLUP
?
MY BOY, HOW CAN I EVER THANK YOU. I NEVER SAW ANYTHING SO BRAVE. LEAPING UNARMED ON THAT FEROCIOUS ANIMAL. YOU SAVED MY LIFE!
AW GEE! ...IT WAS NUTHIN', MR. WEATHERBEE. ...REALLY! NUTHIN' AT ALL!
LISSEN, KID! YOU STAY OUT OF THE BEAR CAVES, SEE? THEM BEARS IS VERY TAME AND YOU'LL SCARE 'EM SO THEY'LL BE SICK FOR A WEEK!
SHHHH! NOT SO LOUD, PLEASE!
THREE CHEERS FOR ARCHIE
Montana
YA KNOW, VERONICA, IT WAS A PRETTY SWELL TRIP.. EVEN IF I DID LOSE THE LUNCH!
YES, ARCHIE, BUT I AM HUNGRY!
WHAT WOULD YOU THINK IF ARCHIE WERE TO BECOME PRESIDENT OF RIVERDALE HIGH? WELL DON'T TRY TO IMAGINE! JUST BUY PEP COMICS AND SEE FOR YOURSELVES!

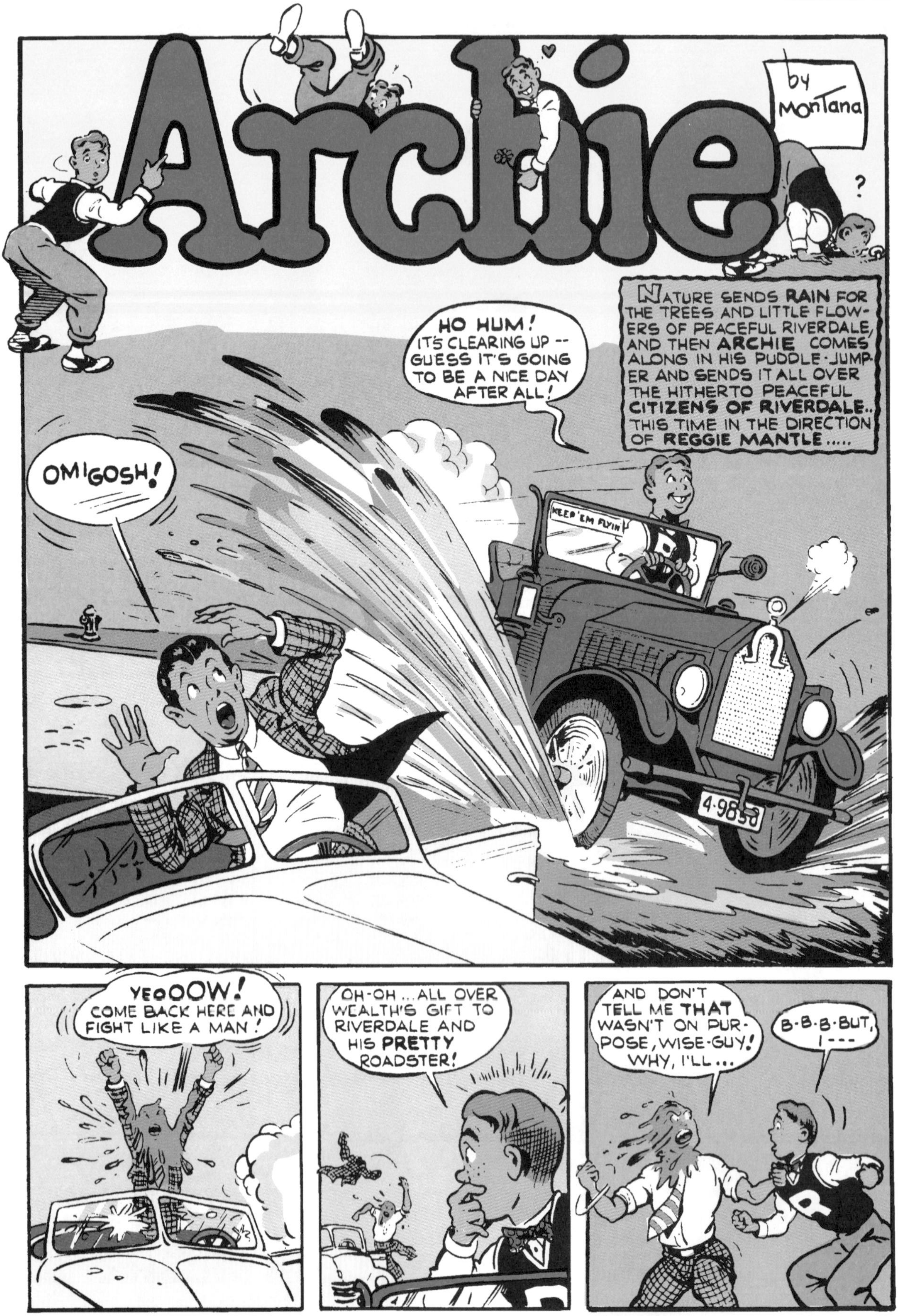
Archie
by MonTana
NATURE SENDS RAIN FOR THE TREES AND LITTLE FLOWERS OF PEACEFUL RIVERDALE, AND THEN ARCHIE COMES ALONG IN HIS PUDDLE-JUMPER AND SENDS IT ALL OVER THE HITHERTO PEACEFUL CITIZENS OF RIVERDALE.. THIS TIME IN THE DIRECTION OF REGGIE MANTLE.....
HO HUM! IT'S CLEARING UP -- GUESS IT'S GOING TO BE A NICE DAY AFTER ALL!
OM'GOSH!
KEEP 'EM FLYIN'
4-985
YEOOOW! COME BACK HERE AND FIGHT LIKE A MAN!
OH-OH ... ALL OVER WEALTH'S GIFT TO RIVERDALE AND HIS PRETTY ROADSTER!
AND DON'T TELL ME THAT WASN'T ON PURPOSE, WISE-GUY! WHY, I'LL ...
B-B-B-BUT, I---

Originally presented in JACKPOT COMICS #6, Summer, 1942

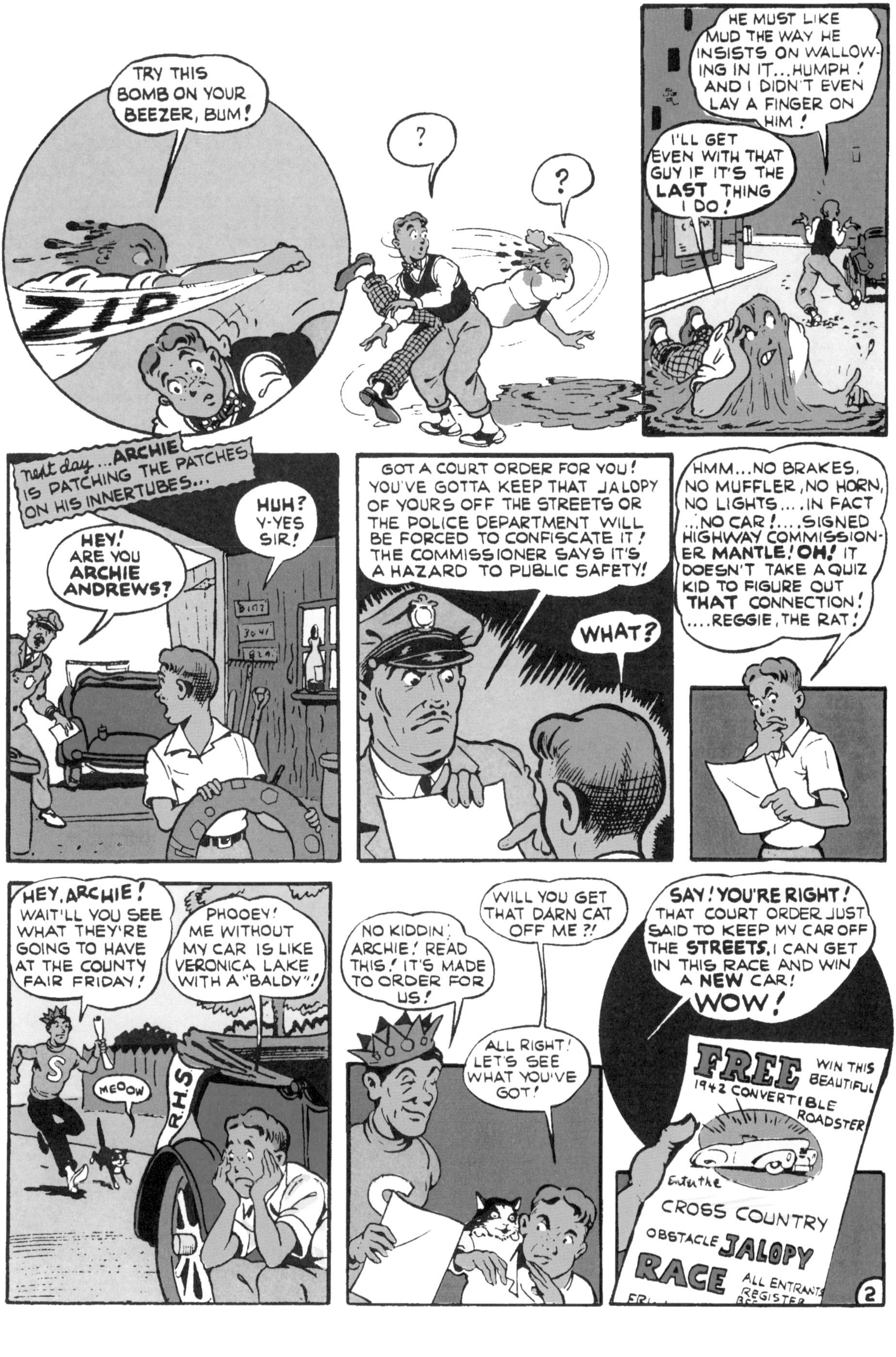
TRY THIS BOMB ON YOUR BEEZER, BUM!
ZIP
?
?
HE MUST LIKE MUD THE WAY HE INSISTS ON WALLOWING IN IT... HUMPH! AND I DIDN'T EVEN LAY A FINGER ON HIM!
I'LL GET EVEN WITH THAT GUY IF IT'S THE LAST THING I DO!
next day... ARCHIE IS PATCHING THE PATCHES ON HIS INNERTUBES...
HEY! ARE YOU ARCHIE ANDREWS?
HUH? Y-YES SIR!
GOT A COURT ORDER FOR YOU! YOU'VE GOTTA KEEP THAT JALOPY OF YOURS OFF THE STREETS OR THE POLICE DEPARTMENT WILL BE FORCED TO CONFISCATE IT! THE COMMISSIONER SAYS IT'S A HAZARD TO PUBLIC SAFETY!
WHAT?
HMM... NO BRAKES, NO MUFFLER, NO HORN, NO LIGHTS.... IN FACT ...NO CAR!.... SIGNED HIGHWAY COMMISSIONER MANTLE! OH! IT DOESN'T TAKE A QUIZ KID TO FIGURE OUT THAT CONNECTION! ....REGGIE, THE RAT!
HEY, ARCHIE! WAIT'LL YOU SEE WHAT THEY'RE GOING TO HAVE AT THE COUNTY FAIR FRIDAY!
PHOOEY! ME WITHOUT MY CAR IS LIKE VERONICA LAKE WITH A "BALDY"!
MEOOW
R.H.S
NO KIDDIN', ARCHIE! READ THIS! IT'S MADE TO ORDER FOR US!
WILL YOU GET THAT DARN CAT OFF ME?!
ALL RIGHT! LET'S SEE WHAT YOU'VE GOT!
SAY! YOU'RE RIGHT! THAT COURT ORDER JUST SAID TO KEEP MY CAR OFF THE STREETS, I CAN GET IN THIS RACE AND WIN A NEW CAR! WOW!
FREE WIN THIS BEAUTIFUL 1942 CONVERTIBLE ROADSTER
Enter the CROSS COUNTRY OBSTACLE JALOPY RACE
ALL ENTRANTS REGISTER
2

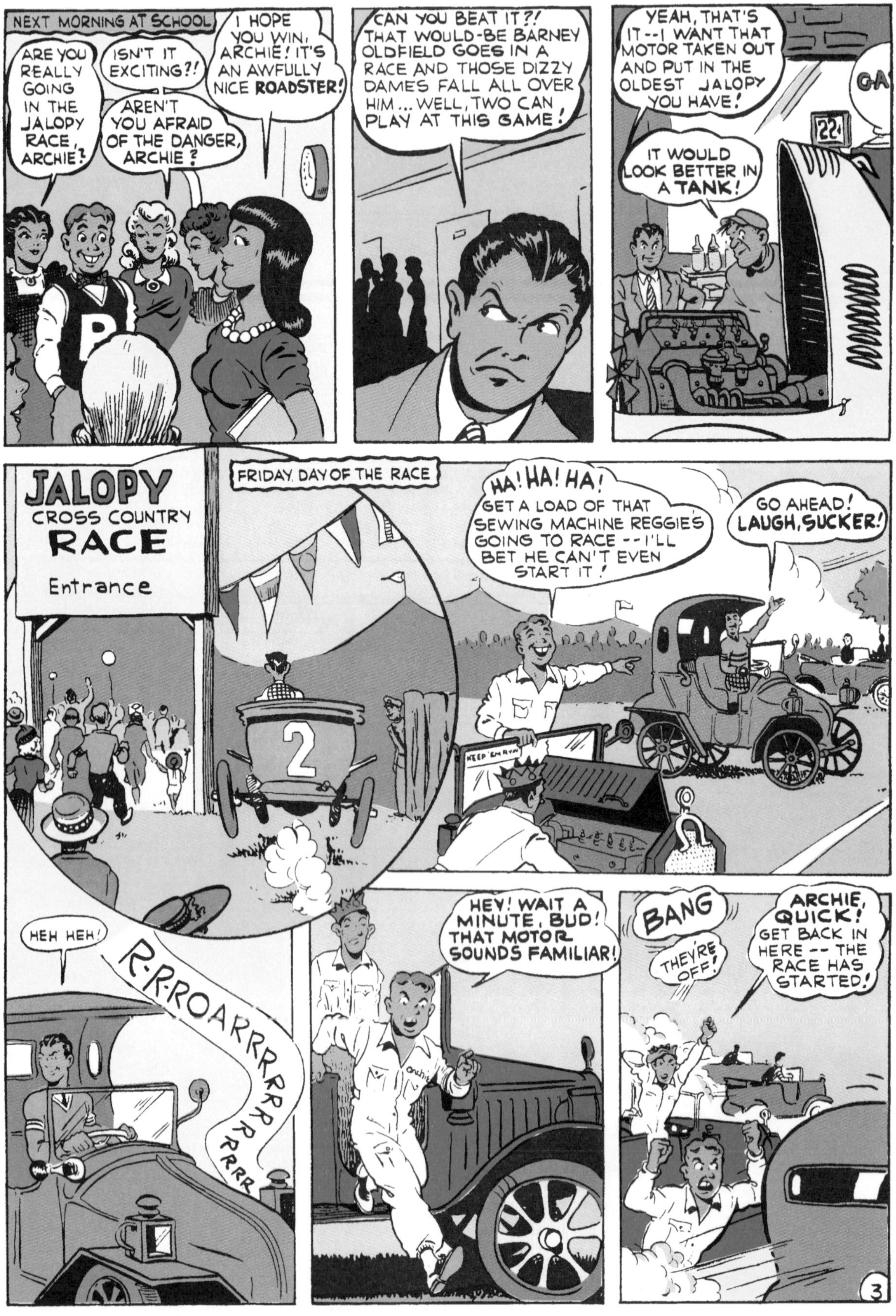
NEXT MORNING AT SCHOOL
ARE YOU REALLY GOING IN THE JALOPY RACE, ARCHIE?
ISN'T IT EXCITING?!
AREN'T YOU AFRAID OF THE DANGER, ARCHIE?
I HOPE YOU WIN, ARCHIE! IT'S AN AWFULLY NICE ROADSTER!
CAN YOU BEAT IT?! THAT WOULD-BE BARNEY OLDFIELD GOES IN A RACE AND THOSE DIZZY DAMES FALL ALL OVER HIM... WELL, TWO CAN PLAY AT THIS GAME!
YEAH, THAT'S IT -- I WANT THAT MOTOR TAKEN OUT AND PUT IN THE OLDEST JALOPY YOU HAVE!
IT WOULD LOOK BETTER IN A TANK!
JALOPY CROSS COUNTRY RACE Entrance
FRIDAY, DAY OF THE RACE
2
HA! HA! HA! GET A LOAD OF THAT SEWING MACHINE REGGIE'S GOING TO RACE -- I'LL BET HE CAN'T EVEN START IT!
GO AHEAD! LAUGH, SUCKER!
HEH HEH!
R-R-ROARRRRRRRRRRR
HEY! WAIT A MINUTE, BUD! THAT MOTOR SOUNDS FAMILIAR!
BANG
THEY'RE OFF!
ARCHIE, QUICK! GET BACK IN HERE -- THE RACE HAS STARTED!
3

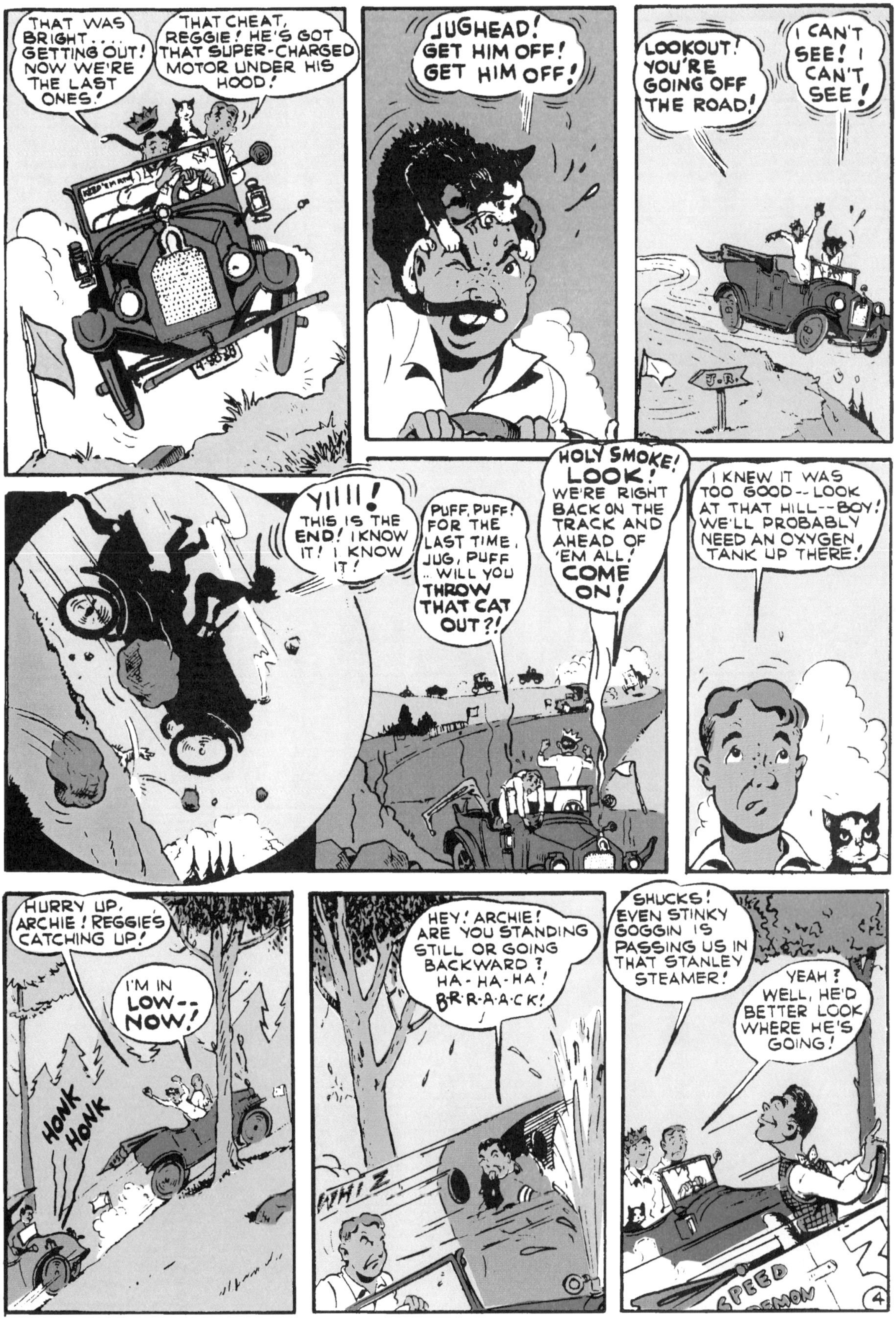
THAT WAS BRIGHT... GETTING OUT! NOW WE'RE THE LAST ONES!
THAT CHEAT, REGGIE! HE'S GOT THAT SUPER-CHARGED MOTOR UNDER HIS HOOD!
JUGHEAD! GET HIM OFF! GET HIM OFF!
LOOKOUT! YOU'RE GOING OFF THE ROAD!
I CAN'T SEE! I CAN'T SEE!
YIIII! THIS IS THE END! I KNOW IT! I KNOW IT!
PUFF, PUFF! FOR THE LAST TIME, JUG, PUFF .. WILL YOU THROW THAT CAT OUT?!
HOLY SMOKE! LOOK! WE'RE RIGHT BACK ON THE TRACK AND AHEAD OF 'EM ALL! COME ON!
I KNEW IT WAS TOO GOOD -- LOOK AT THAT HILL -- BOY! WE'LL PROBABLY NEED AN OXYGEN TANK UP THERE!
HURRY UP, ARCHIE! REGGIE'S CATCHING UP!
I'M IN LOW -- NOW!
HONK HONK
HEY! ARCHIE! ARE YOU STANDING STILL OR GOING BACKWARD? HA-HA-HA! B-R-R-A-A-C-K!
WHIZ
SHUCKS! EVEN STINKY GOGGIN IS PASSING US IN THAT STANLEY STEAMER!
YEAH? WELL, HE'D BETTER LOOK WHERE HE'S GOING!
SPEED DEMON
3
4

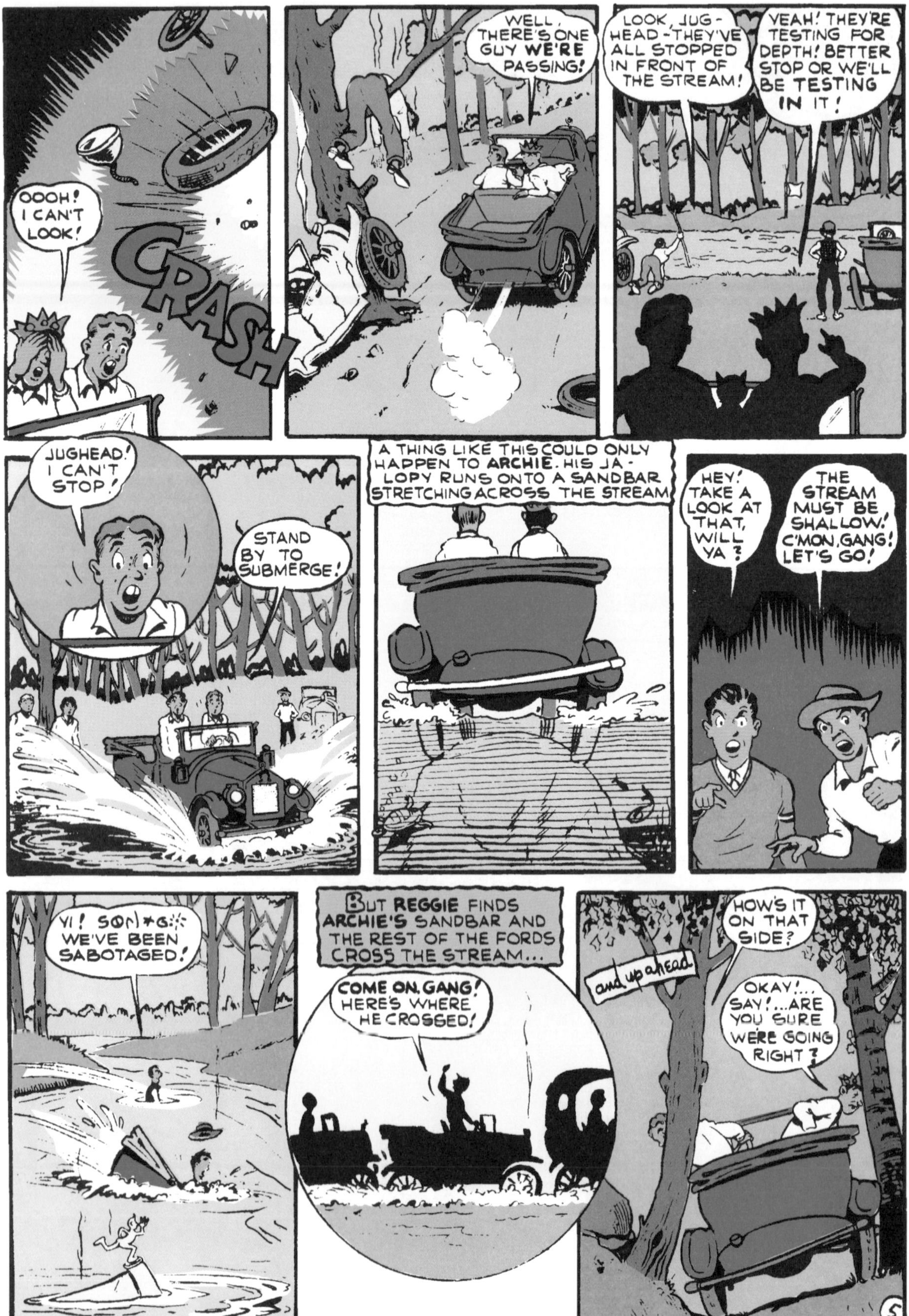
OOOH! I CAN'T LOOK!
CRASH
WELL, THERE'S ONE GUY WE'RE PASSING!
LOOK, JUG-HEAD - THEY'VE ALL STOPPED IN FRONT OF THE STREAM!
YEAH! THEY'RE TESTING FOR DEPTH! BETTER STOP OR WE'LL BE TESTING IN IT!
JUGHEAD! I CAN'T STOP!
STAND BY TO SUBMERGE!
A THING LIKE THIS COULD ONLY HAPPEN TO ARCHIE. HIS JA-LOPY RUNS ONTO A SANDBAR STRETCHING ACROSS THE STREAM
HEY! TAKE A LOOK AT THAT, WILL YA?
THE STREAM MUST BE SHALLOW! C'MON, GANG! LET'S GO!
YI! WE'VE BEEN SABOTAGED!
BUT REGGIE FINDS ARCHIE'S SANDBAR AND THE REST OF THE FORDS CROSS THE STREAM...
COME ON, GANG! HERE'S WHERE HE CROSSED!
and up ahead
HOW'S IT ON THAT SIDE?
OKAY!... SAY!... ARE YOU SURE WE'RE GOING RIGHT?
5

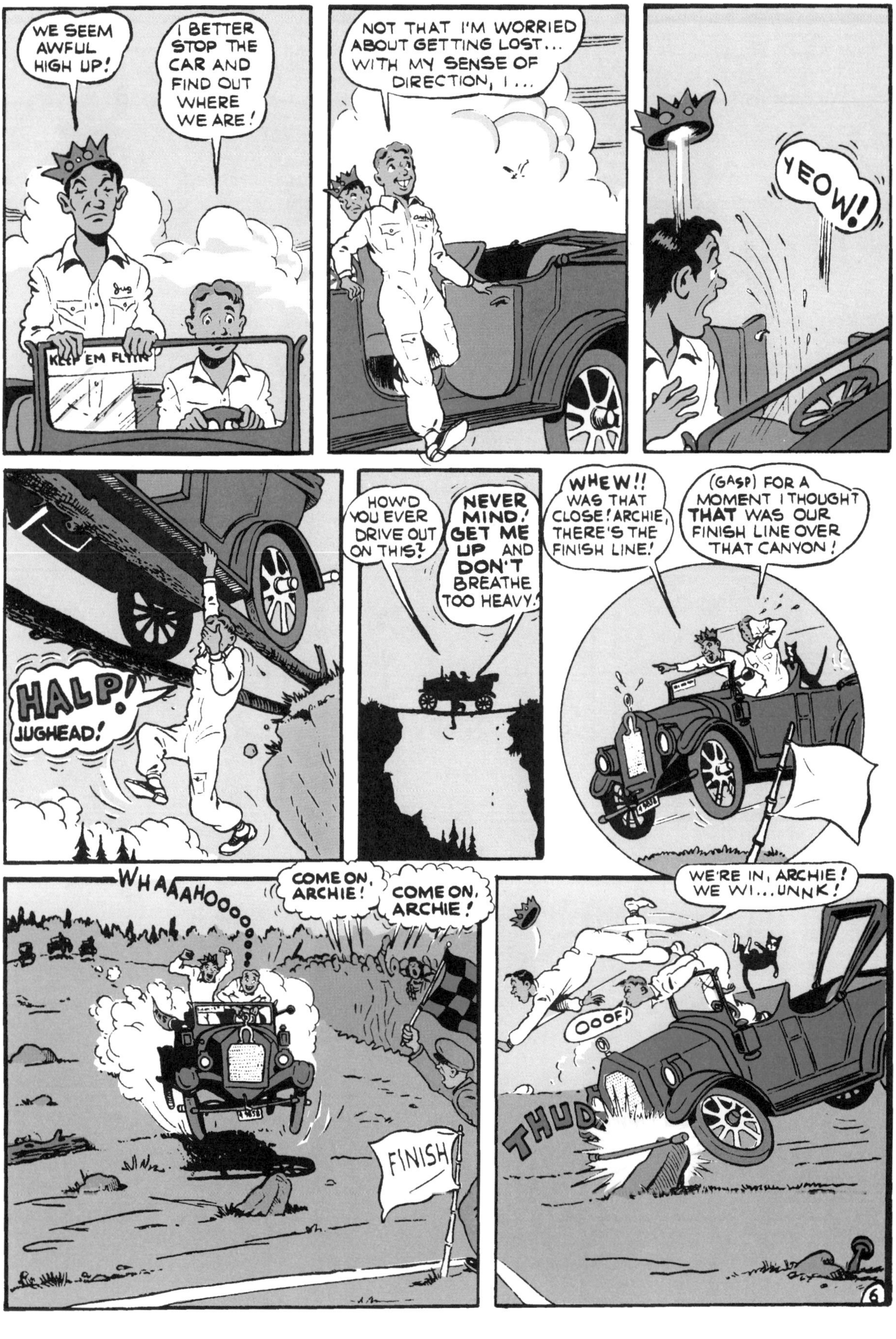
WE SEEM AWFUL HIGH UP!
I BETTER STOP THE CAR AND FIND OUT WHERE WE ARE!
KEEP EM FLYIN
NOT THAT I'M WORRIED ABOUT GETTING LOST... WITH MY SENSE OF DIRECTION, I...
YEOW!
HALP! JUGHEAD!
HOW'D YOU EVER DRIVE OUT ON THIS?
NEVER MIND! GET ME UP AND DON'T BREATHE TOO HEAVY!
WHEW!! WAS THAT CLOSE! ARCHIE, THERE'S THE FINISH LINE!
(GASP) FOR A MOMENT I THOUGHT THAT WAS OUR FINISH LINE OVER THAT CANYON!
WHAAAHOOOOOO
COME ON, ARCHIE!
COME ON, ARCHIE!
FINISH
WE'RE IN, ARCHIE! WE WI...UNNK!
OOOF!
THUD
6

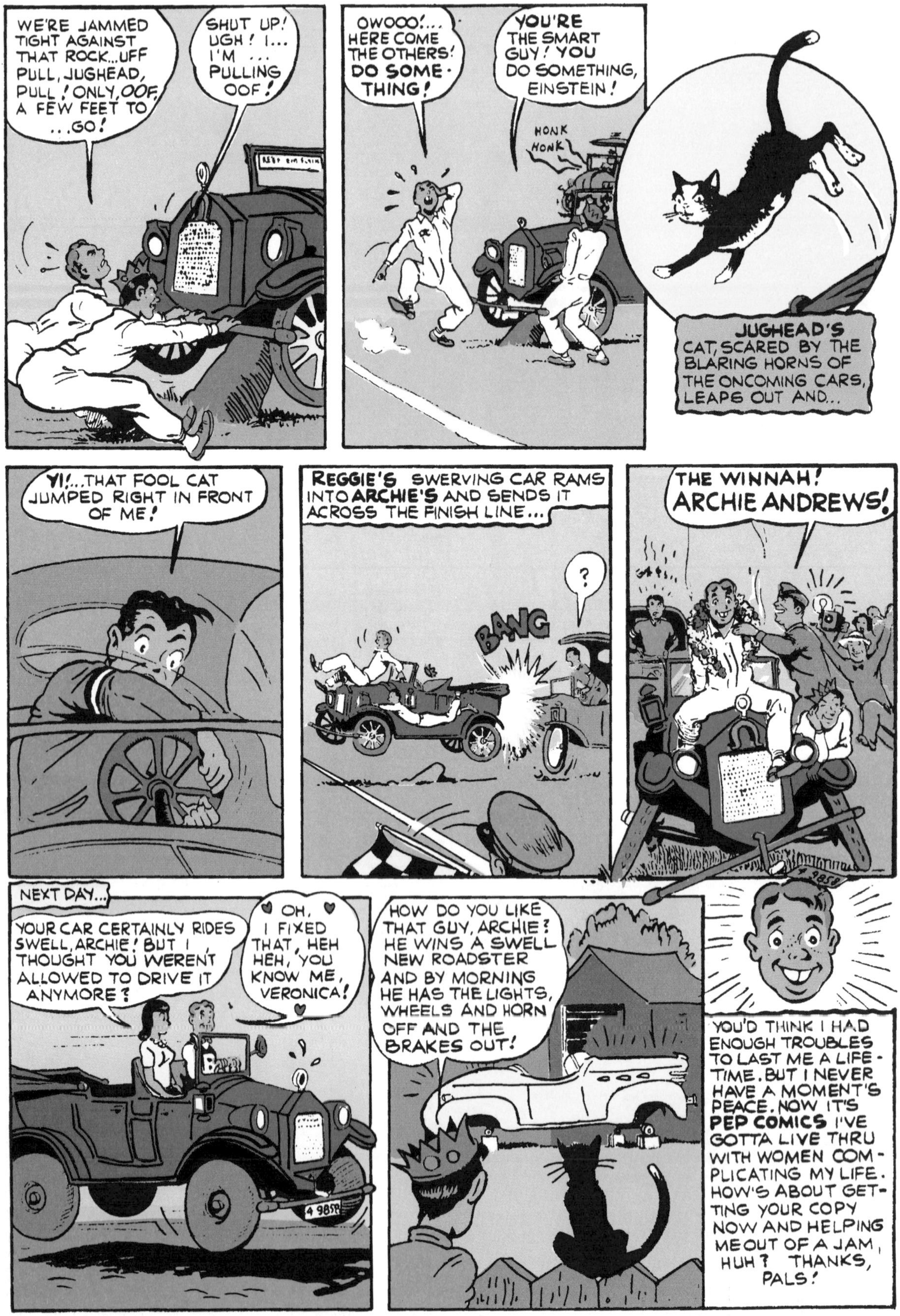

WE'RE JAMMED TIGHT AGAINST THAT ROCK...UFF PULL, JUGHEAD, PULL! ONLY, OOF, A FEW FEET TO ...GO!
SHUT UP! UGH! I... I'M ... PULLING OOF!
OWOOO!... HERE COME THE OTHERS! DO SOME-THING!
YOU'RE THE SMART GUY! YOU DO SOMETHING, EINSTEIN!
HONK HONK
JUGHEAD'S CAT, SCARED BY THE BLARING HORNS OF THE ONCOMING CARS, LEAPS OUT AND...
YI!...THAT FOOL CAT JUMPED RIGHT IN FRONT OF ME!
REGGIE'S SWERVING CAR RAMS INTO ARCHIE'S AND SENDS IT ACROSS THE FINISH LINE...
?
BANG
THE WINNAH! ARCHIE ANDREWS!
4 9858
NEXT DAY...
YOUR CAR CERTAINLY RIDES SWELL, ARCHIE! BUT I THOUGHT YOU WERENT ALLOWED TO DRIVE IT ANYMORE?
OH, I FIXED THAT, HEH HEH, YOU KNOW ME, VERONICA!
4 9858
HOW DO YOU LIKE THAT GUY, ARCHIE? HE WINS A SWELL NEW ROADSTER AND BY MORNING HE HAS THE LIGHTS, WHEELS AND HORN OFF AND THE BRAKES OUT!
YOU'D THINK I HAD ENOUGH TROUBLES TO LAST ME A LIFE-TIME. BUT I NEVER HAVE A MOMENT'S PEACE. NOW IT'S PEP COMICS I'VE GOTTA LIVE THRU WITH WOMEN COM-PLICATING MY LIFE. HOW'S ABOUT GET-TING YOUR COPY NOW AND HELPING ME OUT OF A JAM, HUH? THANKS, PALS!

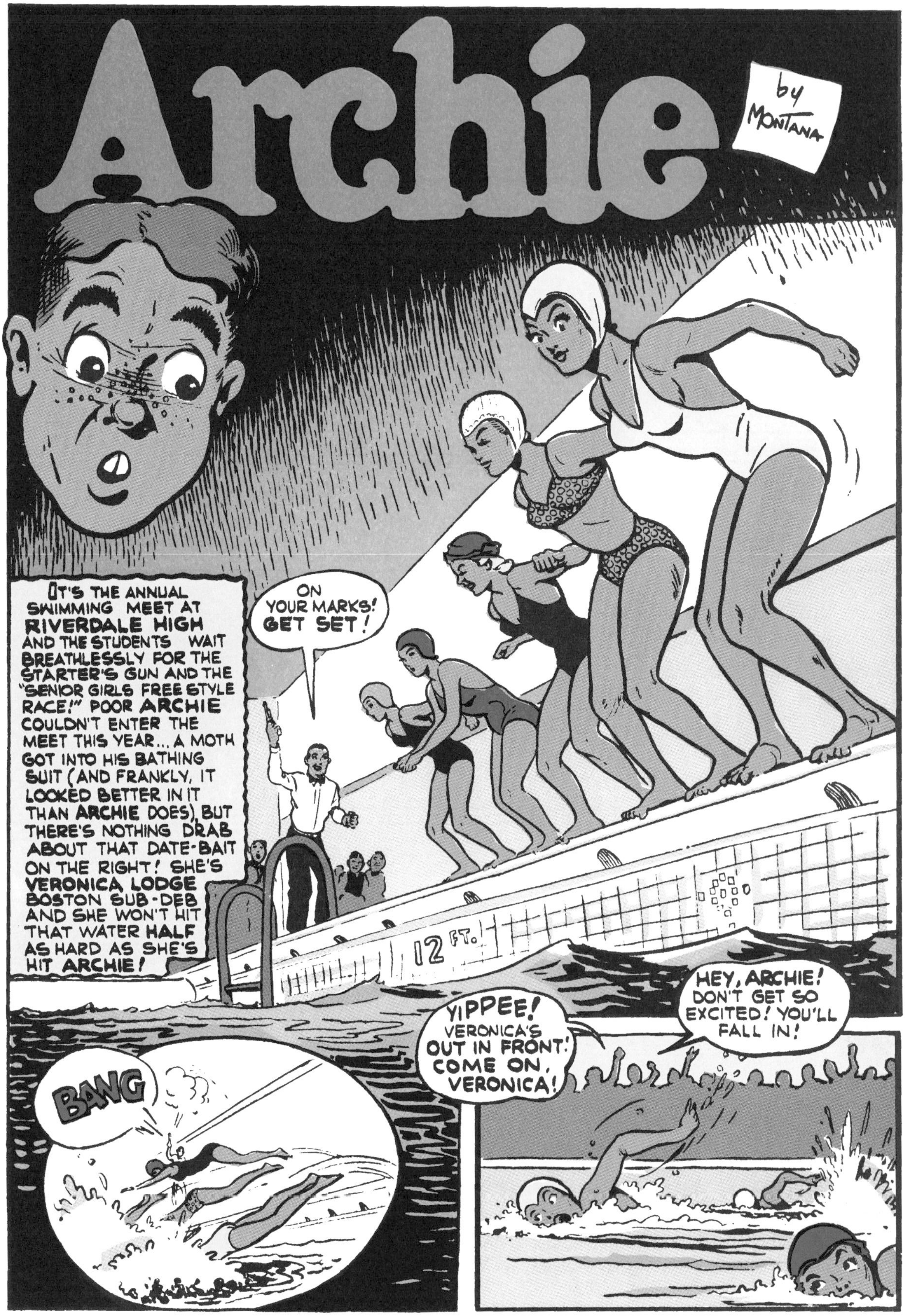
Archie
by MONTANA
IT'S THE ANNUAL SWIMMING MEET AT RIVERDALE HIGH AND THE STUDENTS WAIT BREATHLESSLY FOR THE STARTER'S GUN AND THE "SENIOR GIRLS FREE STYLE RACE!" POOR ARCHIE COULDN'T ENTER THE MEET THIS YEAR... A MOTH GOT INTO HIS BATHING SUIT (AND FRANKLY, IT LOOKED BETTER IN IT THAN ARCHIE DOES), BUT THERE'S NOTHING DRAB ABOUT THAT DATE-BAIT ON THE RIGHT! SHE'S VERONICA LODGE BOSTON SUB-DEB AND SHE WON'T HIT THAT WATER HALF AS HARD AS SHE'S HIT ARCHIE!
ON YOUR MARKS! GET SET!
12 FT.
BANG
YIPPEE! VERONICA'S OUT IN FRONT! COME ON, VERONICA!
HEY, ARCHIE! DON'T GET SO EXCITED! YOU'LL FALL IN!

Originally presented in PEP COMICS #31, September, 1942

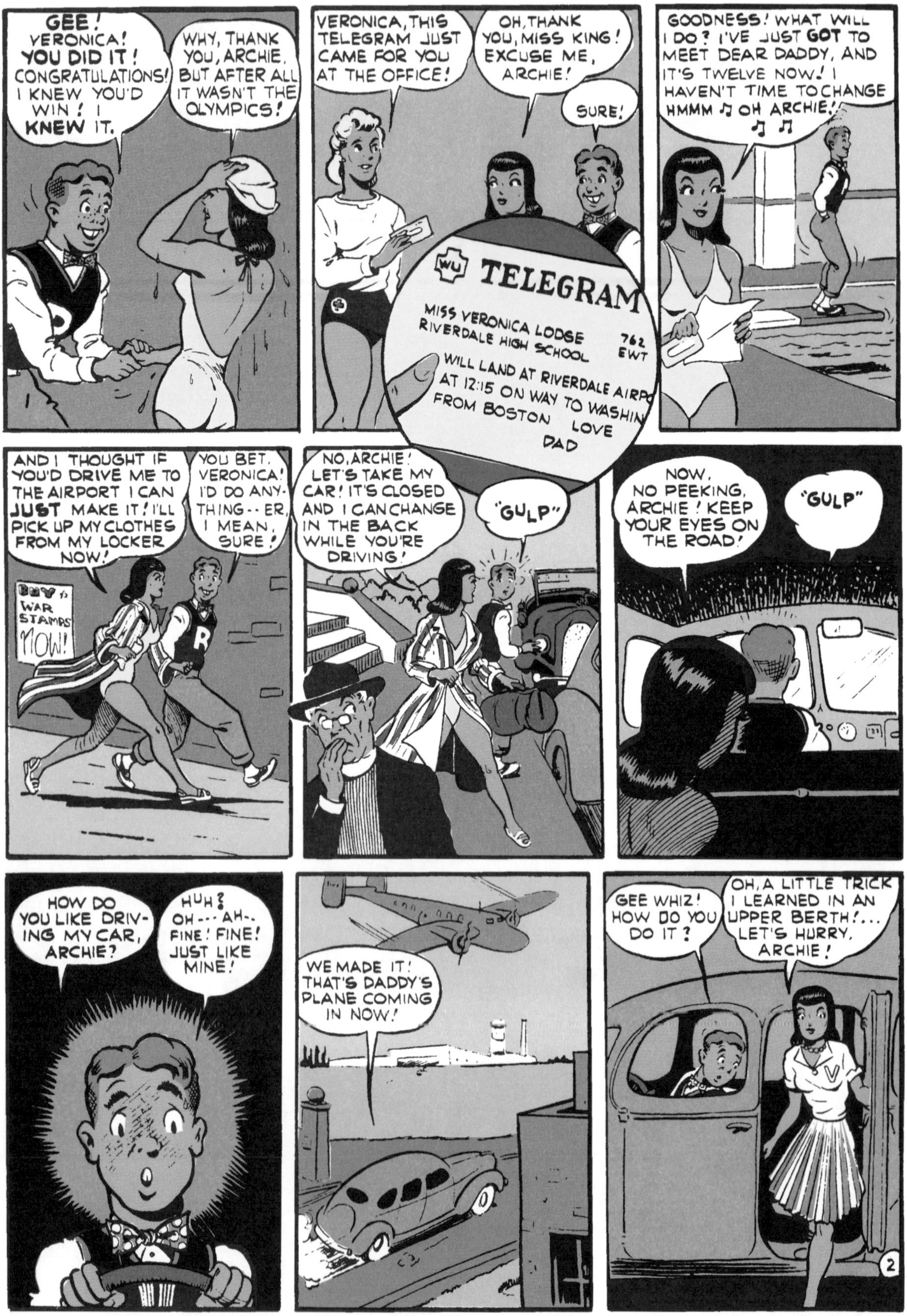
GEE! VERONICA! YOU DID IT! CONGRATULATIONS! I KNEW YOU'D WIN! I KNEW IT.
WHY, THANK YOU, ARCHIE. BUT AFTER ALL IT WASN'T THE OLYMPICS!
VERONICA, THIS TELEGRAM JUST CAME FOR YOU AT THE OFFICE!
OH, THANK YOU, MISS KING! EXCUSE ME, ARCHIE!
SURE!
WU TELEGRAM
MISS VERONICA LODGE RIVERDALE HIGH SCHOOL 762 EWT
WILL LAND AT RIVERDALE AIRP AT 12:15 ON WAY TO WASHIN FROM BOSTON LOVE DAD
GOODNESS! WHAT WILL I DO? I'VE JUST GOT TO MEET DEAR DADDY, AND IT'S TWELVE NOW! I HAVEN'T TIME TO CHANGE HMMM ♫ OH ARCHIE! ♫ ♫
AND I THOUGHT IF YOU'D DRIVE ME TO THE AIRPORT I CAN JUST MAKE IT! I'LL PICK UP MY CLOTHES FROM MY LOCKER NOW!
YOU BET, VERONICA! I'D DO ANY-THING -- ER, I MEAN, SURE!
WAR STAMPS NOW!
NO, ARCHIE! LET'S TAKE MY CAR! IT'S CLOSED AND I CAN CHANGE IN THE BACK WHILE YOU'RE DRIVING!
"GULP"
NOW, NO PEEKING, ARCHIE! KEEP YOUR EYES ON THE ROAD!
"GULP"
HOW DO YOU LIKE DRIV-ING MY CAR, ARCHIE?
HUH? OH --- AH-. FINE! FINE! JUST LIKE MINE!
WE MADE IT! THAT'S DADDY'S PLANE COMING IN NOW!
GEE WHIZ! HOW DO YOU DO IT?
OH, A LITTLE TRICK I LEARNED IN AN UPPER BERTH!... LET'S HURRY, ARCHIE!
2

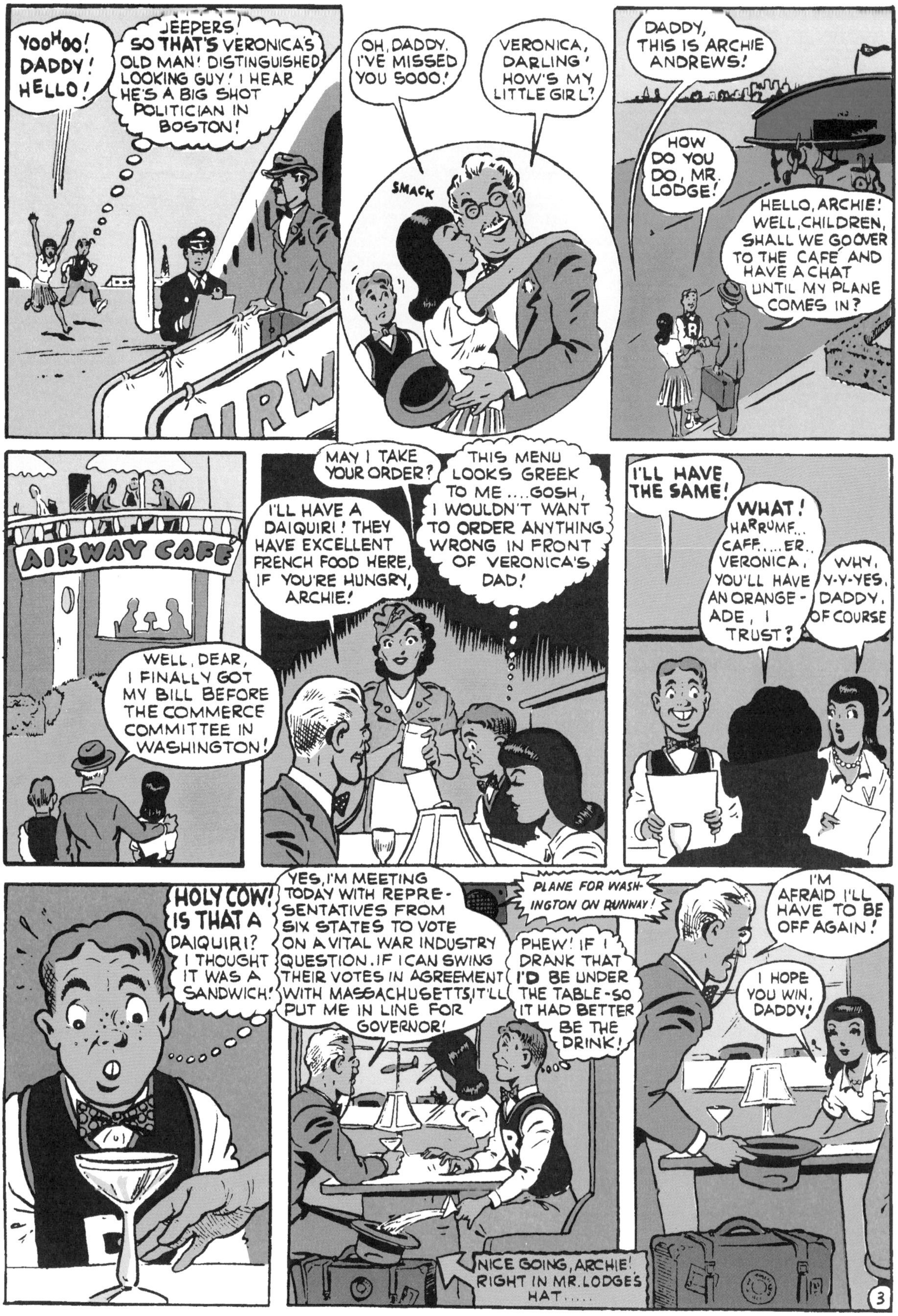
YOOHOO! DADDY! HELLO!
JEEPERS! SO THAT'S VERONICA'S OLD MAN! DISTINGUISHED LOOKING GUY! I HEAR HE'S A BIG SHOT POLITICIAN IN BOSTON!
AIRW
OH, DADDY. I'VE MISSED YOU SOOO!
VERONICA, DARLING! HOW'S MY LITTLE GIRL?
SMACK
DADDY, THIS IS ARCHIE ANDREWS!
HOW DO YOU DO, MR. LODGE!
HELLO, ARCHIE! WELL, CHILDREN, SHALL WE GO OVER TO THE CAFE AND HAVE A CHAT UNTIL MY PLANE COMES IN?
AIRWAY CAFE
WELL, DEAR, I FINALLY GOT MY BILL BEFORE THE COMMERCE COMMITTEE IN WASHINGTON!
MAY I TAKE YOUR ORDER?
I'LL HAVE A DAIQUIRI! THEY HAVE EXCELLENT FRENCH FOOD HERE, IF YOU'RE HUNGRY, ARCHIE!
THIS MENU LOOKS GREEK TO ME....GOSH, I WOULDN'T WANT TO ORDER ANYTHING WRONG IN FRONT OF VERONICA'S DAD!
I'LL HAVE THE SAME!
WHAT! HARRUMF.. CAFF.....ER.. VERONICA, YOU'LL HAVE AN ORANGE-ADE, I TRUST?
WHY, Y-Y-YES, DADDY, OF COURSE
HOLY COW! IS THAT A DAIQUIRI? I THOUGHT IT WAS A SANDWICH!
YES, I'M MEETING TODAY WITH REPRESENTATIVES FROM SIX STATES TO VOTE ON A VITAL WAR INDUSTRY QUESTION. IF I CAN SWING THEIR VOTES IN AGREEMENT WITH MASSACHUSETTS, IT'LL PUT ME IN LINE FOR GOVERNOR!
PLANE FOR WASHINGTON ON RUNWAY!
PHEW! IF I DRANK THAT I'D BE UNDER THE TABLE-SO IT HAD BETTER BE THE DRINK!
NICE GOING, ARCHIE! RIGHT IN MR. LODGE'S HAT.....
I'M AFRAID I'LL HAVE TO BE OFF AGAIN!
I HOPE YOU WIN, DADDY!
3

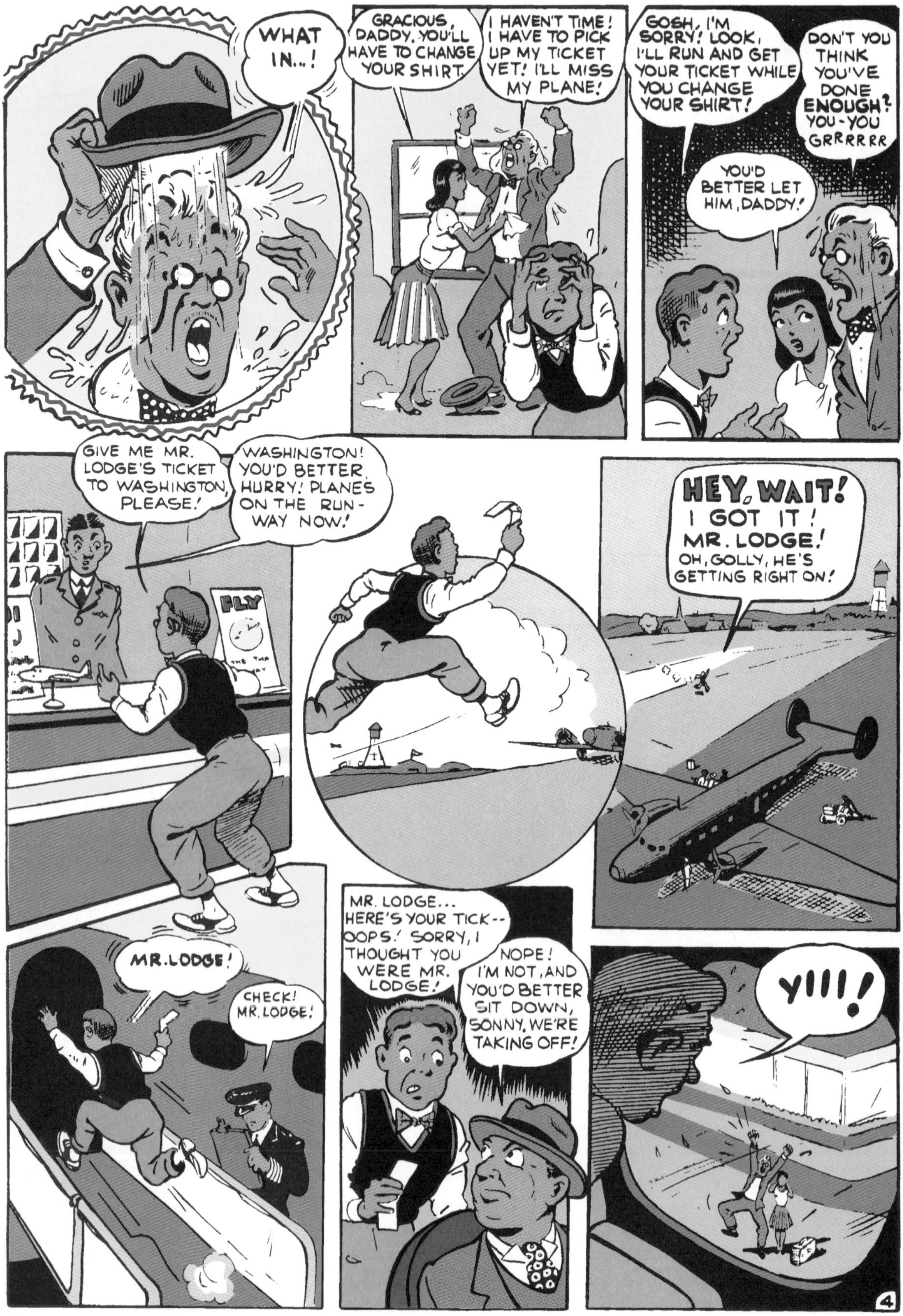
WHAT IN...!
GRACIOUS, DADDY. YOU'LL HAVE TO CHANGE YOUR SHIRT.
I HAVEN'T TIME! I HAVE TO PICK UP MY TICKET YET! I'LL MISS MY PLANE!
GOSH, I'M SORRY! LOOK, I'LL RUN AND GET YOUR TICKET WHILE YOU CHANGE YOUR SHIRT!
DON'T YOU THINK YOU'VE DONE ENOUGH? YOU-YOU GRRRRRR
YOU'D BETTER LET HIM, DADDY!
GIVE ME MR. LODGE'S TICKET TO WASHINGTON, PLEASE!
WASHINGTON! YOU'D BETTER HURRY! PLANES ON THE RUN-WAY NOW!
FLY
HEY, WAIT! I GOT IT! MR. LODGE! OH, GOLLY, HE'S GETTING RIGHT ON!
MR. LODGE!
CHECK! MR. LODGE!
MR. LODGE... HERE'S YOUR TICK-- OOPS! SORRY, I THOUGHT YOU WERE MR. LODGE!
NOPE! I'M NOT, AND YOU'D BETTER SIT DOWN, SONNY, WE'RE TAKING OFF!
YIII!
4

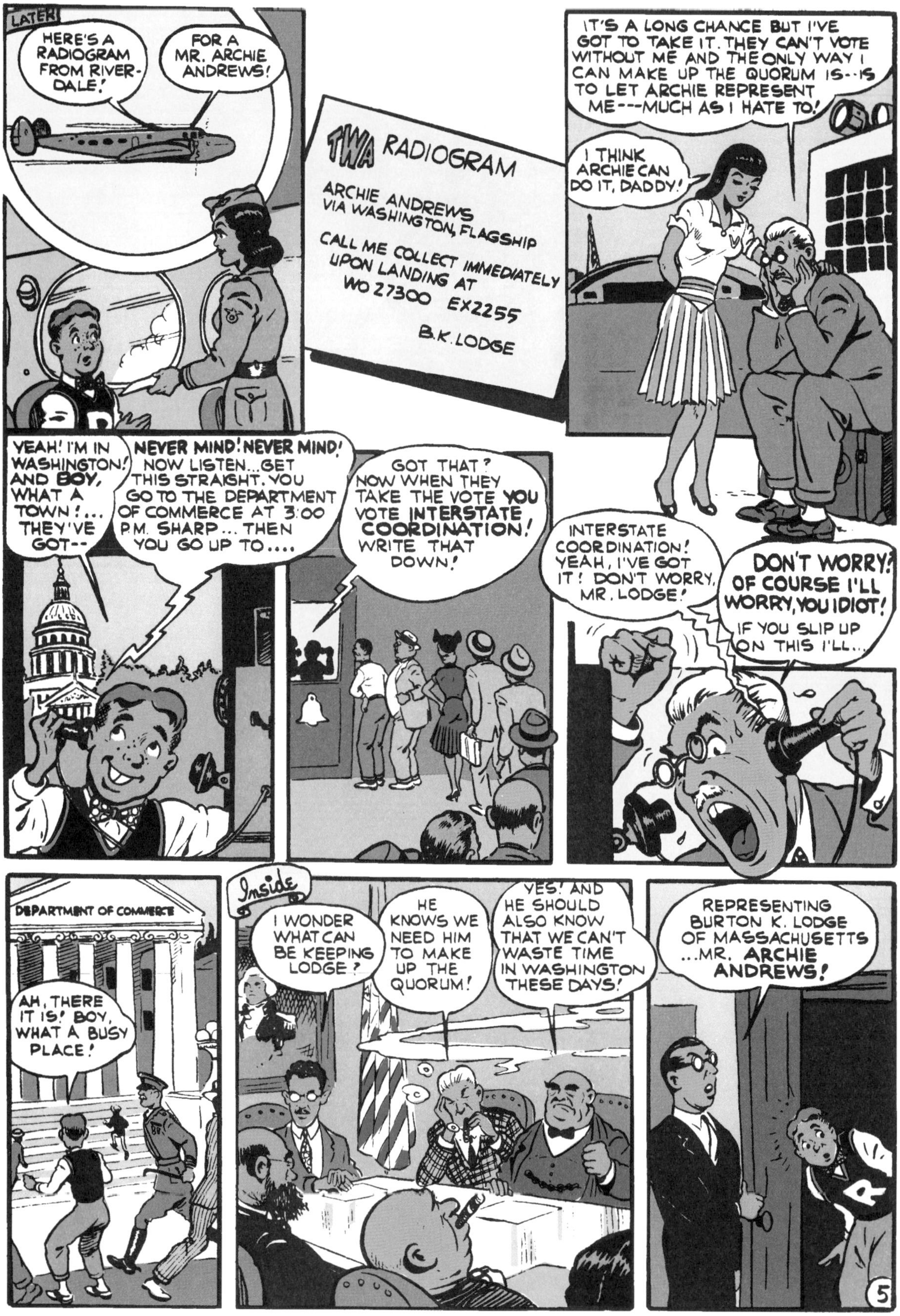
LATER
HERE'S A RADIOGRAM FROM RIVER-DALE!
FOR A MR. ARCHIE ANDREWS!
TWA RADIOGRAM
ARCHIE ANDREWS
VIA WASHINGTON, FLAGSHIP
CALL ME COLLECT IMMEDIATELY
UPON LANDING AT
WO 27300 EX2255
B.K. LODGE
IT'S A LONG CHANCE BUT I'VE GOT TO TAKE IT. THEY CAN'T VOTE WITHOUT ME AND THE ONLY WAY I CAN MAKE UP THE QUORUM IS--IS TO LET ARCHIE REPRESENT ME---MUCH AS I HATE TO!
I THINK ARCHIE CAN DO IT, DADDY!
YEAH! I'M IN WASHINGTON! AND BOY, WHAT A TOWN!... THEY'VE GOT--
NEVER MIND! NEVER MIND! NOW LISTEN...GET THIS STRAIGHT. YOU GO TO THE DEPARTMENT OF COMMERCE AT 3:00 P.M. SHARP... THEN YOU GO UP TO....
GOT THAT? NOW WHEN THEY TAKE THE VOTE YOU VOTE INTERSTATE COORDINATION! WRITE THAT DOWN!
INTERSTATE COORDINATION! YEAH, I'VE GOT IT! DON'T WORRY, MR. LODGE!
DON'T WORRY? OF COURSE I'LL WORRY, YOU IDIOT! IF YOU SLIP UP ON THIS I'LL...
DEPARTMENT OF COMMERCE
AH, THERE IT IS! BOY, WHAT A BUSY PLACE!
Inside
I WONDER WHAT CAN BE KEEPING LODGE?
HE KNOWS WE NEED HIM TO MAKE UP THE QUORUM!
YES! AND HE SHOULD ALSO KNOW THAT WE CAN'T WASTE TIME IN WASHINGTON THESE DAYS!
REPRESENTING BURTON K. LODGE OF MASSACHUSETTS ...MR. ARCHIE ANDREWS!
5

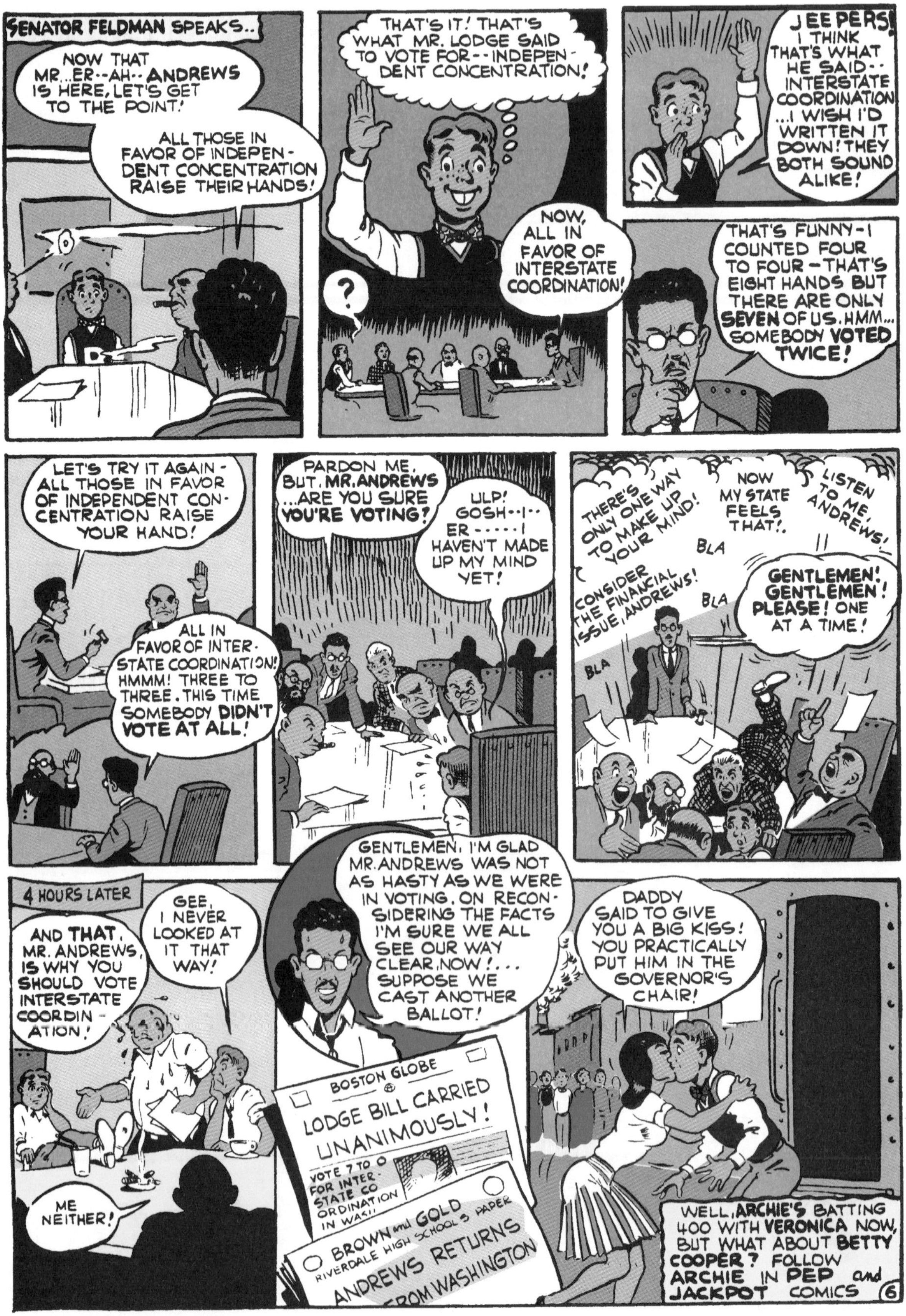
SENATOR FELDMAN SPEAKS..
NOW THAT MR...ER--AH--ANDREWS IS HERE, LET'S GET TO THE POINT!
ALL THOSE IN FAVOR OF INDEPENDENT CONCENTRATION RAISE THEIR HANDS!
THAT'S IT! THAT'S WHAT MR. LODGE SAID TO VOTE FOR--INDEPENDENT CONCENTRATION!
NOW, ALL IN FAVOR OF INTERSTATE COORDINATION!
?
JEEPERS! I THINK THAT'S WHAT HE SAID--INTERSTATE COORDINATION...I WISH I'D WRITTEN IT DOWN! THEY BOTH SOUND ALIKE!
THAT'S FUNNY-I COUNTED FOUR TO FOUR-THAT'S EIGHT HANDS BUT THERE ARE ONLY SEVEN OF US. HMM... SOMEBODY VOTED TWICE!
LET'S TRY IT AGAIN-ALL THOSE IN FAVOR OF INDEPENDENT CONCENTRATION RAISE YOUR HAND!
ALL IN FAVOR OF INTERSTATE COORDINATION! HMMM! THREE TO THREE. THIS TIME SOMEBODY DIDN'T VOTE AT ALL!
PARDON ME, BUT, MR. ANDREWS ...ARE YOU SURE YOU'RE VOTING?
ULP! GOSH--I--ER-----I HAVEN'T MADE UP MY MIND YET!
THERE'S ONLY ONE WAY TO MAKE UP YOUR MIND!
NOW MY STATE FEELS THAT!.
LISTEN TO ME, ANDREWS!
BLA
CONSIDER THE FINANCIAL ISSUE, ANDREWS!
BLA
GENTLEMEN! GENTLEMEN! PLEASE! ONE AT A TIME!
BLA
4 HOURS LATER
AND THAT, MR. ANDREWS, IS WHY YOU SHOULD VOTE INTERSTATE COORDINATION!
GEE, I NEVER LOOKED AT IT THAT WAY!
ME NEITHER!
GENTLEMEN, I'M GLAD MR. ANDREWS WAS NOT AS HASTY AS WE WERE IN VOTING. ON RECONSIDERING THE FACTS I'M SURE WE ALL SEE OUR WAY CLEAR, NOW!... SUPPOSE WE CAST ANOTHER BALLOT!
BOSTON GLOBE
LODGE BILL CARRIED UNANIMOUSLY!
VOTE 7 TO 0 FOR INTERSTATE COORDINATION IN WASH
BROWN and GOLD RIVERDALE HIGH SCHOOL'S PAPER
ANDREWS RETURNS FROM WASHINGTON
DADDY SAID TO GIVE YOU A BIG KISS! YOU PRACTICALLY PUT HIM IN THE GOVERNOR'S CHAIR!
WELL, ARCHIE'S BATTING 400 WITH VERONICA NOW, BUT WHAT ABOUT BETTY COOPER? FOLLOW ARCHIE IN PEP and JACKPOT COMICS
6

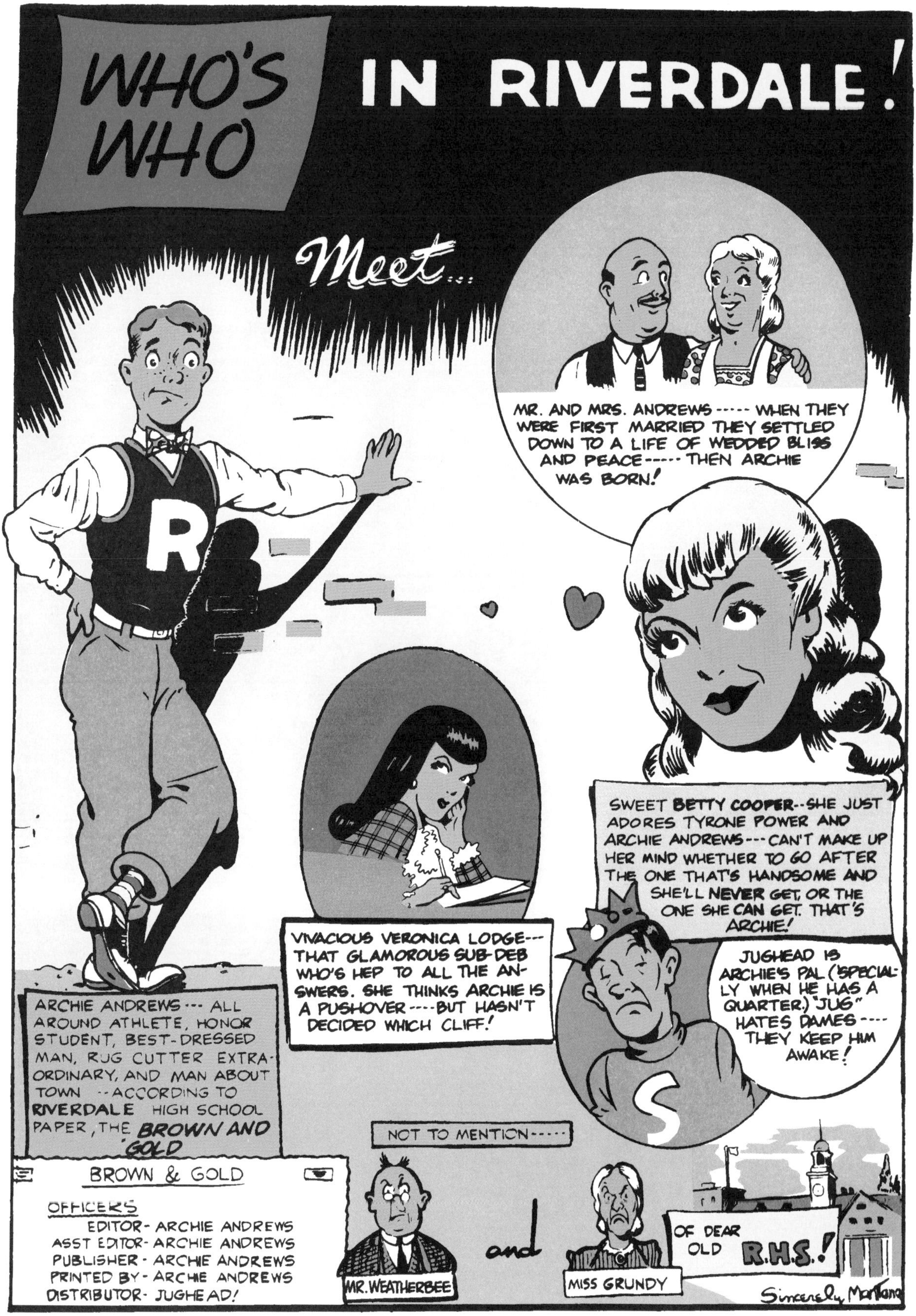
WHO'S WHO IN RIVERDALE!
Meet...
MR. AND MRS. ANDREWS ----- WHEN THEY WERE FIRST MARRIED THEY SETTLED DOWN TO A LIFE OF WEDDED BLISS AND PEACE ----- THEN ARCHIE WAS BORN!
SWEET BETTY COOPER--SHE JUST ADORES TYRONE POWER AND ARCHIE ANDREWS---CAN'T MAKE UP HER MIND WHETHER TO GO AFTER THE ONE THAT'S HANDSOME AND SHE'LL NEVER GET, OR THE ONE SHE CAN GET. THAT'S ARCHIE!
VIVACIOUS VERONICA LODGE--- THAT GLAMOROUS SUB-DEB WHO'S HEP TO ALL THE ANSWERS. SHE THINKS ARCHIE IS A PUSHOVER ----BUT HASN'T DECIDED WHICH CLIFF!
JUGHEAD IS ARCHIE'S PAL ('SPECIALLY WHEN HE HAS A QUARTER.) "JUG" HATES DAMES ---- THEY KEEP HIM AWAKE!
ARCHIE ANDREWS --- ALL AROUND ATHLETE, HONOR STUDENT, BEST-DRESSED MAN, RUG CUTTER EXTRAORDINARY, AND MAN ABOUT TOWN --ACCORDING TO RIVERDALE HIGH SCHOOL PAPER, THE BROWN AND GOLD
BROWN & GOLD
OFFICERS
EDITOR- ARCHIE ANDREWS
ASST EDITOR- ARCHIE ANDREWS
PUBLISHER - ARCHIE ANDREWS
PRINTED BY - ARCHIE ANDREWS
DISTRIBUTOR- JUGHEAD!
NOT TO MENTION-----
MR. WEATHERBEE
and
MISS GRUNDY
OF DEAR OLD R.H.S.!
Sincerely Montana

Originally presented in ARCHIE COMICS #1, Winter, 1942

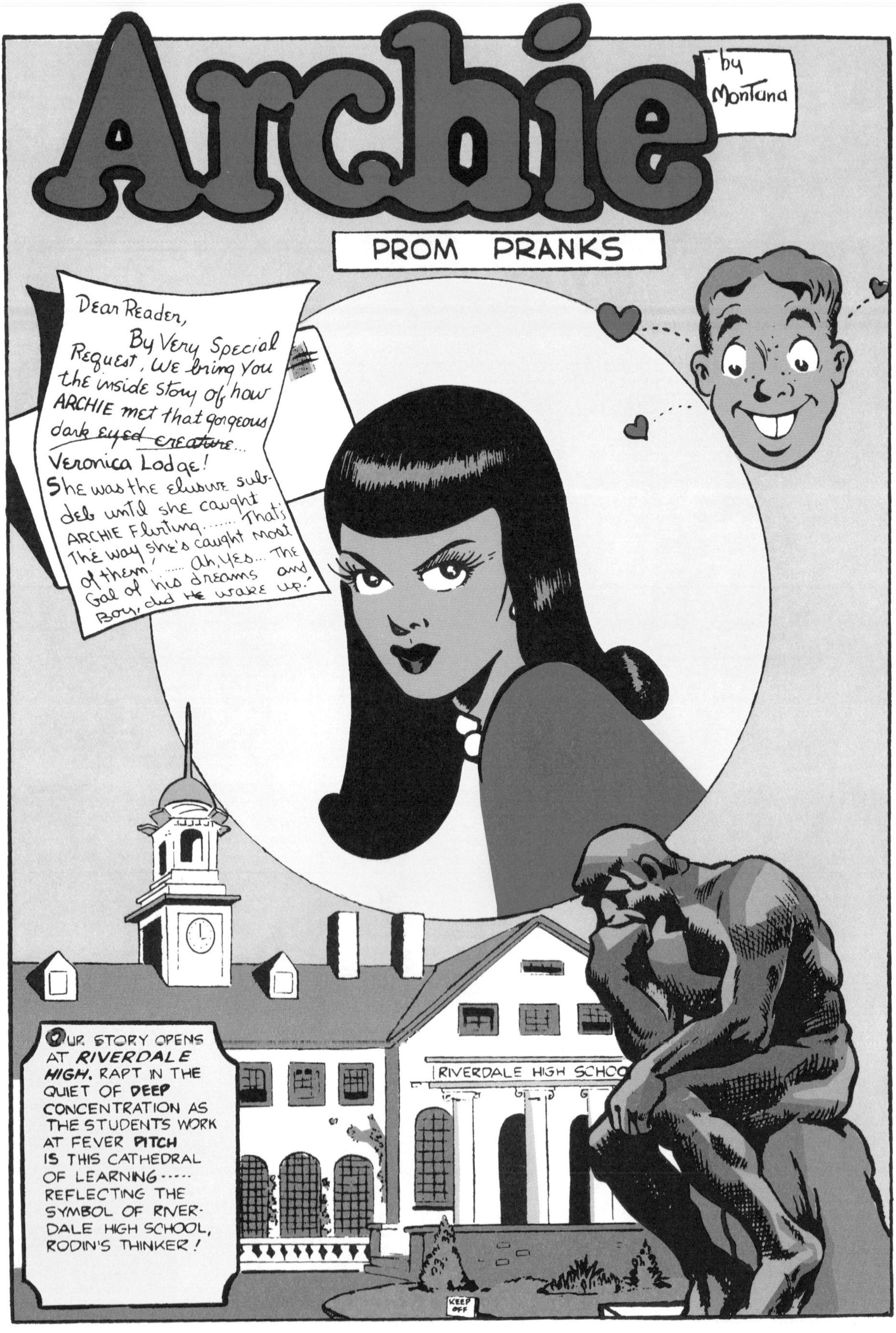
Archie
by Montana
PROM PRANKS
Dear Reader,
By Very Special Request, We bring You the inside story of how ARCHIE met that gorgeous dark eyed creature...
Veronica Lodge!
She was the elusive sub-deb until she caught ARCHIE Flirting...... That's the way she's caught most of them! ...... Ah, Yes... The Gal of his dreams and Boy, did HE wake up!
OUR STORY OPENS AT RIVERDALE HIGH. RAPT IN THE QUIET OF DEEP CONCENTRATION AS THE STUDENTS WORK AT FEVER PITCH IS THIS CATHEDRAL OF LEARNING----- REFLECTING THE SYMBOL OF RIVER-DALE HIGH SCHOOL, RODIN'S THINKER!
RIVERDALE HIGH SCHO
KEEP OFF

Originally presented in ARCHIE COMICS #1, Winter, 1942

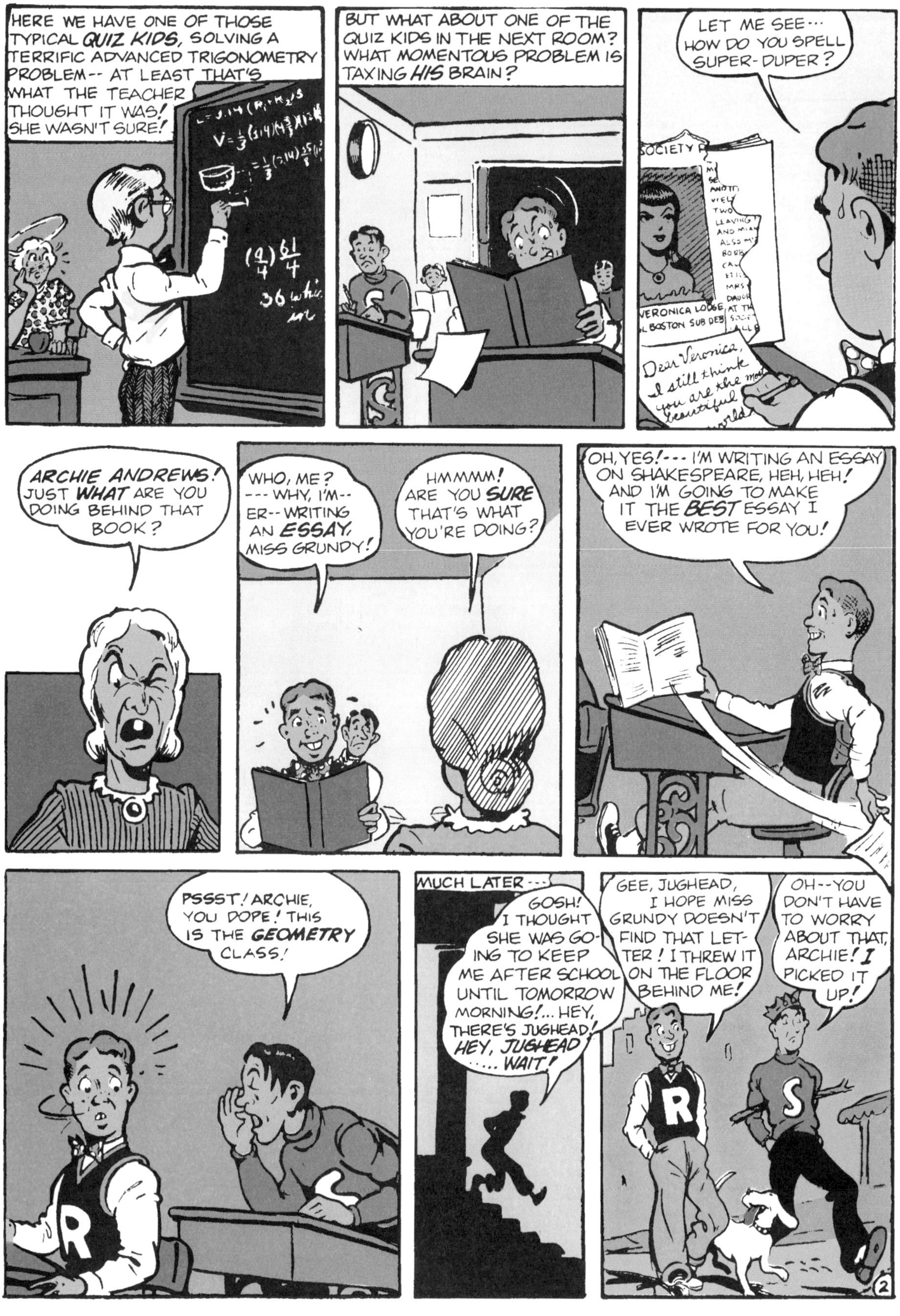
HERE WE HAVE ONE OF THOSE TYPICAL QUIZ KIDS, SOLVING A TERRIFIC ADVANCED TRIGONOMETRY PROBLEM-- AT LEAST THAT'S WHAT THE TEACHER THOUGHT IT WAS! SHE WASN'T SURE!
BUT WHAT ABOUT ONE OF THE QUIZ KIDS IN THE NEXT ROOM? WHAT MOMENTOUS PROBLEM IS TAXING HIS BRAIN?
LET ME SEE... HOW DO YOU SPELL SUPER-DUPER?
SOCIETY
VERONICA LODGE
BOSTON SUB DEB
Dear Veronica, I still think you are the most beautiful
ARCHIE ANDREWS! JUST WHAT ARE YOU DOING BEHIND THAT BOOK?
WHO, ME? --- WHY, I'M-- ER-- WRITING AN ESSAY, MISS GRUNDY!
HMMMM! ARE YOU SURE THAT'S WHAT YOU'RE DOING?
OH, YES!--- I'M WRITING AN ESSAY ON SHAKESPEARE, HEH, HEH! AND I'M GOING TO MAKE IT THE BEST ESSAY I EVER WROTE FOR YOU!
PSSST! ARCHIE, YOU DOPE! THIS IS THE GEOMETRY CLASS!
MUCH LATER---
GOSH! I THOUGHT SHE WAS GOING TO KEEP ME AFTER SCHOOL UNTIL TOMORROW MORNING!... HEY, THERE'S JUGHEAD! HEY, JUGHEAD ..... WAIT!
GEE, JUGHEAD, I HOPE MISS GRUNDY DOESN'T FIND THAT LETTER! I THREW IT ON THE FLOOR BEHIND ME!
OH--YOU DON'T HAVE TO WORRY ABOUT THAT, ARCHIE! I PICKED IT UP!
2

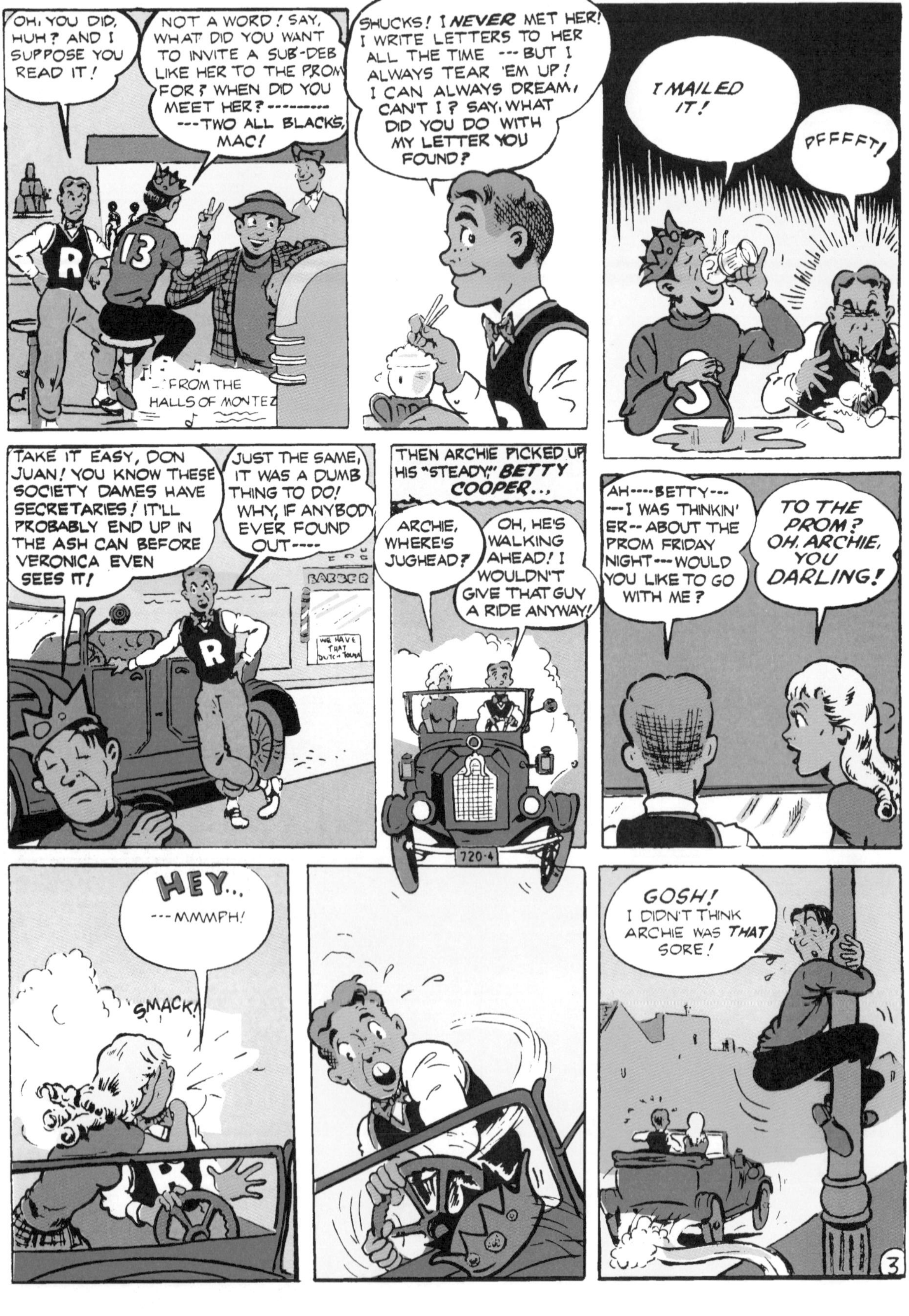
OH, YOU DID, HUH? AND I SUPPOSE YOU READ IT!
NOT A WORD! SAY, WHAT DID YOU WANT TO INVITE A SUB-DEB LIKE HER TO THE PROM FOR? WHEN DID YOU MEET HER? --------- ---TWO ALL BLACKS, MAC!
FROM THE HALLS OF MONTEZ
SHUCKS! I NEVER MET HER! I WRITE LETTERS TO HER ALL THE TIME ---BUT I ALWAYS TEAR 'EM UP! I CAN ALWAYS DREAM, CAN'T I? SAY, WHAT DID YOU DO WITH MY LETTER YOU FOUND?
I MAILED IT!
PFFFFT!
TAKE IT EASY, DON JUAN! YOU KNOW THESE SOCIETY DAMES HAVE SECRETARIES! IT'LL PROBABLY END UP IN THE ASH CAN BEFORE VERONICA EVEN SEES IT!
JUST THE SAME, IT WAS A DUMB THING TO DO! WHY, IF ANYBODY EVER FOUND OUT----
BARBER
WE HAVE THAT DUTCH TOUR
THEN ARCHIE PICKED UP HIS "STEADY," BETTY COOPER...
ARCHIE, WHERE'S JUGHEAD?
OH, HE'S WALKING AHEAD! I WOULDN'T GIVE THAT GUY A RIDE ANYWAY!
720-4
AH----BETTY--- ---I WAS THINKIN' ER-- ABOUT THE PROM FRIDAY NIGHT---WOULD YOU LIKE TO GO WITH ME?
TO THE PROM? OH, ARCHIE, YOU DARLING!
HEY... ---MMMPH!
SMACK!
GOSH! I DIDN'T THINK ARCHIE WAS THAT SORE!
3

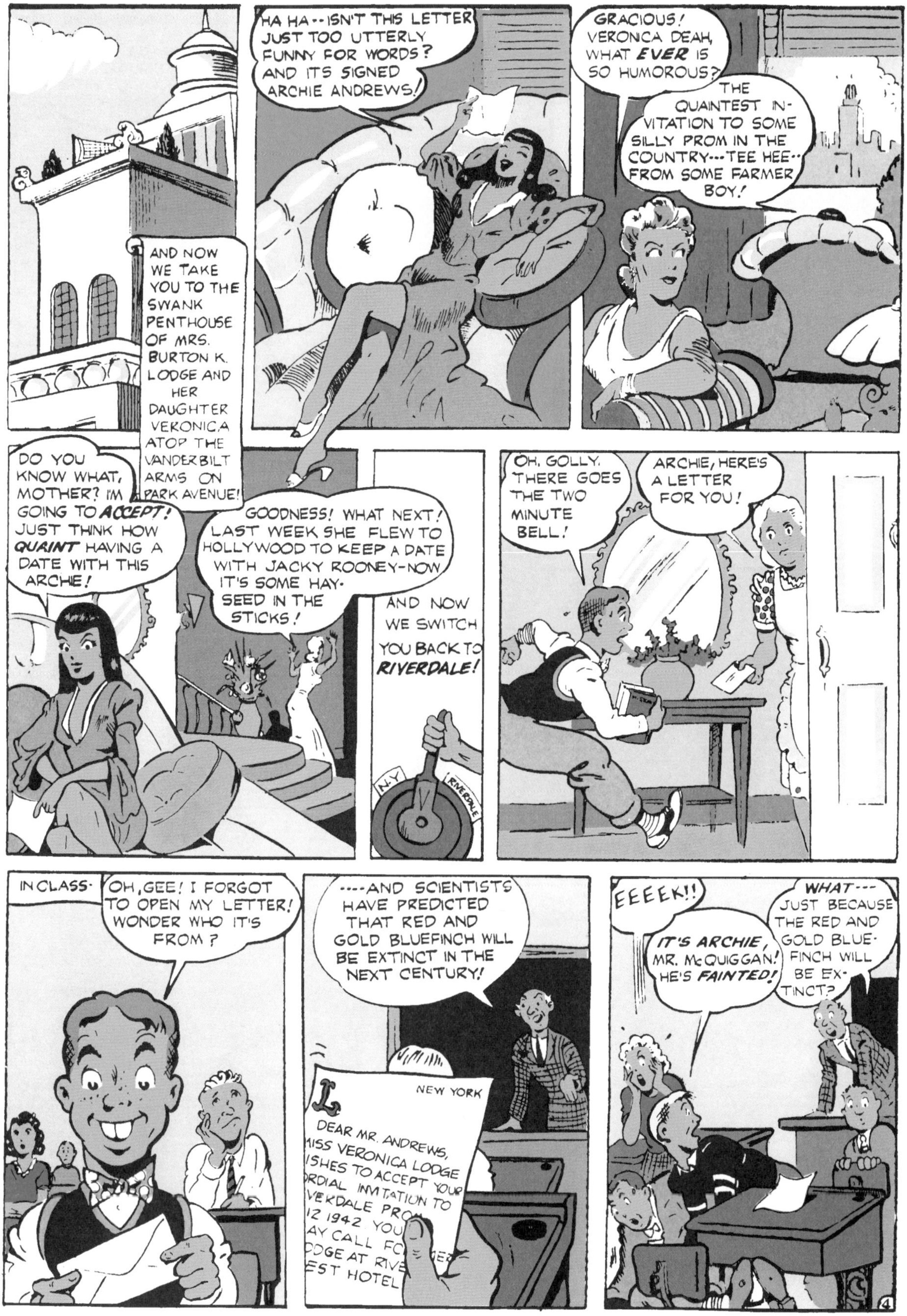
AND NOW WE TAKE YOU TO THE SWANK PENTHOUSE OF MRS. BURTON K. LODGE AND HER DAUGHTER VERONICA ATOP THE VANDERBILT ARMS ON PARK AVENUE!
HA HA--ISN'T THIS LETTER JUST TOO UTTERLY FUNNY FOR WORDS? AND ITS SIGNED ARCHIE ANDREWS!
GRACIOUS! VERONICA DEAH, WHAT EVER IS SO HUMOROUS?
THE QUAINTEST INVITATION TO SOME SILLY PROM IN THE COUNTRY---TEE HEE--FROM SOME FARMER BOY!
DO YOU KNOW WHAT, MOTHER? I'M GOING TO ACCEPT! JUST THINK HOW QUAINT HAVING A DATE WITH THIS ARCHIE!
GOODNESS! WHAT NEXT! LAST WEEK SHE FLEW TO HOLLYWOOD TO KEEP A DATE WITH JACKY ROONEY-NOW IT'S SOME HAY-SEED IN THE STICKS!
AND NOW WE SWITCH YOU BACK TO RIVERDALE!
N.Y
RIVERDALE
OH, GOLLY. THERE GOES THE TWO MINUTE BELL!
ARCHIE, HERE'S A LETTER FOR YOU!
IN CLASS-
OH, GEE! I FORGOT TO OPEN MY LETTER! WONDER WHO IT'S FROM?
----AND SCIENTISTS HAVE PREDICTED THAT RED AND GOLD BLUEFINCH WILL BE EXTINCT IN THE NEXT CENTURY!
NEW YORK
DEAR MR. ANDREWS, MISS VERONICA LODGE ISHES TO ACCEPT YOUR ORDIAL INVITATION TO VERDALE PROM 12 1942 YOU AY CALL FO ODGE AT RIVE EST HOTEL
EEEEK!!
IT'S ARCHIE, MR. McQUIGGAN! HE'S FAINTED!
WHAT--- JUST BECAUSE THE RED AND GOLD BLUEFINCH WILL BE EXTINCT?
4

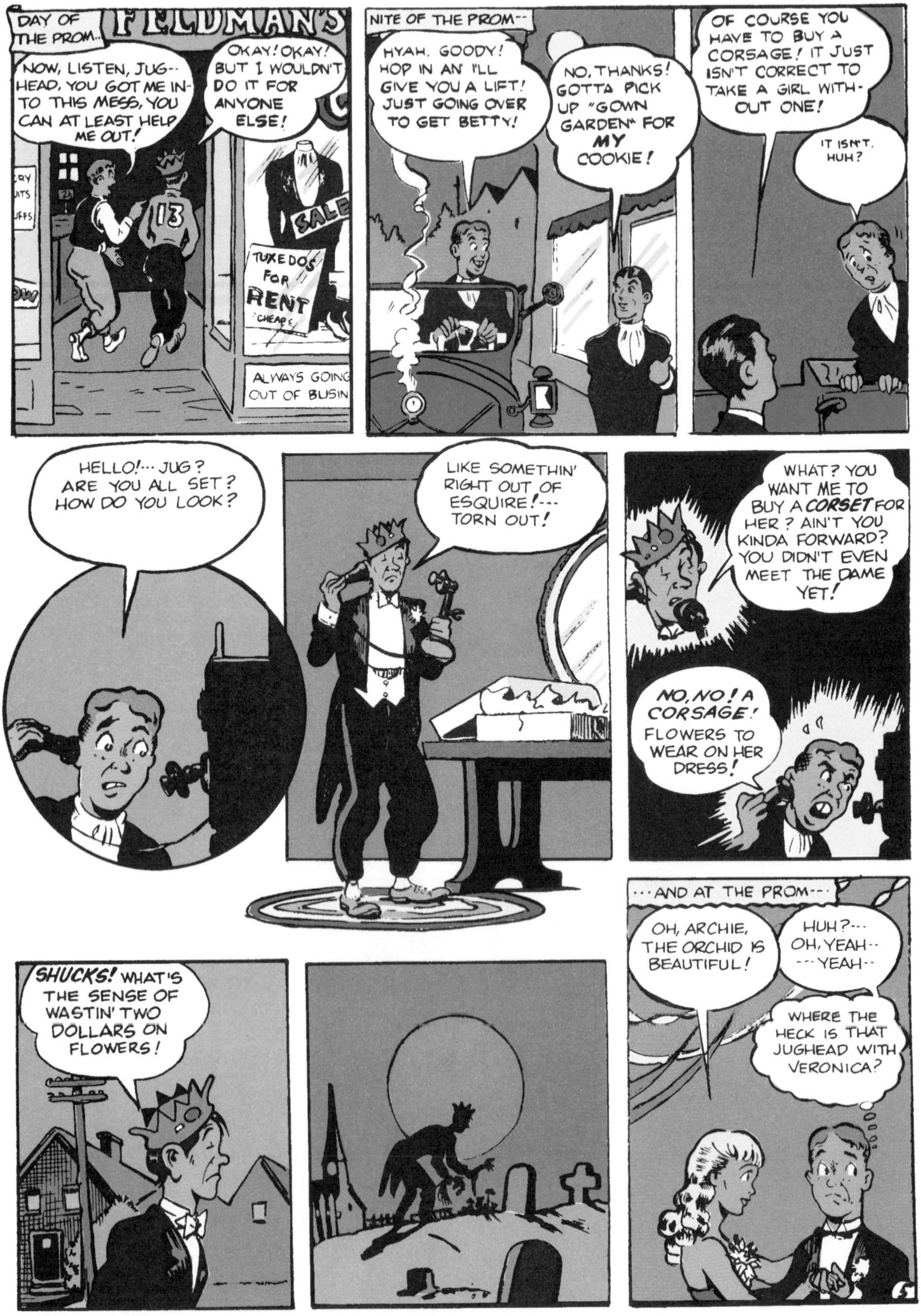
DAY OF THE PROM..
FELDMAN'S
NOW, LISTEN, JUG-- HEAD, YOU GOT ME IN- TO THIS MESS, YOU CAN AT LEAST HELP ME OUT!
OKAY! OKAY! BUT I WOULDN'T DO IT FOR ANYONE ELSE!
SALE
TUXEDOS FOR RENT CHEAP
ALWAYS GOING OUT OF BUSIN
NITE OF THE PROM--
HYAH, GOODY! HOP IN AN' I'LL GIVE YOU A LIFT! JUST GOING OVER TO GET BETTY!
NO, THANKS! GOTTA PICK UP "GOWN GARDEN" FOR MY COOKIE!
OF COURSE YOU HAVE TO BUY A CORSAGE! IT JUST ISN'T CORRECT TO TAKE A GIRL WITH- OUT ONE!
IT ISN'T, HUH?
HELLO!... JUG? ARE YOU ALL SET? HOW DO YOU LOOK?
LIKE SOMETHIN' RIGHT OUT OF ESQUIRE!--- TORN OUT!
WHAT? YOU WANT ME TO BUY A CORSET FOR HER? AIN'T YOU KINDA FORWARD? YOU DIDN'T EVEN MEET THE DAME YET!
NO, NO! A CORSAGE! FLOWERS TO WEAR ON HER DRESS!
SHUCKS! WHAT'S THE SENSE OF WASTIN' TWO DOLLARS ON FLOWERS!
...AND AT THE PROM...
OH, ARCHIE, THE ORCHID IS BEAUTIFUL!
HUH?... OH, YEAH-- --- YEAH--
WHERE THE HECK IS THAT JUGHEAD WITH VERONICA?

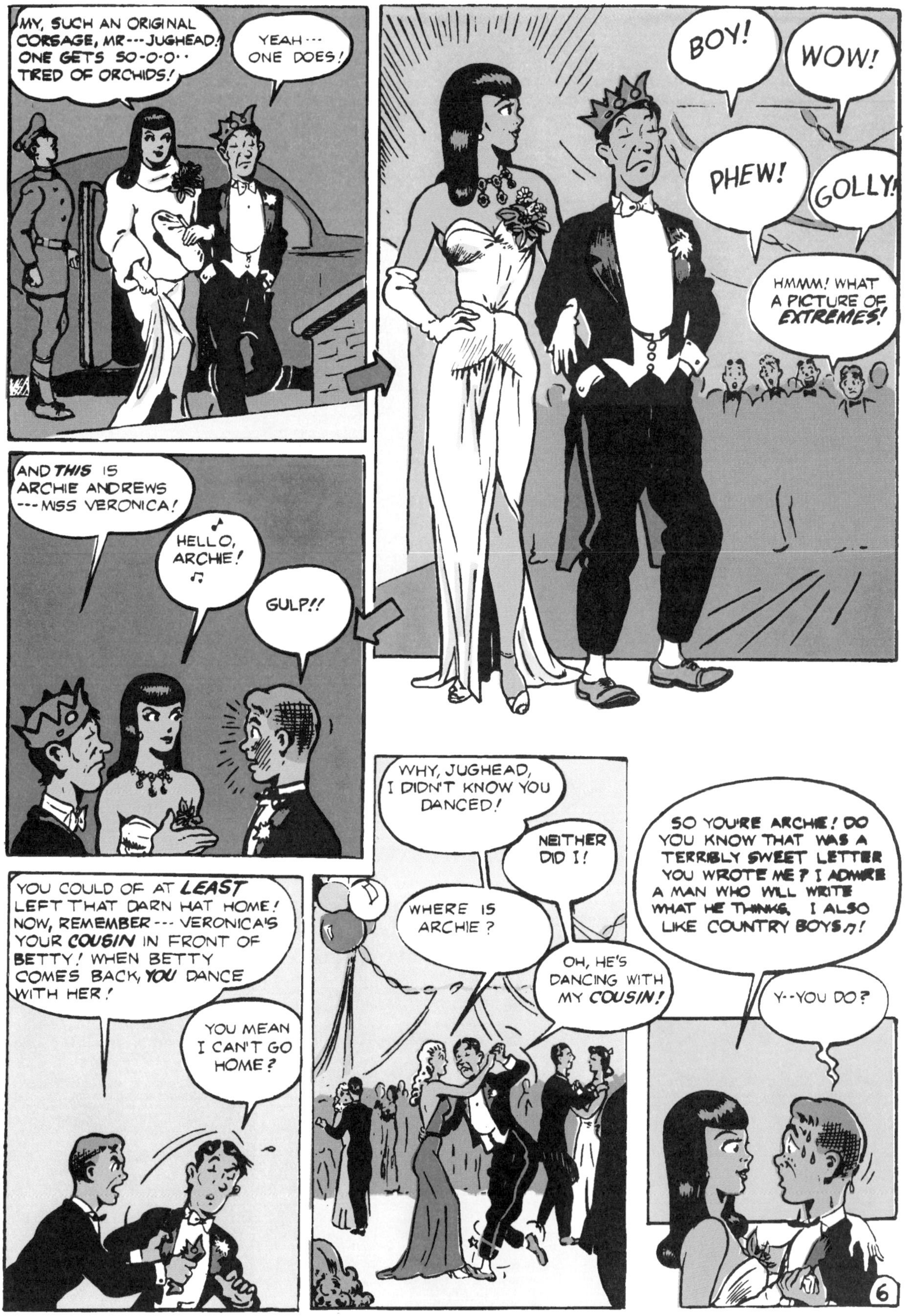
MY, SUCH AN ORIGINAL CORSAGE, MR---JUGHEAD! ONE GETS SO-O-O-- TIRED OF ORCHIDS!
YEAH--- ONE DOES!
BOY!
WOW!
PHEW!
GOLLY!
HMMM! WHAT A PICTURE OF EXTREMES!
AND THIS IS ARCHIE ANDREWS ---MISS VERONICA!
HELLO, ARCHIE!
GULP!!
YOU COULD OF AT LEAST LEFT THAT DARN HAT HOME! NOW, REMEMBER--- VERONICA'S YOUR COUSIN IN FRONT OF BETTY! WHEN BETTY COMES BACK, YOU DANCE WITH HER!
YOU MEAN I CAN'T GO HOME?
WHY, JUGHEAD, I DIDN'T KNOW YOU DANCED!
NEITHER DID I!
WHERE IS ARCHIE?
OH, HE'S DANCING WITH MY COUSIN!
SO YOU'RE ARCHIE! DO YOU KNOW THAT WAS A TERRIBLY SWEET LETTER YOU WROTE ME? I ADMIRE A MAN WHO WILL WRITE WHAT HE THINKS. I ALSO LIKE COUNTRY BOYS!
Y--YOU DO?
6

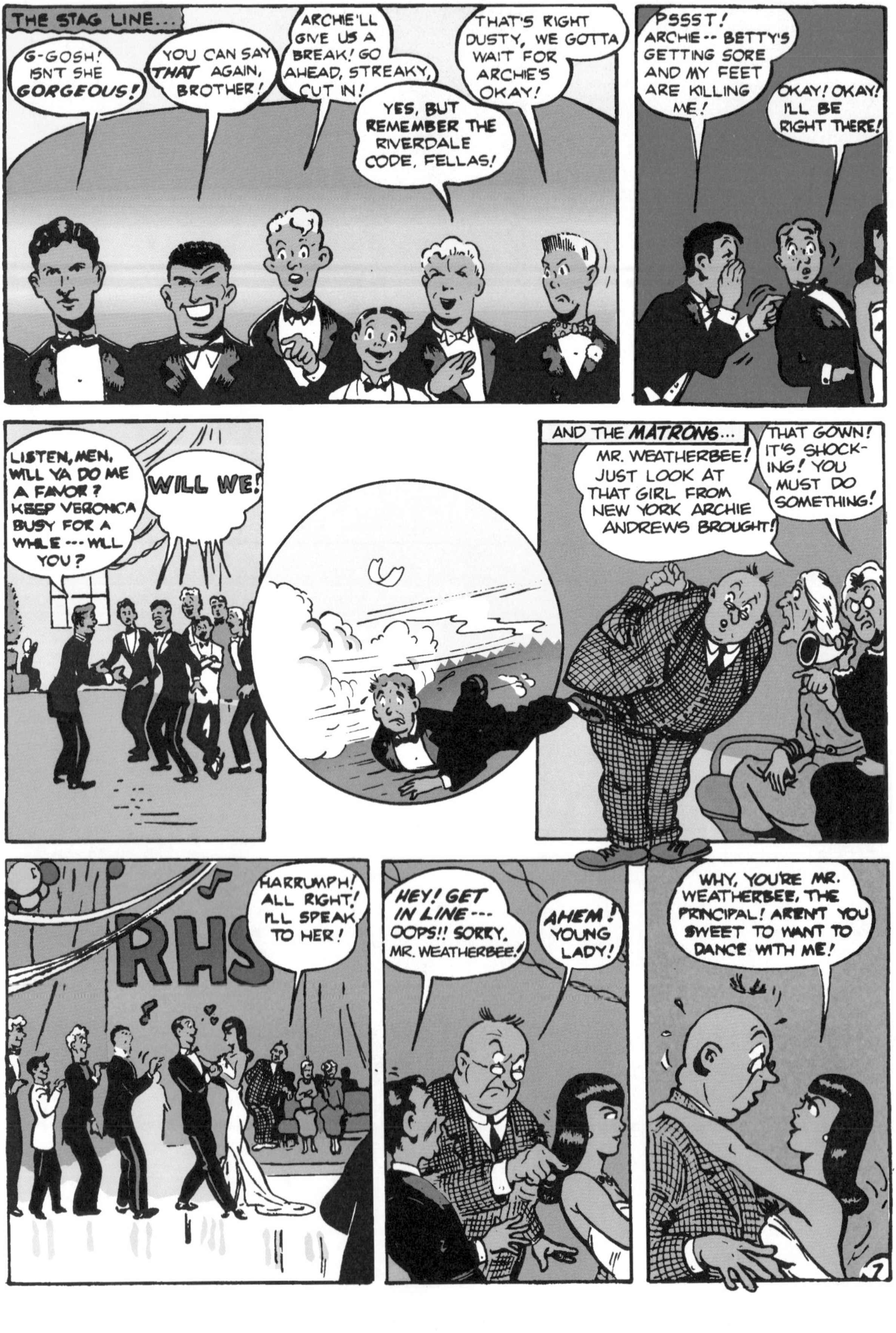
THE STAG LINE...
G-GOSH! ISN'T SHE GORGEOUS!
YOU CAN SAY THAT AGAIN, BROTHER!
ARCHIE'LL GIVE US A BREAK! GO AHEAD, STREAKY, CUT IN!
YES, BUT REMEMBER THE RIVERDALE CODE, FELLAS!
THAT'S RIGHT DUSTY, WE GOTTA WAIT FOR ARCHIE'S OKAY!
PSSST! ARCHIE -- BETTY'S GETTING SORE AND MY FEET ARE KILLING ME!
OKAY! OKAY! I'LL BE RIGHT THERE!
LISTEN, MEN, WILL YA DO ME A FAVOR? KEEP VERONICA BUSY FOR A WHILE --- WILL YOU?
WILL WE!
AND THE MATRONS...
MR. WEATHERBEE! JUST LOOK AT THAT GIRL FROM NEW YORK ARCHIE ANDREWS BROUGHT!
THAT GOWN! IT'S SHOCKING! YOU MUST DO SOMETHING!
HARRUMPH! ALL RIGHT! I'LL SPEAK TO HER!
RHS
HEY! GET IN LINE --- OOPS!! SORRY, MR. WEATHERBEE!
AHEM! YOUNG LADY!
WHY, YOU'RE MR. WEATHERBEE, THE PRINCIPAL! AREN'T YOU SWEET TO WANT TO DANCE WITH ME!
7

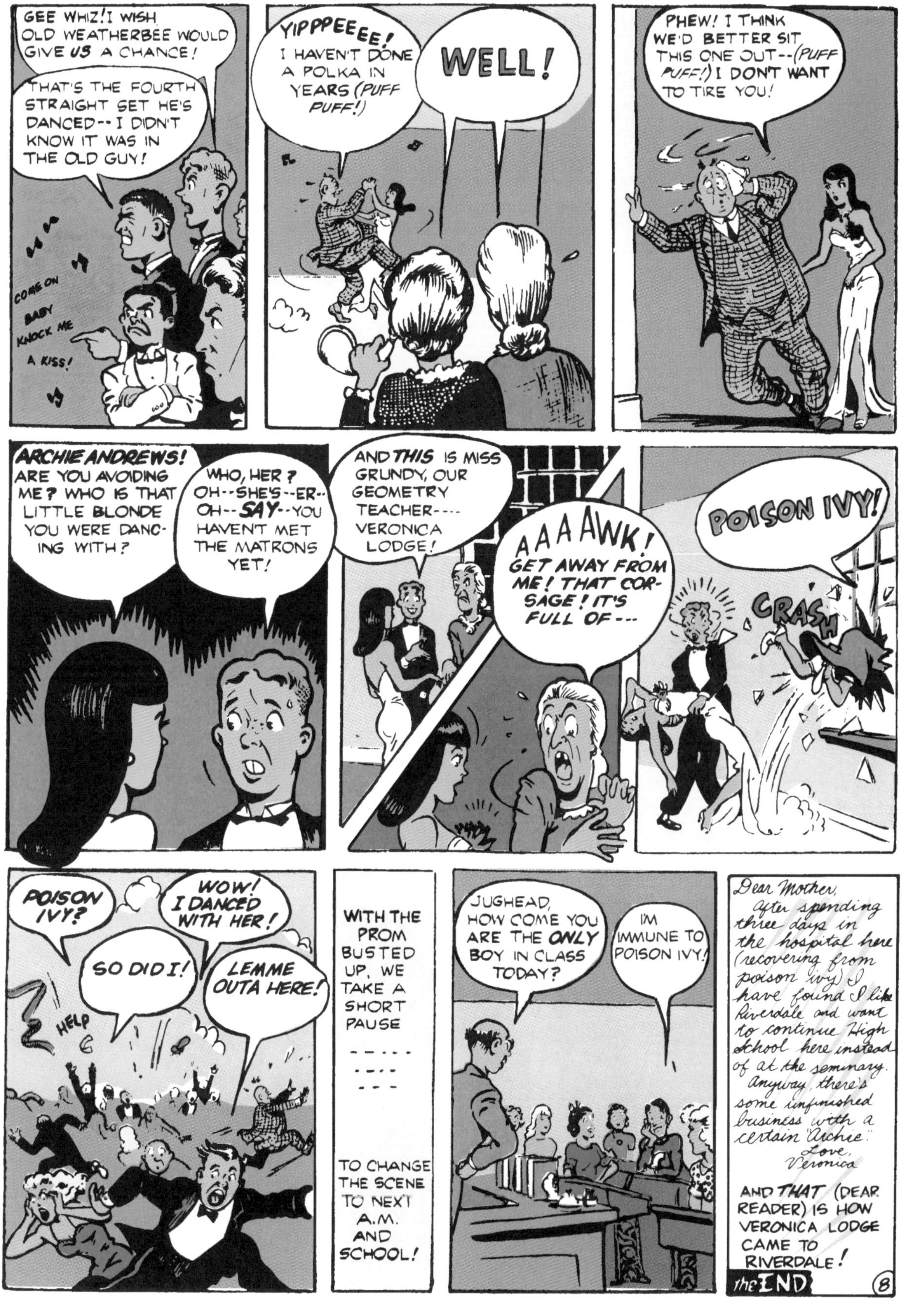
GEE WHIZ! I WISH OLD WEATHERBEE WOULD GIVE US A CHANCE!
THAT'S THE FOURTH STRAIGHT SET HE'S DANCED-- I DIDN'T KNOW IT WAS IN THE OLD GUY!
COME ON BABY KNOCK ME A KISS!
YIPPPEEEEE! I HAVEN'T DONE A POLKA IN YEARS (PUFF PUFF!)
WELL!
PHEW! I THINK WE'D BETTER SIT THIS ONE OUT--(PUFF PUFF!) I DON'T WANT TO TIRE YOU!
ARCHIE ANDREWS! ARE YOU AVOIDING ME? WHO IS THAT LITTLE BLONDE YOU WERE DANCING WITH?
WHO, HER? OH--SHE'S--ER--OH--SAY--YOU HAVEN'T MET THE MATRONS YET!
AND THIS IS MISS GRUNDY, OUR GEOMETRY TEACHER---- VERONICA LODGE!
AAAAWK! GET AWAY FROM ME! THAT CORSAGE! IT'S FULL OF---
POISON IVY!
CRASH
POISON IVY?
WOW! I DANCED WITH HER!
SO DID I!
LEMME OUTA HERE!
HELP
WITH THE PROM BUSTED UP, WE TAKE A SHORT PAUSE
TO CHANGE THE SCENE TO NEXT A.M. AND SCHOOL!
JUGHEAD, HOW COME YOU ARE THE ONLY BOY IN CLASS TODAY?
I'M IMMUNE TO POISON IVY!
Dear Mother, After spending three days in the hospital here (recovering from poison ivy) I have found I like Riverdale and want to continue High School here instead of at the seminary. Anyway, there's some unfinished business with a certain "Archie." Love, Veronica
AND THAT (DEAR READER) IS HOW VERONICA LODGE CAME TO RIVERDALE!
the END
8

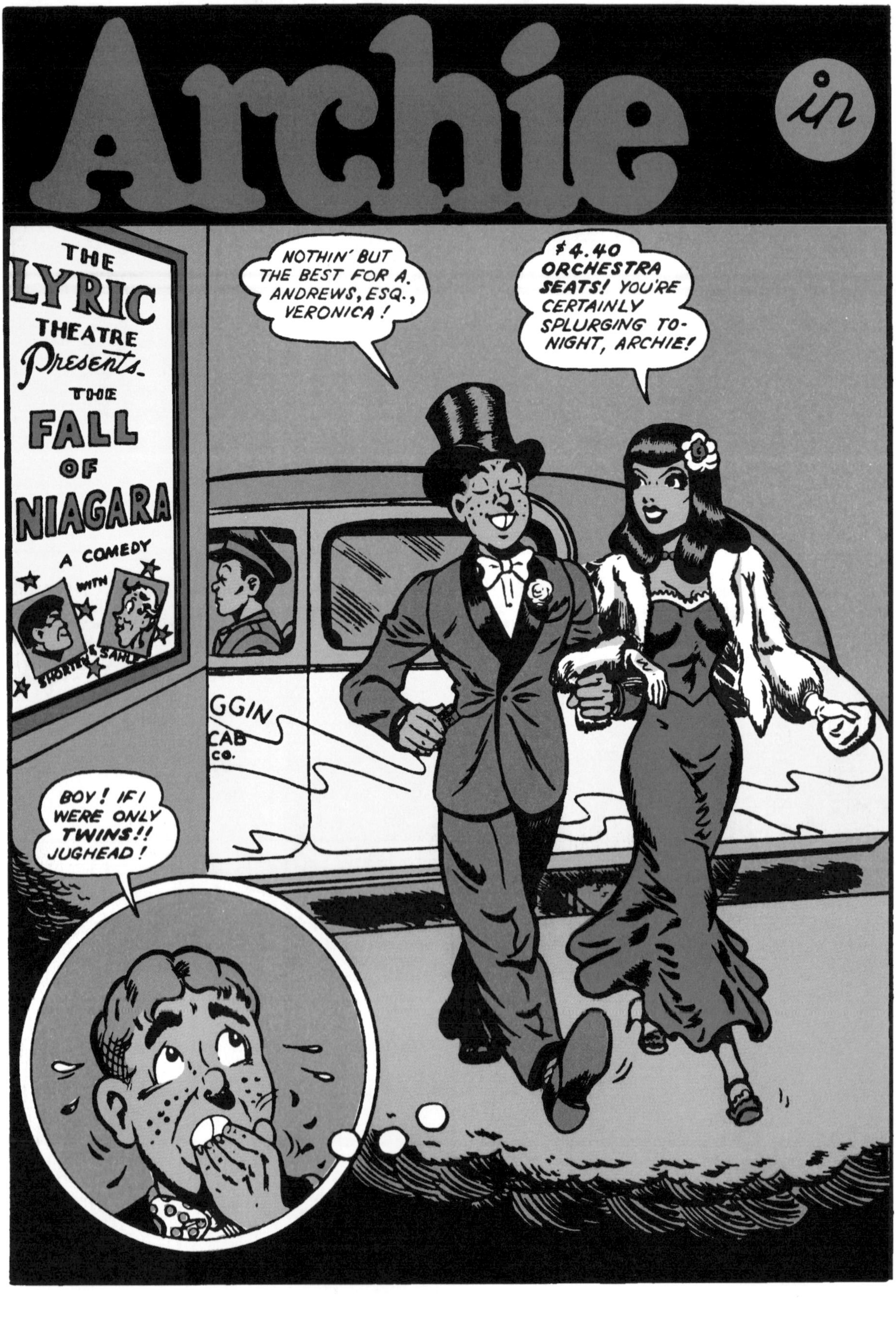
Archie in
THE LYRIC THEATRE Presents THE FALL OF NIAGARA A COMEDY WITH SHORTEY & SAHL
NOTHIN' BUT THE BEST FOR A. ANDREWS, ESQ., VERONICA!
$4.40 ORCHESTRA SEATS! YOU'RE CERTAINLY SPLURGING TO-NIGHT, ARCHIE!
GGIN CAB CO.
BOY! IF I WERE ONLY TWINS!! JUGHEAD!

Originally presented in ARCHIE COMICS #7, March-April, 1944

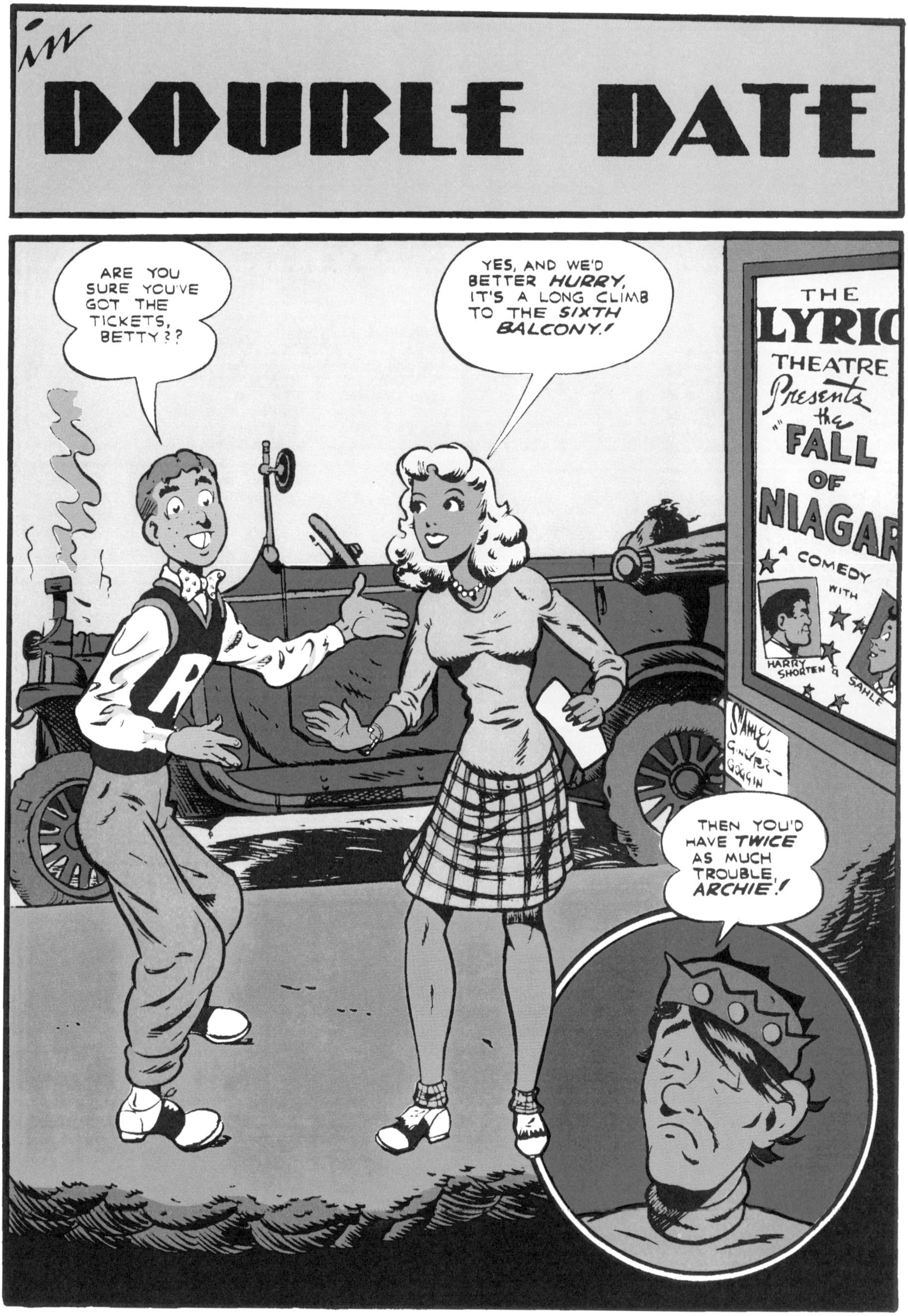
in
DOUBLE DATE
ARE YOU SURE YOU'VE GOT THE TICKETS, BETTY??
YES, AND WE'D BETTER HURRY, IT'S A LONG CLIMB TO THE SIXTH BALCONY!
THE LYRIC THEATRE Presents the "FALL OF NIAGAR
A COMEDY WITH
HARRY SHORTEN & SAHLE
THEN YOU'D HAVE TWICE AS MUCH TROUBLE, ARCHIE!

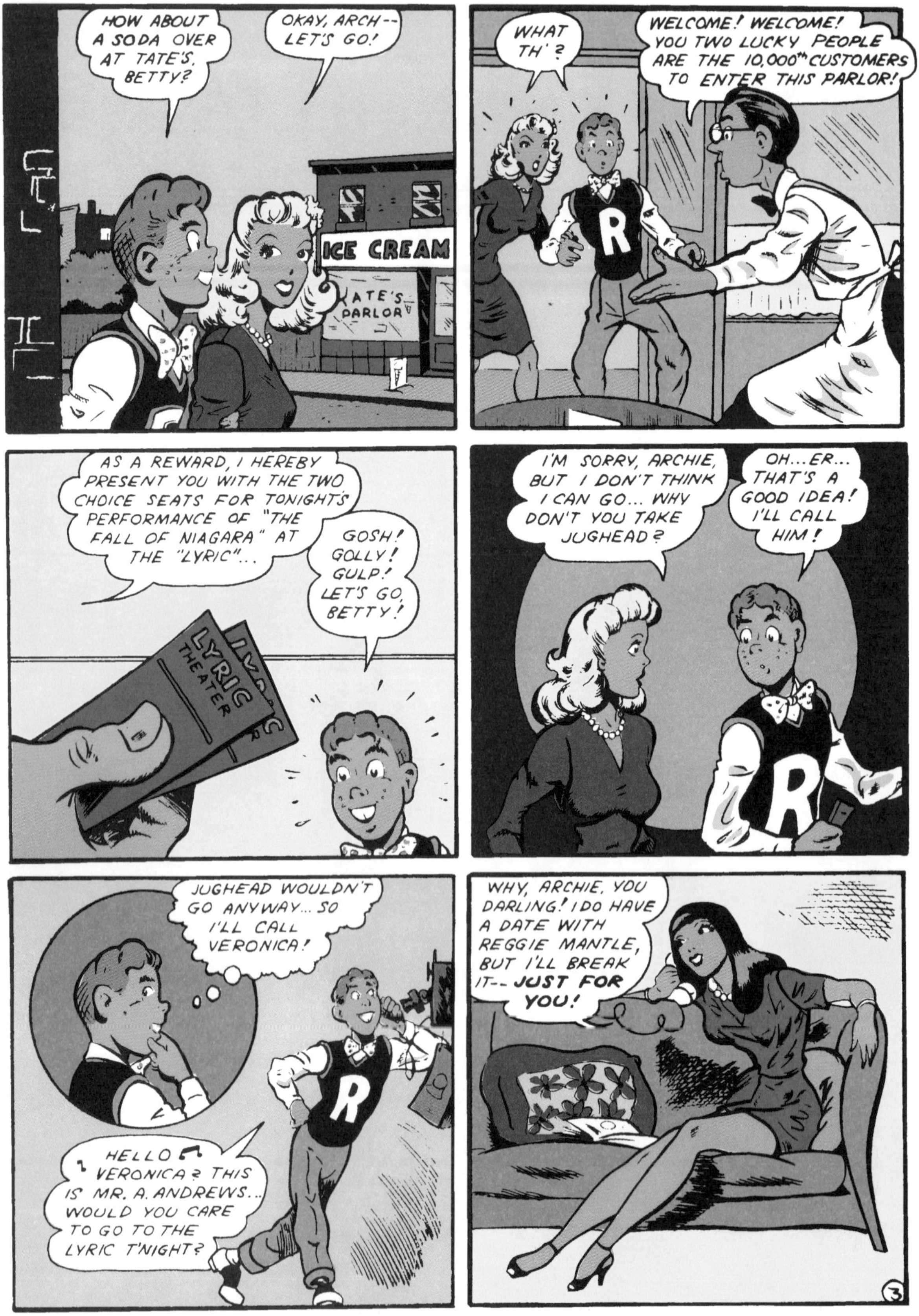
HOW ABOUT A SODA OVER AT TATE'S, BETTY?
OKAY, ARCH-- LET'S GO!
ICE CREAM
TATE'S PARLOR
WHAT TH'?
WELCOME! WELCOME! YOU TWO LUCKY PEOPLE ARE THE 10,000TH CUSTOMERS TO ENTER THIS PARLOR!
AS A REWARD, I HEREBY PRESENT YOU WITH THE TWO CHOICE SEATS FOR TONIGHT'S PERFORMANCE OF "THE FALL OF NIAGARA" AT THE "LYRIC"...
GOSH! GOLLY! GULP! LET'S GO, BETTY!
LYRIC THEATER
I'M SORRY, ARCHIE, BUT I DON'T THINK I CAN GO... WHY DON'T YOU TAKE JUGHEAD?
OH...ER... THAT'S A GOOD IDEA! I'LL CALL HIM!
JUGHEAD WOULDN'T GO ANYWAY... SO I'LL CALL VERONICA!
HELLO VERONICA? THIS IS MR. A. ANDREWS... WOULD YOU CARE TO GO TO THE LYRIC T'NIGHT?
WHY, ARCHIE, YOU DARLING! I DO HAVE A DATE WITH REGGIE MANTLE, BUT I'LL BREAK IT-- **JUST FOR YOU!**
3

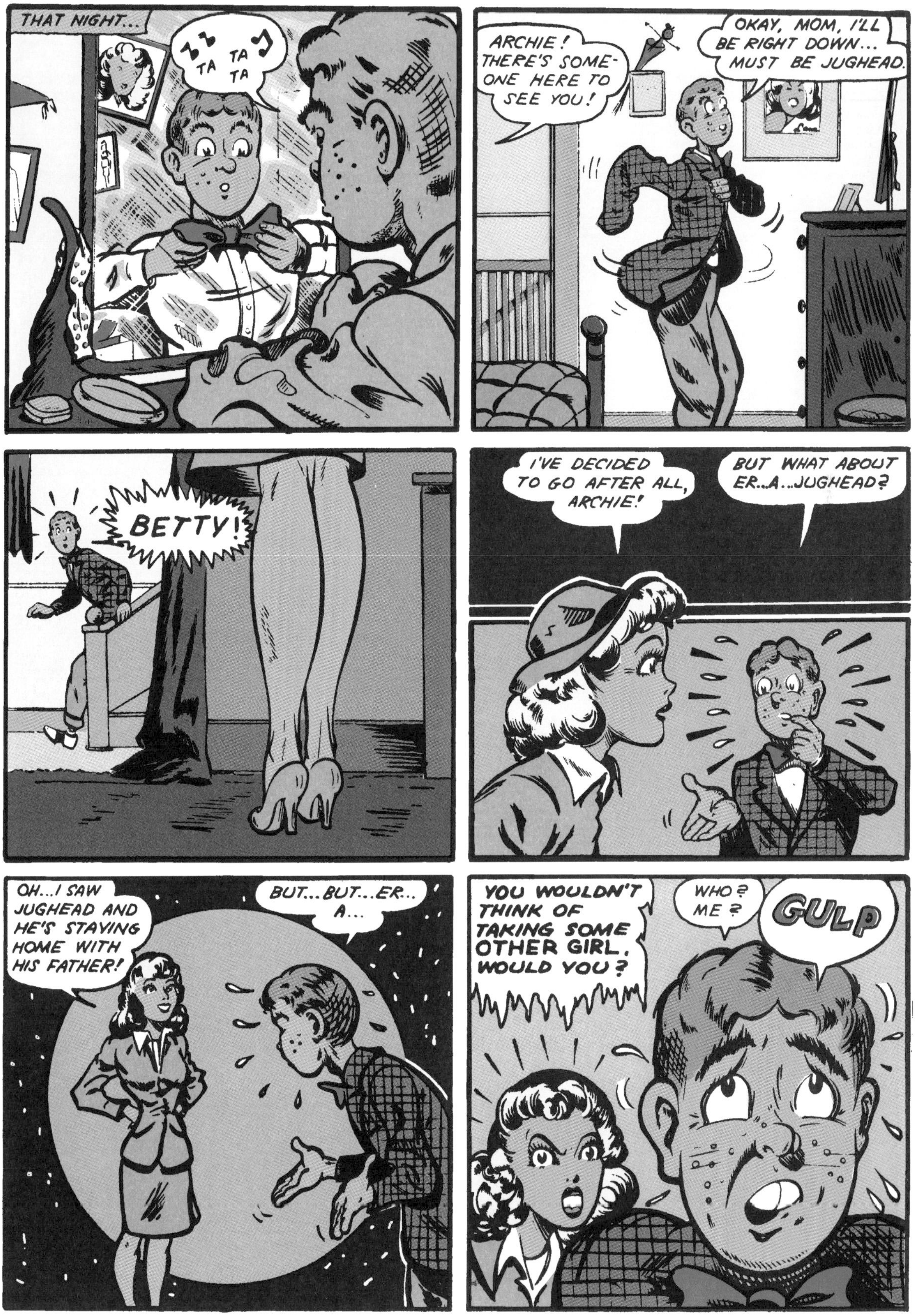
THAT NIGHT...
TA TA TA
ARCHIE! THERE'S SOMEONE HERE TO SEE YOU!
OKAY, MOM, I'LL BE RIGHT DOWN... MUST BE JUGHEAD.
BETTY!
I'VE DECIDED TO GO AFTER ALL, ARCHIE!
BUT WHAT ABOUT ER...A...JUGHEAD?
OH...I SAW JUGHEAD AND HE'S STAYING HOME WITH HIS FATHER!
BUT...BUT...ER... A...
YOU WOULDN'T THINK OF TAKING SOME OTHER GIRL, WOULD YOU?
WHO? ME?
GULP

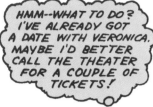

HMM--WHAT TO DO? I'VE ALREADY GOT A DATE WITH VERONICA. MAYBE I'D BETTER CALL THE THEATER FOR A COUPLE OF TICKETS!

YOU WAIT THERE, BETTY! I'LL BE RIGHT BACK!

HELLO! LYRIC THEATER? THIS IS MR. ANDREWS! DO YOU HAVE TWO TICKETS FOR TONIGHT'S SHOW?

YEAH... JUST TWO--THEY'RE $4.40--EACH!

WHAT? YEOW'E! 4.40? EACH?

I'LL TAKE THEM!

GOSH...$8.80 FOR TWO TICKETS...THERE'S ONLY $2.19 HERE!

ER...A...BETTY! COULD YOU A... LOAN ME $6.61? IT'S AN EMER- GENCY!

WELL...IF IT'S AN EMERGENCY, I GUESS IT'S ALL RIGHT!

I WON'T BE GONE LONG, BETTY... RELAX FOR A WHILE...

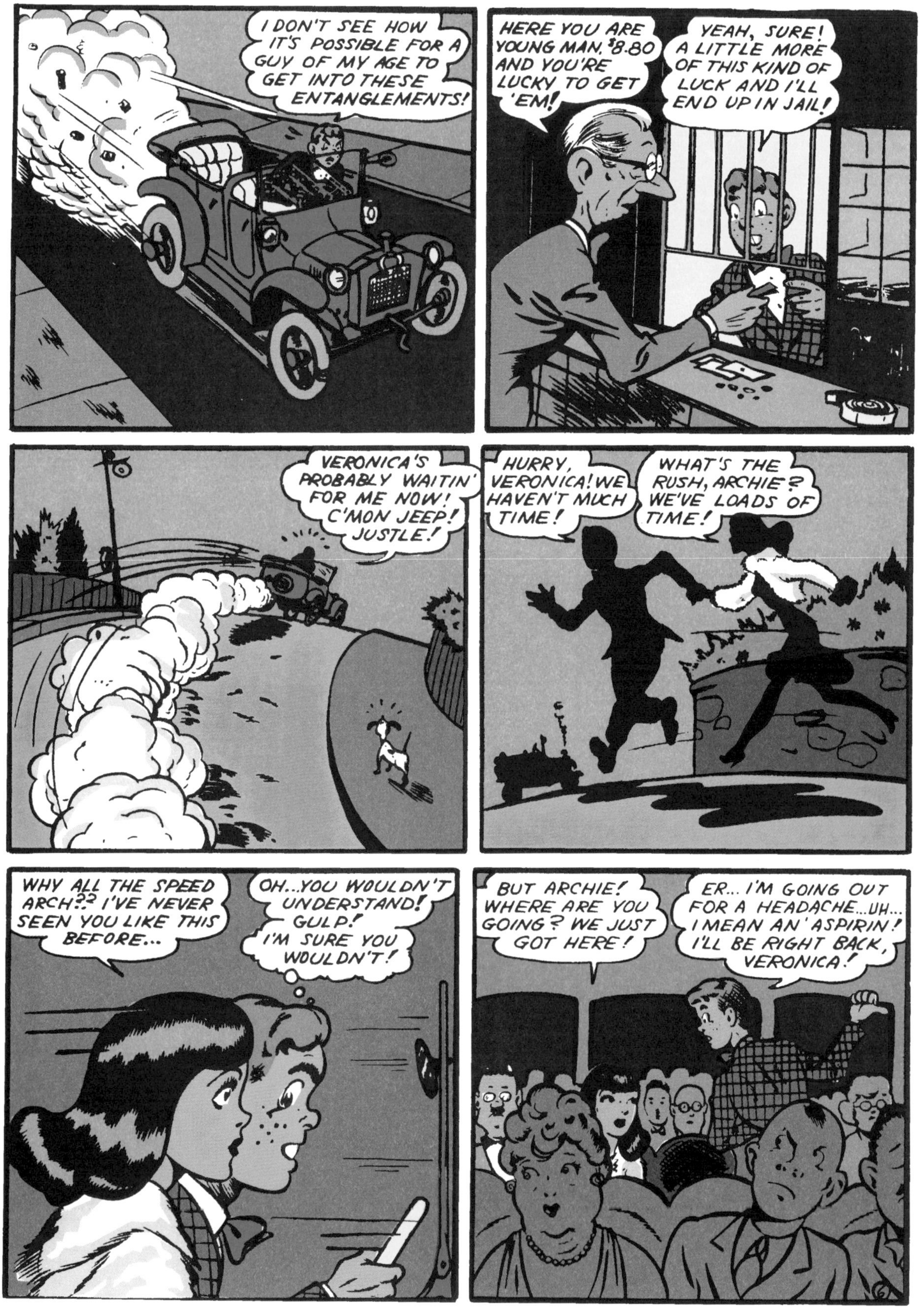
I DON'T SEE HOW IT'S POSSIBLE FOR A GUY OF MY AGE TO GET INTO THESE ENTANGLEMENTS!
HERE YOU ARE YOUNG MAN, $8.80 AND YOU'RE LUCKY TO GET 'EM!
YEAH, SURE! A LITTLE MORE OF THIS KIND OF LUCK AND I'LL END UP IN JAIL!
VERONICA'S PROBABLY WAITIN' FOR ME NOW! C'MON JEEP! JUSTLE!
HURRY, VERONICA! WE HAVEN'T MUCH TIME!
WHAT'S THE RUSH, ARCHIE? WE'VE LOADS OF TIME!
WHY ALL THE SPEED ARCH?? I'VE NEVER SEEN YOU LIKE THIS BEFORE...
OH...YOU WOULDN'T UNDERSTAND! GULP! I'M SURE YOU WOULDN'T!
BUT ARCHIE! WHERE ARE YOU GOING? WE JUST GOT HERE!
ER... I'M GOING OUT FOR A HEADACHE...UH... I MEAN AN 'ASPIRIN'! I'LL BE RIGHT BACK, VERONICA!

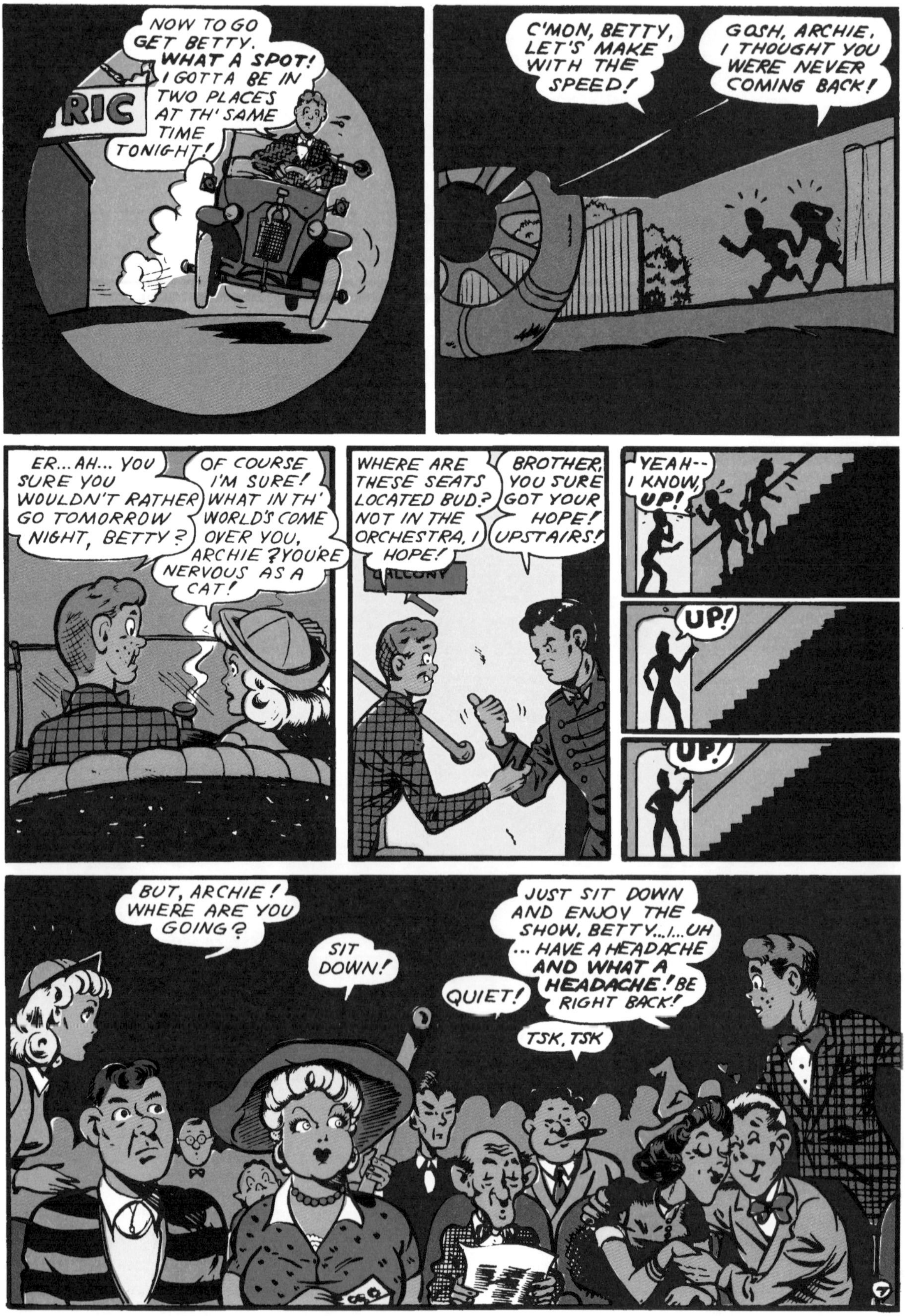
NOW TO GO GET BETTY. WHAT A SPOT! I GOTTA BE IN TWO PLACES AT TH' SAME TIME TONIGHT!
RIC
C'MON, BETTY, LET'S MAKE WITH THE SPEED!
GOSH, ARCHIE, I THOUGHT YOU WERE NEVER COMING BACK!
ER... AH... YOU SURE YOU WOULDN'T RATHER GO TOMORROW NIGHT, BETTY?
OF COURSE I'M SURE! WHAT IN TH' WORLD'S COME OVER YOU, ARCHIE? YOU'RE NERVOUS AS A CAT!
WHERE ARE THESE SEATS LOCATED BUD? NOT IN THE ORCHESTRA, I HOPE!
BROTHER, YOU SURE GOT YOUR HOPE! UPSTAIRS!
YEAH-- I KNOW, UP!
UP!
UP!
BUT, ARCHIE! WHERE ARE YOU GOING?
SIT DOWN!
QUIET!
JUST SIT DOWN AND ENJOY THE SHOW, BETTY... I... UH ... HAVE A HEADACHE AND WHAT A HEADACHE! BE RIGHT BACK!
TSK, TSK
7

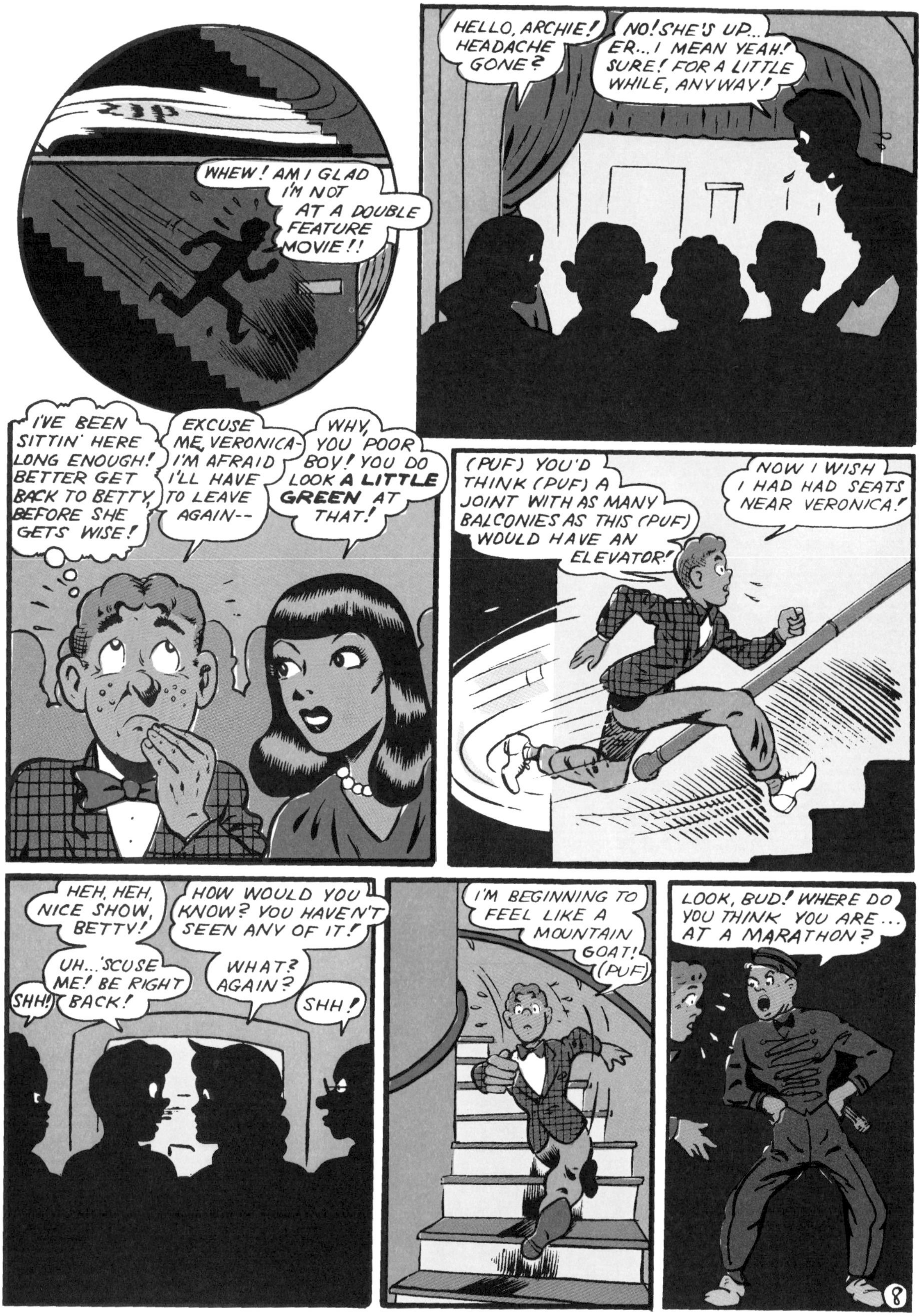
WHEW! AM I GLAD I'M NOT AT A DOUBLE FEATURE MOVIE!!
HELLO, ARCHIE! HEADACHE GONE?
NO! SHE'S UP... ER... I MEAN YEAH! SURE! FOR A LITTLE WHILE, ANYWAY!
I'VE BEEN SITTIN' HERE LONG ENOUGH! BETTER GET BACK TO BETTY, BEFORE SHE GETS WISE!
EXCUSE ME, VERONICA-I'M AFRAID I'LL HAVE TO LEAVE AGAIN--
WHY, YOU POOR BOY! YOU DO LOOK **A LITTLE GREEN** AT THAT!
(PUF) YOU'D THINK (PUF) A JOINT WITH AS MANY BALCONIES AS THIS (PUF) WOULD HAVE AN ELEVATOR!
NOW I WISH I HAD HAD SEATS NEAR VERONICA!
HEH, HEH, NICE SHOW, BETTY!
HOW WOULD YOU KNOW? YOU HAVEN'T SEEN ANY OF IT!
UH...'SCUSE ME! BE RIGHT BACK!
WHAT? AGAIN?
SHH!
SHH!
I'M BEGINNING TO FEEL LIKE A MOUNTAIN GOAT! (PUF)
LOOK, BUD! WHERE DO YOU THINK YOU ARE... AT A MARATHON?
8

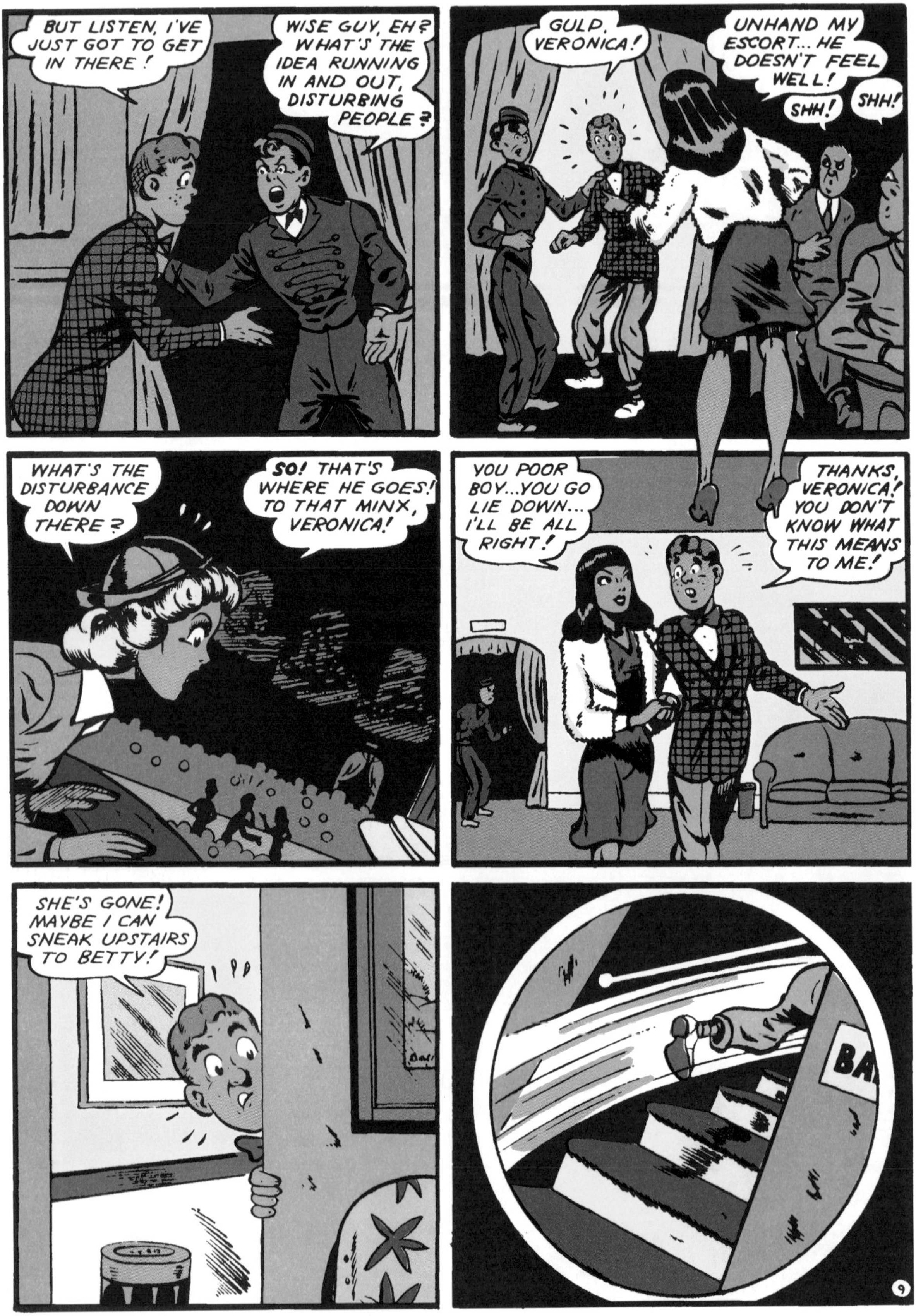
BUT LISTEN, I'VE JUST GOT TO GET IN THERE!
WISE GUY, EH? WHAT'S THE IDEA RUNNING IN AND OUT, DISTURBING PEOPLE?
GULP. VERONICA!
UNHAND MY ESCORT... HE DOESN'T FEEL WELL!
SHH!
SHH!
WHAT'S THE DISTURBANCE DOWN THERE?
SO! THAT'S WHERE HE GOES! TO THAT MINX, VERONICA!
YOU POOR BOY...YOU GO LIE DOWN... I'LL BE ALL RIGHT!
THANKS, VERONICA! YOU DON'T KNOW WHAT THIS MEANS TO ME!
SHE'S GONE! MAYBE I CAN SNEAK UPSTAIRS TO BETTY!
9

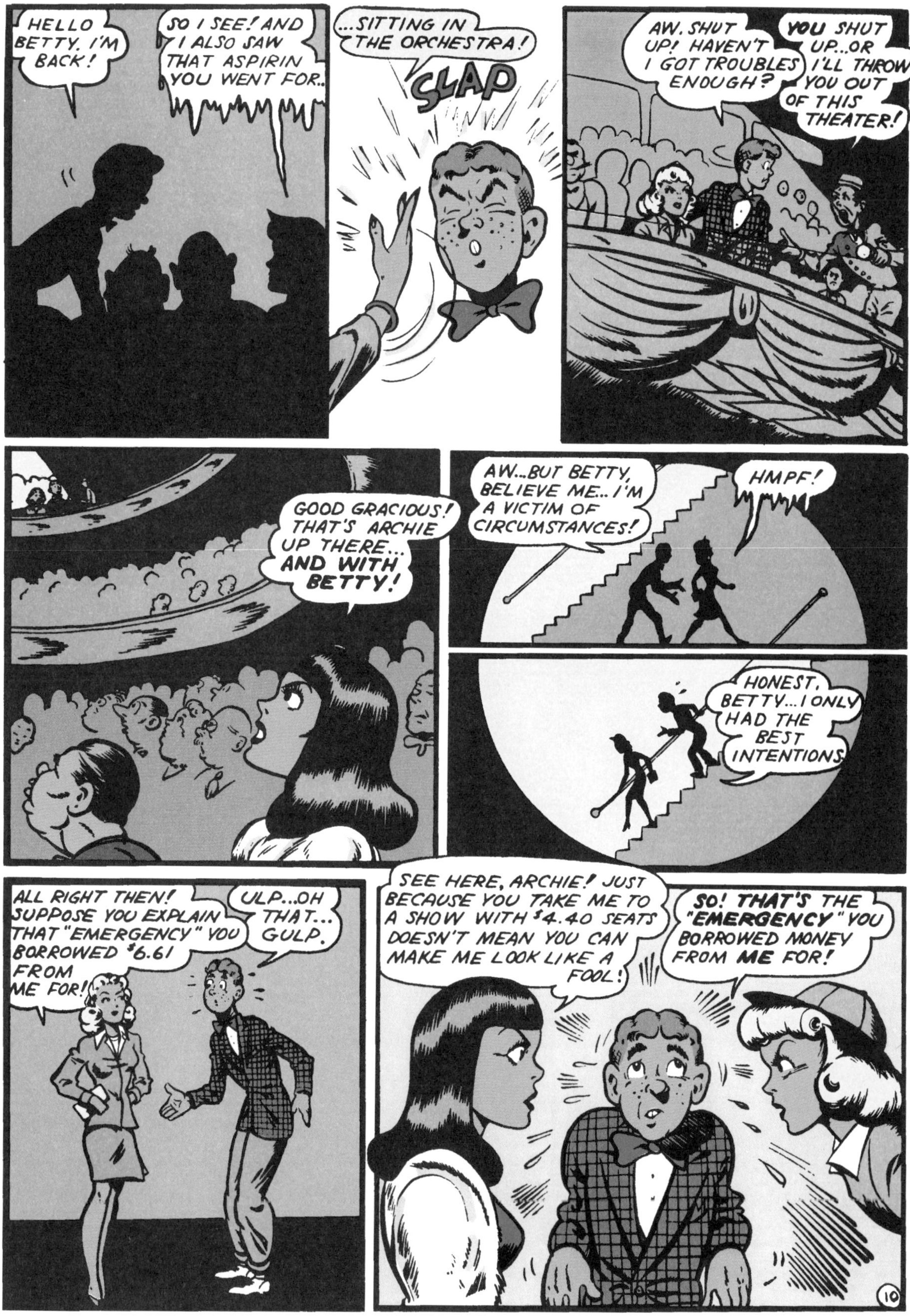
HELLO BETTY, I'M BACK!
SO I SEE! AND I ALSO SAW THAT ASPIRIN YOU WENT FOR...
...SITTING IN THE ORCHESTRA!
SLAP
AW, SHUT UP! HAVEN'T I GOT TROUBLES ENOUGH?
YOU SHUT UP...OR I'LL THROW YOU OUT OF THIS THEATER!
GOOD GRACIOUS! THAT'S ARCHIE UP THERE... AND WITH BETTY!
AW...BUT BETTY, BELIEVE ME...I'M A VICTIM OF CIRCUMSTANCES!
HMPF!
HONEST, BETTY...I ONLY HAD THE BEST INTENTIONS
ALL RIGHT THEN! SUPPOSE YOU EXPLAIN THAT "EMERGENCY" YOU BORROWED $6.61 FROM ME FOR!
ULP...OH THAT... GULP.
SEE HERE, ARCHIE! JUST BECAUSE YOU TAKE ME TO A SHOW WITH $4.40 SEATS DOESN'T MEAN YOU CAN MAKE ME LOOK LIKE A FOOL!
SO! THAT'S THE "EMERGENCY" YOU BORROWED MONEY FROM ME FOR!
10

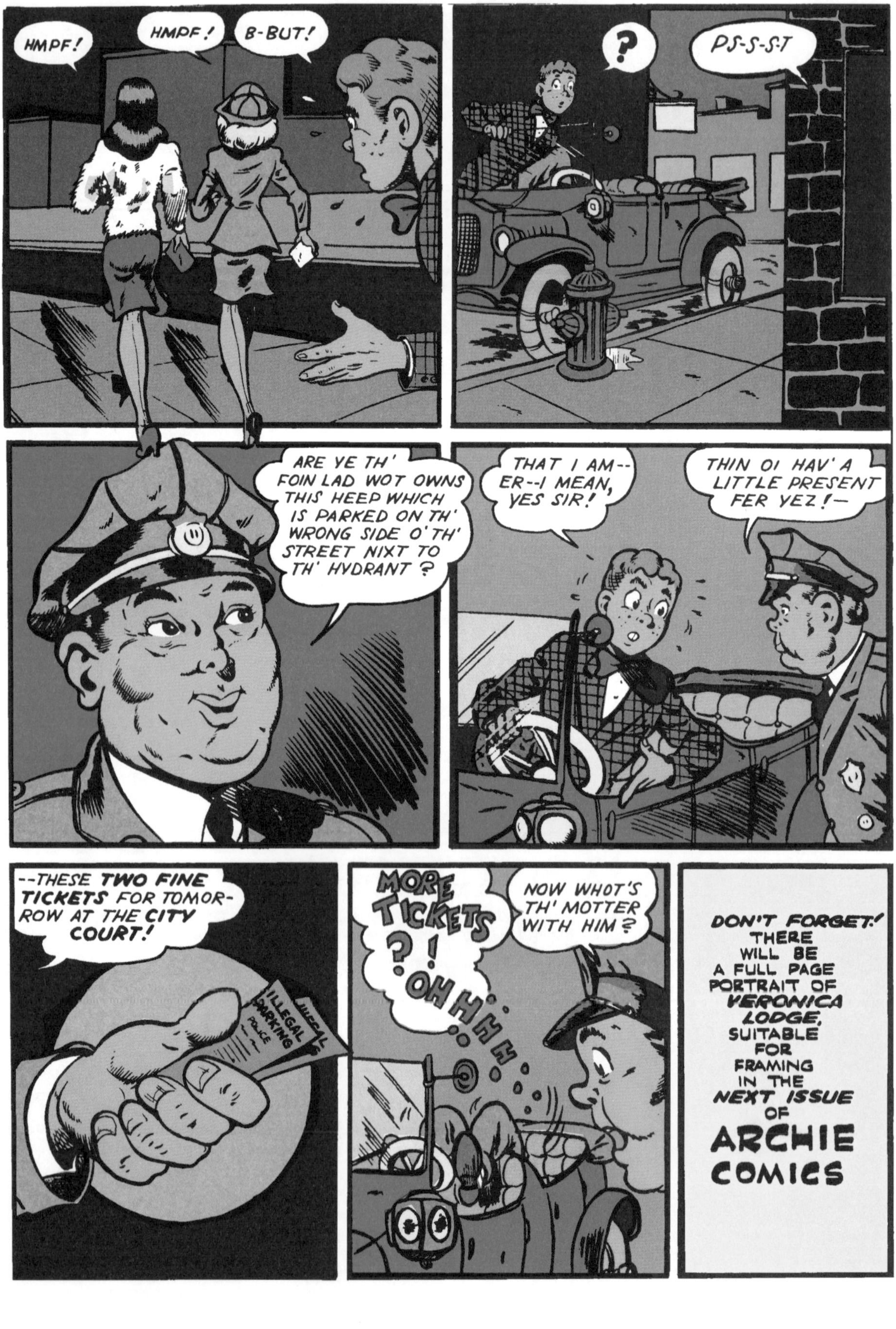
HMPF!
HMPF!
B-BUT!
?
PS-S-S-T
ARE YE TH' FOIN LAD WOT OWNS THIS HEEP WHICH IS PARKED ON TH' WRONG SIDE O'TH' STREET NIXT TO TH' HYDRANT?
THAT I AM--ER--I MEAN, YES SIR!
THIN OI HAV' A LITTLE PRESENT FER YEZ!—
--THESE TWO FINE TICKETS FOR TOMORROW AT THE CITY COURT!
ILLEGAL PARKING POLICE
ILLEGAL
MORE TICKETS ? ! OHHHHH
NOW WHOT'S TH' MOTTER WITH HIM?
DON'T FORGET! THERE WILL BE A FULL PAGE PORTRAIT OF VERONICA LODGE, SUITABLE FOR FRAMING IN THE NEXT ISSUE OF ARCHIE COMICS

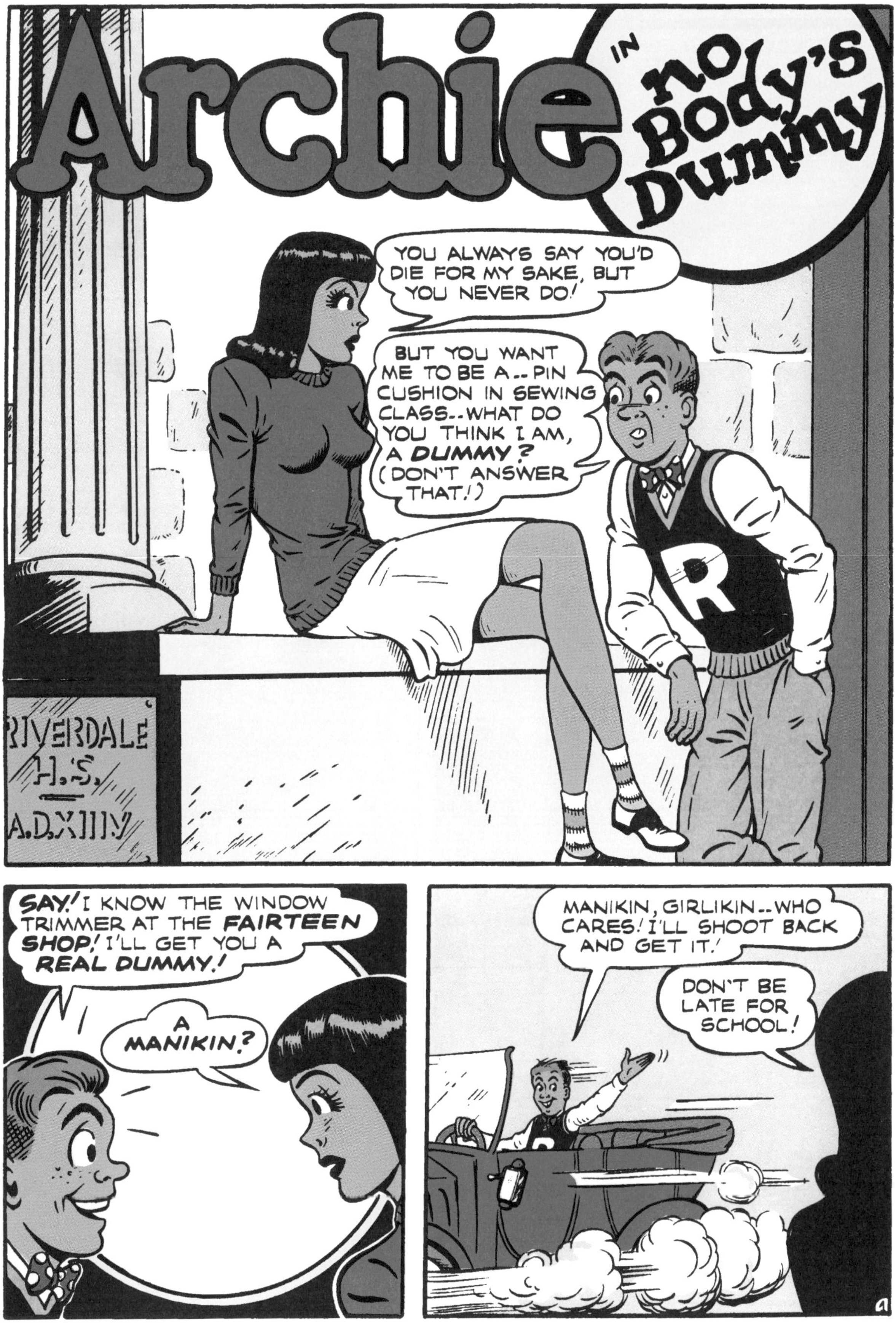
Archie
IN
no Body's Dummy
YOU ALWAYS SAY YOU'D DIE FOR MY SAKE, BUT YOU NEVER DO!
BUT YOU WANT ME TO BE A.. PIN CUSHION IN SEWING CLASS..WHAT DO YOU THINK I AM, A DUMMY? (DON'T ANSWER THAT!)
RIVERDALE H.S. A.D.XIIIV
SAY! I KNOW THE WINDOW TRIMMER AT THE FAIRTEEN SHOP! I'LL GET YOU A REAL DUMMY!
A MANIKIN?
MANIKIN, GIRLIKIN.. WHO CARES! I'LL SHOOT BACK AND GET IT!
DON'T BE LATE FOR SCHOOL!
a

Originally presented in PEP COMICS #64, November, 1947

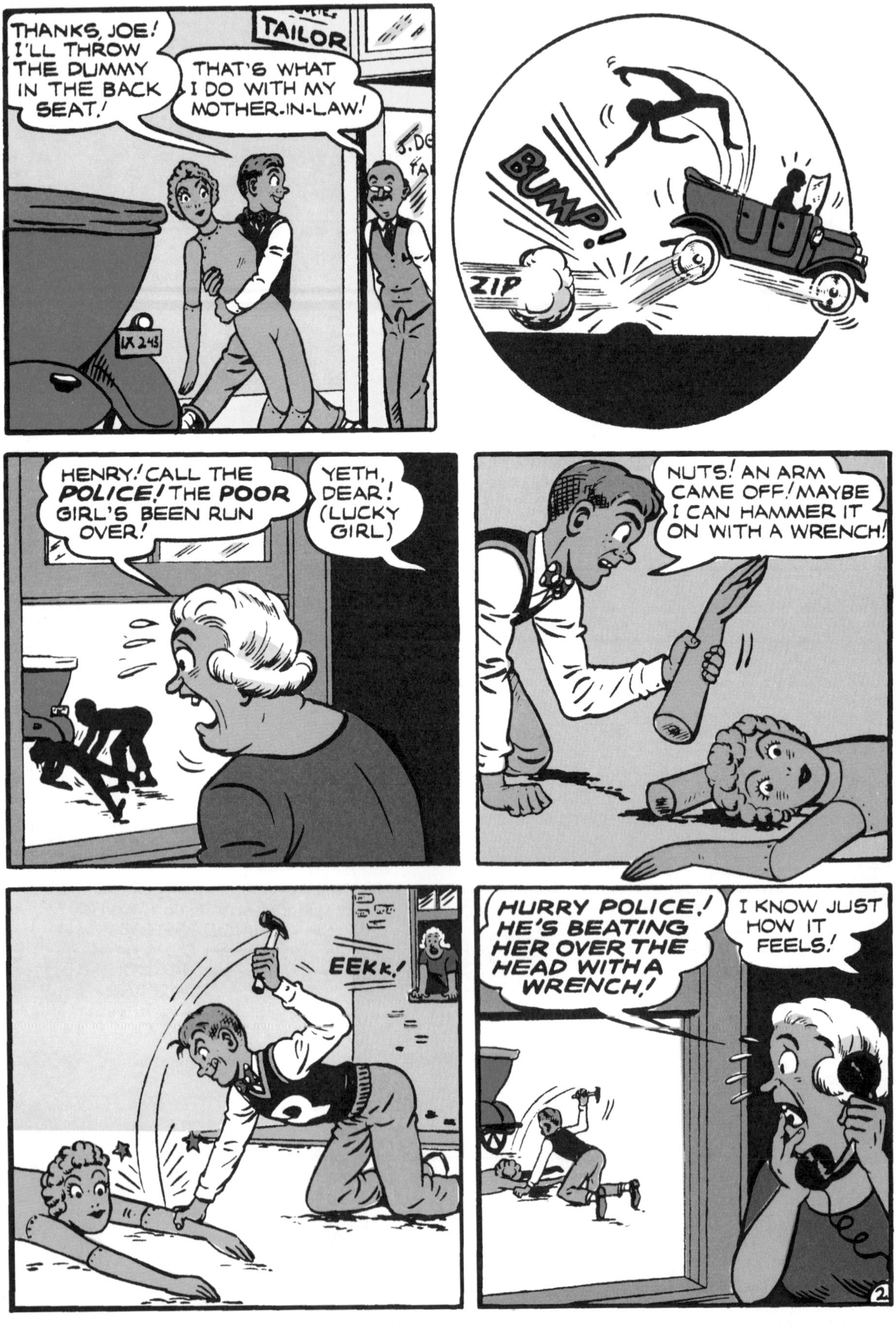
TAILOR
THANKS, JOE! I'LL THROW THE DUMMY IN THE BACK SEAT!
THAT'S WHAT I DO WITH MY MOTHER-IN-LAW!
LX 243
BUMP!
ZIP
HENRY! CALL THE POLICE! THE POOR GIRL'S BEEN RUN OVER!
YETH, DEAR! (LUCKY GIRL)
NUTS! AN ARM CAME OFF! MAYBE I CAN HAMMER IT ON WITH A WRENCH!
EEKK!
HURRY POLICE! HE'S BEATING HER OVER THE HEAD WITH A WRENCH!
I KNOW JUST HOW IT FEELS!
2

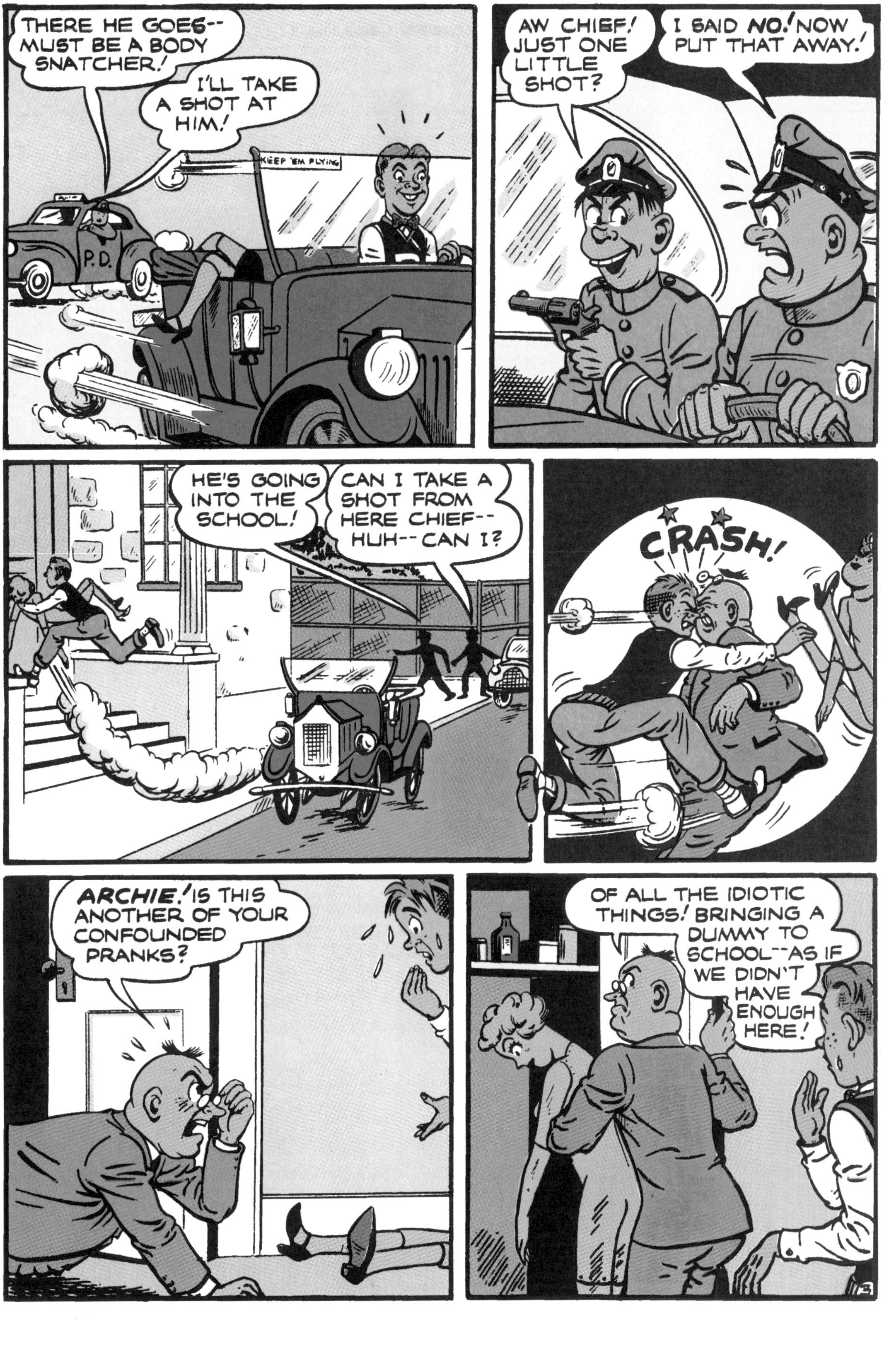
THERE HE GOES-- MUST BE A BODY SNATCHER!
I'LL TAKE A SHOT AT HIM!
KEEP 'EM FLYING
AW CHIEF! JUST ONE LITTLE SHOT?
I SAID NO! NOW PUT THAT AWAY!
HE'S GOING INTO THE SCHOOL!
CAN I TAKE A SHOT FROM HERE CHIEF-- HUH-- CAN I?
CRASH!
ARCHIE! IS THIS ANOTHER OF YOUR CONFOUNDED PRANKS?
OF ALL THE IDIOTIC THINGS! BRINGING A DUMMY TO SCHOOL--AS IF WE DIDN'T HAVE ENOUGH HERE!

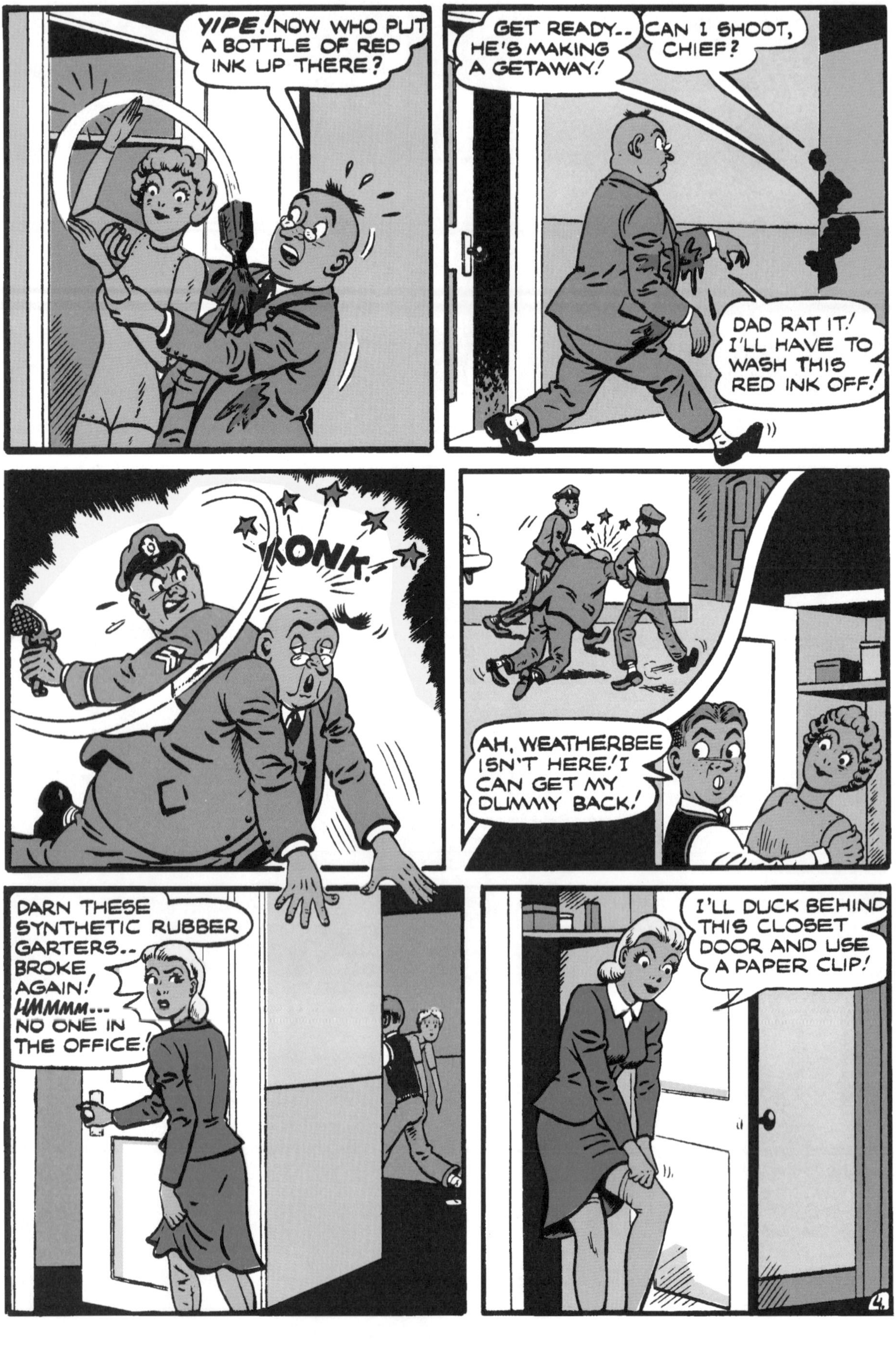
YIPE! NOW WHO PUT A BOTTLE OF RED INK UP THERE?
GET READY.. HE'S MAKING A GETAWAY!
CAN I SHOOT, CHIEF?
DAD RAT IT! I'LL HAVE TO WASH THIS RED INK OFF!
KONK!
AH, WEATHERBEE ISN'T HERE! I CAN GET MY DUMMY BACK!
DARN THESE SYNTHETIC RUBBER GARTERS.. BROKE AGAIN! HMMMM... NO ONE IN THE OFFICE!
I'LL DUCK BEHIND THIS CLOSET DOOR AND USE A PAPER CLIP!
4

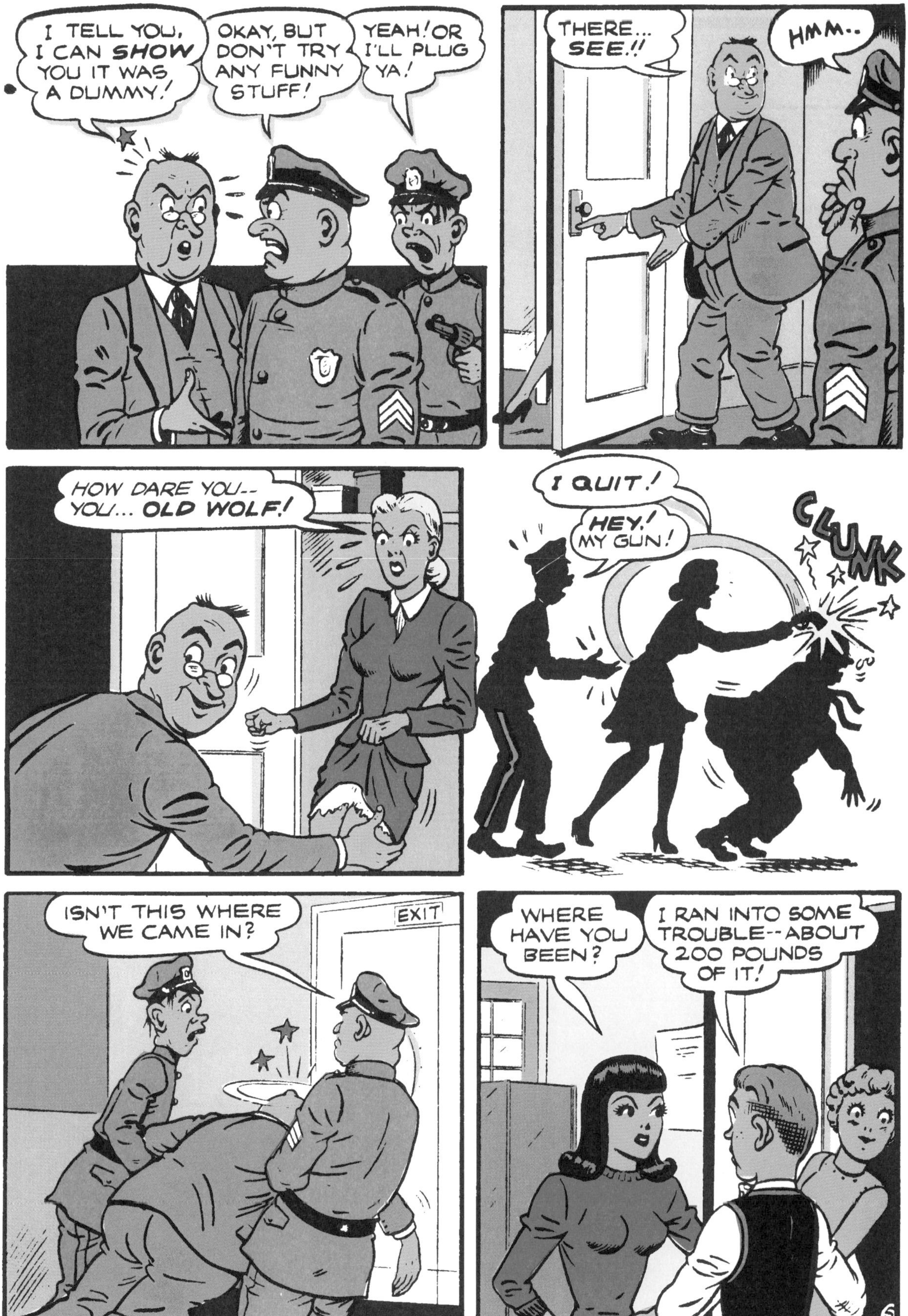
I TELL YOU, I CAN **SHOW** YOU IT WAS A DUMMY!
OKAY, BUT DON'T TRY ANY FUNNY STUFF!
YEAH! OR I'LL PLUG YA!
THERE... **SEE!!**
HMM..
HOW DARE YOU-- YOU... **OLD WOLF!**
I QUIT!
HEY! MY GUN!
CLUNK
ISN'T THIS WHERE WE CAME IN?
EXIT
WHERE HAVE YOU BEEN?
I RAN INTO SOME TROUBLE--ABOUT 200 POUNDS OF IT!
5

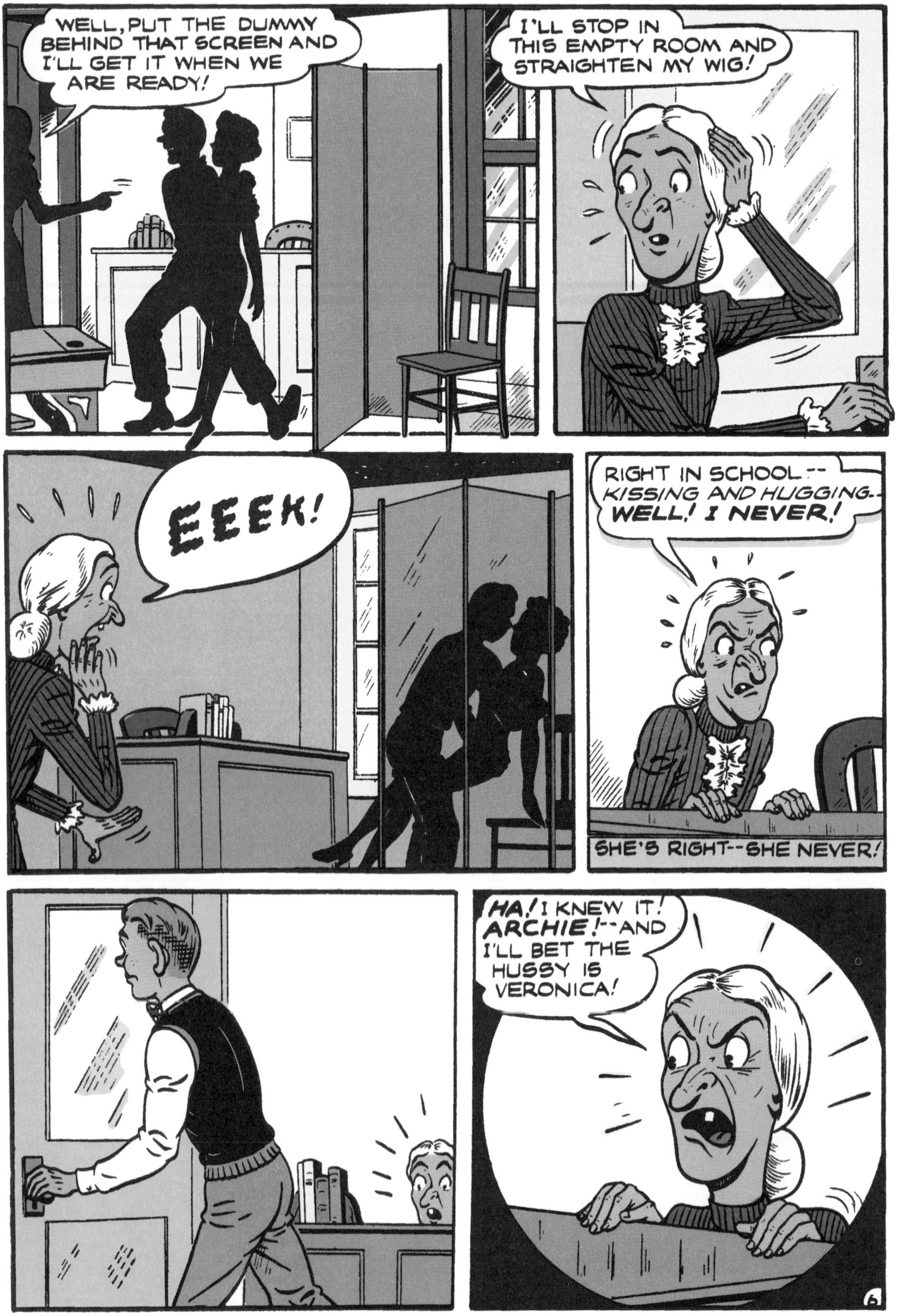
WELL, PUT THE DUMMY BEHIND THAT SCREEN AND I'LL GET IT WHEN WE ARE READY!
I'LL STOP IN THIS EMPTY ROOM AND STRAIGHTEN MY WIG!
EEEK!
RIGHT IN SCHOOL-- KISSING AND HUGGING-- WELL! I NEVER!
SHE'S RIGHT--SHE NEVER!
HA! I KNEW IT! ARCHIE!--AND I'LL BET THE HUSSY IS VERONICA!
6

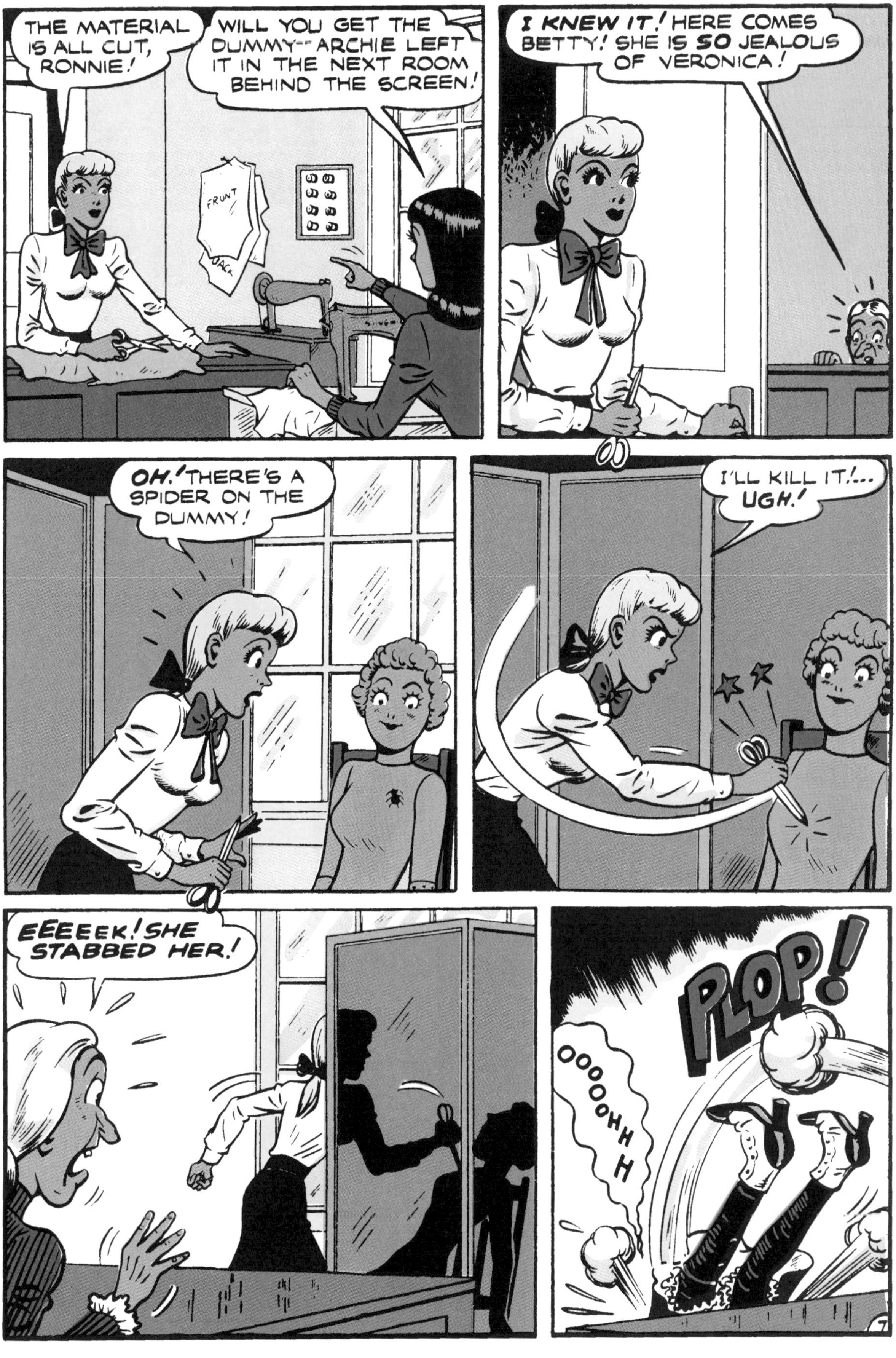
THE MATERIAL IS ALL CUT, RONNIE!
WILL YOU GET THE DUMMY--ARCHIE LEFT IT IN THE NEXT ROOM BEHIND THE SCREEN!
FRONT
I KNEW IT! HERE COMES BETTY! SHE IS SO JEALOUS OF VERONICA!
OH! THERE'S A SPIDER ON THE DUMMY!
I'LL KILL IT!... UGH!
EEEEEK! SHE STABBED HER!
PLOP!
OOOOOHHH
7

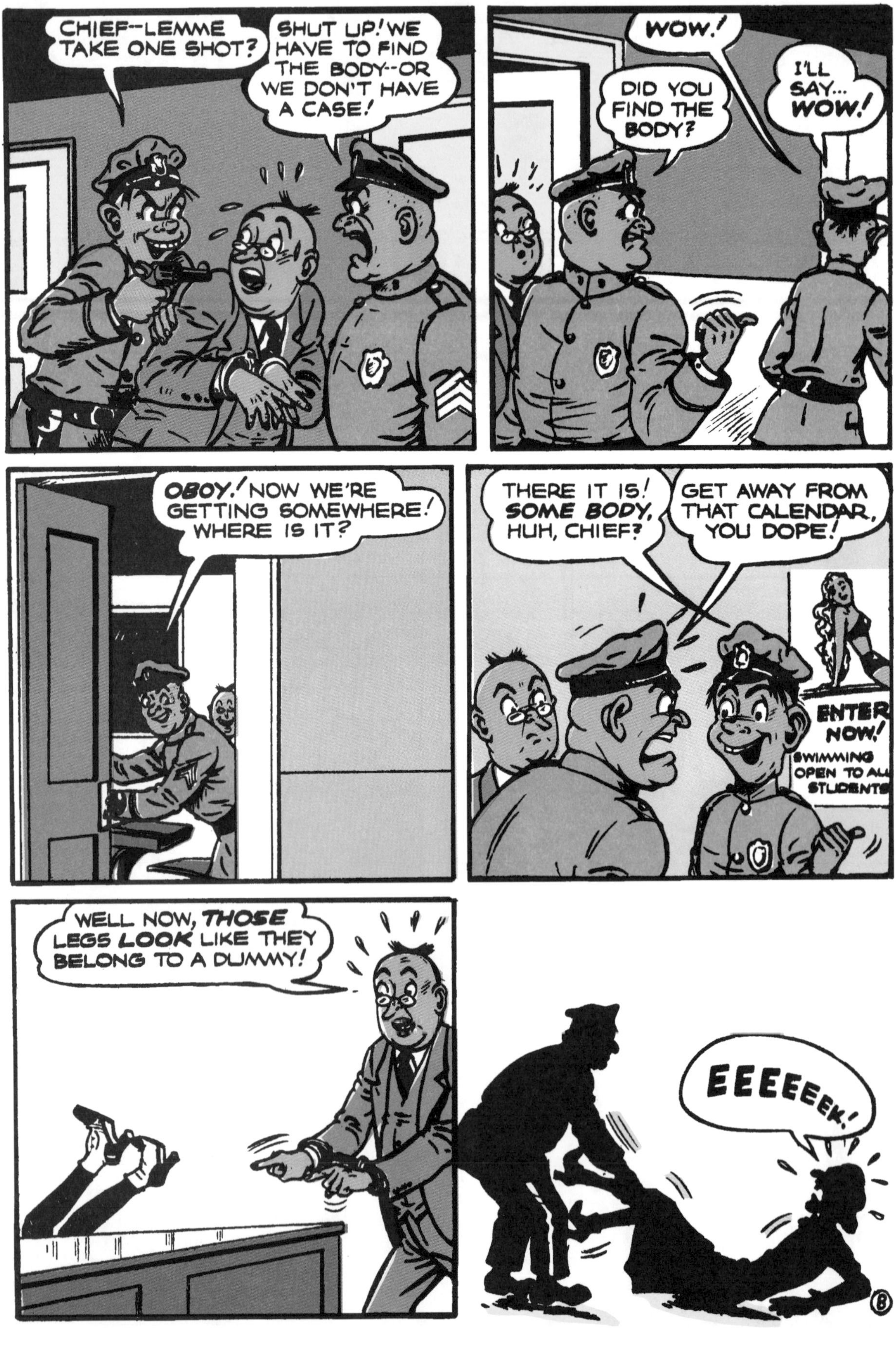
CHIEF--LEMME TAKE ONE SHOT?
SHUT UP! WE HAVE TO FIND THE BODY--OR WE DON'T HAVE A CASE!
WOW!
DID YOU FIND THE BODY?
I'LL SAY... WOW!
OBOY! NOW WE'RE GETTING SOMEWHERE! WHERE IS IT?
THERE IT IS! SOME BODY, HUH, CHIEF?
GET AWAY FROM THAT CALENDAR, YOU DOPE!
ENTER NOW!
SWIMMING OPEN TO ALL STUDENTS
WELL NOW, THOSE LEGS LOOK LIKE THEY BELONG TO A DUMMY!
EEEEEEEK!
8

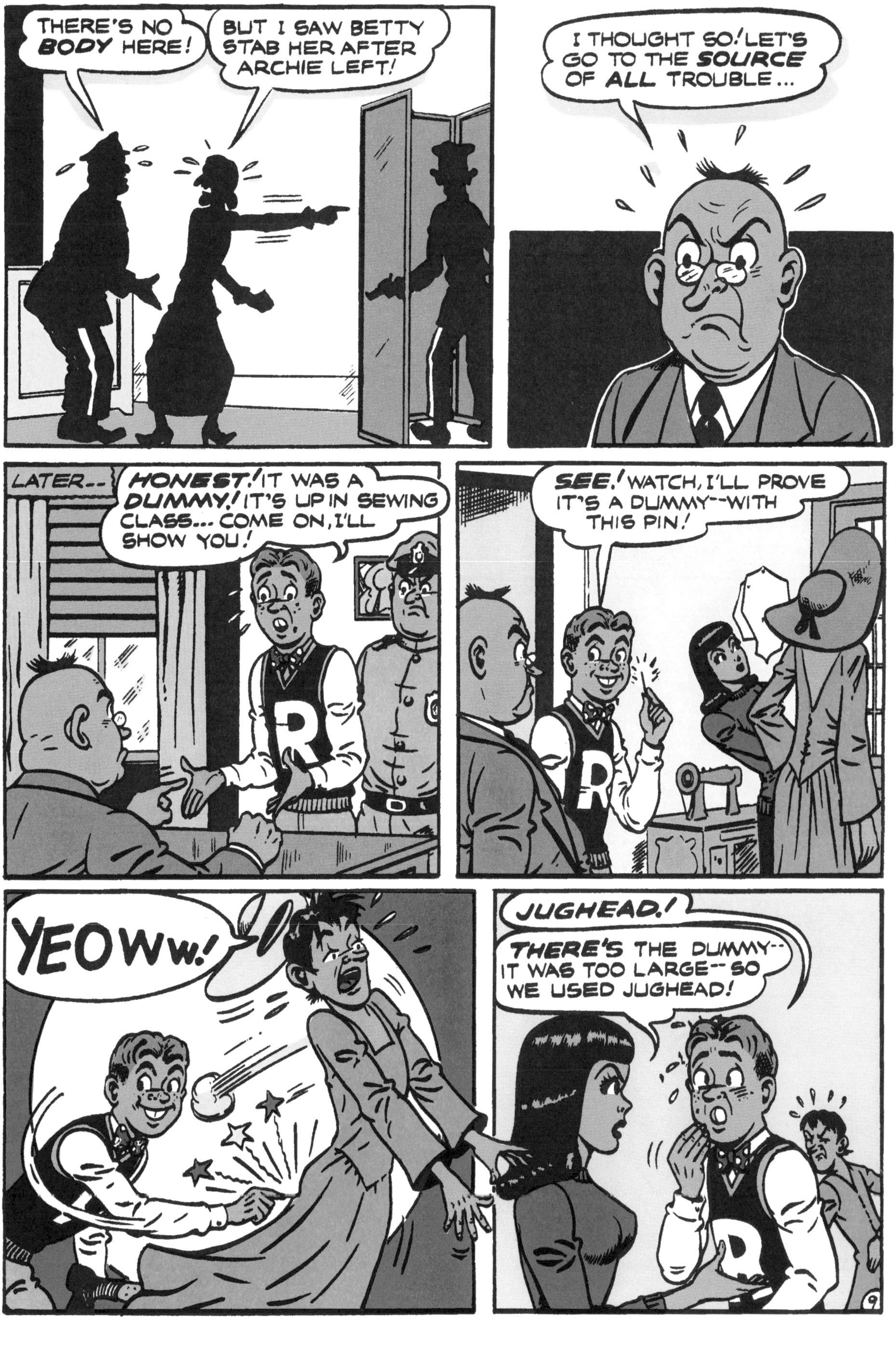
THERE'S NO BODY HERE!
BUT I SAW BETTY STAB HER AFTER ARCHIE LEFT!
I THOUGHT SO! LET'S GO TO THE SOURCE OF ALL TROUBLE...
LATER--
HONEST! IT WAS A DUMMY! IT'S UP IN SEWING CLASS... COME ON, I'LL SHOW YOU!
SEE! WATCH, I'LL PROVE IT'S A DUMMY--WITH THIS PIN!
YEOWW!
JUGHEAD!
THERE'S THE DUMMY-- IT WAS TOO LARGE-- SO WE USED JUGHEAD!
9

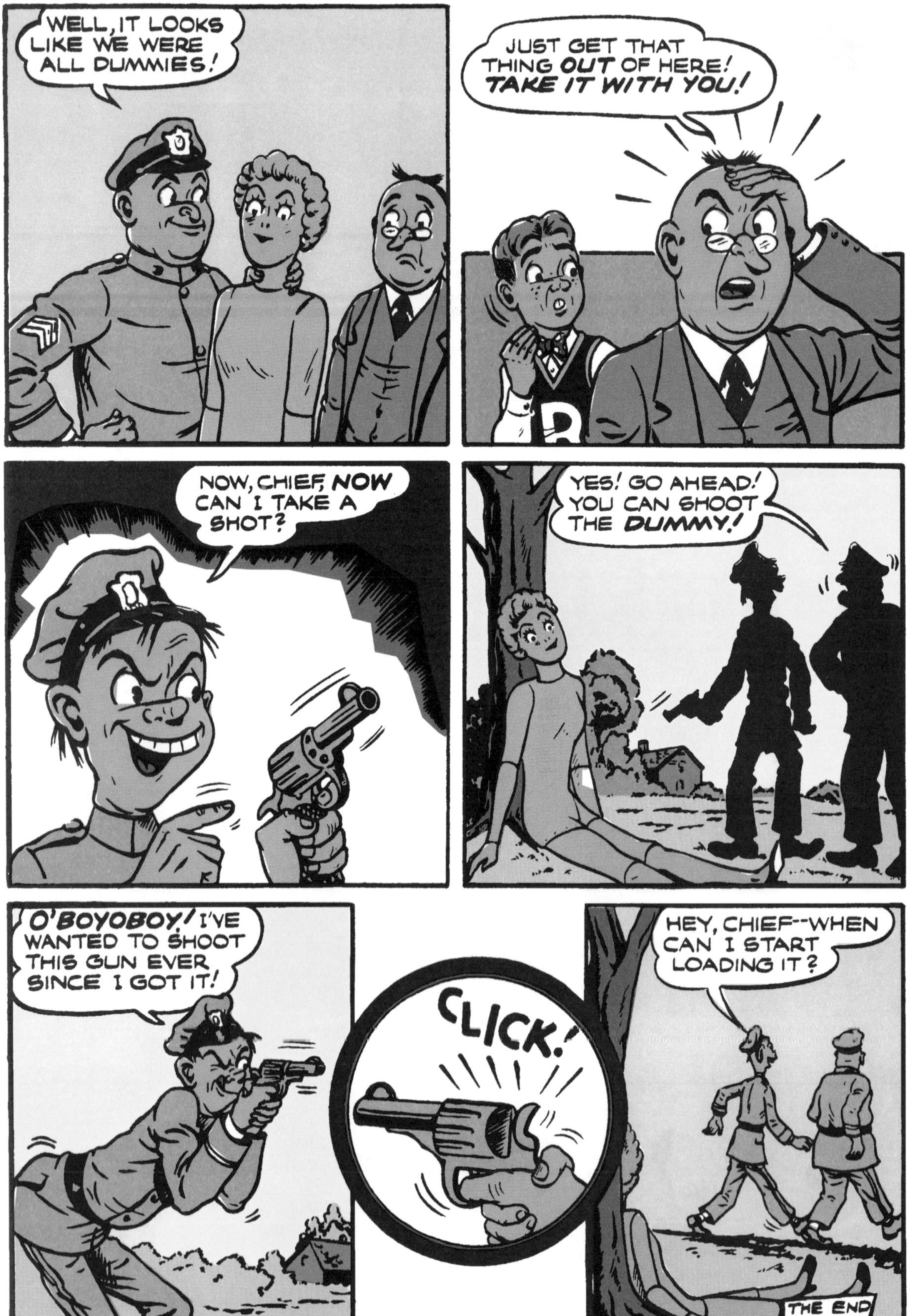
WELL, IT LOOKS LIKE WE WERE ALL DUMMIES!
JUST GET THAT THING OUT OF HERE! TAKE IT WITH YOU!
NOW, CHIEF, NOW CAN I TAKE A SHOT?
YES! GO AHEAD! YOU CAN SHOOT THE DUMMY!
O'BOYOBOY! I'VE WANTED TO SHOOT THIS GUN EVER SINCE I GOT IT!
CLICK!
HEY, CHIEF--WHEN CAN I START LOADING IT?
THE END

1940's ARCHIE COMIC BOOK COVERS

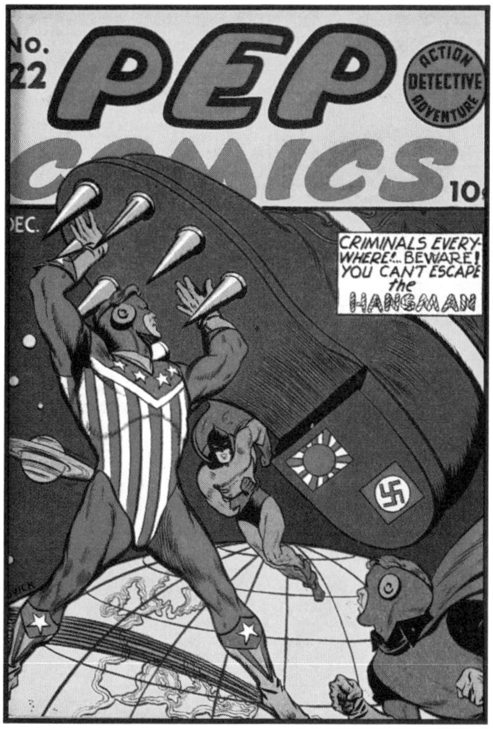
NO. 22
PEP
ACTION DETECTIVE ADVENTURE
COMICS
10¢
DEC.
CRIMINALS EVERY-WHERE!... BEWARE! YOU CAN'T ESCAPE the HANGMAN

PEP COMICS #22, DECEMBER, 1941
Contains the very first Archie story.

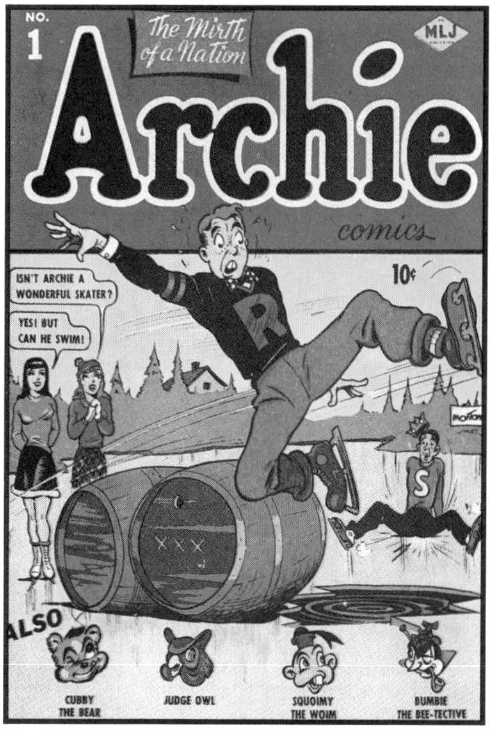
NO. 1
The Mirth of a Nation
MLJ
Archie
comics
10¢
ISN'T ARCHIE A WONDERFUL SKATER?
YES! BUT CAN HE SWIM!
ALSO
CUBBY THE BEAR
JUDGE OWL
SQUOIMY THE WOIM
BUMBIE THE BEE-TECTIVE

ARCHIE COMICS #1, WINTER, 1942
Archie gets his own title. First title to concentrate primarily on Archie and friends.

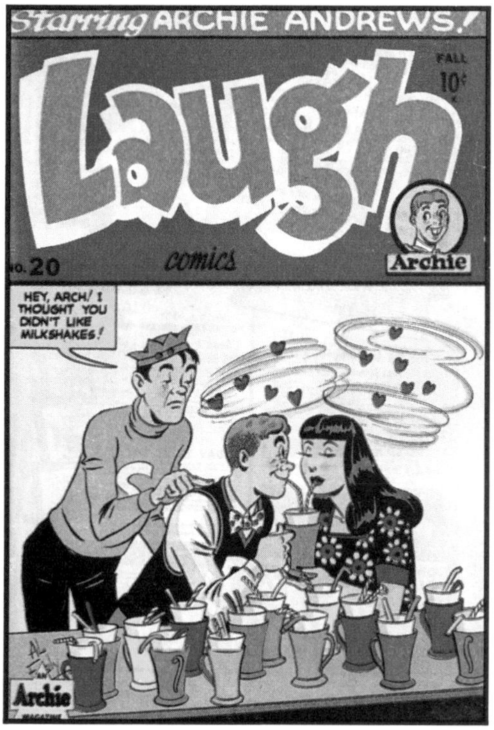
Starring ARCHIE ANDREWS!
FALL
10¢
Laugh
comics
NO. 20
Archie
HEY, ARCH! I THOUGHT YOU DIDN'T LIKE MILKSHAKES!
Archie

LAUGH COMICS #20, FALL, 1946
Second title specifically created to showcase the exploits of Archie. Numbering system continues from various hero titles.

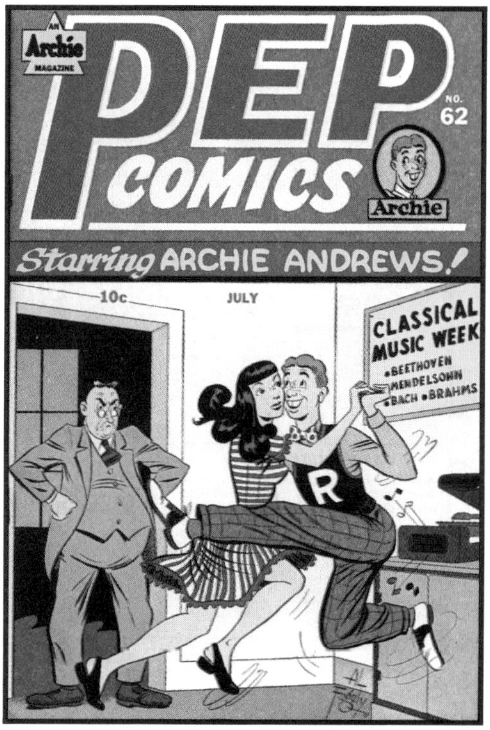
Archie
PEP
NO. 62
COMICS
Archie
Starring ARCHIE ANDREWS!
10c
JULY
CLASSICAL MUSIC WEEK
•BEETHOVEN
•MENDELSOHN
•BACH •BRAHMS

PEP COMICS #62, JULY, 1947
Cover is exemplary of 1940's Americana as it depicts the characters dancing the Jitterbug.

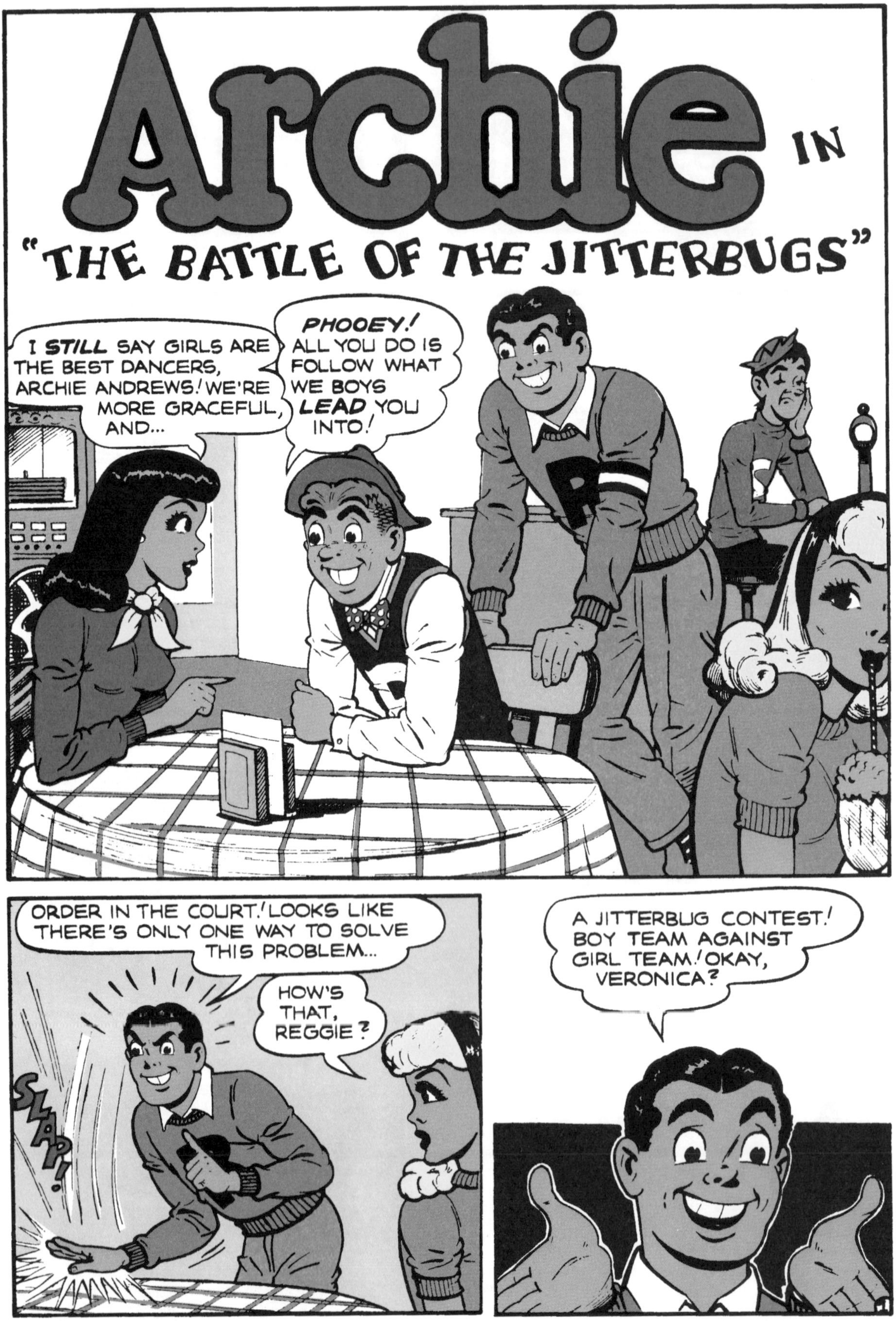
Archie IN
"THE BATTLE OF THE JITTERBUGS"
I STILL SAY GIRLS ARE THE BEST DANCERS, ARCHIE ANDREWS! WE'RE MORE GRACEFUL, AND...
PHOOEY! ALL YOU DO IS FOLLOW WHAT WE BOYS LEAD YOU INTO!
ORDER IN THE COURT! LOOKS LIKE THERE'S ONLY ONE WAY TO SOLVE THIS PROBLEM...
HOW'S THAT, REGGIE?
SLAP!
A JITTERBUG CONTEST! BOY TEAM AGAINST GIRL TEAM! OKAY, VERONICA?

Originally presented in ARCHIE COMICS #30, January-February, 1948

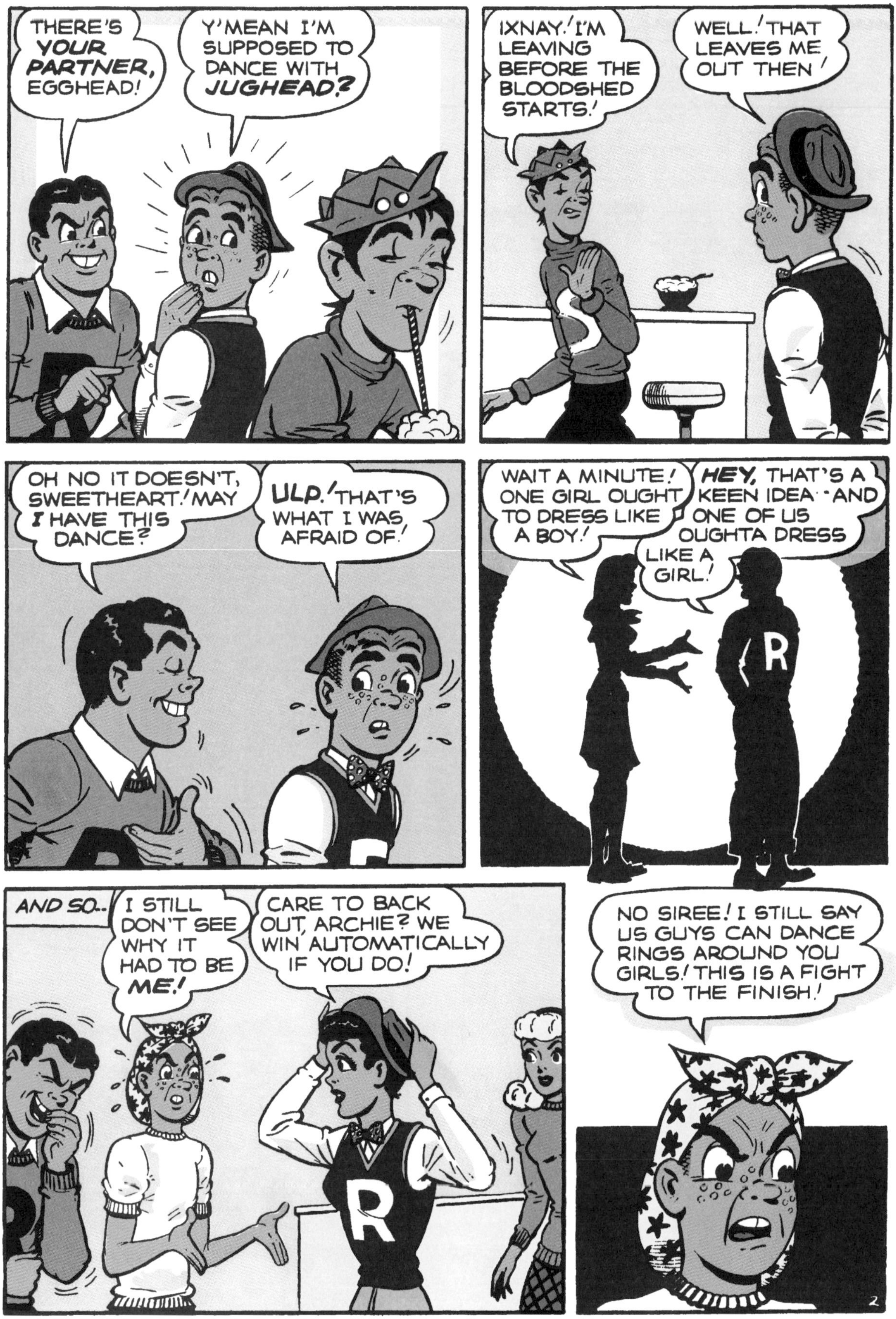
THERE'S YOUR PARTNER, EGGHEAD!
Y'MEAN I'M SUPPOSED TO DANCE WITH JUGHEAD?
IXNAY! I'M LEAVING BEFORE THE BLOODSHED STARTS!
WELL! THAT LEAVES ME OUT THEN!
OH NO IT DOESN'T, SWEETHEART! MAY I HAVE THIS DANCE?
ULP! THAT'S WHAT I WAS AFRAID OF!
WAIT A MINUTE! ONE GIRL OUGHT TO DRESS LIKE A BOY!
HEY, THAT'S A KEEN IDEA--AND ONE OF US OUGHTA DRESS LIKE A GIRL!
AND SO..
I STILL DON'T SEE WHY IT HAD TO BE ME!
CARE TO BACK OUT, ARCHIE? WE WIN AUTOMATICALLY IF YOU DO!
NO SIREE! I STILL SAY US GUYS CAN DANCE RINGS AROUND YOU GIRLS! THIS IS A FIGHT TO THE FINISH!
2

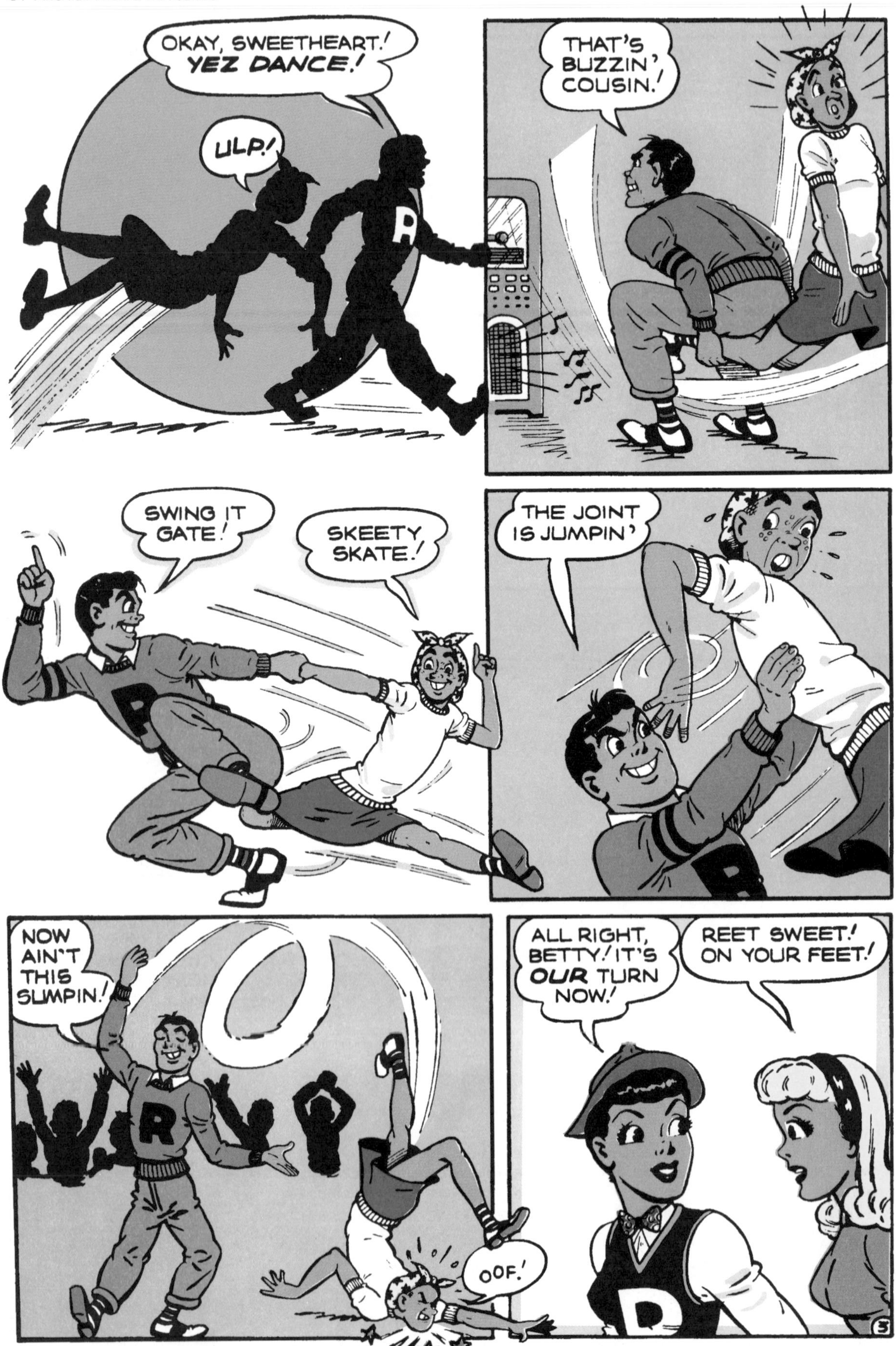
OKAY, SWEETHEART! YEZ DANCE!
ULP!
THAT'S BUZZIN' COUSIN!
SWING IT GATE!
SKEETY SKATE!
THE JOINT IS JUMPIN'
NOW AIN'T THIS SUMPIN!
OOF!
ALL RIGHT, BETTY! IT'S OUR TURN NOW!
REET SWEET! ON YOUR FEET!
3

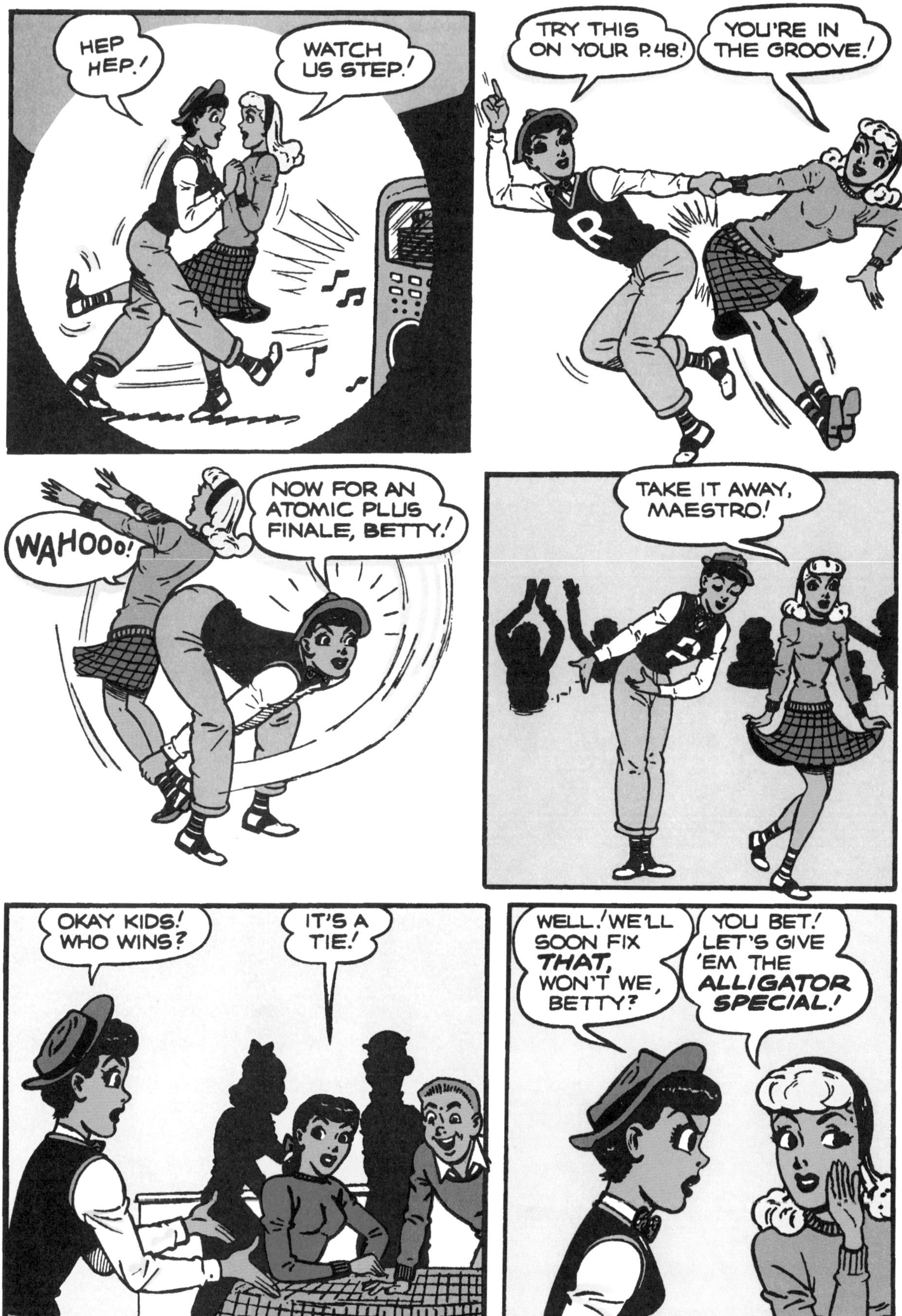
HEP HEP!
WATCH US STEP!
TRY THIS ON YOUR P.48!
YOU'RE IN THE GROOVE!
WAHOOo!
NOW FOR AN ATOMIC PLUS FINALE, BETTY!
TAKE IT AWAY, MAESTRO!
OKAY KIDS! WHO WINS?
IT'S A TIE!
WELL! WE'LL SOON FIX THAT, WON'T WE, BETTY?
YOU BET! LET'S GIVE 'EM THE ALLIGATOR SPECIAL!

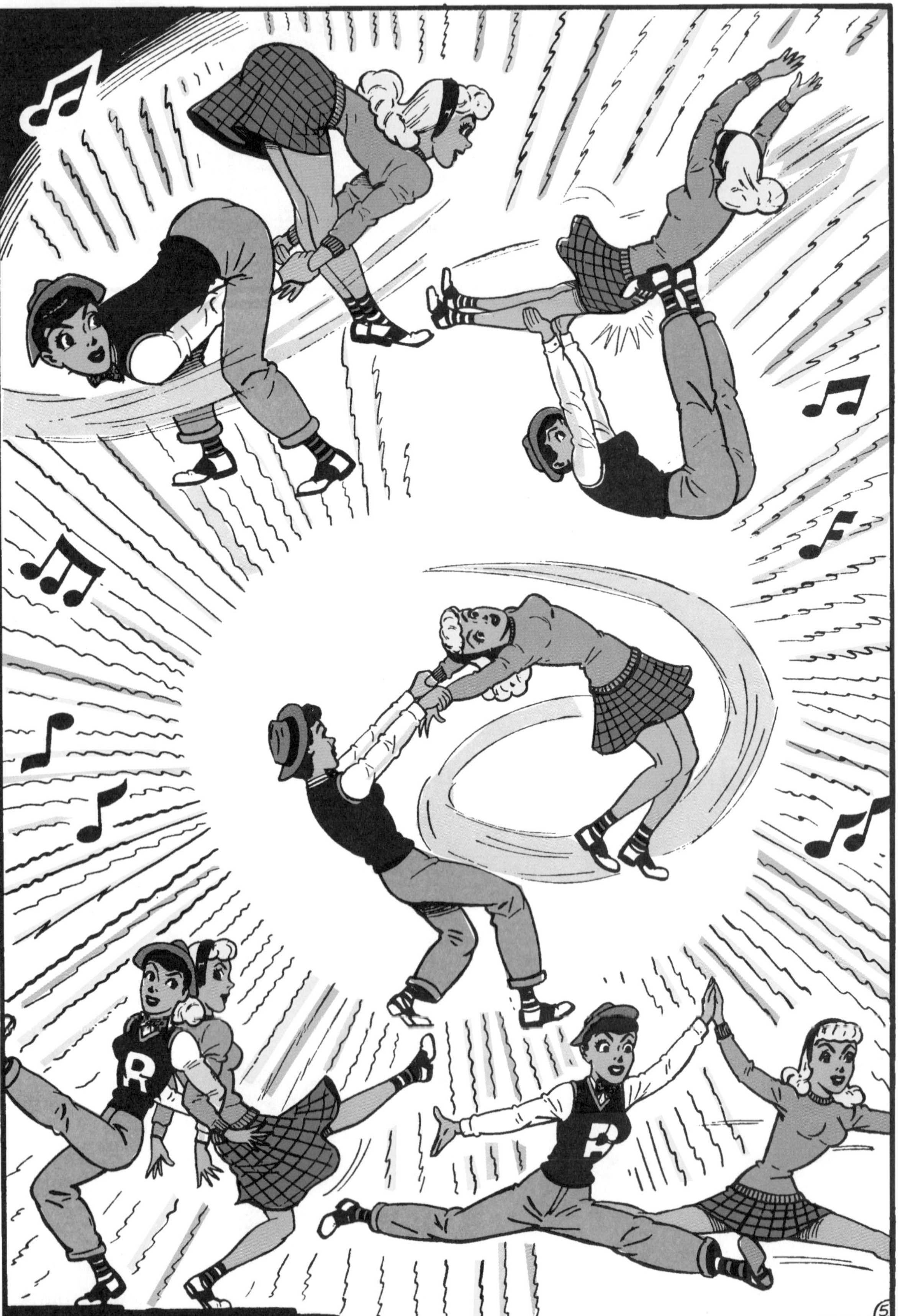
5

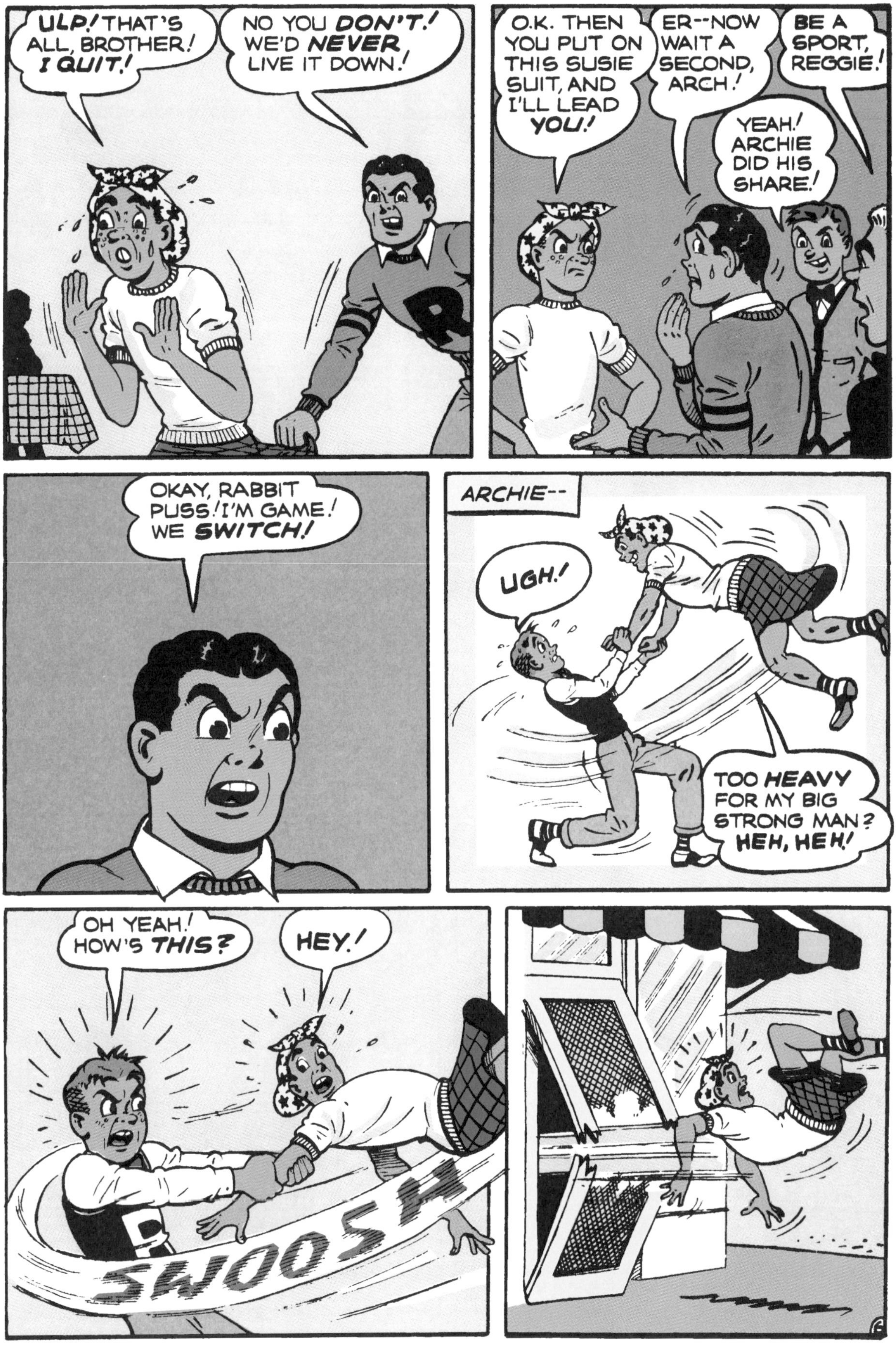
ULP! THAT'S ALL, BROTHER! I QUIT!
NO YOU DON'T! WE'D NEVER LIVE IT DOWN!
O.K. THEN YOU PUT ON THIS SUSIE SUIT, AND I'LL LEAD YOU!
ER--NOW WAIT A SECOND, ARCH!
BE A SPORT, REGGIE!
YEAH! ARCHIE DID HIS SHARE!
OKAY, RABBIT PUSS! I'M GAME! WE SWITCH!
ARCHIE--
UGH!
TOO HEAVY FOR MY BIG STRONG MAN? HEH, HEH!
OH YEAH! HOW'S THIS?
HEY!
SWOOSH

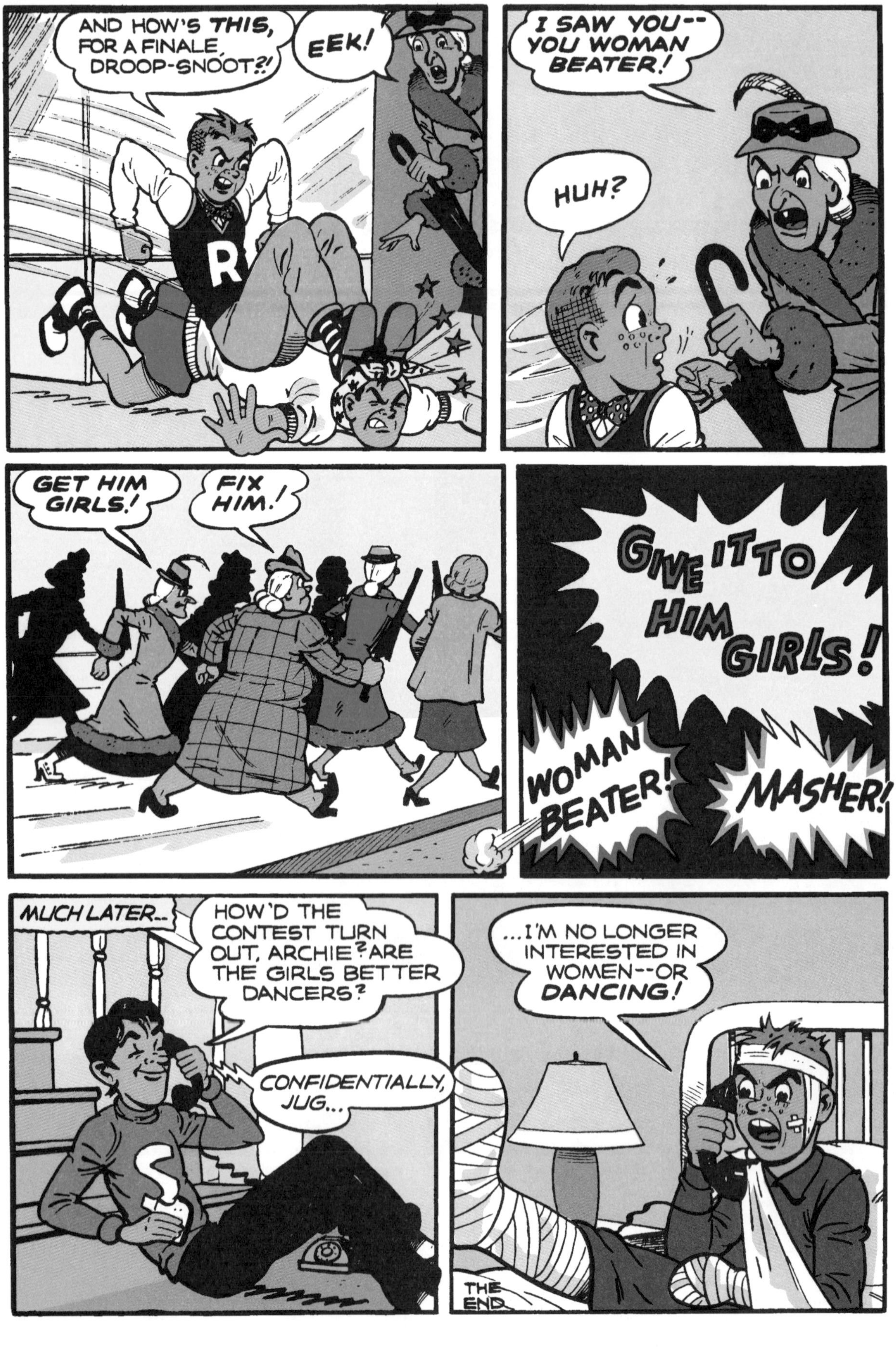
AND HOW'S THIS, FOR A FINALE, DROOP-SNOOT?!
EEK!
I SAW YOU--YOU WOMAN BEATER!
HUH?
GET HIM GIRLS!
FIX HIM.!
GIVE IT TO HIM GIRLS!
WOMAN BEATER!
MASHER!
MUCH LATER..
HOW'D THE CONTEST TURN OUT, ARCHIE? ARE THE GIRLS BETTER DANCERS?
CONFIDENTIALLY, JUG...
...I'M NO LONGER INTERESTED IN WOMEN--OR DANCING!
THE END

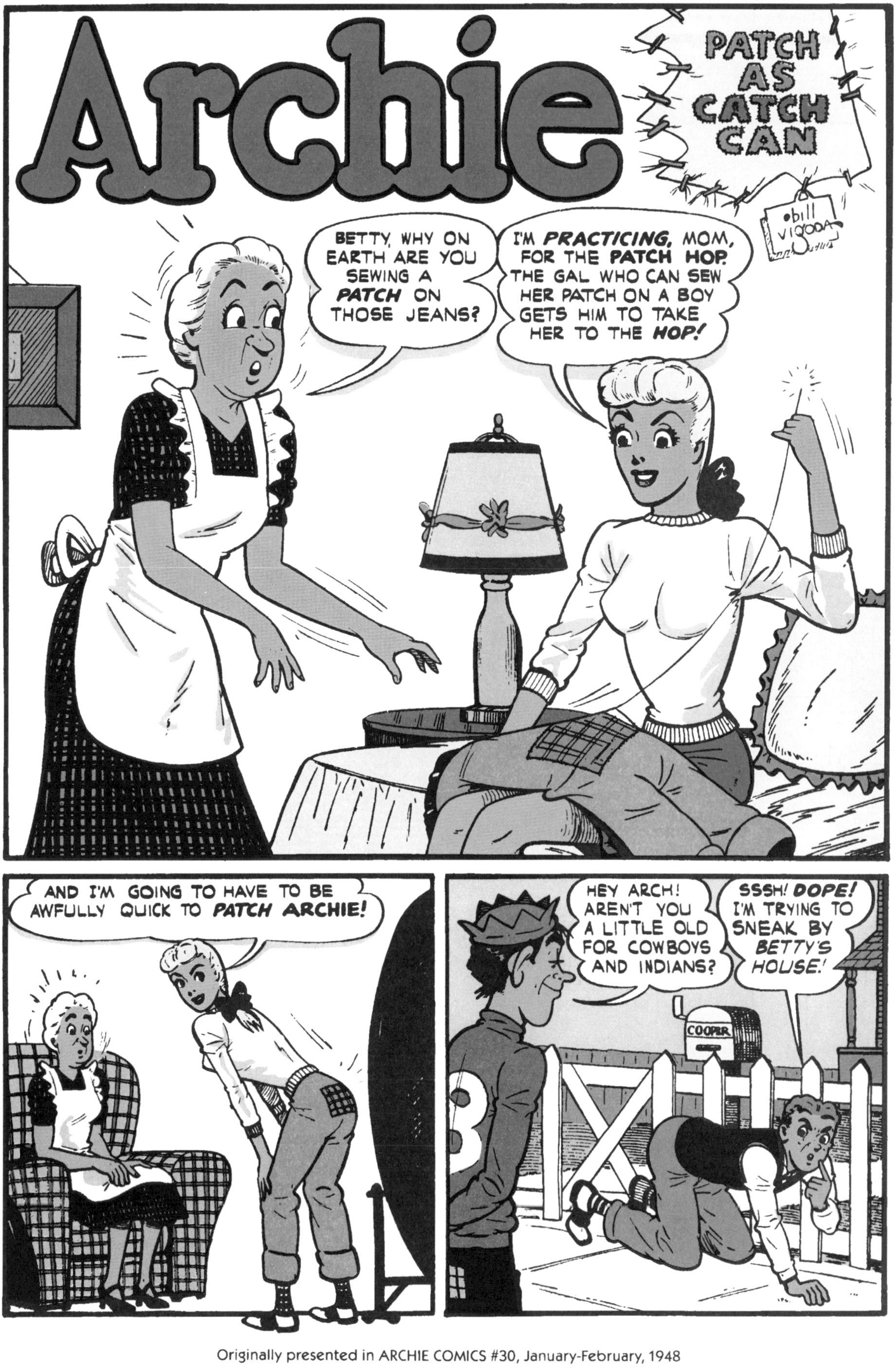
Archie
PATCH AS CATCH CAN
BETTY, WHY ON EARTH ARE YOU SEWING A PATCH ON THOSE JEANS?
I'M PRACTICING, MOM, FOR THE PATCH HOP. THE GAL WHO CAN SEW HER PATCH ON A BOY GETS HIM TO TAKE HER TO THE HOP!
AND I'M GOING TO HAVE TO BE AWFULLY QUICK TO PATCH ARCHIE!
HEY ARCH! AREN'T YOU A LITTLE OLD FOR COWBOYS AND INDIANS?
SSSH! DOPE! I'M TRYING TO SNEAK BY BETTY'S HOUSE!
COOPER

Originally presented in ARCHIE COMICS #30, January-February, 1948

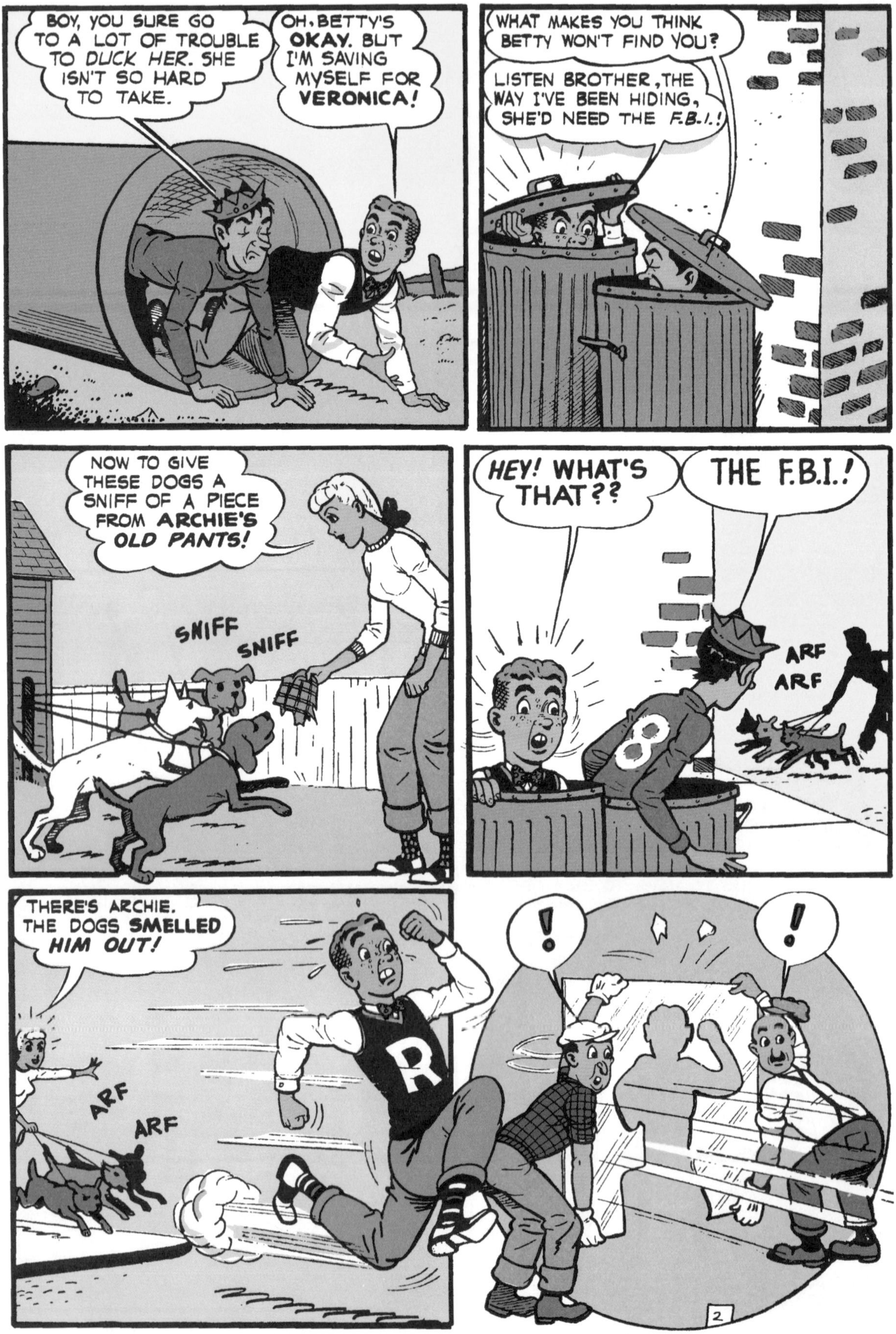
BOY, YOU SURE GO TO A LOT OF TROUBLE TO DUCK HER. SHE ISN'T SO HARD TO TAKE.
OH, BETTY'S OKAY. BUT I'M SAVING MYSELF FOR VERONICA!
WHAT MAKES YOU THINK BETTY WON'T FIND YOU?
LISTEN BROTHER, THE WAY I'VE BEEN HIDING, SHE'D NEED THE F.B.I.!
NOW TO GIVE THESE DOGS A SNIFF OF A PIECE FROM ARCHIE'S OLD PANTS!
SNIFF
SNIFF
HEY! WHAT'S THAT??
THE F.B.I.!
ARF
ARF
THERE'S ARCHIE. THE DOGS SMELLED HIM OUT!
ARF
ARF
!
!
2

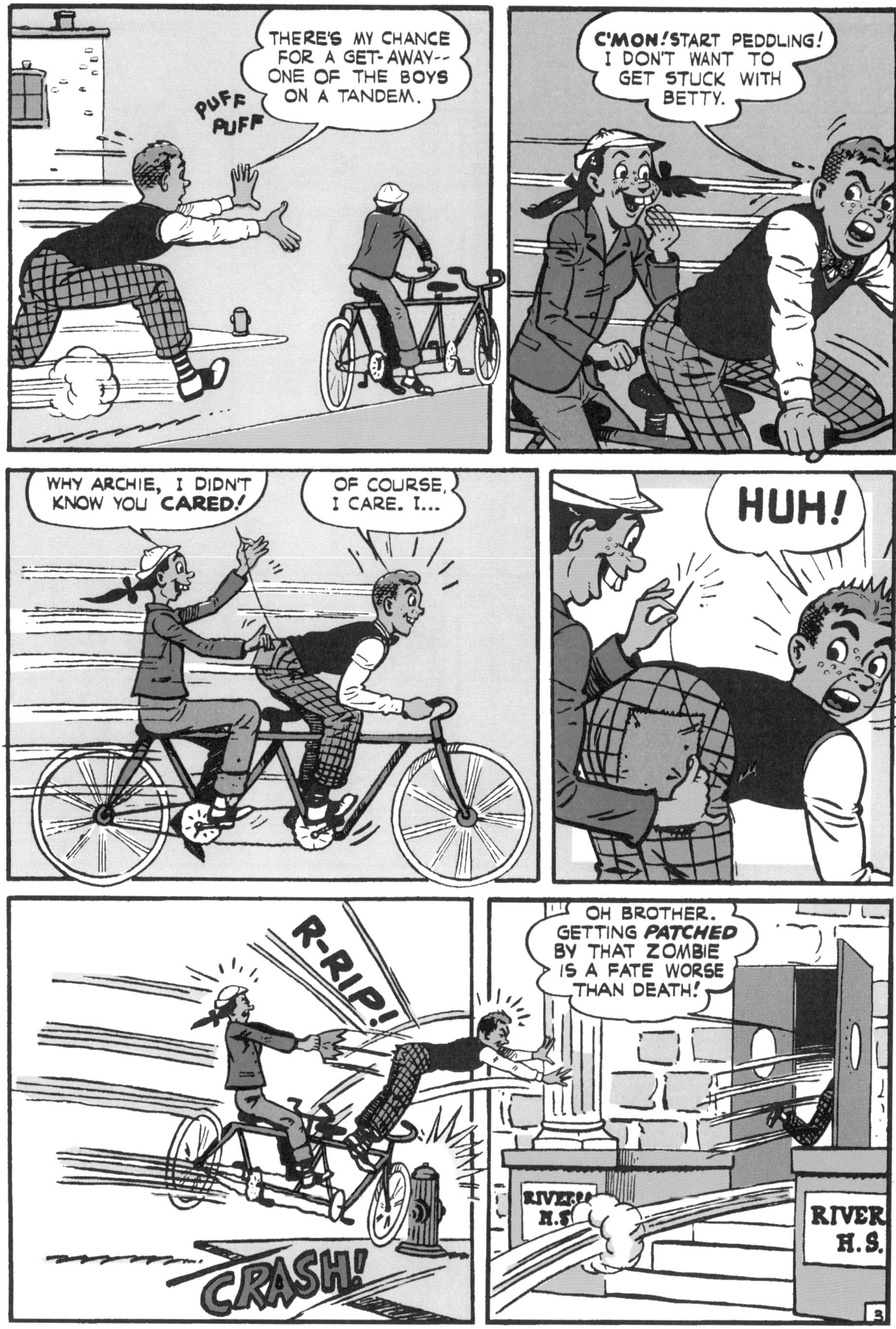
THERE'S MY CHANCE FOR A GET-AWAY-- ONE OF THE BOYS ON A TANDEM.
PUFF PUFF
C'MON! START PEDDLING! I DON'T WANT TO GET STUCK WITH BETTY.
WHY ARCHIE, I DIDN'T KNOW YOU CARED!
OF COURSE, I CARE. I...
HUH!
R-RIP!
CRASH!
OH BROTHER. GETTING PATCHED BY THAT ZOMBIE IS A FATE WORSE THAN DEATH!
RIVER H.S.
RIVER H.S.
3

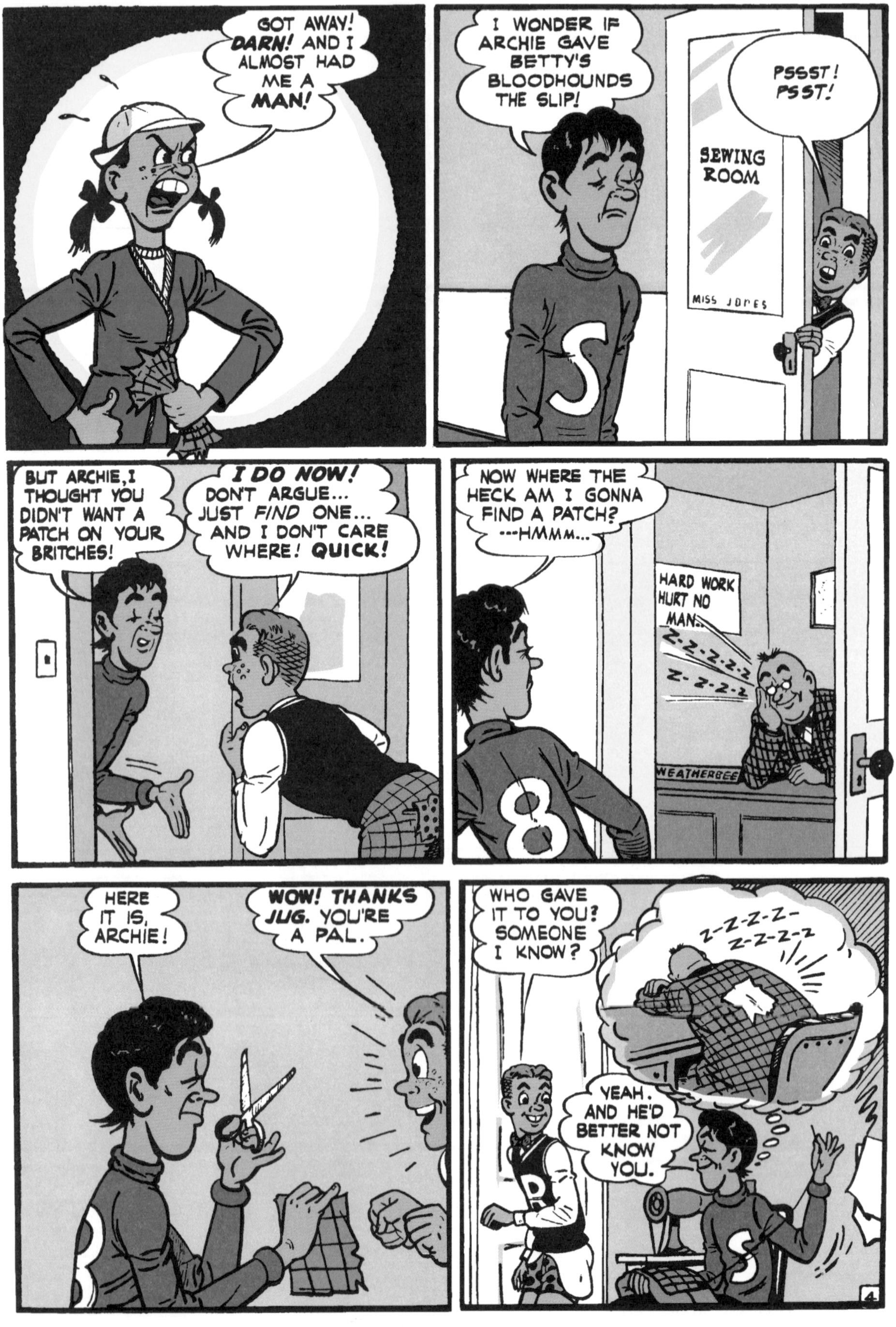
GOT AWAY! DARN! AND I ALMOST HAD ME A MAN!
I WONDER IF ARCHIE GAVE BETTY'S BLOODHOUNDS THE SLIP!
SEWING ROOM
MISS JONES
PSSST! PSST!
BUT ARCHIE, I THOUGHT YOU DIDN'T WANT A PATCH ON YOUR BRITCHES!
I DO NOW! DON'T ARGUE... JUST FIND ONE... AND I DON'T CARE WHERE! QUICK!
NOW WHERE THE HECK AM I GONNA FIND A PATCH? ---HMMM...
HARD WORK HURT NO MAN.
Z-Z-Z-Z-Z
Z-Z-Z-Z
WEATHERBEE
HERE IT IS, ARCHIE!
WOW! THANKS JUG. YOU'RE A PAL.
WHO GAVE IT TO YOU? SOMEONE I KNOW?
Z-Z-Z-Z- Z-Z-Z-Z
YEAH. AND HE'D BETTER NOT KNOW YOU.
4

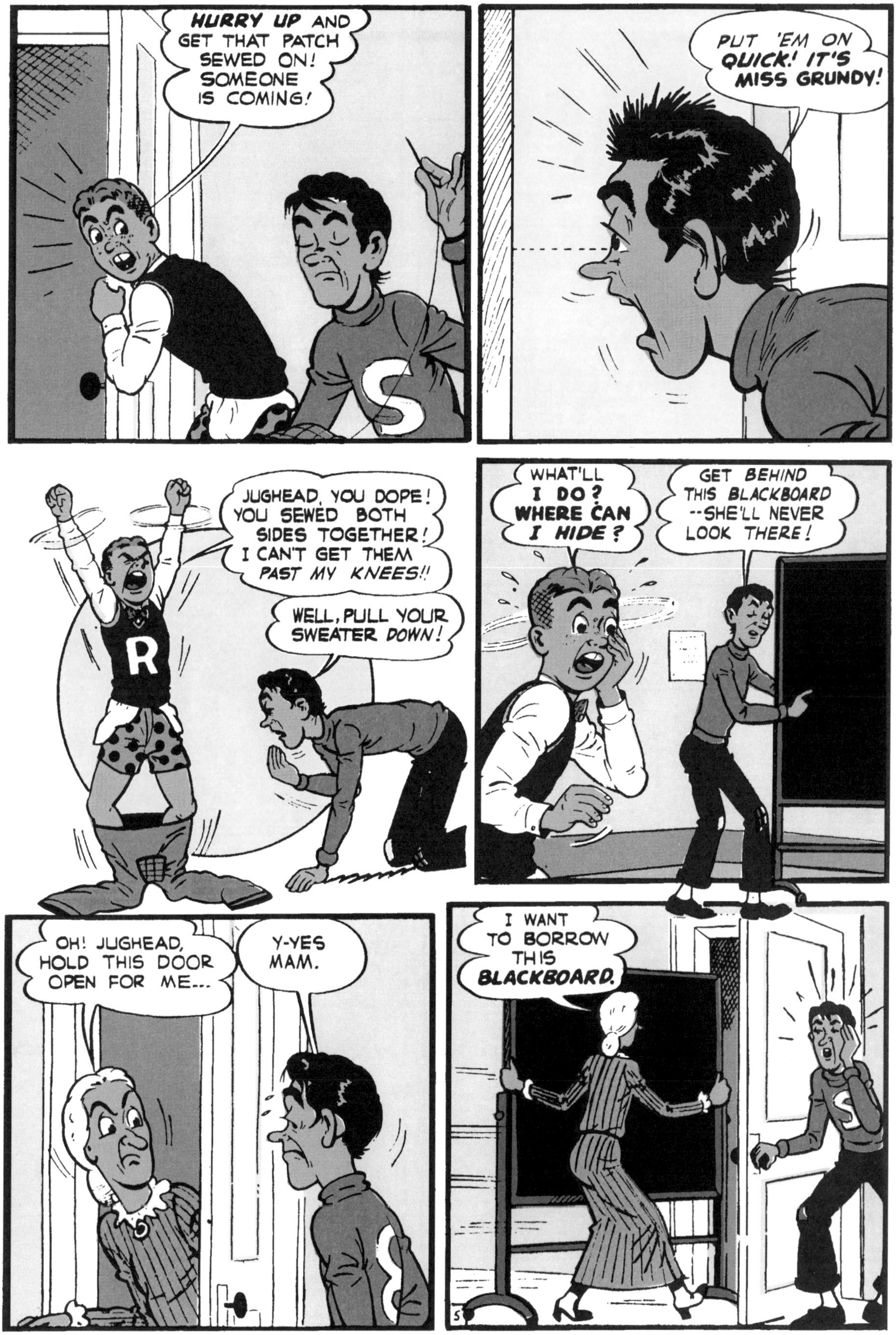
HURRY UP AND GET THAT PATCH SEWED ON! SOMEONE IS COMING!
PUT 'EM ON QUICK! IT'S MISS GRUNDY!
JUGHEAD, YOU DOPE! YOU SEWED BOTH SIDES TOGETHER! I CAN'T GET THEM PAST MY KNEES!!
WELL, PULL YOUR SWEATER DOWN!
WHAT'LL I DO? WHERE CAN I HIDE?
GET BEHIND THIS BLACKBOARD --SHE'LL NEVER LOOK THERE!
OH! JUGHEAD, HOLD THIS DOOR OPEN FOR ME...
Y-YES MAM.
I WANT TO BORROW THIS BLACKBOARD.

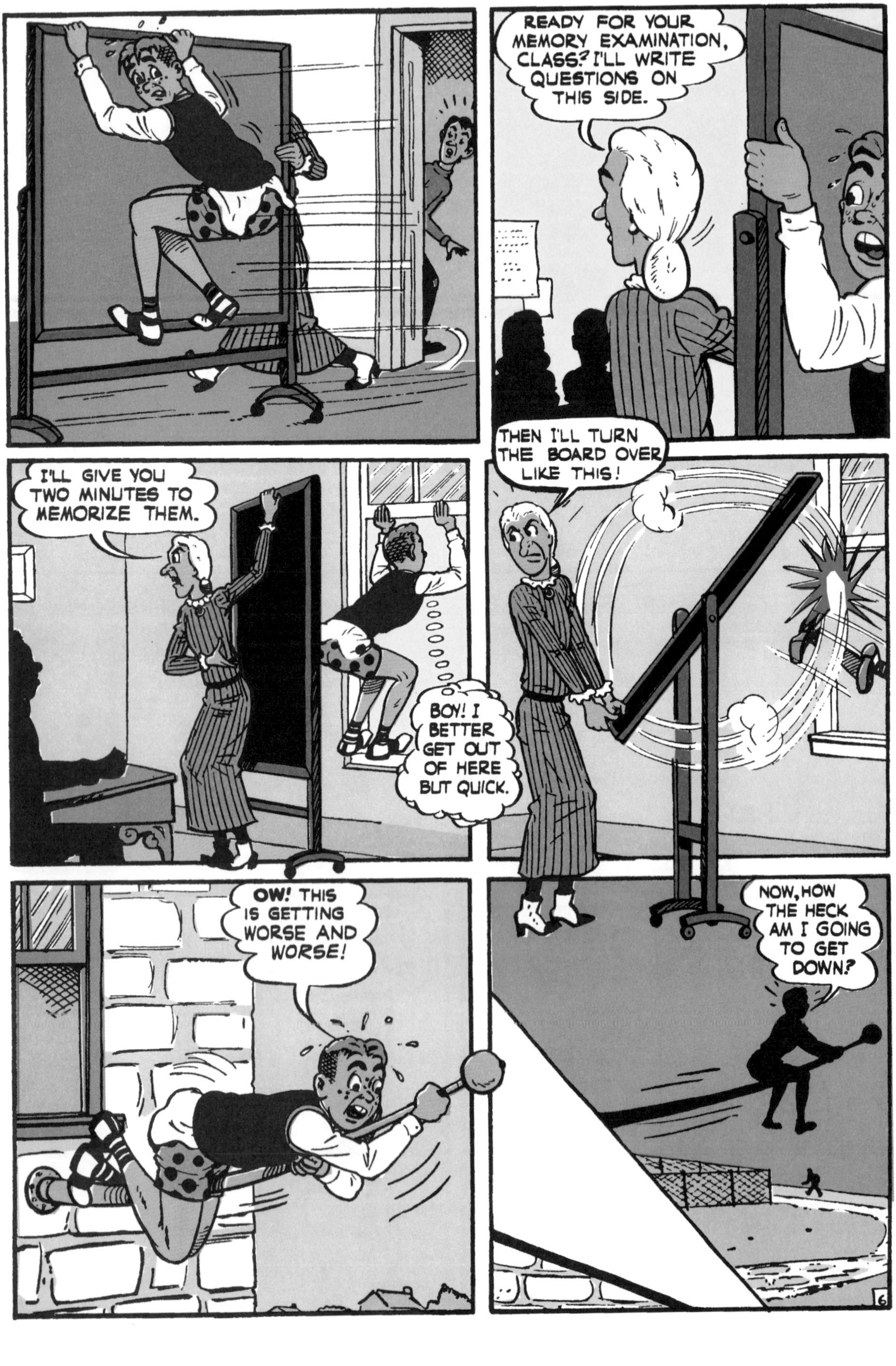
READY FOR YOUR MEMORY EXAMINATION, CLASS? I'LL WRITE QUESTIONS ON THIS SIDE.
I'LL GIVE YOU TWO MINUTES TO MEMORIZE THEM.
BOY! I BETTER GET OUT OF HERE BUT QUICK.
THEN I'LL TURN THE BOARD OVER LIKE THIS!
OW! THIS IS GETTING WORSE AND WORSE!
NOW, HOW THE HECK AM I GOING TO GET DOWN?
6

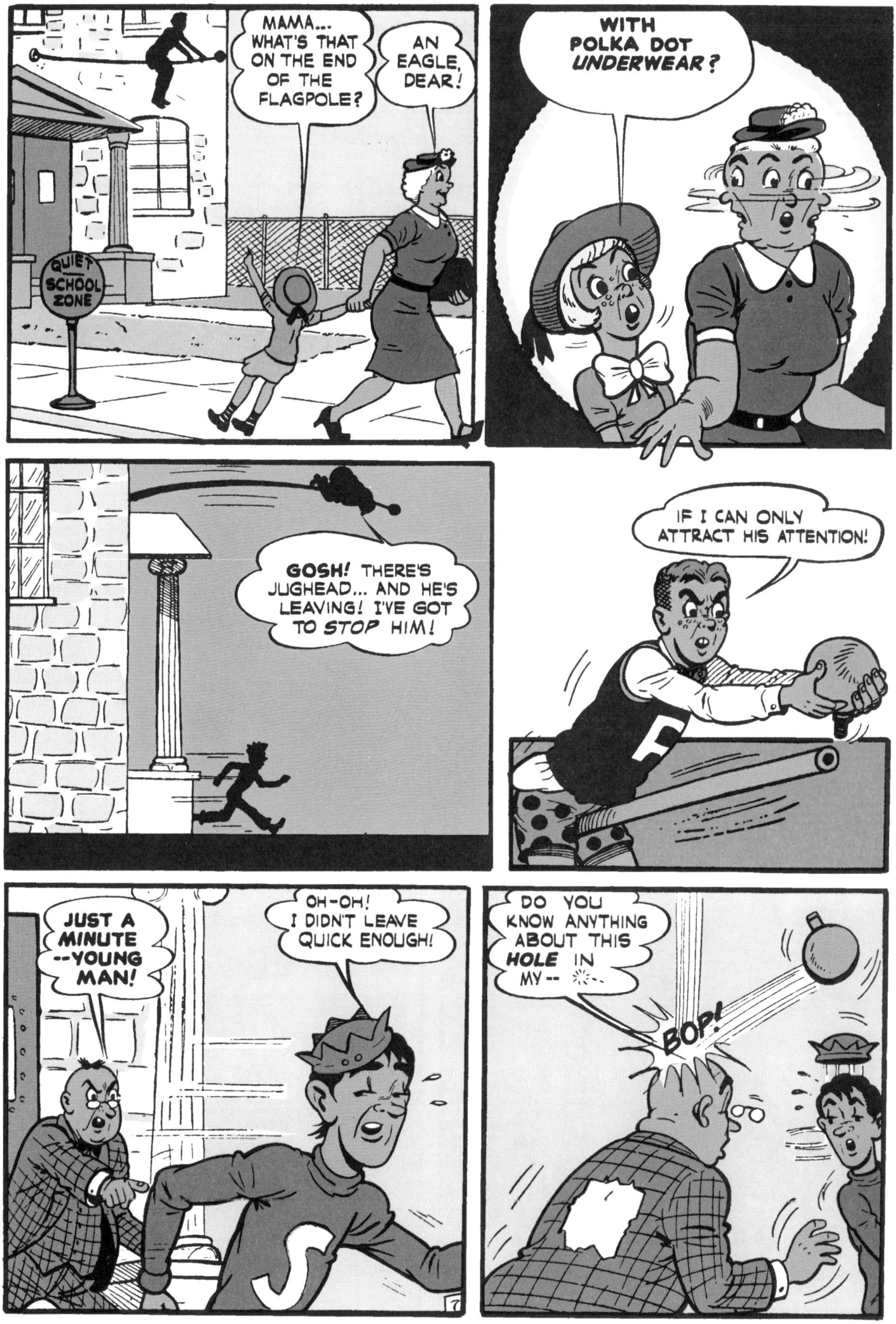
MAMA... WHAT'S THAT ON THE END OF THE FLAGPOLE?
AN EAGLE, DEAR!
QUIET SCHOOL ZONE
WITH POLKA DOT *UNDERWEAR*?
GOSH! THERE'S JUGHEAD... AND HE'S LEAVING! I'VE GOT TO *STOP* HIM!
IF I CAN ONLY ATTRACT HIS ATTENTION!
JUST A MINUTE --YOUNG MAN!
OH-OH! I DIDN'T LEAVE QUICK ENOUGH!
DO YOU KNOW ANYTHING ABOUT THIS **HOLE** IN MY--
BOP!

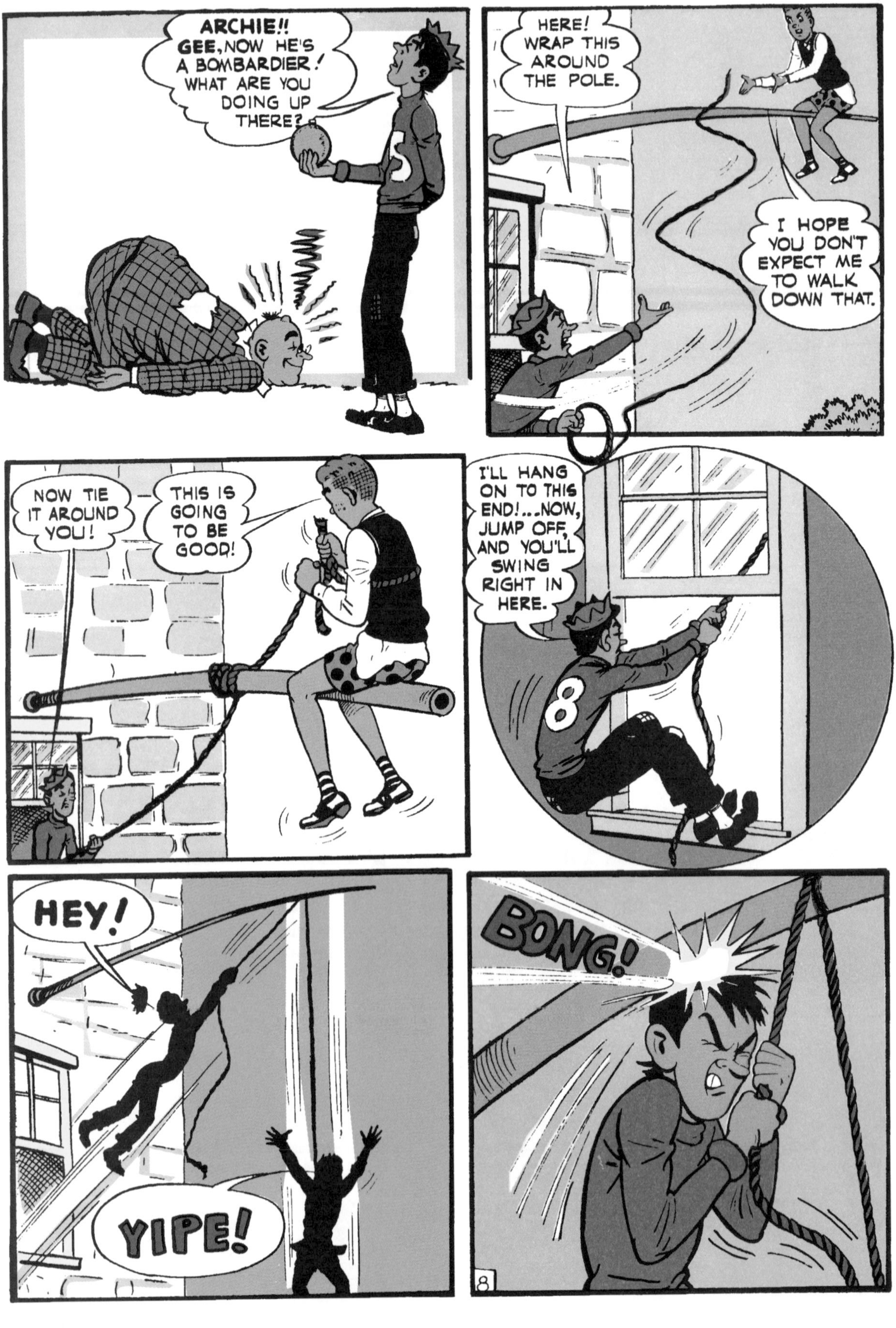
ARCHIE!! GEE, NOW HE'S A BOMBARDIER! WHAT ARE YOU DOING UP THERE?
HERE! WRAP THIS AROUND THE POLE.
I HOPE YOU DON'T EXPECT ME TO WALK DOWN THAT.
NOW TIE IT AROUND YOU!
THIS IS GOING TO BE GOOD!
I'LL HANG ON TO THIS END!...NOW, JUMP OFF, AND YOU'LL SWING RIGHT IN HERE.
HEY!
YIPE!
BONG!
8

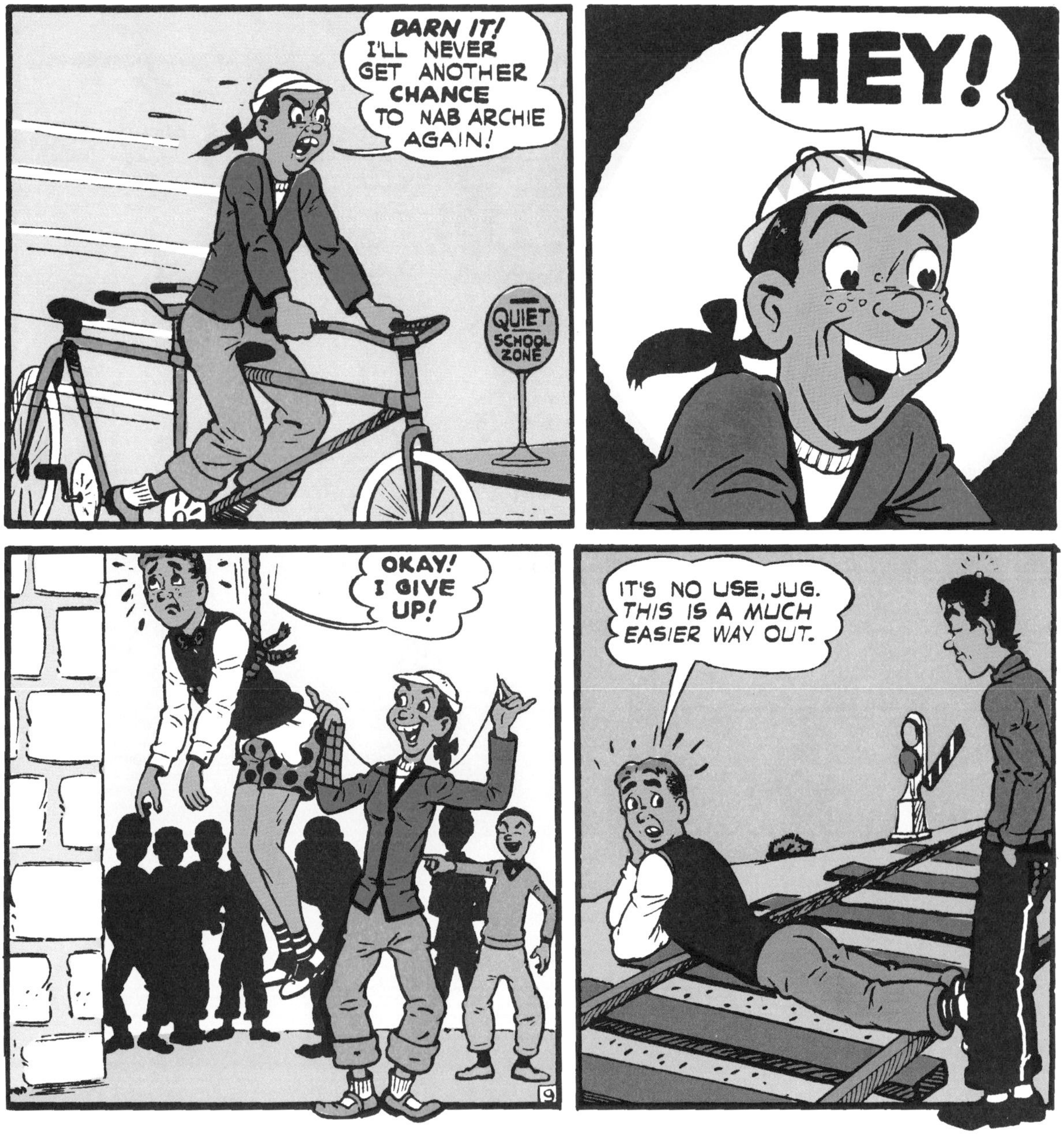
DARN IT! I'LL NEVER GET ANOTHER CHANCE TO NAB ARCHIE AGAIN!
QUIET SCHOOL ZONE
HEY!
OKAY! I GIVE UP!
9
IT'S NO USE, JUG. THIS IS A MUCH EASIER WAY OUT.

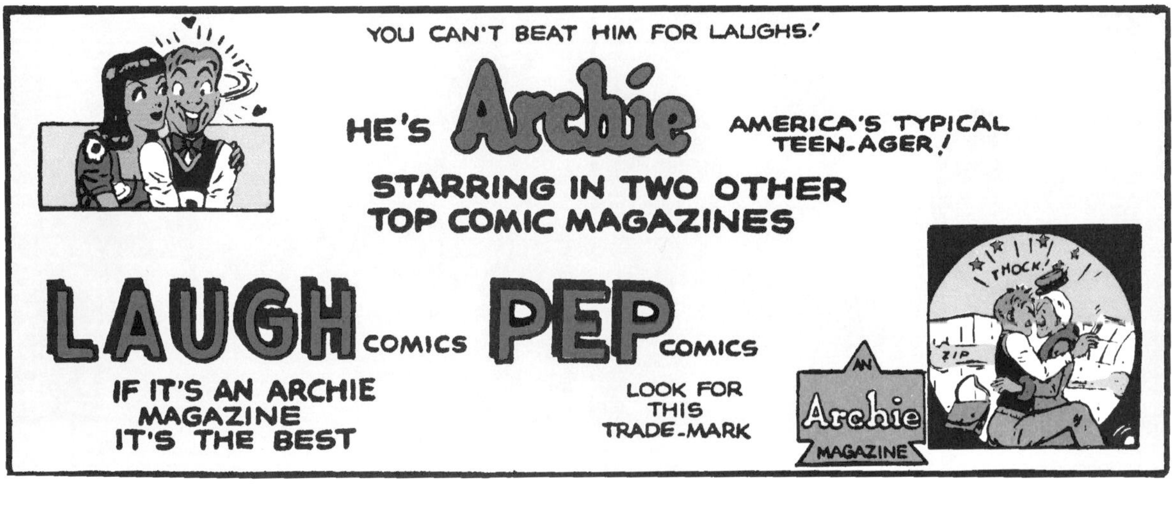
YOU CAN'T BEAT HIM FOR LAUGHS!
HE'S Archie AMERICA'S TYPICAL TEEN-AGER!
STARRING IN TWO OTHER TOP COMIC MAGAZINES
LAUGH COMICS PEP COMICS
IF IT'S AN ARCHIE MAGAZINE IT'S THE BEST
LOOK FOR THIS TRADE-MARK
AN Archie MAGAZINE
THOCK!
ZIP

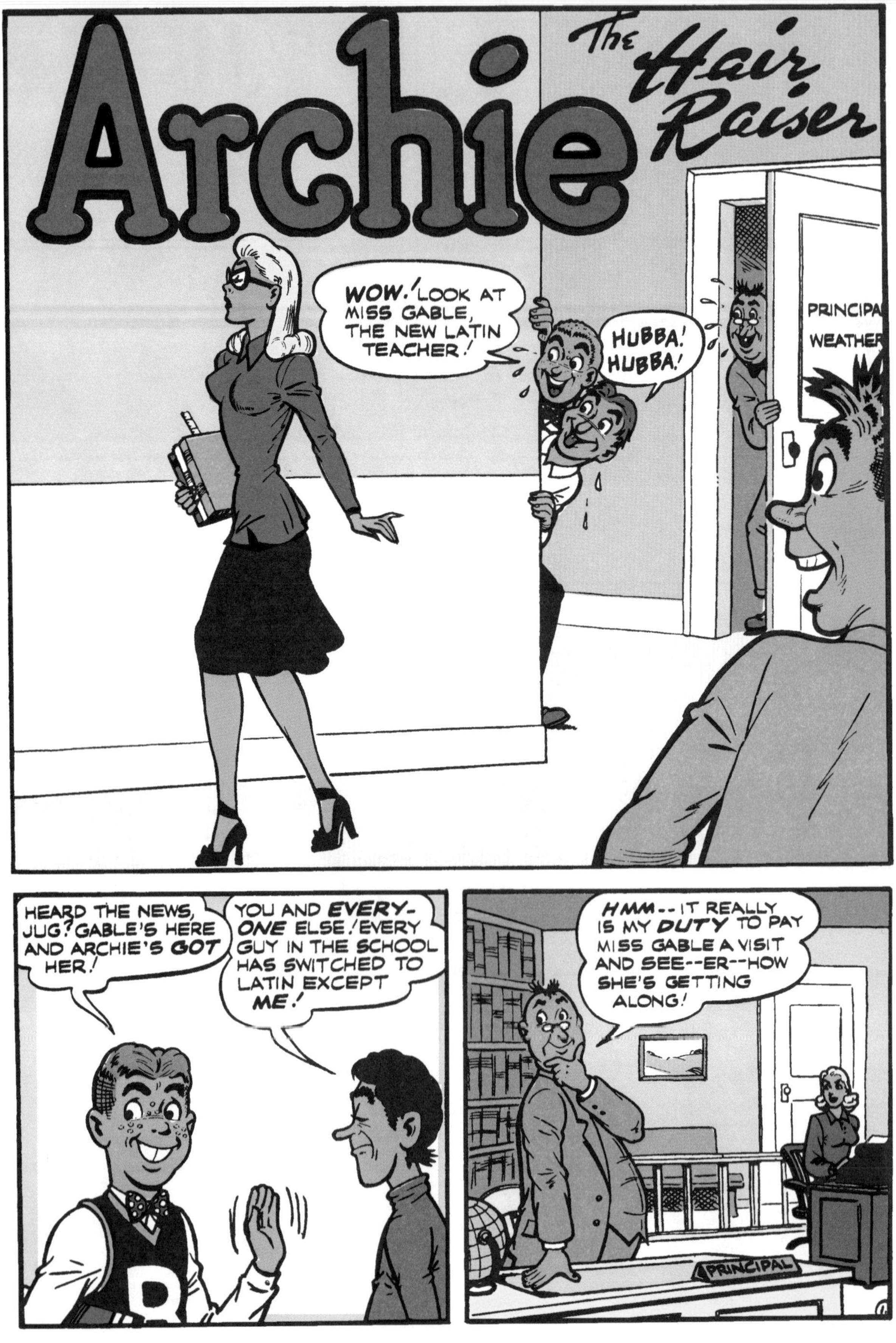
Archie
The Hair Raiser
WOW! LOOK AT MISS GABLE, THE NEW LATIN TEACHER!
HUBBA! HUBBA!
PRINCIPA
WEATHER
HEARD THE NEWS, JUG? GABLE'S HERE AND ARCHIE'S GOT HER!
YOU AND EVERY-ONE ELSE! EVERY GUY IN THE SCHOOL HAS SWITCHED TO LATIN EXCEPT ME!
HMM-- IT REALLY IS MY DUTY TO PAY MISS GABLE A VISIT AND SEE--ER--HOW SHE'S GETTING ALONG!
PRINCIPAL

Originally presented in ARCHIE COMICS #34, September-October, 1948

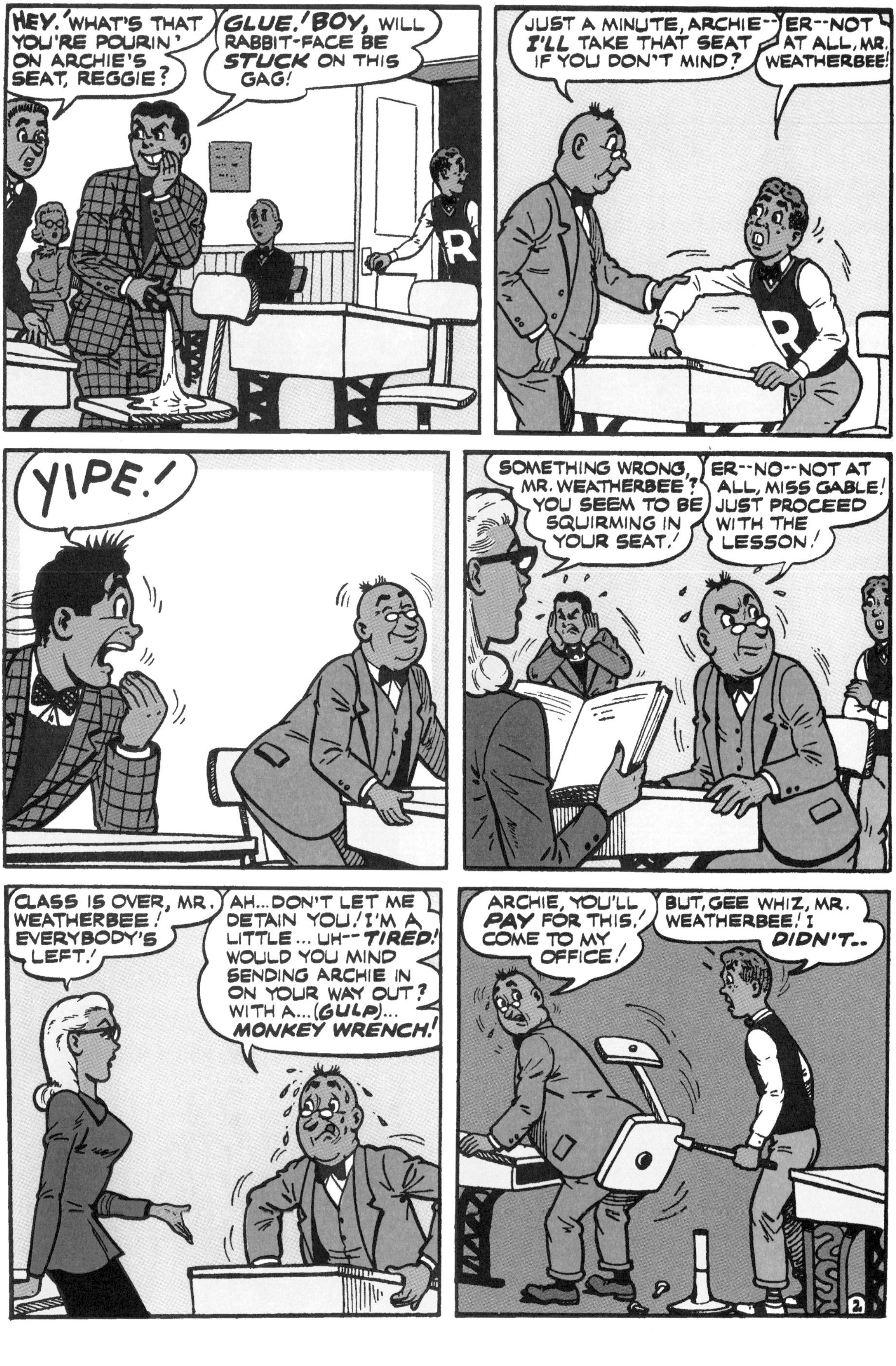
HEY! WHAT'S THAT YOU'RE POURIN' ON ARCHIE'S SEAT, REGGIE?
GLUE! BOY, WILL RABBIT-FACE BE STUCK ON THIS GAG!
JUST A MINUTE, ARCHIE-- I'LL TAKE THAT SEAT IF YOU DON'T MIND?
ER--NOT AT ALL, MR. WEATHERBEE!
YIPE!
SOMETHING WRONG, MR. WEATHERBEE? YOU SEEM TO BE SQUIRMING IN YOUR SEAT!
ER--NO--NOT AT ALL, MISS GABLE! JUST PROCEED WITH THE LESSON!
CLASS IS OVER, MR. WEATHERBEE! EVERYBODY'S LEFT!
AH...DON'T LET ME DETAIN YOU! I'M A LITTLE ... UH-- TIRED! WOULD YOU MIND SENDING ARCHIE IN ON YOUR WAY OUT? WITH A...(GULP)... MONKEY WRENCH!
ARCHIE, YOU'LL PAY FOR THIS! COME TO MY OFFICE!
BUT, GEE WHIZ, MR. WEATHERBEE! I DIDN'T..
2

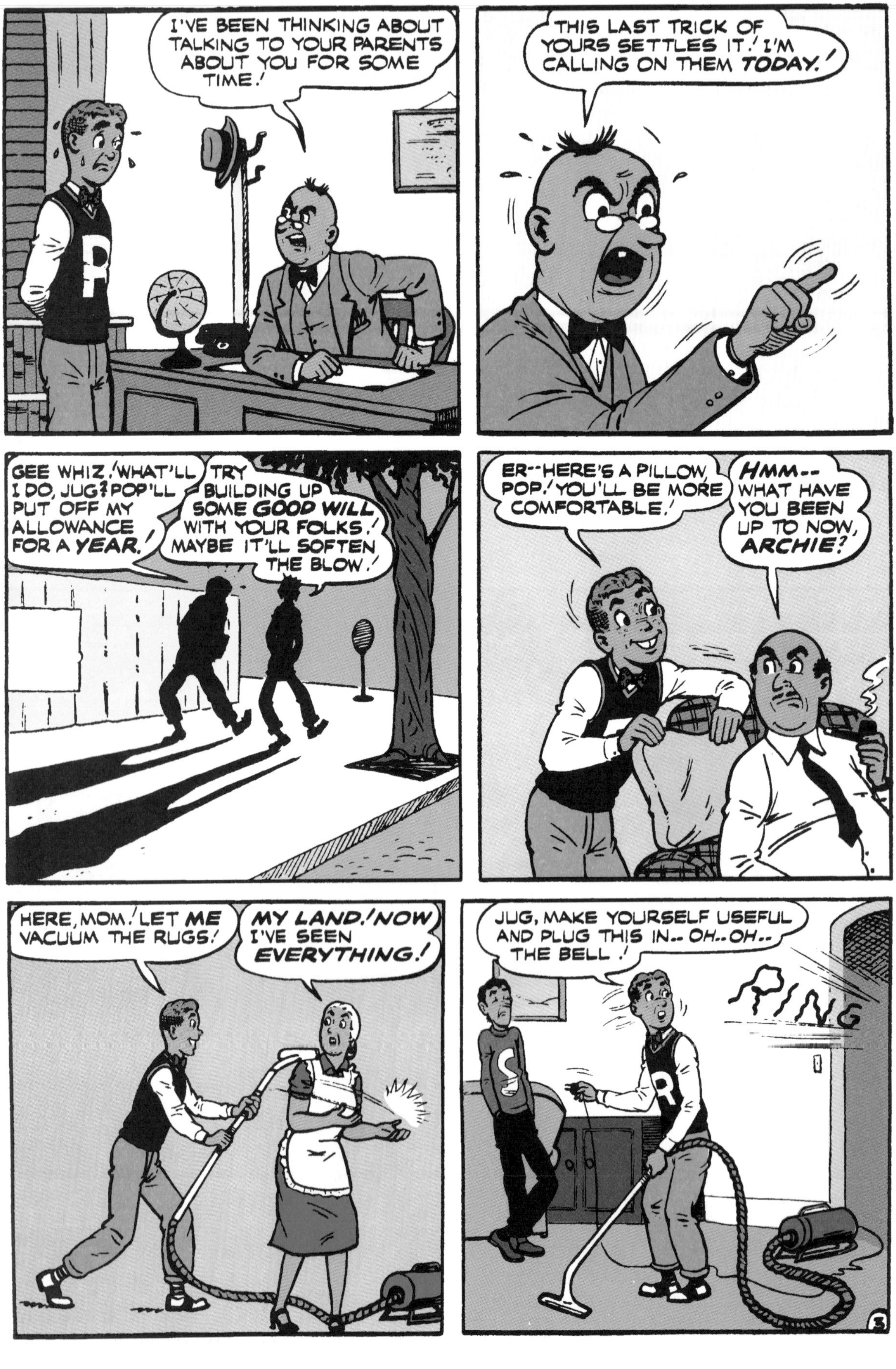
I'VE BEEN THINKING ABOUT TALKING TO YOUR PARENTS ABOUT YOU FOR SOME TIME!
THIS LAST TRICK OF YOURS SETTLES IT! I'M CALLING ON THEM TODAY!
GEE WHIZ! WHAT'LL I DO, JUG? POP'LL PUT OFF MY ALLOWANCE FOR A YEAR!
TRY BUILDING UP SOME GOOD WILL WITH YOUR FOLKS! MAYBE IT'LL SOFTEN THE BLOW!
ER--HERE'S A PILLOW, POP! YOU'LL BE MORE COMFORTABLE!
HMM-- WHAT HAVE YOU BEEN UP TO NOW, ARCHIE?
HERE, MOM! LET ME VACUUM THE RUGS!
MY LAND! NOW I'VE SEEN EVERYTHING!
JUG, MAKE YOURSELF USEFUL AND PLUG THIS IN-- OH--OH-- THE BELL!
PING
3

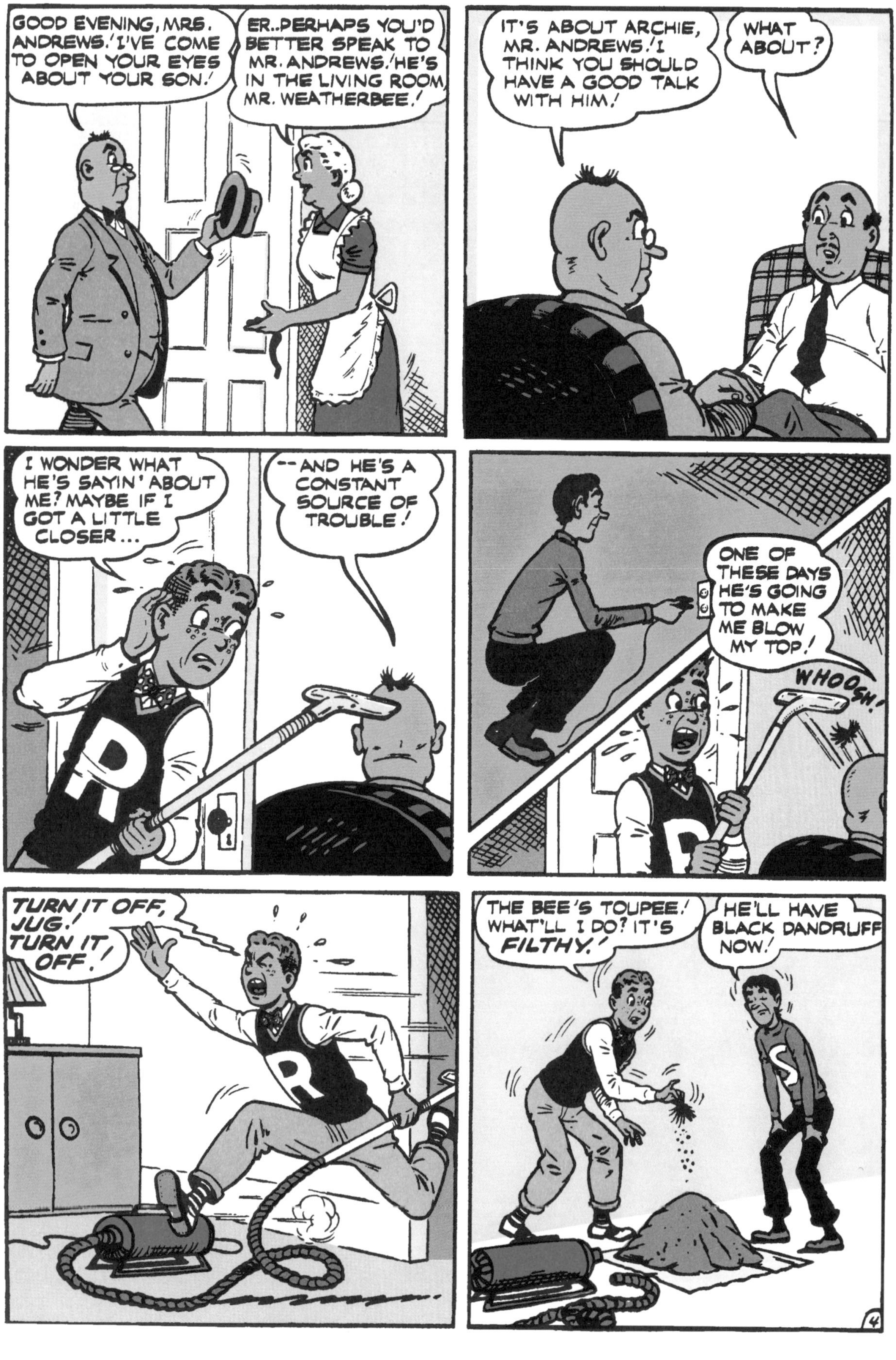
GOOD EVENING, MRS. ANDREWS.! I'VE COME TO OPEN YOUR EYES ABOUT YOUR SON.!
ER..PERHAPS YOU'D BETTER SPEAK TO MR. ANDREWS.! HE'S IN THE LIVING ROOM MR. WEATHERBEE.!
IT'S ABOUT ARCHIE, MR. ANDREWS.! I THINK YOU SHOULD HAVE A GOOD TALK WITH HIM.!
WHAT ABOUT?
I WONDER WHAT HE'S SAYIN' ABOUT ME? MAYBE IF I GOT A LITTLE CLOSER...
--AND HE'S A CONSTANT SOURCE OF TROUBLE.!
ONE OF THESE DAYS HE'S GOING TO MAKE ME BLOW MY TOP.!
WHOOOSH!
TURN IT OFF, JUG.! TURN IT OFF.!
THE BEE'S TOUPEE.! WHAT'LL I DO? IT'S FILTHY.!
HE'LL HAVE BLACK DANDRUFF NOW.!
4

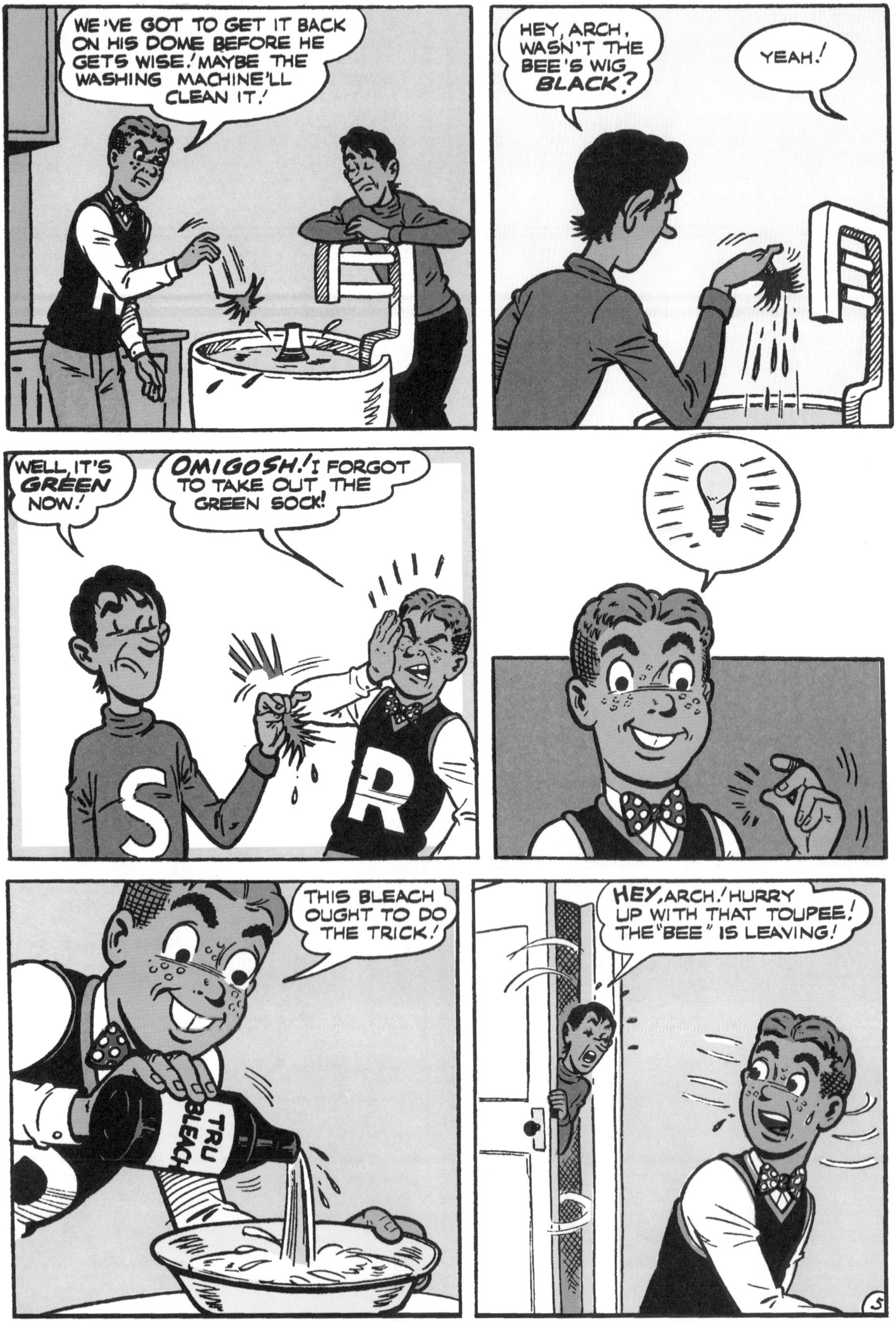
WE'VE GOT TO GET IT BACK ON HIS DOME BEFORE HE GETS WISE! MAYBE THE WASHING MACHINE'LL CLEAN IT!
HEY, ARCH, WASN'T THE BEE'S WIG BLACK?
YEAH!
WELL, IT'S GREEN NOW!
OMIGOSH! I FORGOT TO TAKE OUT THE GREEN SOCK!
THIS BLEACH OUGHT TO DO THE TRICK!
TRU BLEACH
HEY, ARCH! HURRY UP WITH THAT TOUPEE! THE "BEE" IS LEAVING!
5

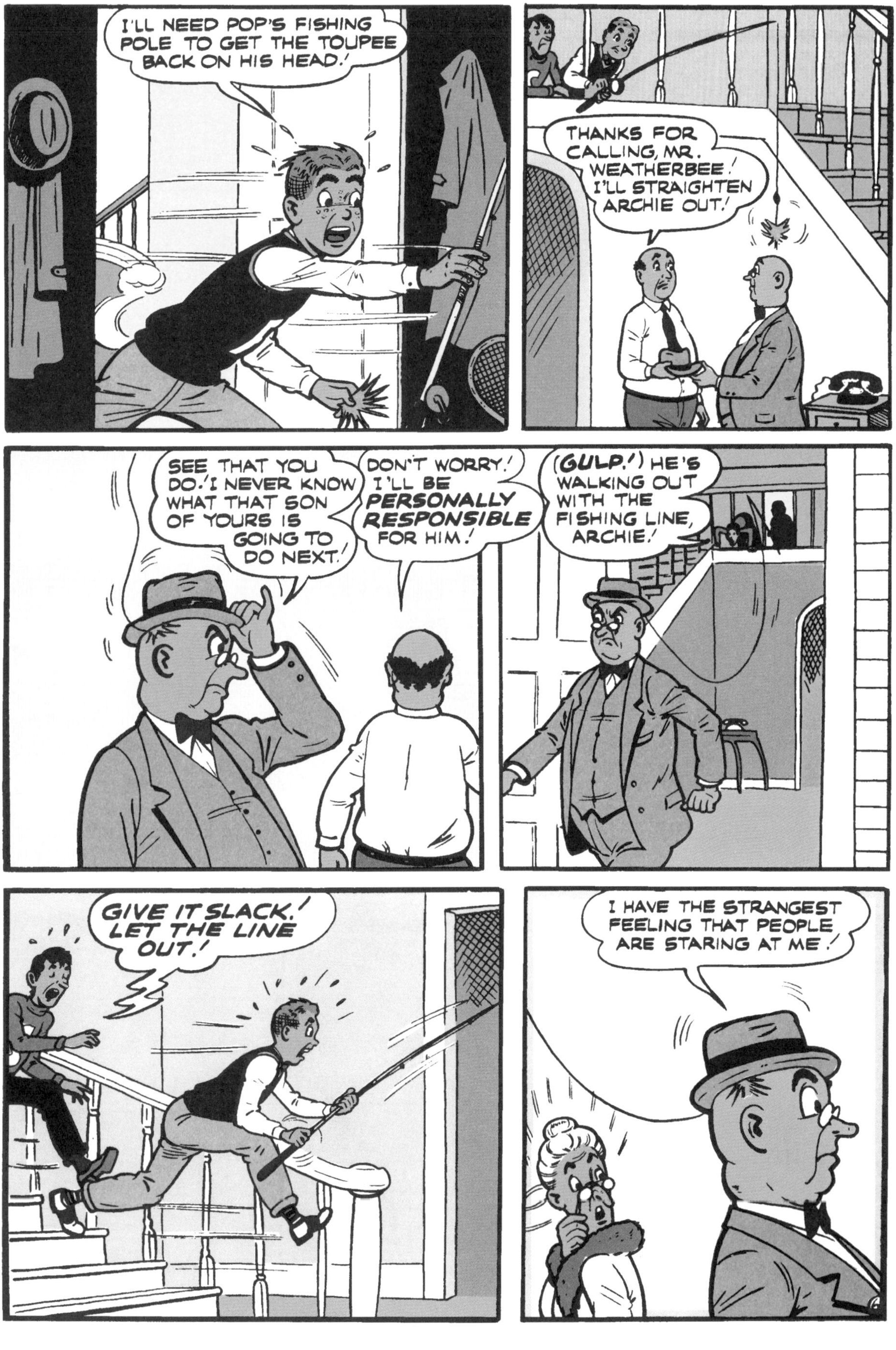
I'LL NEED POP'S FISHING POLE TO GET THE TOUPEE BACK ON HIS HEAD!
THANKS FOR CALLING, MR. WEATHERBEE! I'LL STRAIGHTEN ARCHIE OUT!
SEE THAT YOU DO! I NEVER KNOW WHAT THAT SON OF YOURS IS GOING TO DO NEXT!
DON'T WORRY! I'LL BE PERSONALLY RESPONSIBLE FOR HIM!
(GULP!) HE'S WALKING OUT WITH THE FISHING LINE, ARCHIE!
GIVE IT SLACK! LET THE LINE OUT!
I HAVE THE STRANGEST FEELING THAT PEOPLE ARE STARING AT ME!

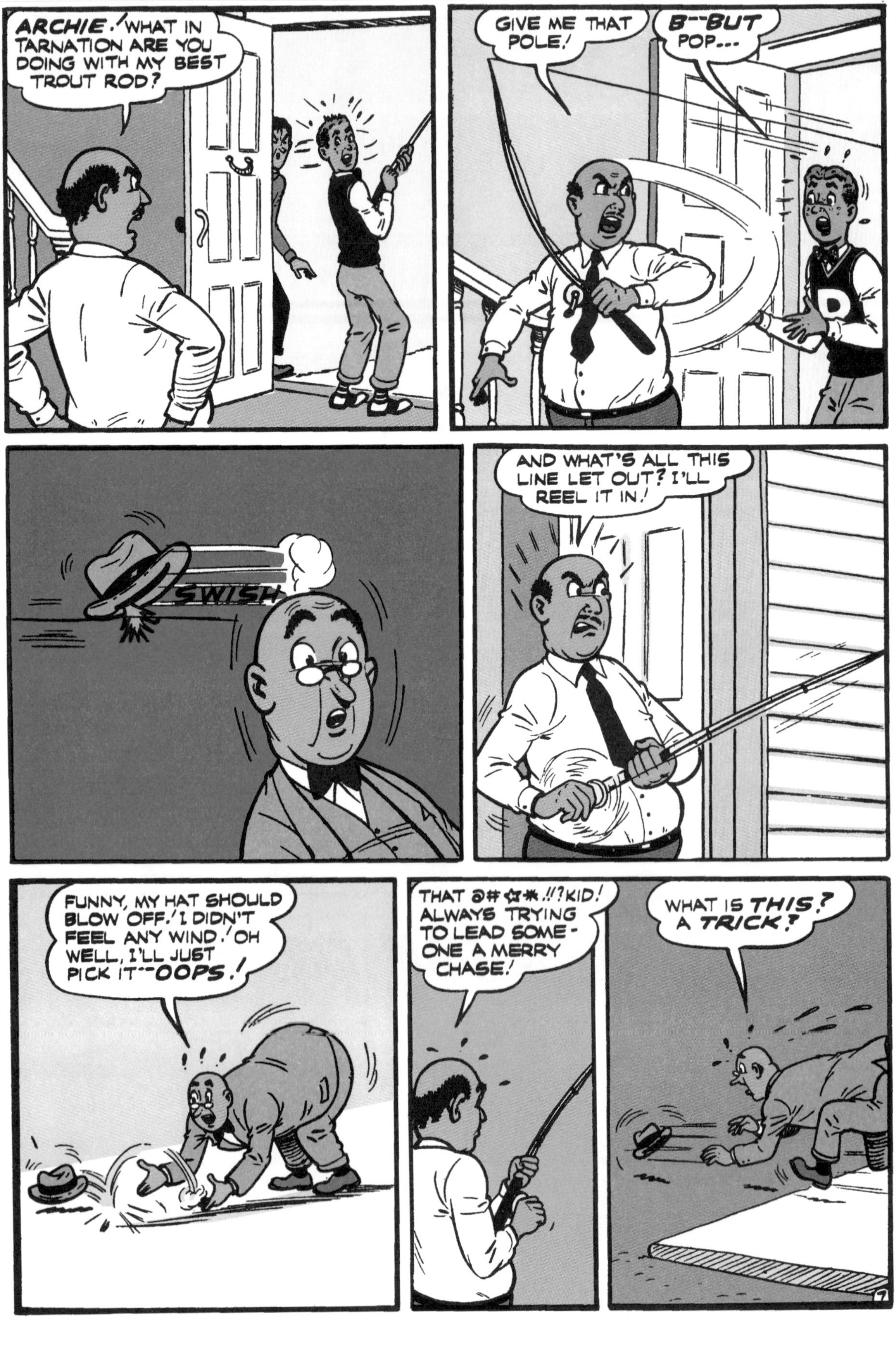
ARCHIE! WHAT IN TARNATION ARE YOU DOING WITH MY BEST TROUT ROD?
GIVE ME THAT POLE!
B--BUT POP...
SWISH
AND WHAT'S ALL THIS LINE LET OUT? I'LL REEL IT IN!
FUNNY, MY HAT SHOULD BLOW OFF! I DIDN'T FEEL ANY WIND! OH WELL, I'LL JUST PICK IT--OOPS!
THAT @#✿*!!?KID! ALWAYS TRYING TO LEAD SOME-ONE A MERRY CHASE!
WHAT IS THIS? A TRICK?
7

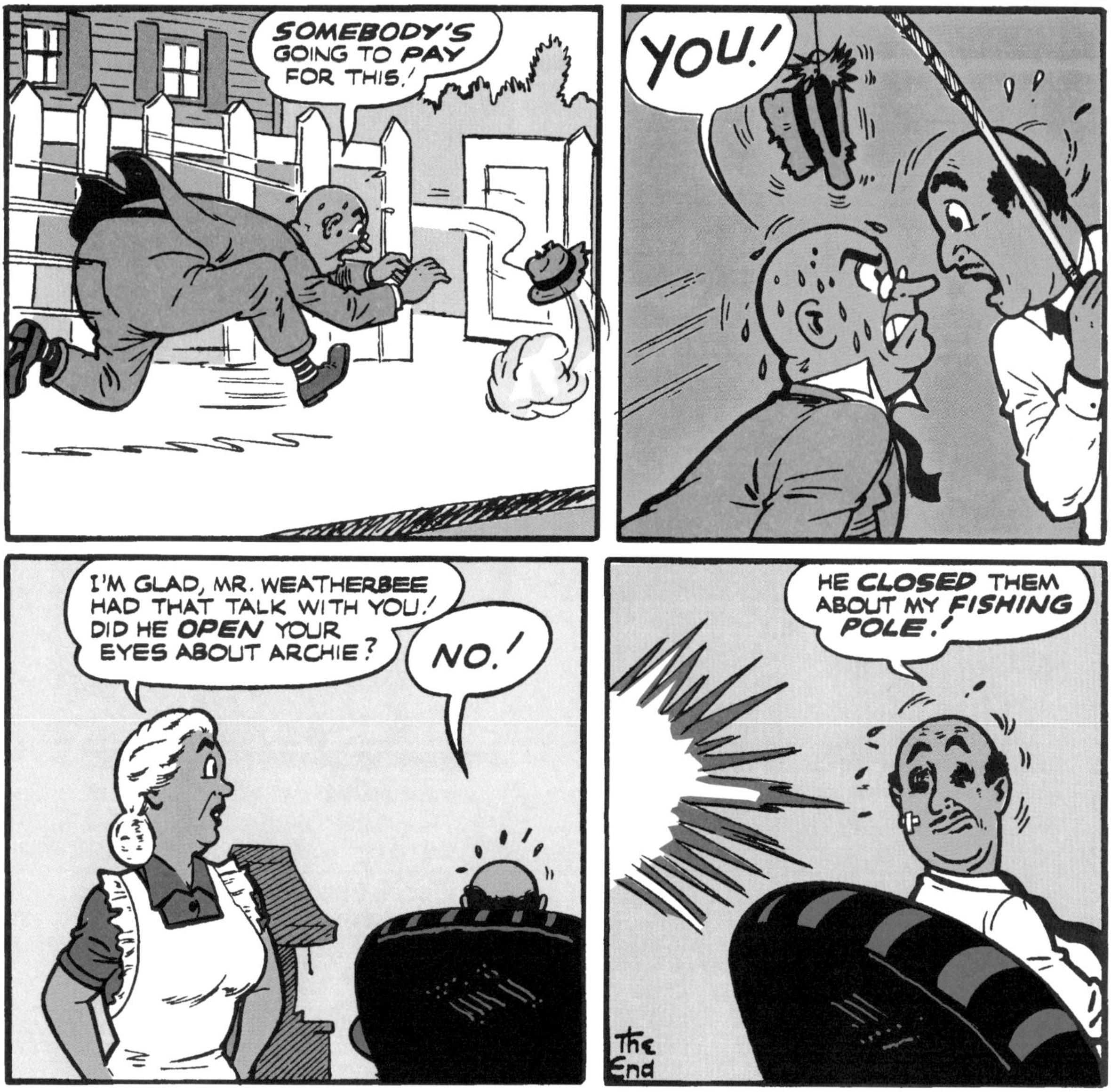
SOMEBODY'S GOING TO PAY FOR THIS!
YOU!
I'M GLAD, MR. WEATHERBEE HAD THAT TALK WITH YOU! DID HE OPEN YOUR EYES ABOUT ARCHIE?
NO.!
HE CLOSED THEM ABOUT MY FISHING POLE.!
The End

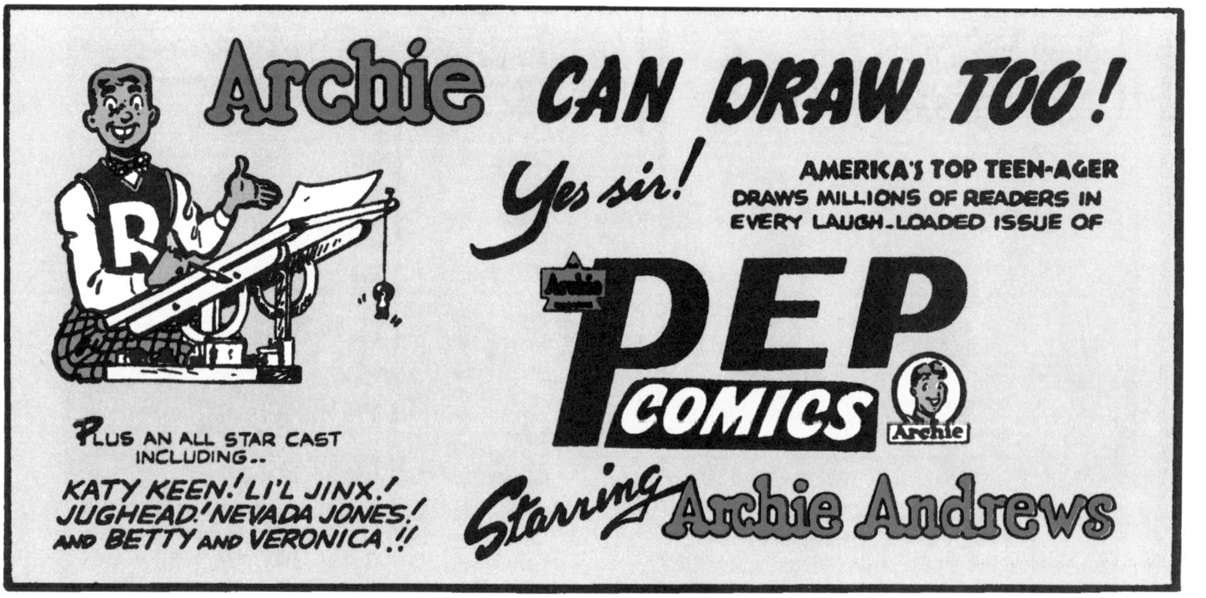

1940's ARCHIE COMIC BOOK COVERS

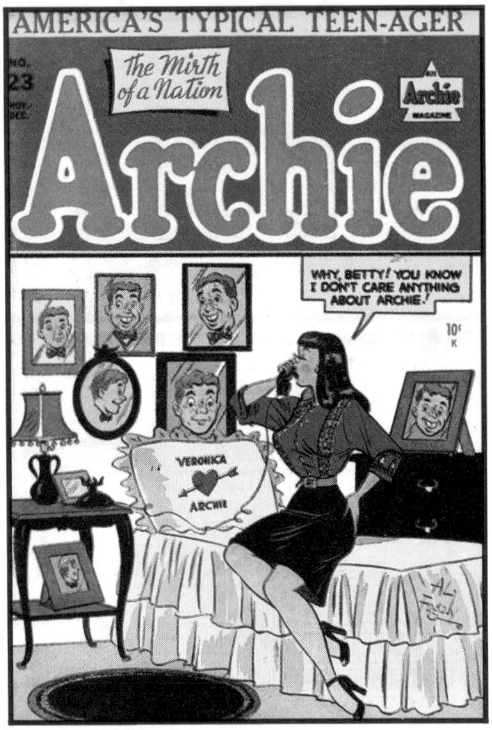
AMERICA'S TYPICAL TEEN-AGER
NO. 23
NOV.-DEC.
The Mirth of a Nation
Archie
WHY, BETTY! YOU KNOW I DON'T CARE ANYTHING ABOUT ARCHIE!
10¢
VERONICA
ARCHIE

ARCHIE COMICS #23, NOVEMBER–DECEMBER, 1946
Cover depicts the "Veronica side" of the Archie/Veronica/Betty love-triangle.

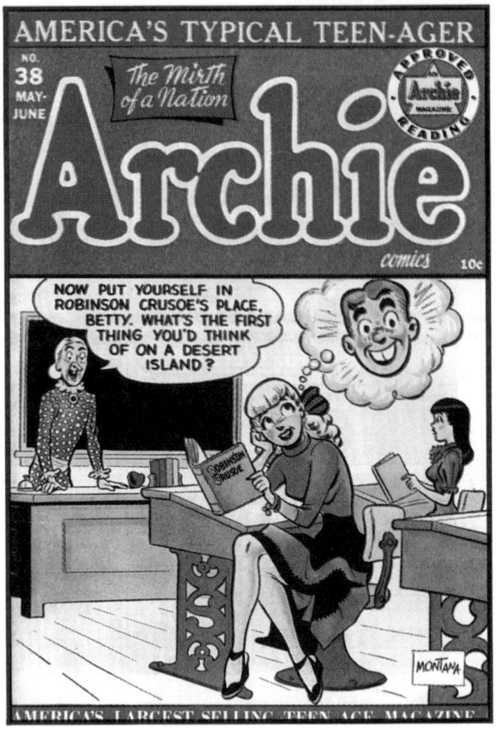
AMERICA'S TYPICAL TEEN-AGER
NO. 38
MAY-JUNE
The Mirth of a Nation
APPROVED READING
Archie
comics
10¢
NOW PUT YOURSELF IN ROBINSON CRUSOE'S PLACE, BETTY. WHAT'S THE FIRST THING YOU'D THINK OF ON A DESERT ISLAND?
ROBINSON CRUSOE
MONTANA

ARCHIE COMICS #38, MAY–JUNE, 1949
Depicts the "Betty side" of the Archie/Veronica/Betty love-triangle.

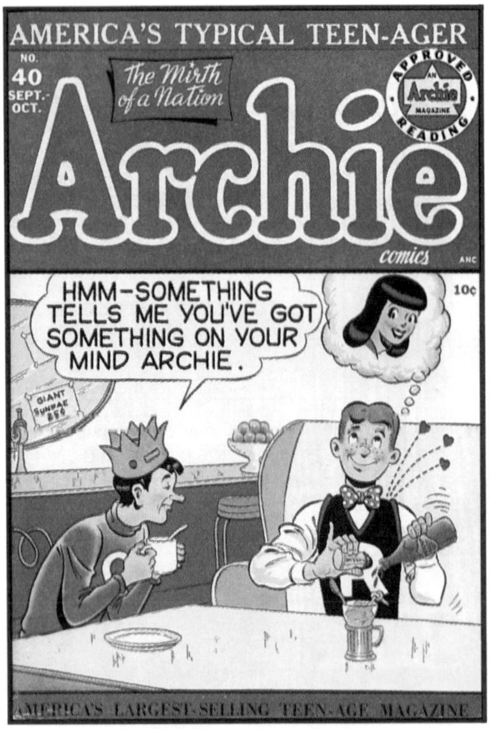
AMERICA'S TYPICAL TEEN-AGER
NO. 40
SEPT.-OCT.
The Mirth of a Nation
APPROVED READING
Archie
comics
10¢
HMM–SOMETHING TELLS ME YOU'VE GOT SOMETHING ON YOUR MIND ARCHIE.
AMERICA'S LARGEST-SELLING TEEN-AGE MAGAZINE

ARCHIE COMICS #40, SEPTEMBER–OCTOBER, 1949
Depicts the "Archie side" of the Archie/Veronica/Betty love-triangle.

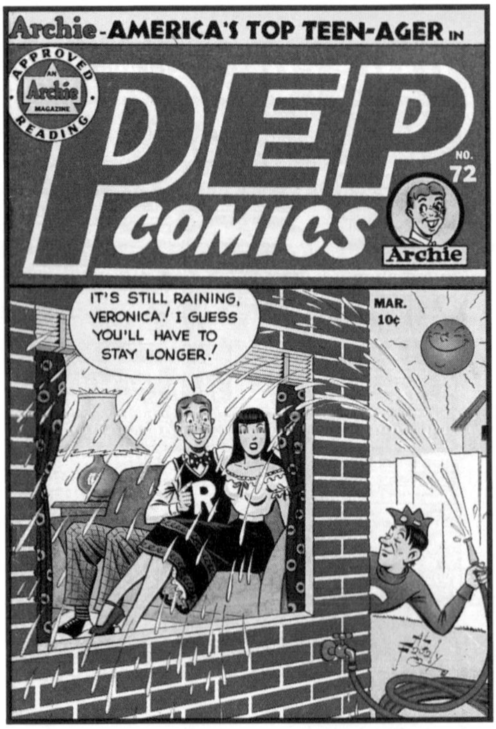
Archie-AMERICA'S TOP TEEN-AGER IN
APPROVED READING
PEP COMICS
NO. 72
Archie
IT'S STILL RAINING, VERONICA! I GUESS YOU'LL HAVE TO STAY LONGER!
MAR. 10¢

PEP COMICS #72, MARCH, 1949
One of the most colorful and creative covers of the 1940s.

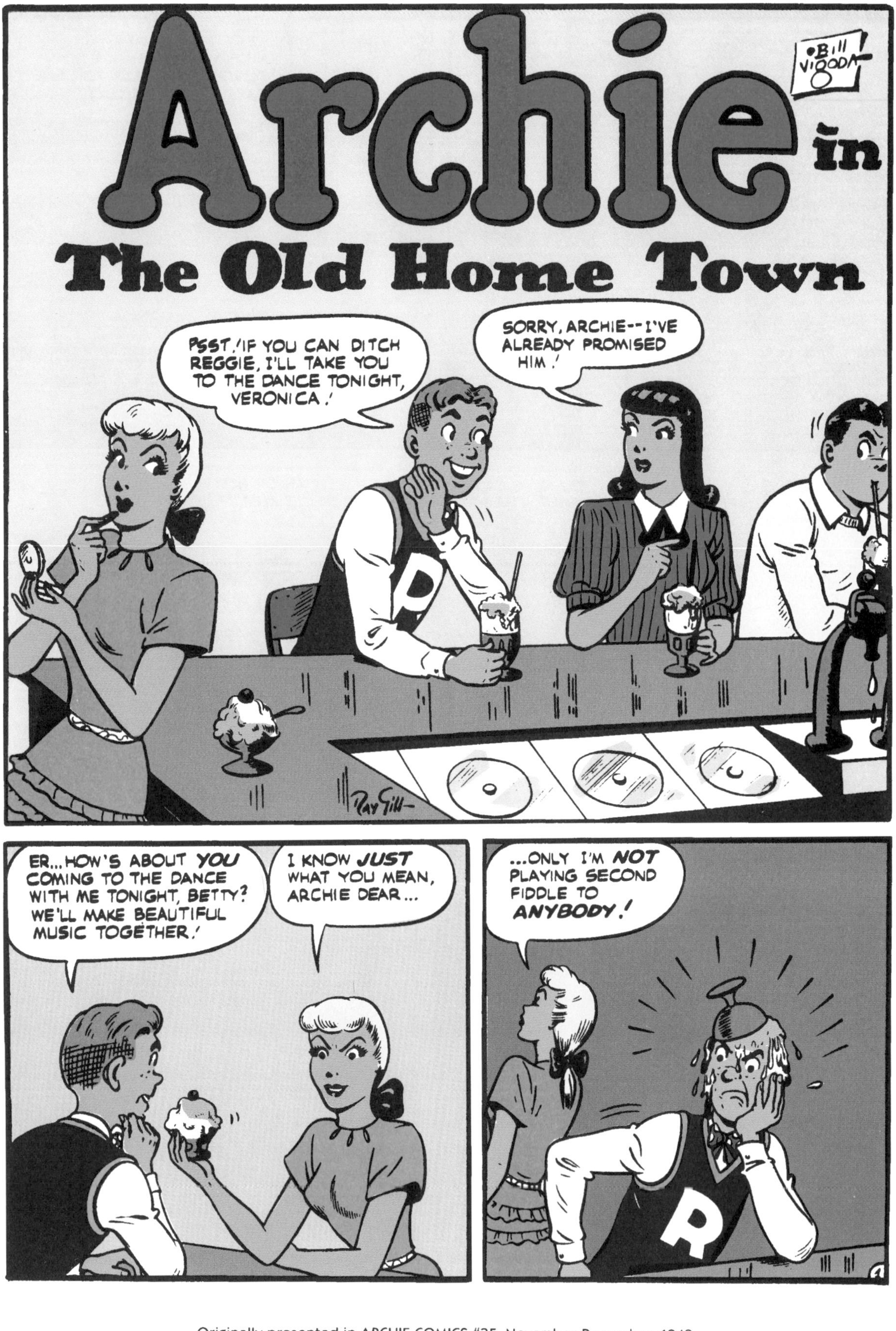
Archie in
The Old Home Town
PSST.! IF YOU CAN DITCH REGGIE, I'LL TAKE YOU TO THE DANCE TONIGHT, VERONICA.!
SORRY, ARCHIE--I'VE ALREADY PROMISED HIM.!
ER...HOW'S ABOUT YOU COMING TO THE DANCE WITH ME TONIGHT, BETTY? WE'LL MAKE BEAUTIFUL MUSIC TOGETHER.!
I KNOW JUST WHAT YOU MEAN, ARCHIE DEAR...
...ONLY I'M NOT PLAYING SECOND FIDDLE TO ANYBODY.!

Originally presented in ARCHIE COMICS #35, November-December, 1948

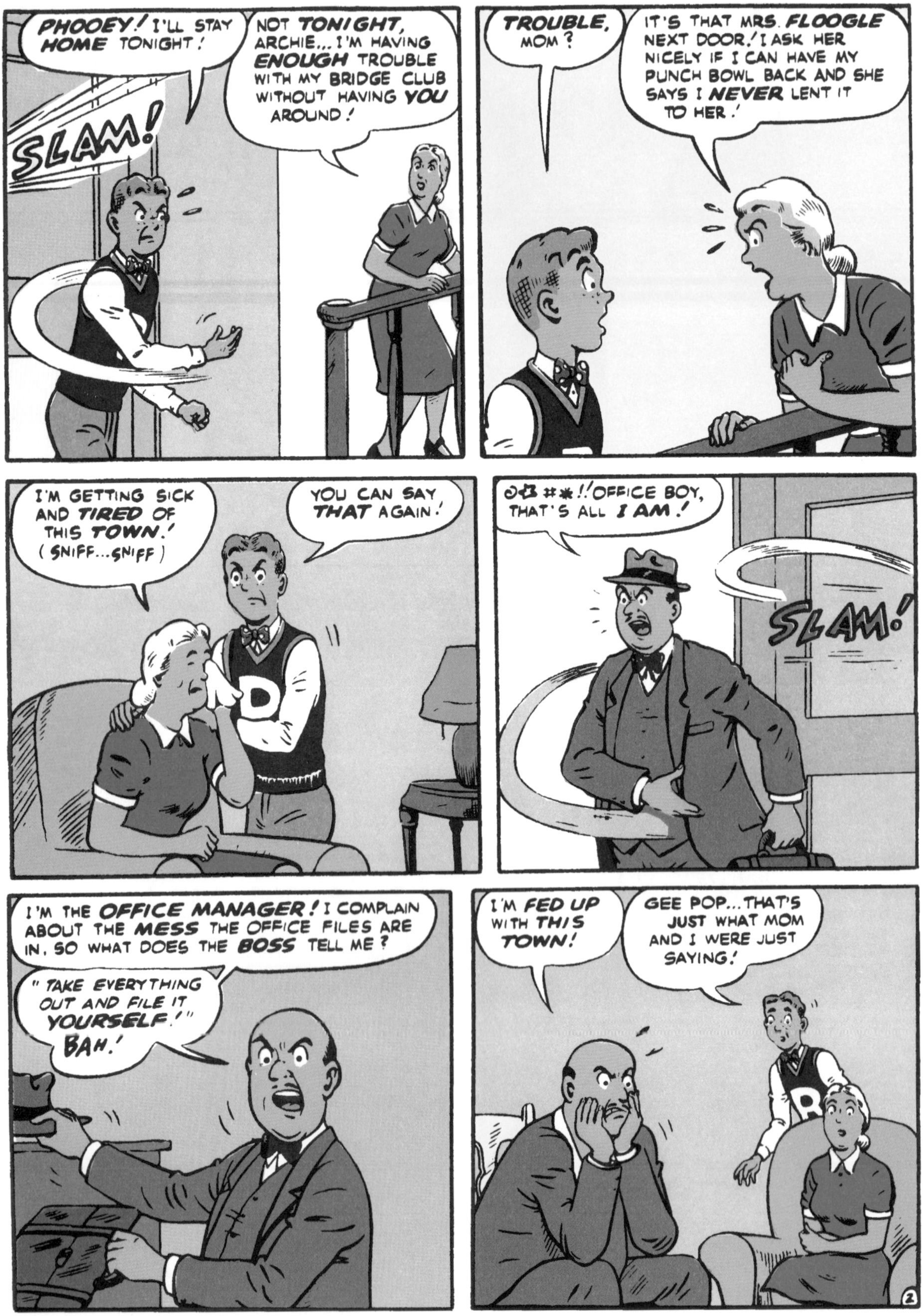
PHOOEY! I'LL STAY HOME TONIGHT!
SLAM!
NOT TONIGHT, ARCHIE... I'M HAVING ENOUGH TROUBLE WITH MY BRIDGE CLUB WITHOUT HAVING YOU AROUND!
TROUBLE, MOM?
IT'S THAT MRS. FLOOGLE NEXT DOOR! I ASK HER NICELY IF I CAN HAVE MY PUNCH BOWL BACK AND SHE SAYS I NEVER LENT IT TO HER!
I'M GETTING SICK AND TIRED OF THIS TOWN! (SNIFF...SNIFF)
YOU CAN SAY THAT AGAIN!
#*!! OFFICE BOY, THAT'S ALL I AM!
SLAM!
I'M THE OFFICE MANAGER! I COMPLAIN ABOUT THE MESS THE OFFICE FILES ARE IN. SO WHAT DOES THE BOSS TELL ME?
"TAKE EVERYTHING OUT AND FILE IT YOURSELF!" BAH!
I'M FED UP WITH THIS TOWN!
GEE POP... THAT'S JUST WHAT MOM AND I WERE JUST SAYING!
2

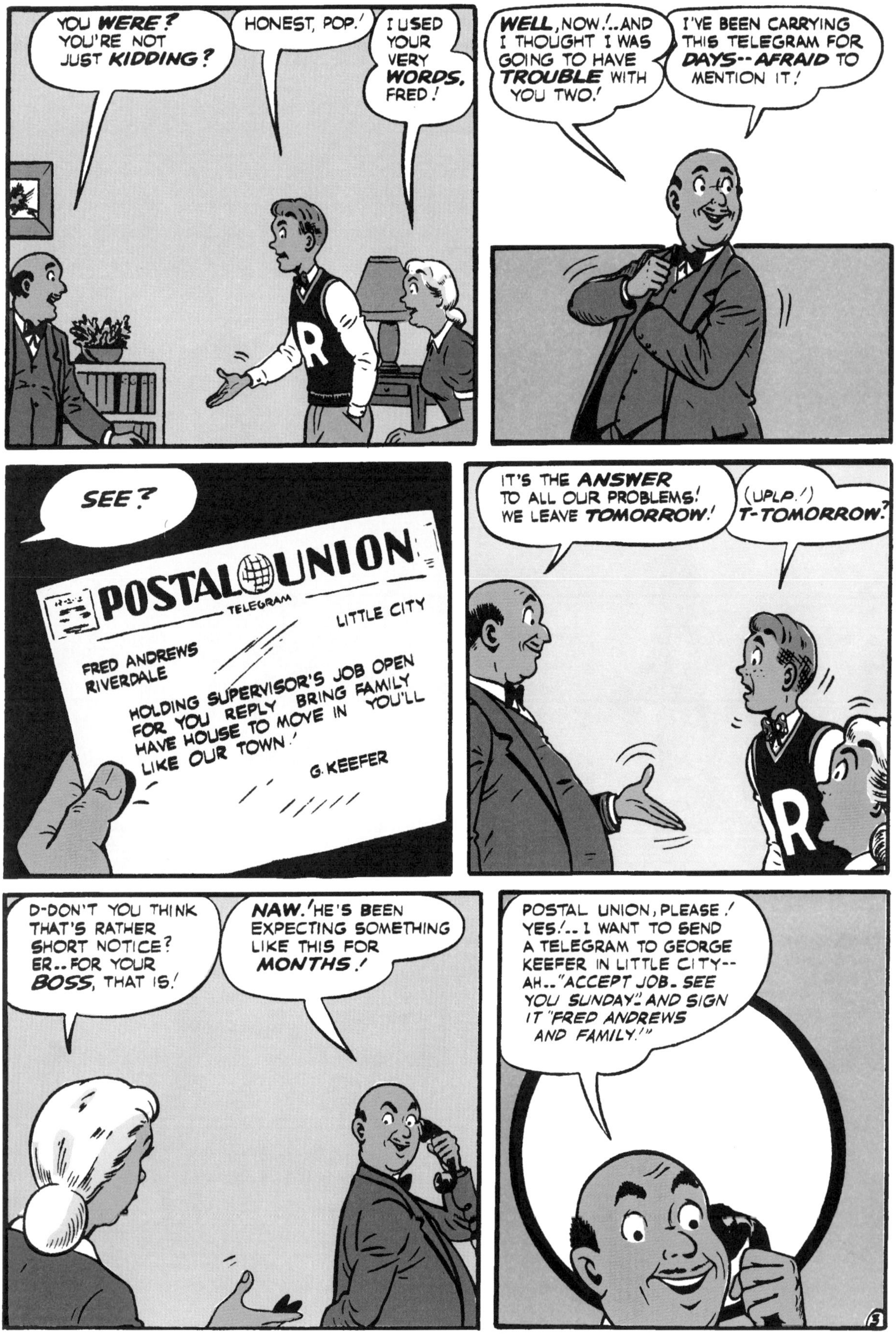
YOU WERE? YOU'RE NOT JUST KIDDING?
HONEST, POP.!
I USED YOUR VERY WORDS, FRED!
WELL, NOW.!..AND I THOUGHT I WAS GOING TO HAVE TROUBLE WITH YOU TWO.!
I'VE BEEN CARRYING THIS TELEGRAM FOR DAYS--AFRAID TO MENTION IT.!
SEE?
POSTAL UNION
TELEGRAM
LITTLE CITY
FRED ANDREWS
RIVERDALE
HOLDING SUPERVISOR'S JOB OPEN FOR YOU REPLY BRING FAMILY HAVE HOUSE TO MOVE IN YOU'LL LIKE OUR TOWN.
G. KEEFER
IT'S THE ANSWER TO ALL OUR PROBLEMS! WE LEAVE TOMORROW!
(UPLP.!) T-TOMORROW?
D-DON'T YOU THINK THAT'S RATHER SHORT NOTICE? ER..FOR YOUR BOSS, THAT IS!
NAW.! HE'S BEEN EXPECTING SOMETHING LIKE THIS FOR MONTHS.!
POSTAL UNION, PLEASE.! YES!.. I WANT TO SEND A TELEGRAM TO GEORGE KEEFER IN LITTLE CITY-- AH.."ACCEPT JOB. SEE YOU SUNDAY." AND SIGN IT "FRED ANDREWS AND FAMILY!"

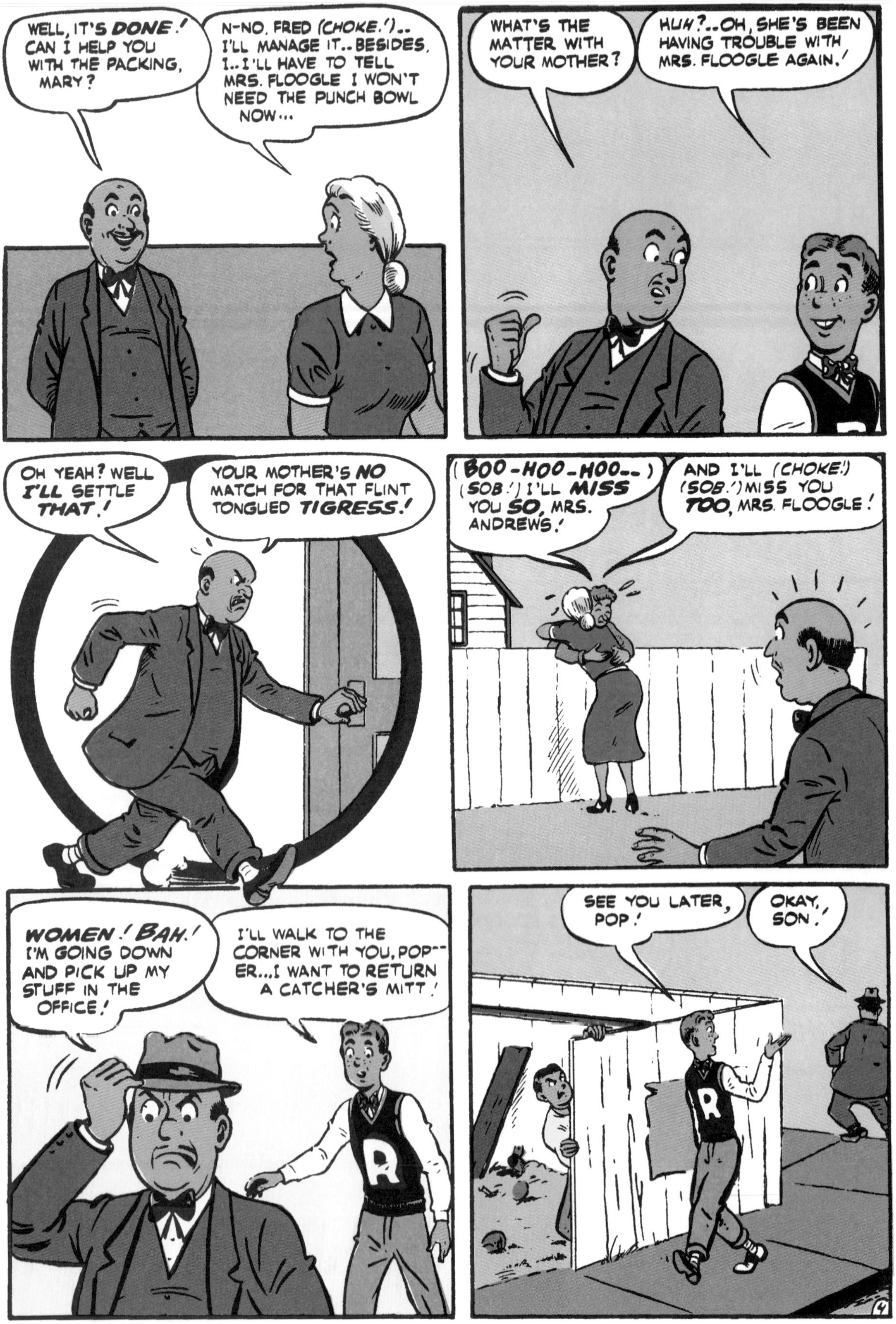
WELL, IT'S DONE! CAN I HELP YOU WITH THE PACKING, MARY?
N-NO, FRED (CHOKE!).. I'LL MANAGE IT.. BESIDES, I..I'LL HAVE TO TELL MRS. FLOOGLE I WON'T NEED THE PUNCH BOWL NOW...
WHAT'S THE MATTER WITH YOUR MOTHER?
HUH?..OH, SHE'S BEEN HAVING TROUBLE WITH MRS. FLOOGLE AGAIN!
OH YEAH? WELL I'LL SETTLE THAT!
YOUR MOTHER'S NO MATCH FOR THAT FLINT TONGUED TIGRESS!
(BOO-HOO-HOO--) (SOB!) I'LL MISS YOU SO, MRS. ANDREWS!
AND I'LL (CHOKE!) (SOB!) MISS YOU TOO, MRS. FLOOGLE!
WOMEN! BAH! I'M GOING DOWN AND PICK UP MY STUFF IN THE OFFICE!
I'LL WALK TO THE CORNER WITH YOU, POP-- ER...I WANT TO RETURN A CATCHER'S MITT!
SEE YOU LATER, POP!
OKAY, SON!
4

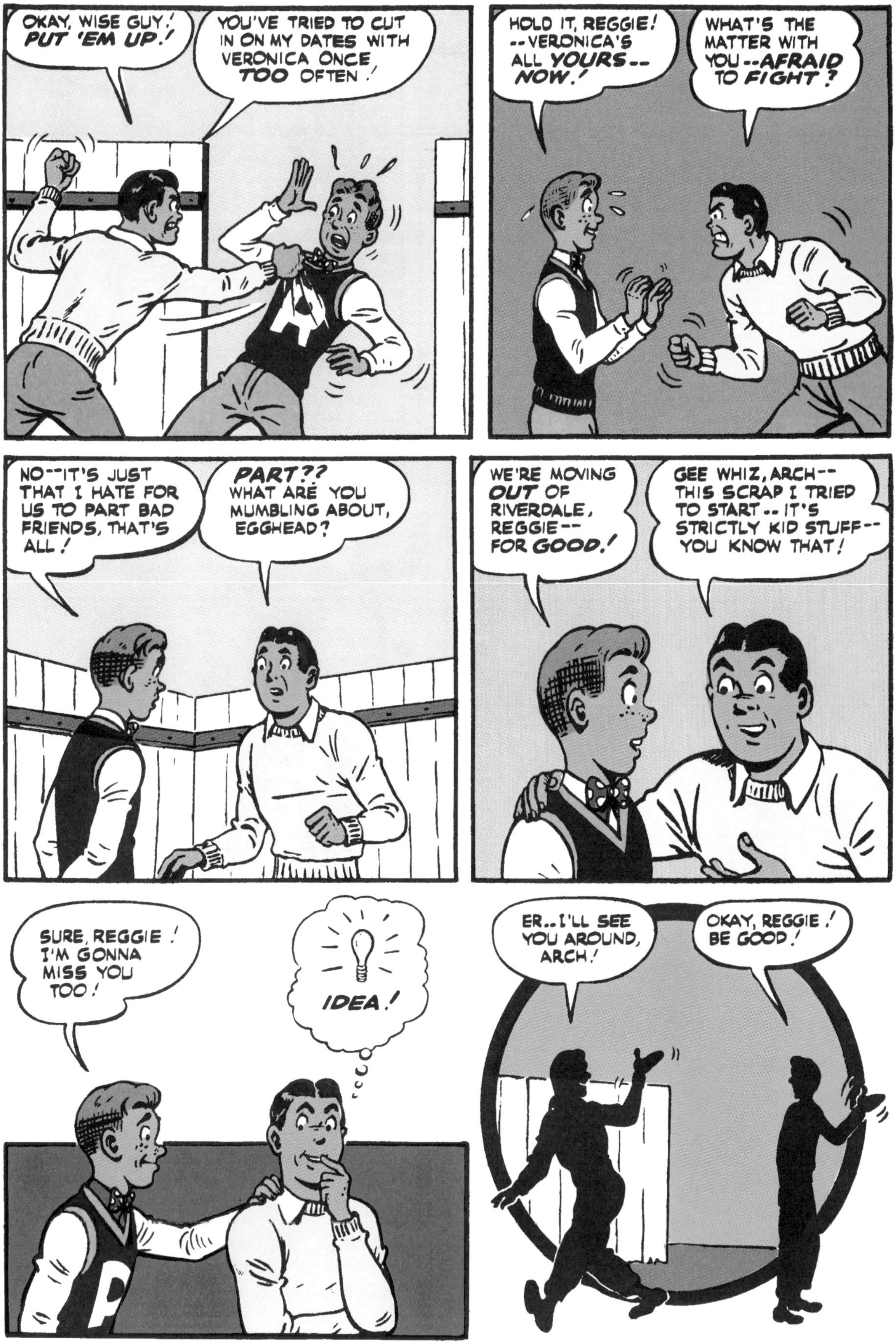
OKAY, WISE GUY! PUT 'EM UP!
YOU'VE TRIED TO CUT IN ON MY DATES WITH VERONICA ONCE TOO OFTEN!
HOLD IT, REGGIE! --VERONICA'S ALL YOURS--NOW!
WHAT'S THE MATTER WITH YOU--AFRAID TO FIGHT?
NO--IT'S JUST THAT I HATE FOR US TO PART BAD FRIENDS, THAT'S ALL!
PART?? WHAT ARE YOU MUMBLING ABOUT, EGGHEAD?
WE'RE MOVING OUT OF RIVERDALE, REGGIE--FOR GOOD!
GEE WHIZ, ARCH--THIS SCRAP I TRIED TO START--IT'S STRICTLY KID STUFF--YOU KNOW THAT!
SURE, REGGIE! I'M GONNA MISS YOU TOO!
IDEA!
ER..I'LL SEE YOU AROUND, ARCH!
OKAY, REGGIE! BE GOOD!

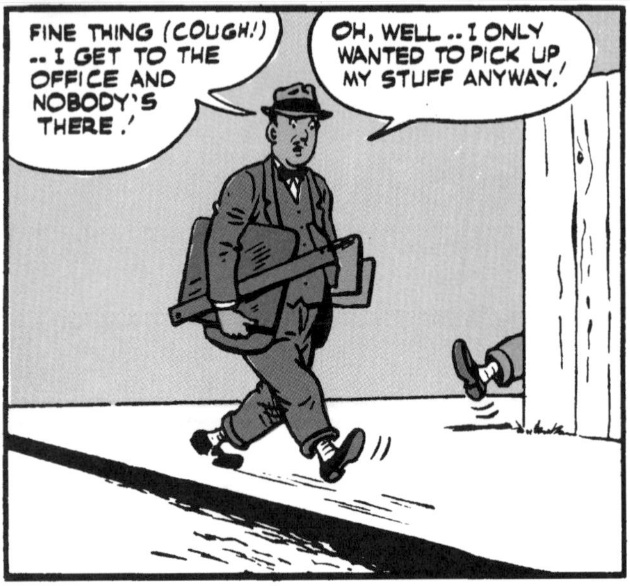
FINE THING (COUGH!) -- I GET TO THE OFFICE AND NOBODY'S THERE!
OH, WELL -- I ONLY WANTED TO PICK UP MY STUFF ANYWAY!

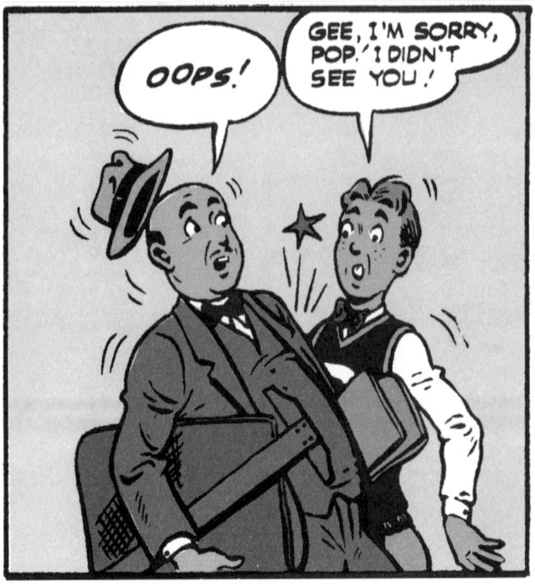
OOPS!
GEE, I'M SORRY, POP! I DIDN'T SEE YOU!

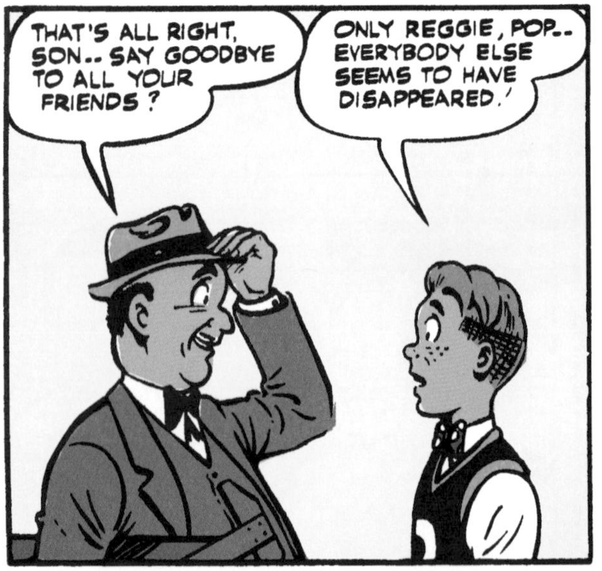
THAT'S ALL RIGHT, SON -- SAY GOODBYE TO ALL YOUR FRIENDS?
ONLY REGGIE, POP -- EVERYBODY ELSE SEEMS TO HAVE DISAPPEARED!

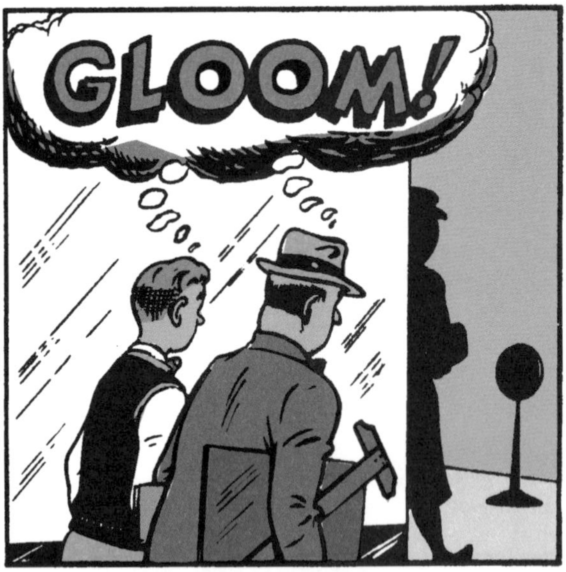
GLOOM!

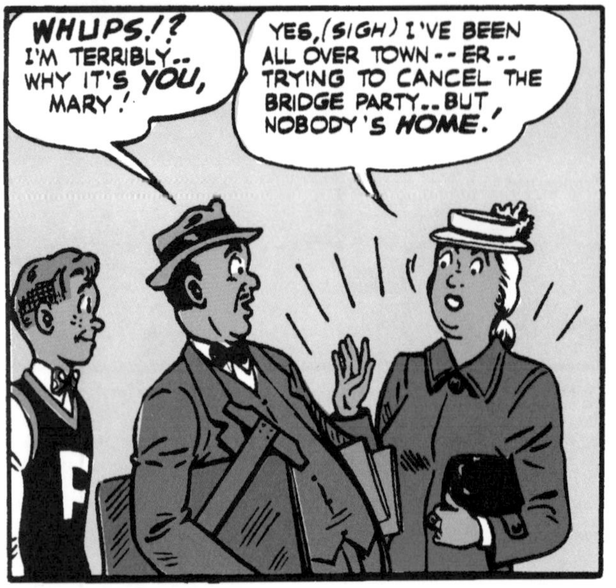
WHUPS!? I'M TERRIBLY -- WHY IT'S YOU, MARY!
YES, (SIGH) I'VE BEEN ALL OVER TOWN -- ER -- TRYING TO CANCEL THE BRIDGE PARTY -- BUT, NOBODY'S HOME!

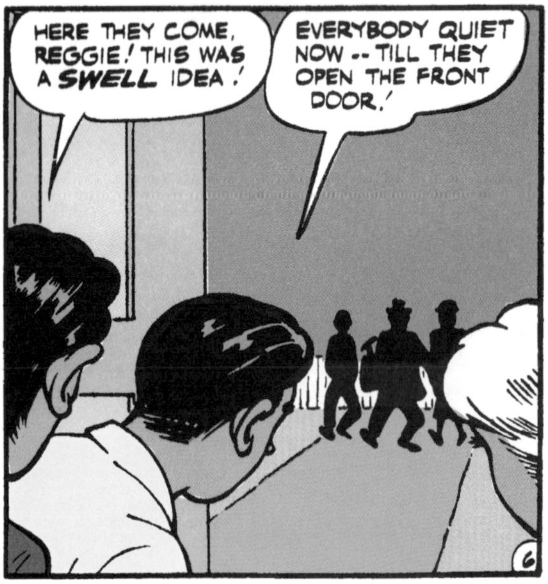
HERE THEY COME, REGGIE! THIS WAS A SWELL IDEA!
EVERYBODY QUIET NOW -- TILL THEY OPEN THE FRONT DOOR!
6

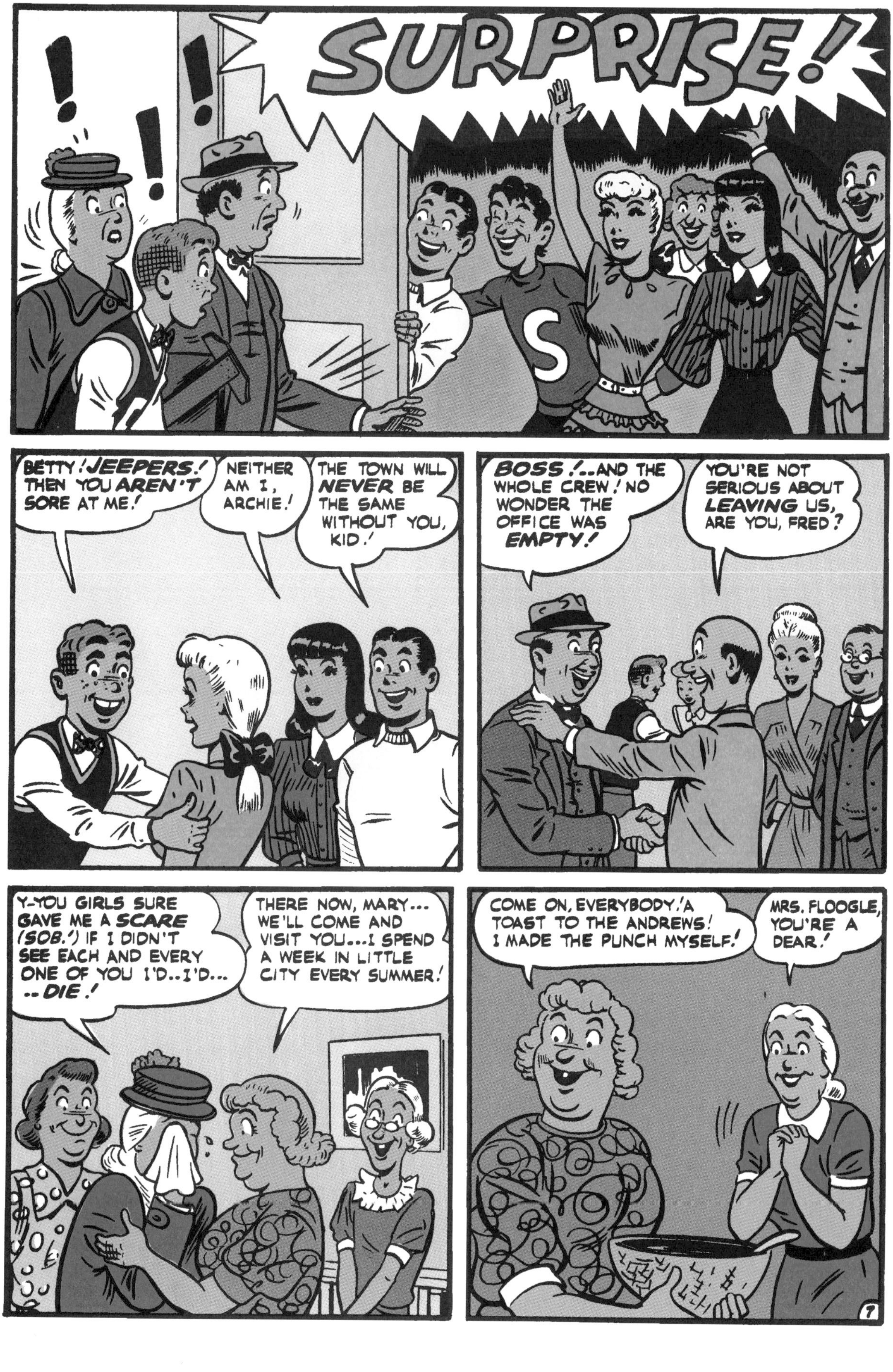
SURPRISE!
BETTY! JEEPERS! THEN YOU AREN'T SORE AT ME!
NEITHER AM I, ARCHIE!
THE TOWN WILL NEVER BE THE SAME WITHOUT YOU, KID!
BOSS!..AND THE WHOLE CREW! NO WONDER THE OFFICE WAS EMPTY!
YOU'RE NOT SERIOUS ABOUT LEAVING US, ARE YOU, FRED?
Y-YOU GIRLS SURE GAVE ME A SCARE (SOB.') IF I DIDN'T SEE EACH AND EVERY ONE OF YOU I'D..I'D... ..DIE!
THERE NOW, MARY... WE'LL COME AND VISIT YOU...I SPEND A WEEK IN LITTLE CITY EVERY SUMMER!
COME ON, EVERYBODY! A TOAST TO THE ANDREWS! I MADE THE PUNCH MYSELF!
MRS. FLOOGLE, YOU'RE A DEAR!
7

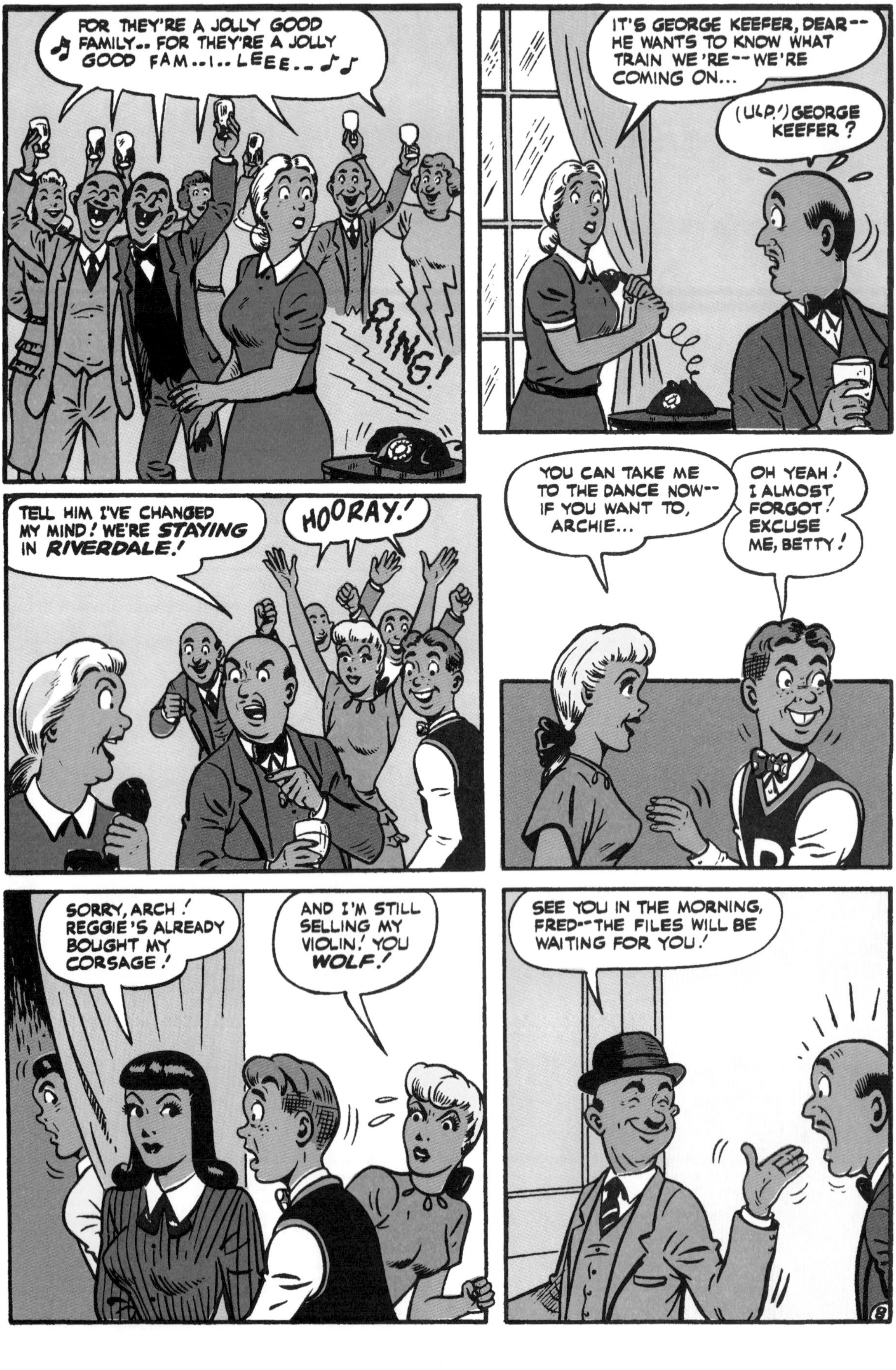
FOR THEY'RE A JOLLY GOOD FAMILY.. FOR THEY'RE A JOLLY GOOD FAM..I..LEEE..
RING!
IT'S GEORGE KEEFER, DEAR-- HE WANTS TO KNOW WHAT TRAIN WE'RE--WE'RE COMING ON...
(ULP!) GEORGE KEEFER?
TELL HIM I'VE CHANGED MY MIND! WE'RE STAYING IN RIVERDALE!
HOORAY!
YOU CAN TAKE ME TO THE DANCE NOW-- IF YOU WANT TO, ARCHIE...
OH YEAH! I ALMOST FORGOT! EXCUSE ME, BETTY!
SORRY, ARCH! REGGIE'S ALREADY BOUGHT MY CORSAGE!
AND I'M STILL SELLING MY VIOLIN! YOU WOLF!
SEE YOU IN THE MORNING, FRED--THE FILES WILL BE WAITING FOR YOU!
8

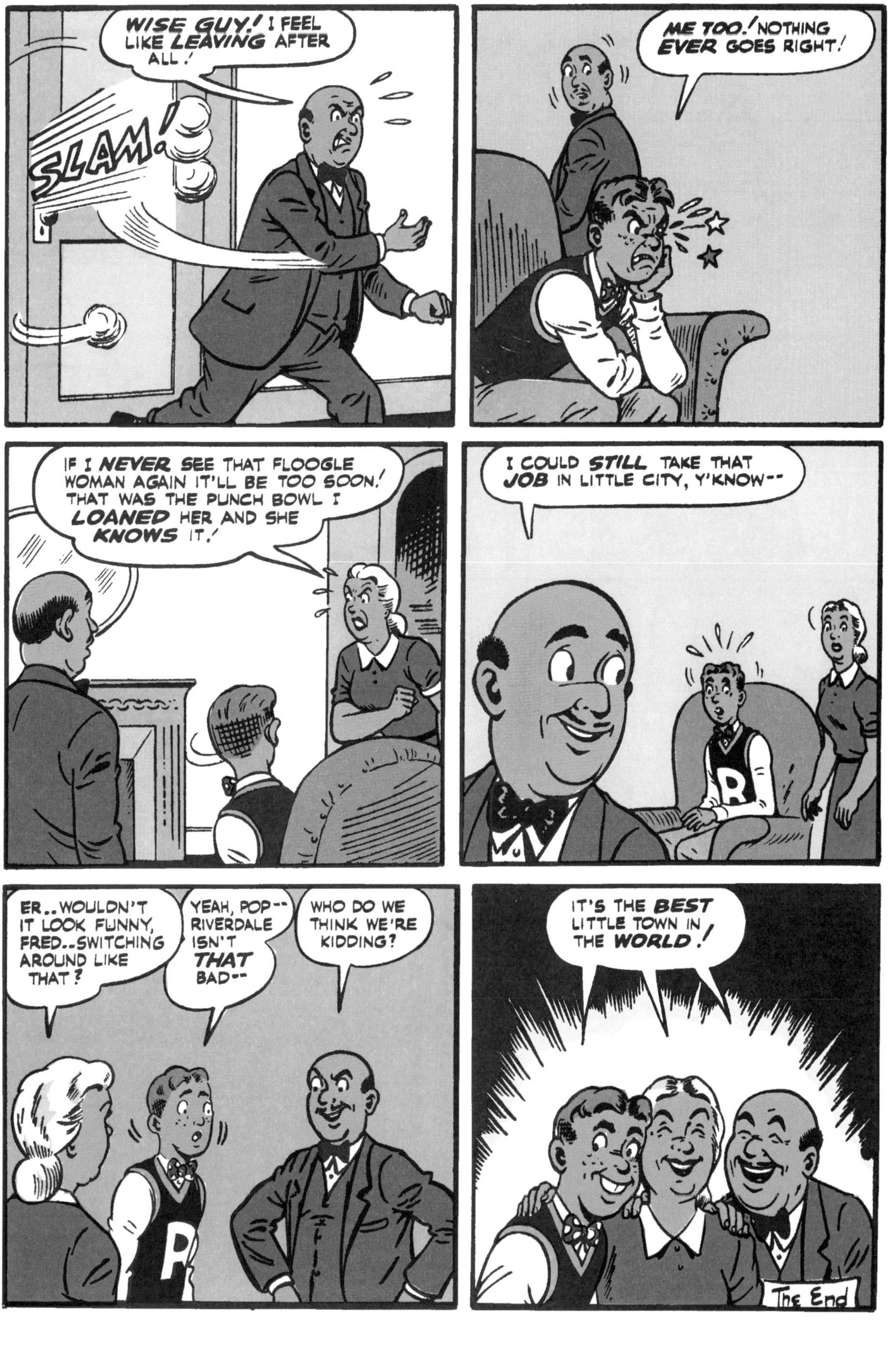
WISE GUY! I FEEL LIKE LEAVING AFTER ALL!
SLAM!
ME TOO! NOTHING EVER GOES RIGHT!
IF I NEVER SEE THAT FLOOGLE WOMAN AGAIN IT'LL BE TOO SOON! THAT WAS THE PUNCH BOWL I LOANED HER AND SHE KNOWS IT!
I COULD STILL TAKE THAT JOB IN LITTLE CITY, Y'KNOW--
ER.. WOULDN'T IT LOOK FUNNY, FRED.. SWITCHING AROUND LIKE THAT?
YEAH, POP-- RIVERDALE ISN'T THAT BAD--
WHO DO WE THINK WE'RE KIDDING?
IT'S THE BEST LITTLE TOWN IN THE WORLD!
The End

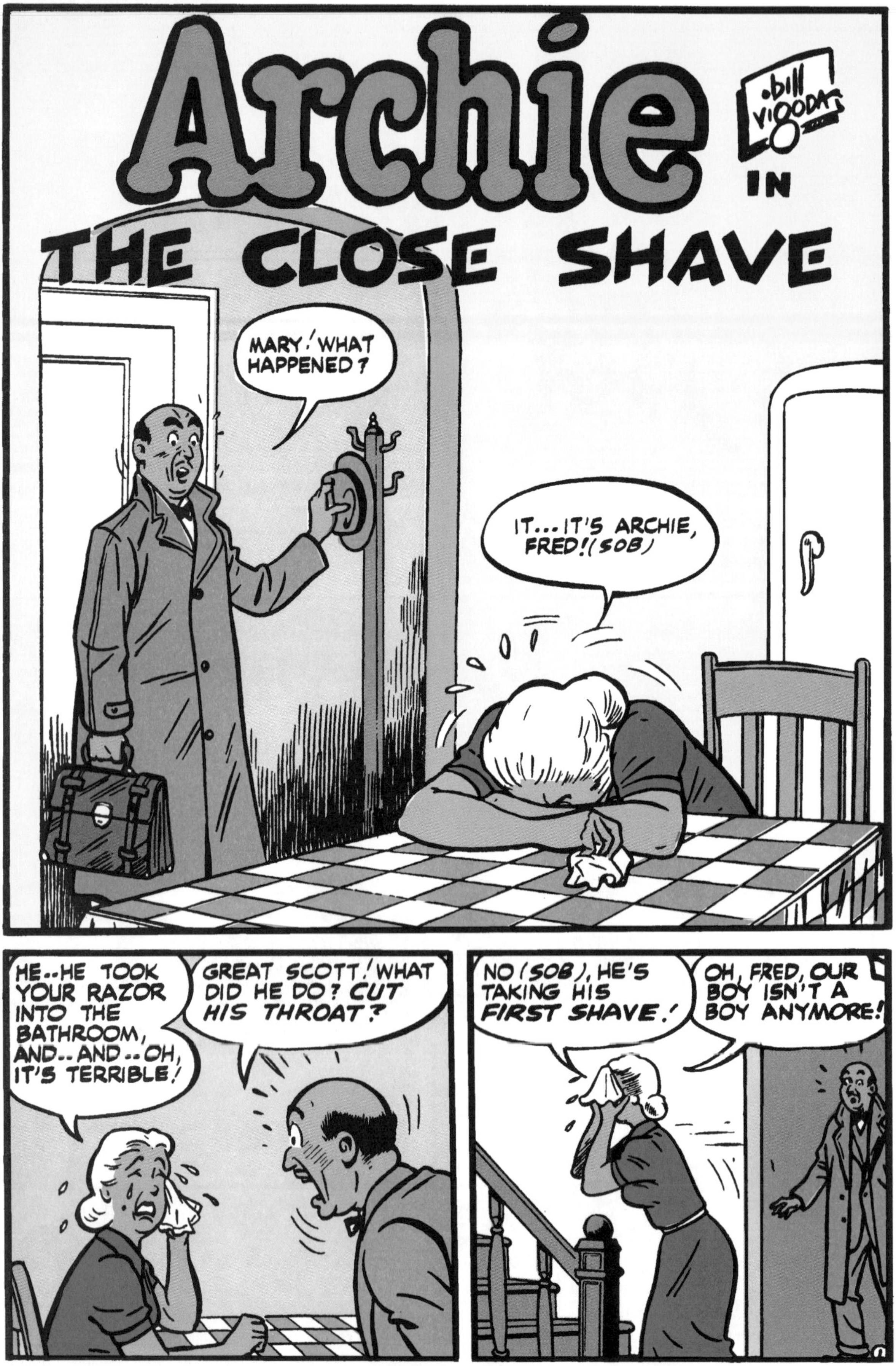
Archie
bill VIGODA
IN
THE CLOSE SHAVE
MARY! WHAT HAPPENED?
IT...IT'S ARCHIE, FRED! (SOB)
HE..HE TOOK YOUR RAZOR INTO THE BATHROOM, AND..AND..OH, IT'S TERRIBLE!
GREAT SCOTT! WHAT DID HE DO? CUT HIS THROAT?
NO (SOB), HE'S TAKING HIS FIRST SHAVE!
OH, FRED, OUR BOY ISN'T A BOY ANYMORE!

Originally presented in ARCHIE COMICS #40, September-October, 1949

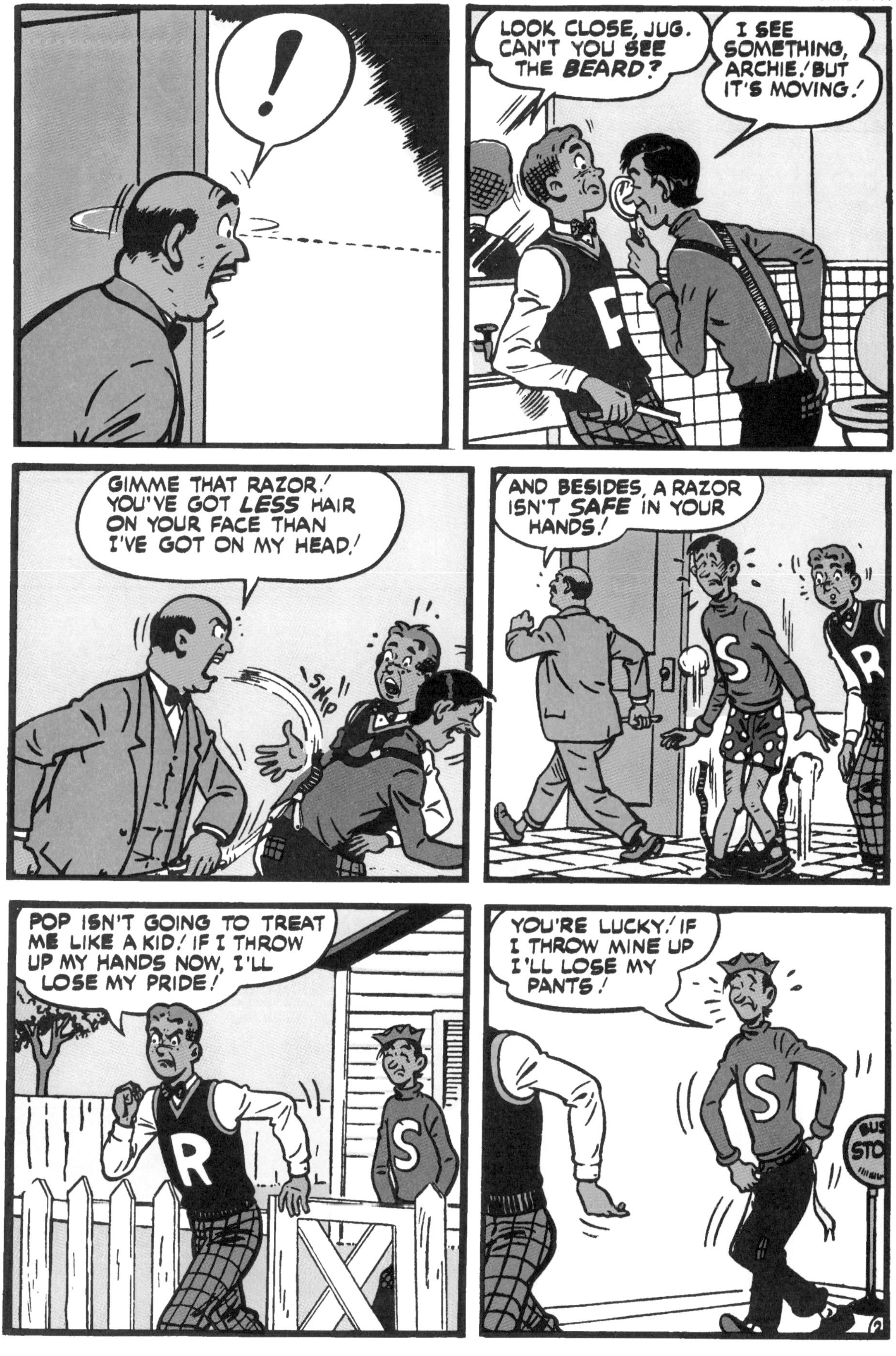
!
LOOK CLOSE, JUG. CAN'T YOU SEE THE BEARD?
I SEE SOMETHING, ARCHIE! BUT IT'S MOVING!
GIMME THAT RAZOR! YOU'VE GOT LESS HAIR ON YOUR FACE THAN I'VE GOT ON MY HEAD!
SNIP
AND BESIDES, A RAZOR ISN'T SAFE IN YOUR HANDS!
POP ISN'T GOING TO TREAT ME LIKE A KID! IF I THROW UP MY HANDS NOW, I'LL LOSE MY PRIDE!
YOU'RE LUCKY! IF I THROW MINE UP I'LL LOSE MY PANTS!

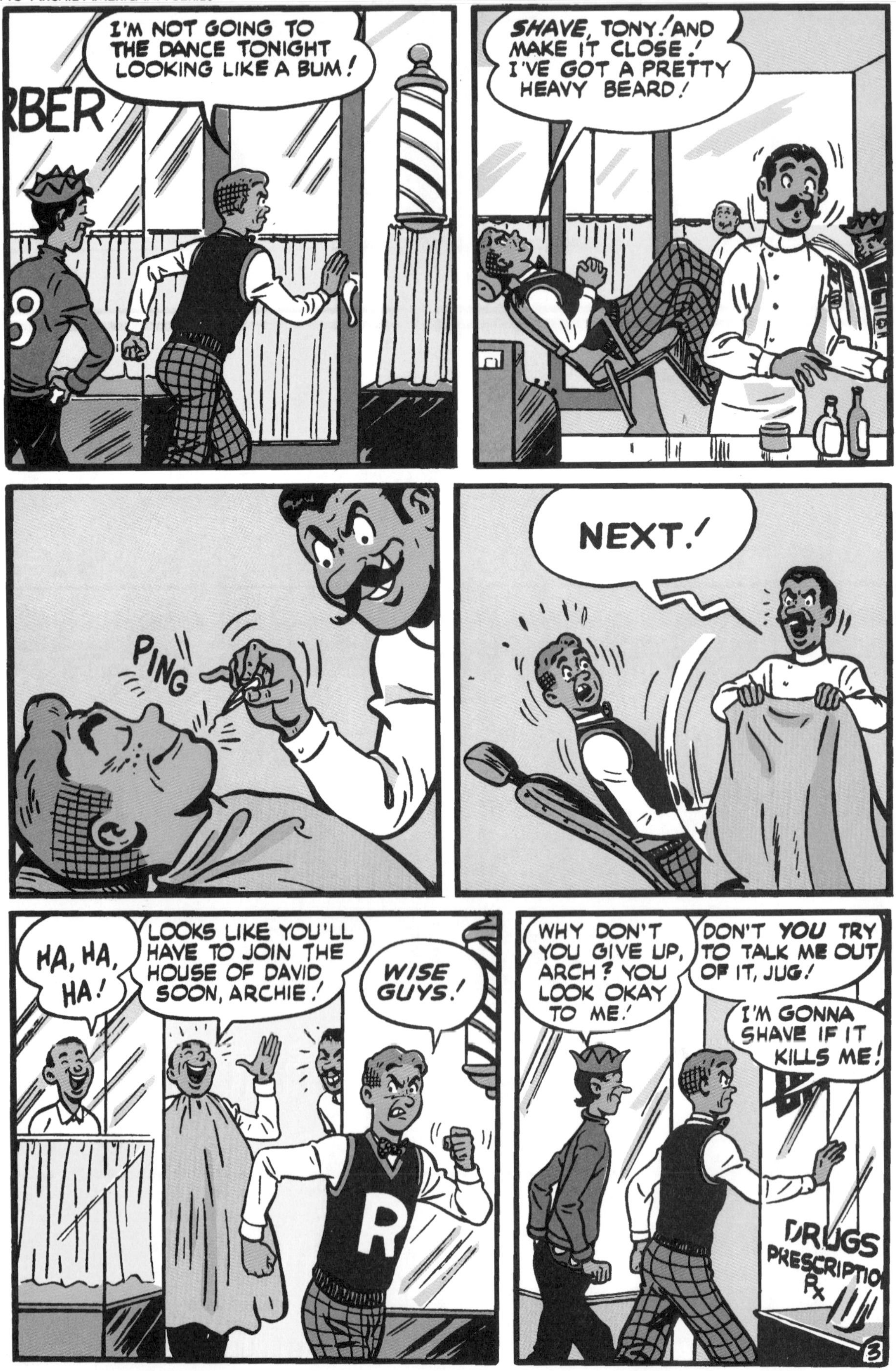

I'M NOT GOING TO THE DANCE TONIGHT LOOKING LIKE A BUM!
RBER
SHAVE, TONY! AND MAKE IT CLOSE! I'VE GOT A PRETTY HEAVY BEARD!
PING
NEXT.!
HA, HA, HA!
LOOKS LIKE YOU'LL HAVE TO JOIN THE HOUSE OF DAVID SOON, ARCHIE!
WISE GUYS!
WHY DON'T YOU GIVE UP, ARCH? YOU LOOK OKAY TO ME!
DON'T YOU TRY TO TALK ME OUT OF IT, JUG!
I'M GONNA SHAVE IF IT KILLS ME!
DRUGS
PRESCRIPTIO
Rx
3

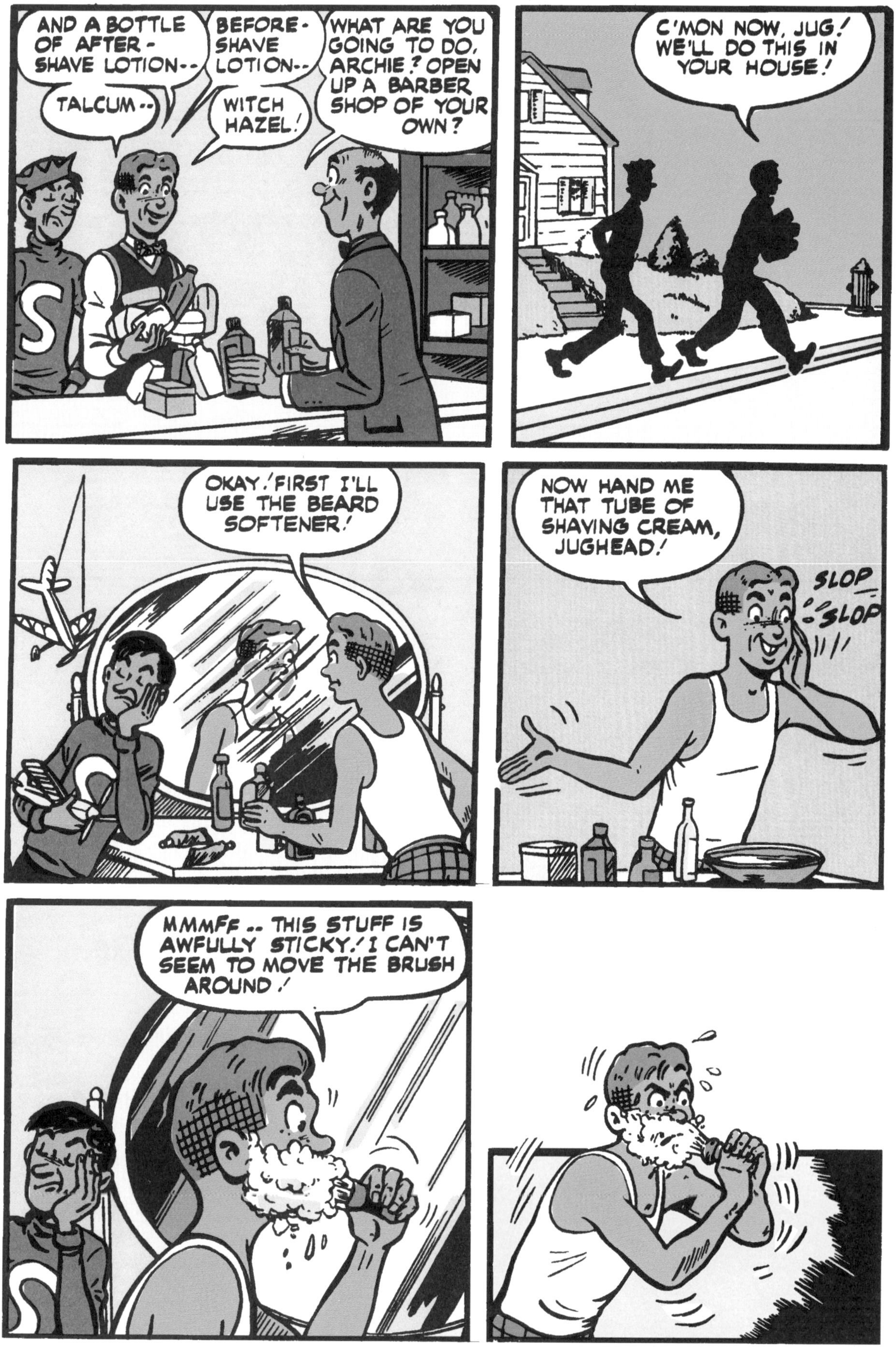
AND A BOTTLE OF AFTER-SHAVE LOTION--
BEFORE-SHAVE LOTION--
WHAT ARE YOU GOING TO DO, ARCHIE? OPEN UP A BARBER SHOP OF YOUR OWN?
TALCUM--
WITCH HAZEL!
C'MON NOW, JUG! WE'LL DO THIS IN YOUR HOUSE!
OKAY! FIRST I'LL USE THE BEARD SOFTENER!
NOW HAND ME THAT TUBE OF SHAVING CREAM, JUGHEAD!
SLOP
SLOP
MMMFF .. THIS STUFF IS AWFULLY STICKY! I CAN'T SEEM TO MOVE THE BRUSH AROUND!

YIPE! ARCH, I GAVE YOU MY TUBE OF AIRPLANE GLUE BY MISTAKE!
GET IT OFF! GET IT OFF!
THUD!
THAT EVENING..
OH, ARCHIE! YOU REALLY SHOULDN'T HAVE TAKEN ME TO THIS DANCE WITHOUT A SHAVE!
THE END

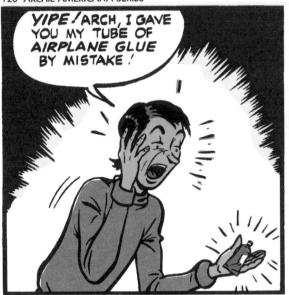

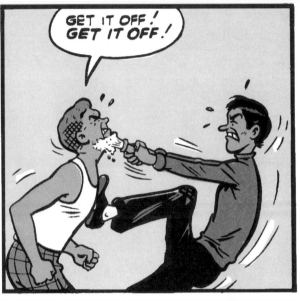

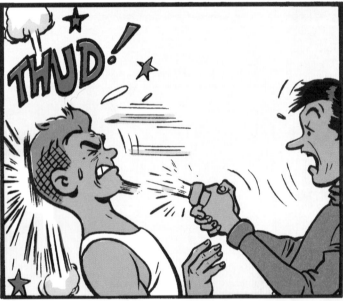

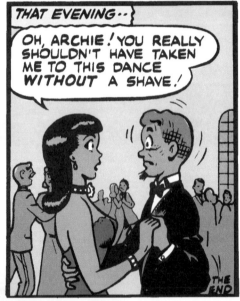

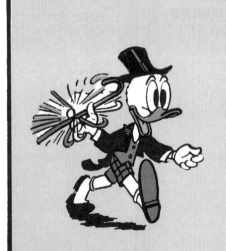

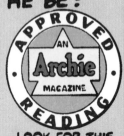

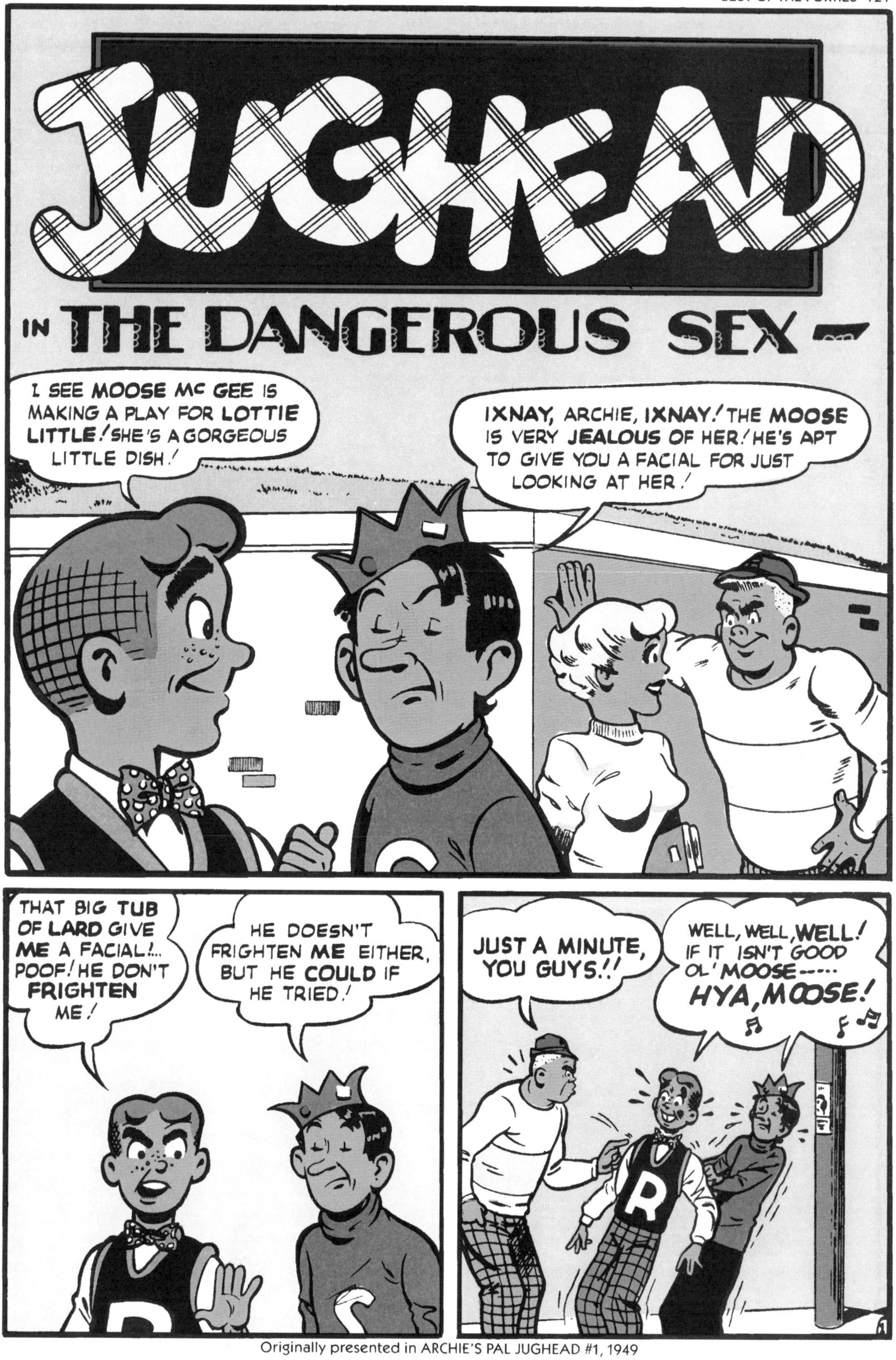
JUGHEAD
IN THE DANGEROUS SEX—
I SEE MOOSE MC GEE IS MAKING A PLAY FOR LOTTIE LITTLE! SHE'S A GORGEOUS LITTLE DISH!
IXNAY, ARCHIE, IXNAY! THE MOOSE IS VERY JEALOUS OF HER! HE'S APT TO GIVE YOU A FACIAL FOR JUST LOOKING AT HER!
THAT BIG TUB OF LARD GIVE ME A FACIAL!... POOF! HE DON'T FRIGHTEN ME!
HE DOESN'T FRIGHTEN ME EITHER, BUT HE COULD IF HE TRIED!
JUST A MINUTE, YOU GUYS!!
WELL, WELL, WELL! IF IT ISN'T GOOD OL' MOOSE----- HYA, MOOSE!

Originally presented in ARCHIE'S PAL JUGHEAD #1, 1949

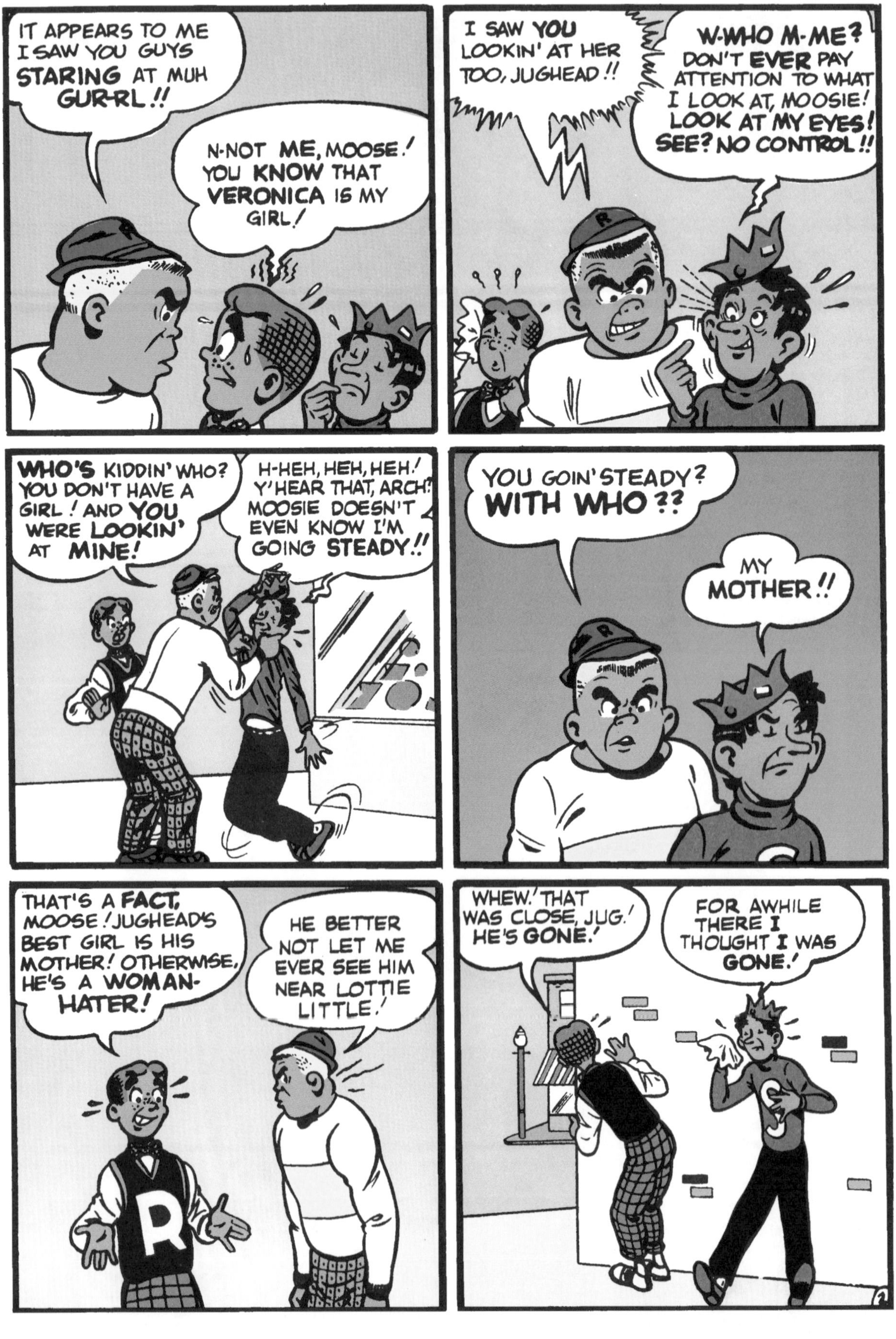
IT APPEARS TO ME I SAW YOU GUYS STARING AT MUH GUR-RL!!
N-NOT ME, MOOSE! YOU KNOW THAT VERONICA IS MY GIRL!
I SAW YOU LOOKIN' AT HER TOO, JUGHEAD!!
W-WHO M-ME? DON'T EVER PAY ATTENTION TO WHAT I LOOK AT, MOOSIE! LOOK AT MY EYES! SEE? NO CONTROL!!
WHO'S KIDDIN' WHO? YOU DON'T HAVE A GIRL! AND YOU WERE LOOKIN' AT MINE!
H-HEH, HEH, HEH! Y'HEAR THAT, ARCH? MOOSIE DOESN'T EVEN KNOW I'M GOING STEADY!!
YOU GOIN' STEADY? WITH WHO??
MY MOTHER!!
THAT'S A FACT, MOOSE! JUGHEAD'S BEST GIRL IS HIS MOTHER! OTHERWISE, HE'S A WOMAN-HATER!
HE BETTER NOT LET ME EVER SEE HIM NEAR LOTTIE LITTLE!
WHEW! THAT WAS CLOSE, JUG! HE'S GONE!
FOR AWHILE THERE I THOUGHT I WAS GONE!

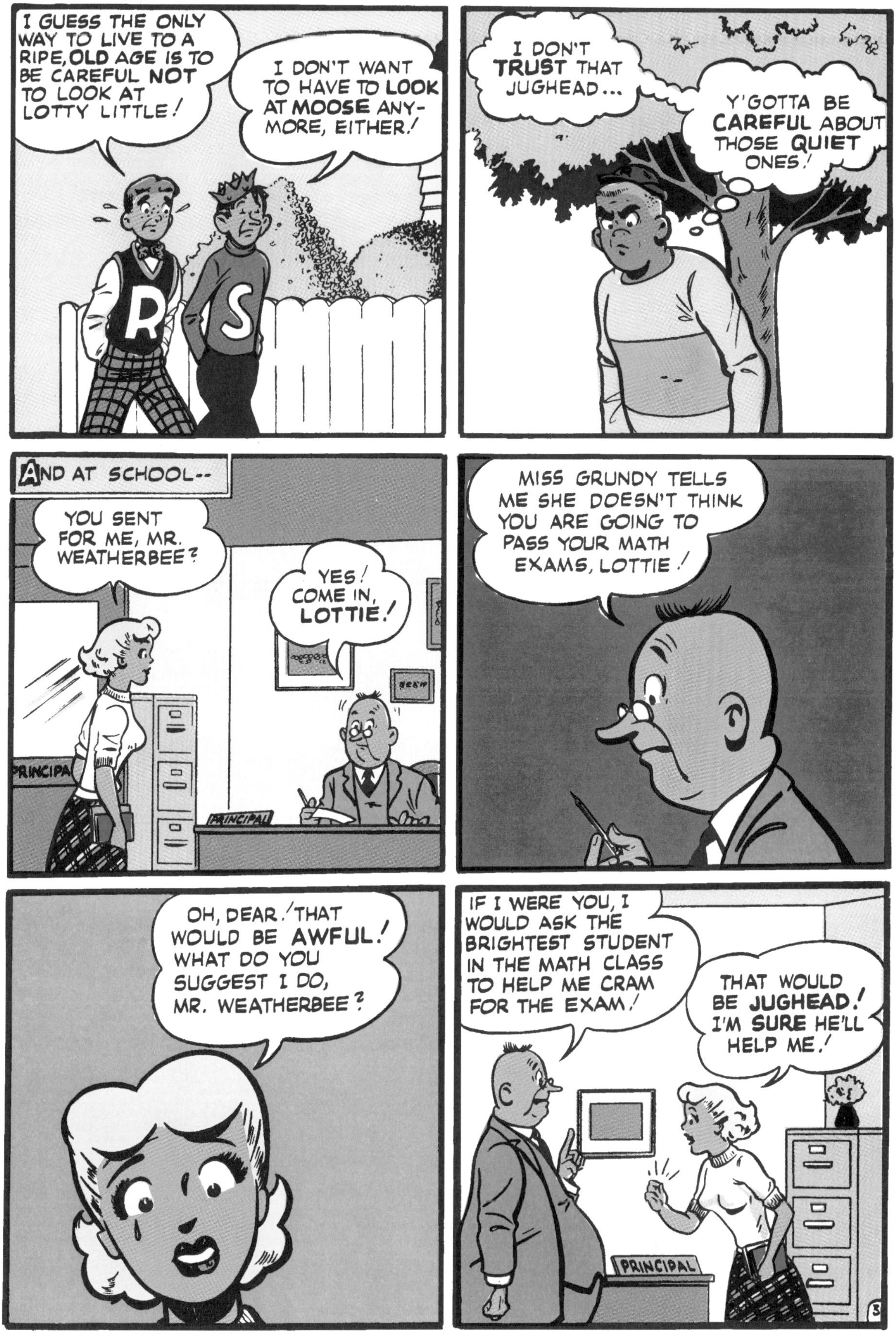
I GUESS THE ONLY WAY TO LIVE TO A RIPE, OLD AGE IS TO BE CAREFUL NOT TO LOOK AT LOTTY LITTLE!
I DON'T WANT TO HAVE TO LOOK AT MOOSE ANY-MORE, EITHER!
I DON'T TRUST THAT JUGHEAD...
Y'GOTTA BE CAREFUL ABOUT THOSE QUIET ONES!
AND AT SCHOOL--
YOU SENT FOR ME, MR. WEATHERBEE?
YES! COME IN, LOTTIE!
PRINCIPAL
PRINCIPAL
MISS GRUNDY TELLS ME SHE DOESN'T THINK YOU ARE GOING TO PASS YOUR MATH EXAMS, LOTTIE!
OH, DEAR! THAT WOULD BE AWFUL! WHAT DO YOU SUGGEST I DO, MR. WEATHERBEE?
IF I WERE YOU, I WOULD ASK THE BRIGHTEST STUDENT IN THE MATH CLASS TO HELP ME CRAM FOR THE EXAM!
THAT WOULD BE JUGHEAD! I'M SURE HE'LL HELP ME!
PRINCIPAL
3

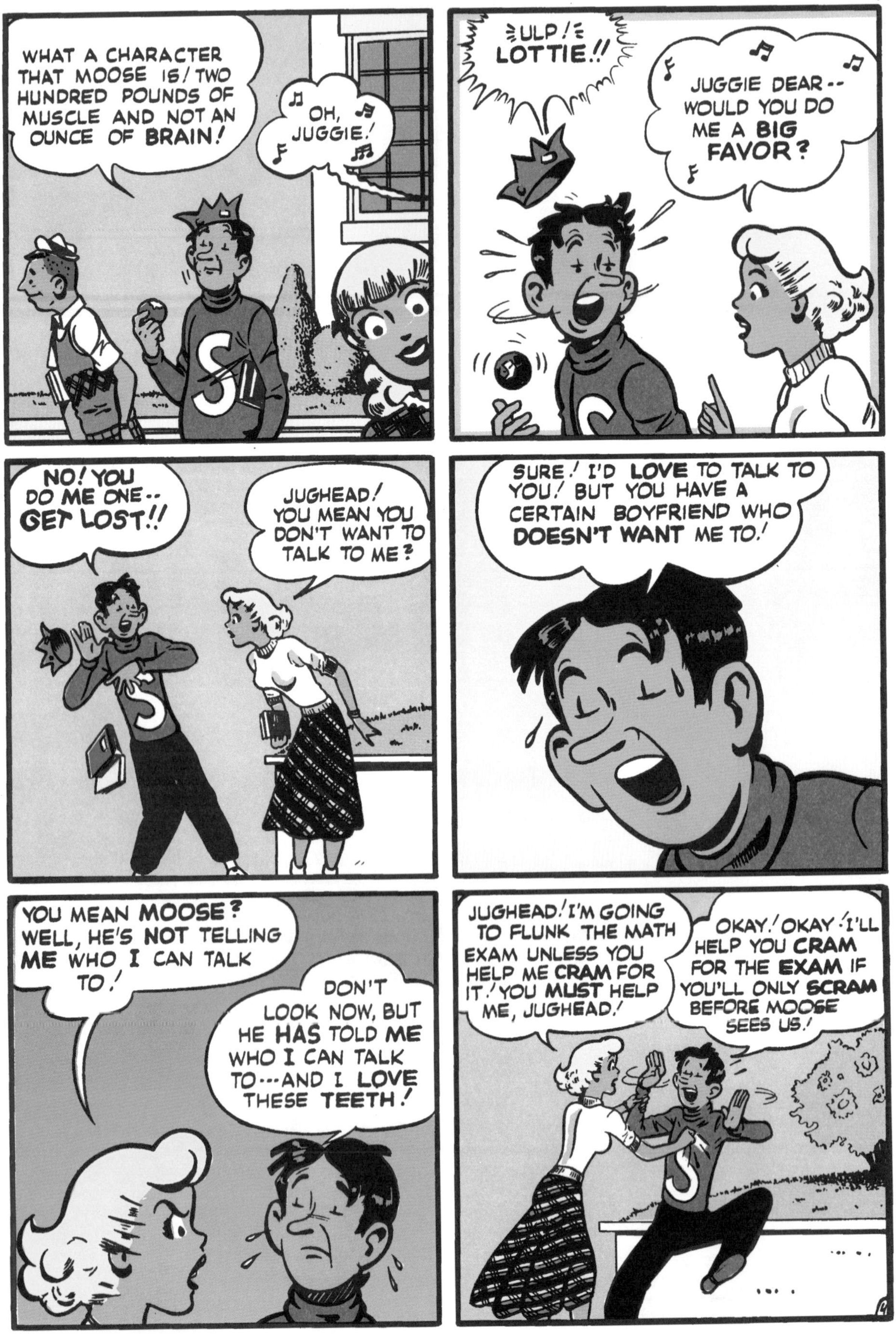
WHAT A CHARACTER THAT MOOSE IS! TWO HUNDRED POUNDS OF MUSCLE AND NOT AN OUNCE OF BRAIN!
OH, JUGGIE!
ULP! LOTTIE!!
JUGGIE DEAR -- WOULD YOU DO ME A BIG FAVOR?
NO! YOU DO ME ONE -- GET LOST!!
JUGHEAD! YOU MEAN YOU DON'T WANT TO TALK TO ME?
SURE! I'D LOVE TO TALK TO YOU! BUT YOU HAVE A CERTAIN BOYFRIEND WHO DOESN'T WANT ME TO!
YOU MEAN MOOSE? WELL, HE'S NOT TELLING ME WHO I CAN TALK TO!
DON'T LOOK NOW, BUT HE HAS TOLD ME WHO I CAN TALK TO---AND I LOVE THESE TEETH!
JUGHEAD! I'M GOING TO FLUNK THE MATH EXAM UNLESS YOU HELP ME CRAM FOR IT! YOU MUST HELP ME, JUGHEAD!
OKAY! OKAY! I'LL HELP YOU CRAM FOR THE EXAM IF YOU'LL ONLY SCRAM BEFORE MOOSE SEES US!

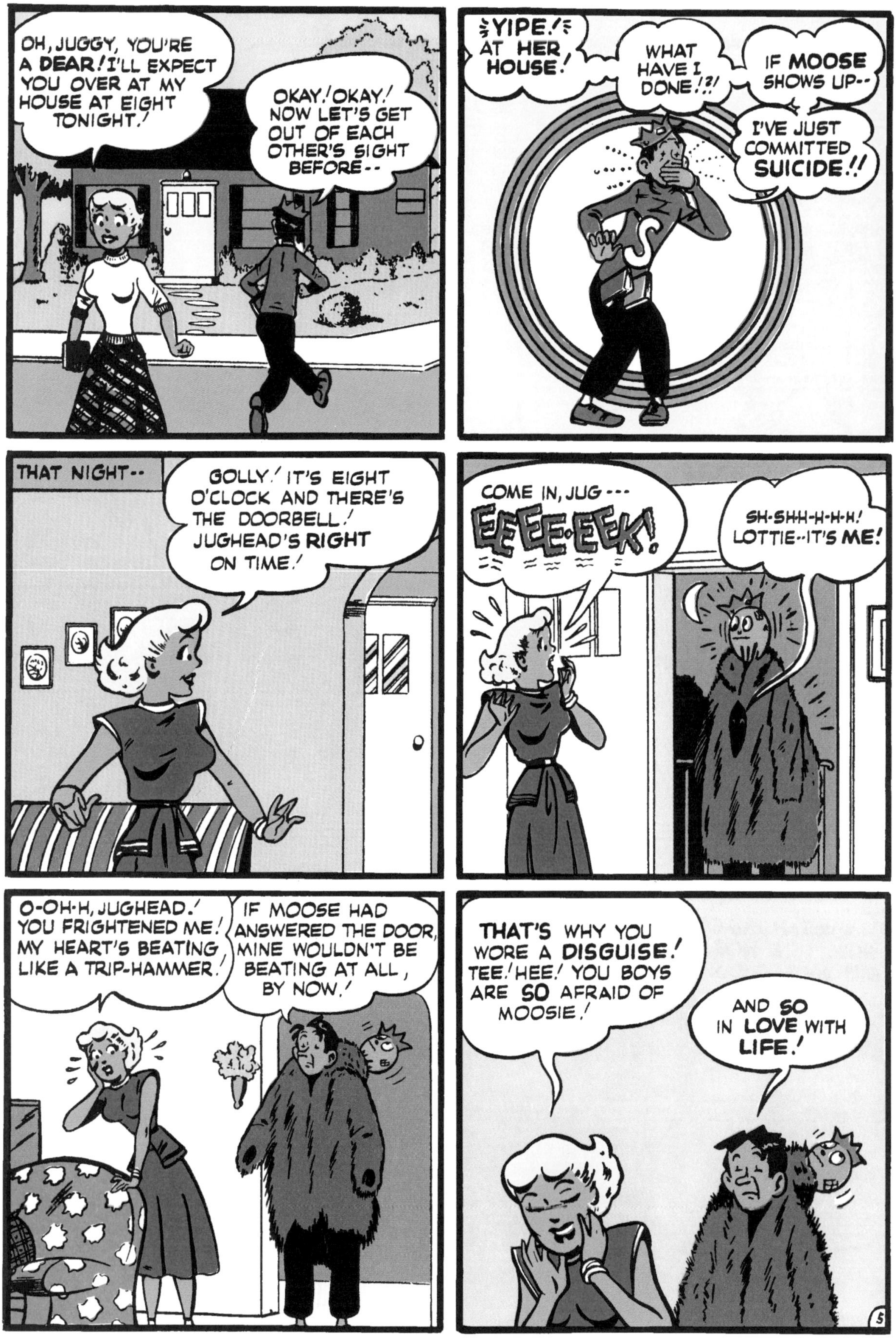
OH, JUGGY, YOU'RE A DEAR! I'LL EXPECT YOU OVER AT MY HOUSE AT EIGHT TONIGHT!
OKAY! OKAY! NOW LET'S GET OUT OF EACH OTHER'S SIGHT BEFORE--
YIPE! AT HER HOUSE!
WHAT HAVE I DONE!?!
IF MOOSE SHOWS UP--
I'VE JUST COMMITTED SUICIDE!!
THAT NIGHT--
GOLLY! IT'S EIGHT O'CLOCK AND THERE'S THE DOORBELL! JUGHEAD'S RIGHT ON TIME!
COME IN, JUG---
EEEEEEK!
SH-SHH-H-H-H! LOTTIE--IT'S ME!
O-OH-H, JUGHEAD! YOU FRIGHTENED ME! MY HEART'S BEATING LIKE A TRIP-HAMMER!
IF MOOSE HAD ANSWERED THE DOOR, MINE WOULDN'T BE BEATING AT ALL, BY NOW!
THAT'S WHY YOU WORE A DISGUISE! TEE! HEE! YOU BOYS ARE SO AFRAID OF MOOSIE!
AND SO IN LOVE WITH LIFE!
5

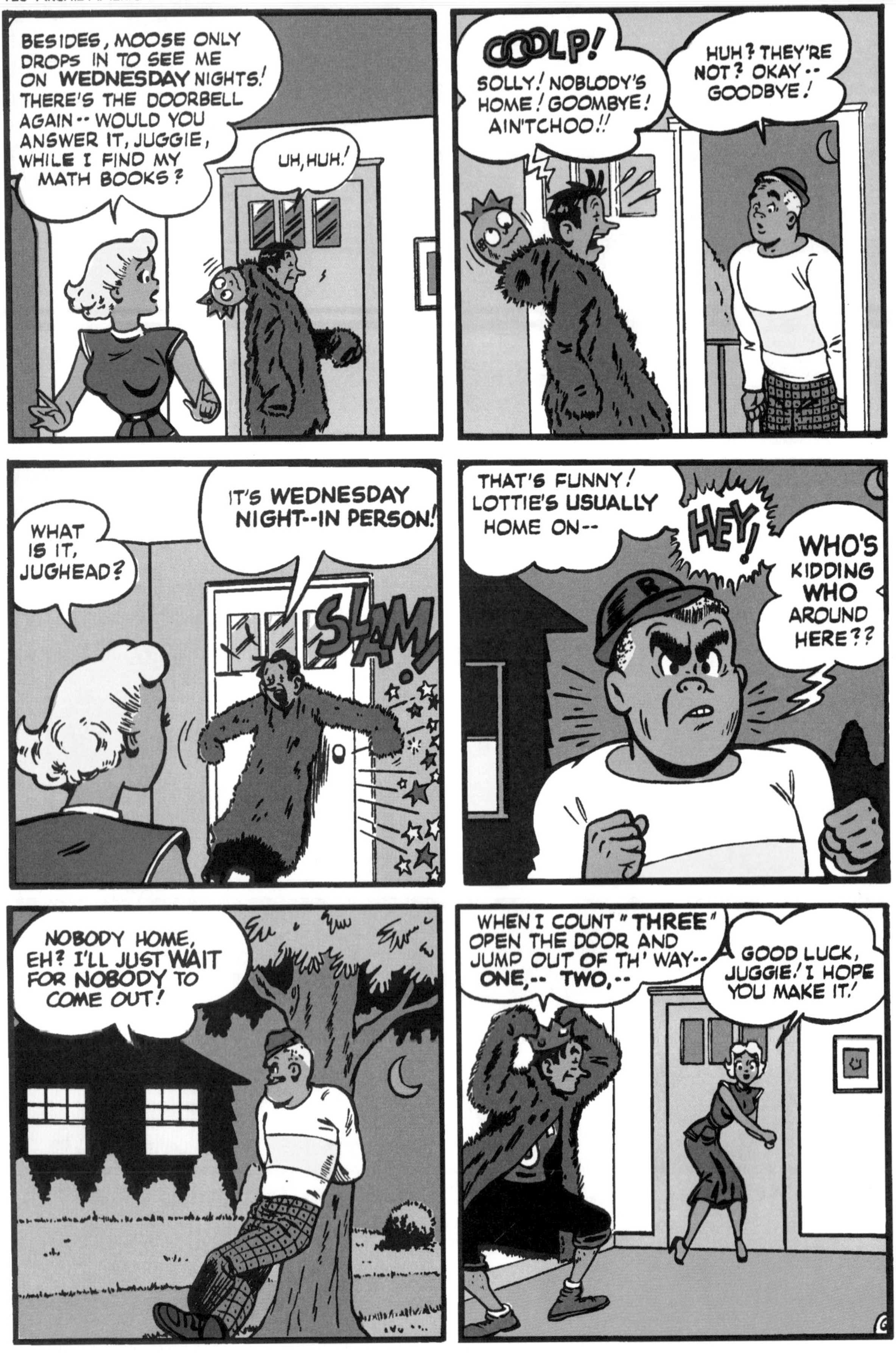
BESIDES, MOOSE ONLY DROPS IN TO SEE ME ON WEDNESDAY NIGHTS! THERE'S THE DOORBELL AGAIN -- WOULD YOU ANSWER IT, JUGGIE, WHILE I FIND MY MATH BOOKS?
UH, HUH!
COOLP!
SOLLY! NOBLODY'S HOME! GOOMBYE! AIN'TCHOO!!
HUH? THEY'RE NOT? OKAY -- GOODBYE!
WHAT IS IT, JUGHEAD?
IT'S WEDNESDAY NIGHT--IN PERSON!
SLAM
THAT'S FUNNY! LOTTIE'S USUALLY HOME ON--
HEY!
WHO'S KIDDING WHO AROUND HERE??
NOBODY HOME, EH? I'LL JUST WAIT FOR NOBODY TO COME OUT!
WHEN I COUNT "THREE" OPEN THE DOOR AND JUMP OUT OF TH' WAY-- ONE,-- TWO,--
GOOD LUCK, JUGGIE! I HOPE YOU MAKE IT!

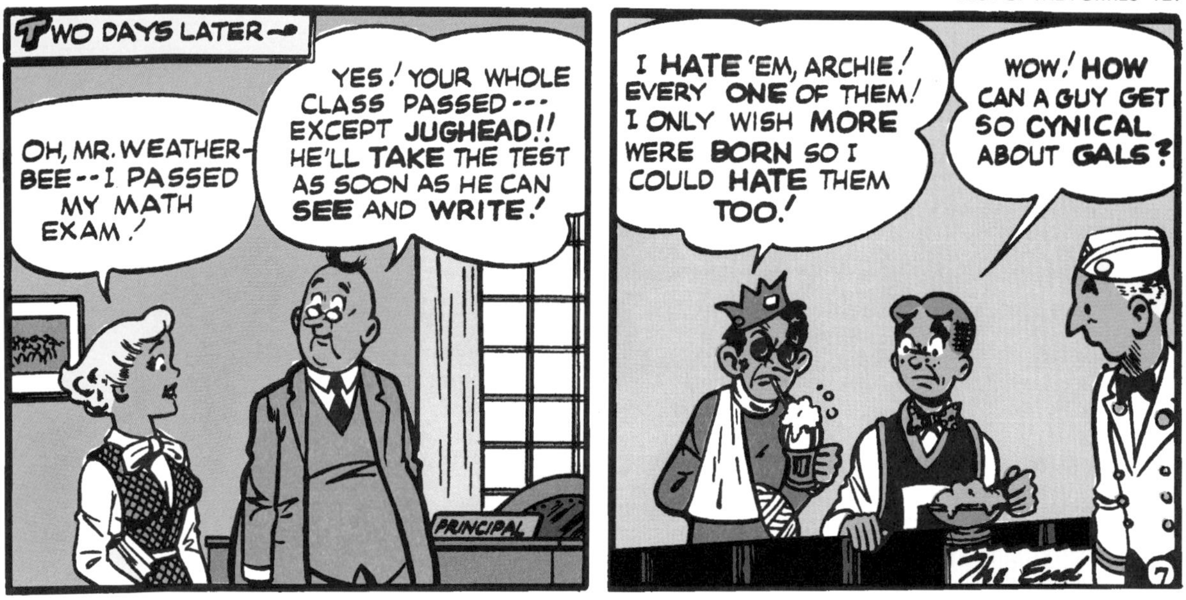
TWO DAYS LATER
OH, MR. WEATHERBEE--I PASSED MY MATH EXAM!
YES! YOUR WHOLE CLASS PASSED--- EXCEPT JUGHEAD!! HE'LL TAKE THE TEST AS SOON AS HE CAN SEE AND WRITE!
PRINCIPAL
I HATE 'EM, ARCHIE! EVERY ONE OF THEM! I ONLY WISH MORE WERE BORN SO I COULD HATE THEM TOO!
WOW! HOW CAN A GUY GET SO CYNICAL ABOUT GALS?
The End
7

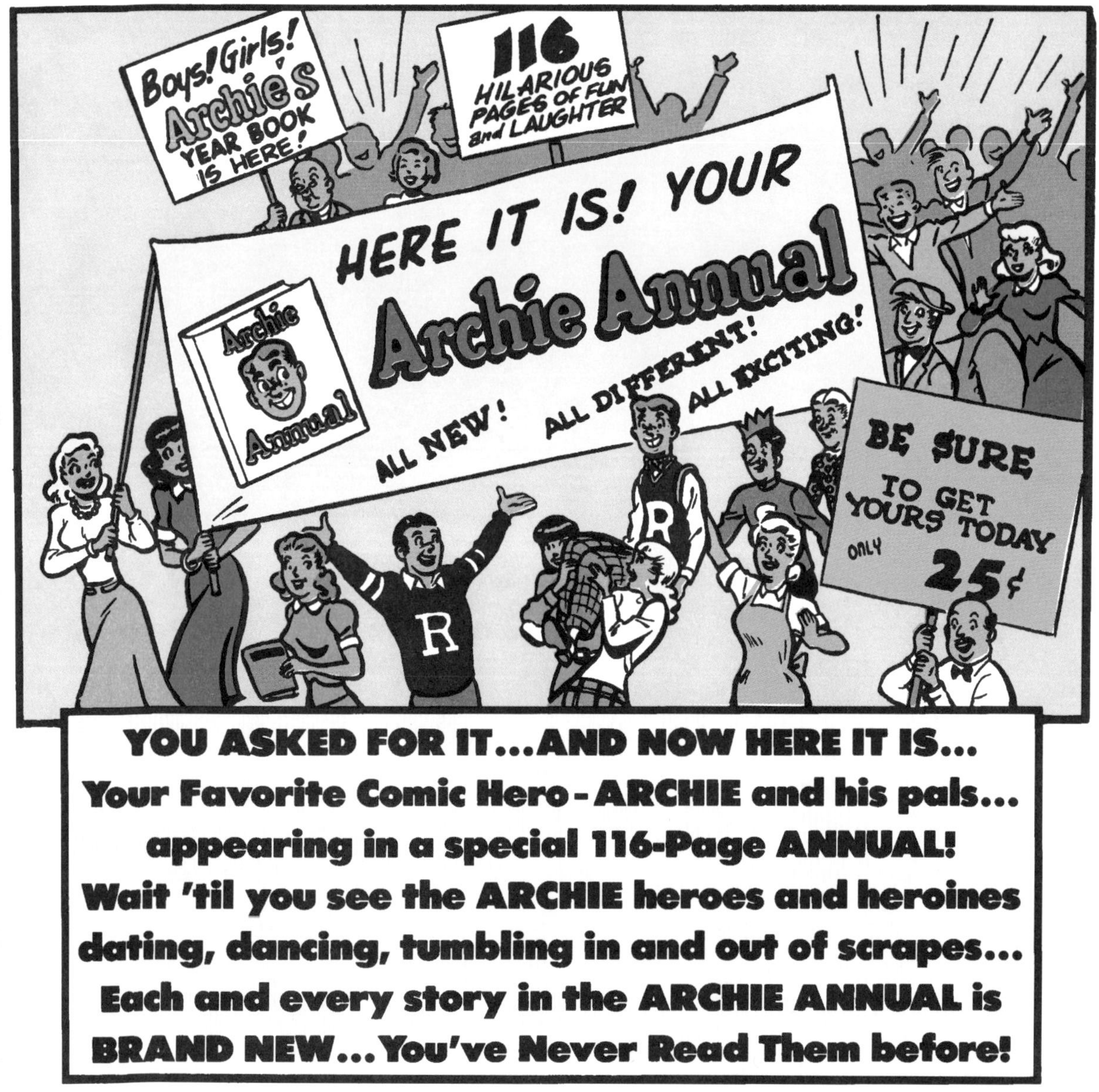
Boys! Girls! Archie's YEAR BOOK IS HERE!
116 HILARIOUS PAGES OF FUN and LAUGHTER
HERE IT IS! YOUR
Archie Annual
Archie Annual
ALL NEW!
ALL DIFFERENT!
ALL EXCITING!
BE SURE TO GET YOURS TODAY
ONLY 25¢

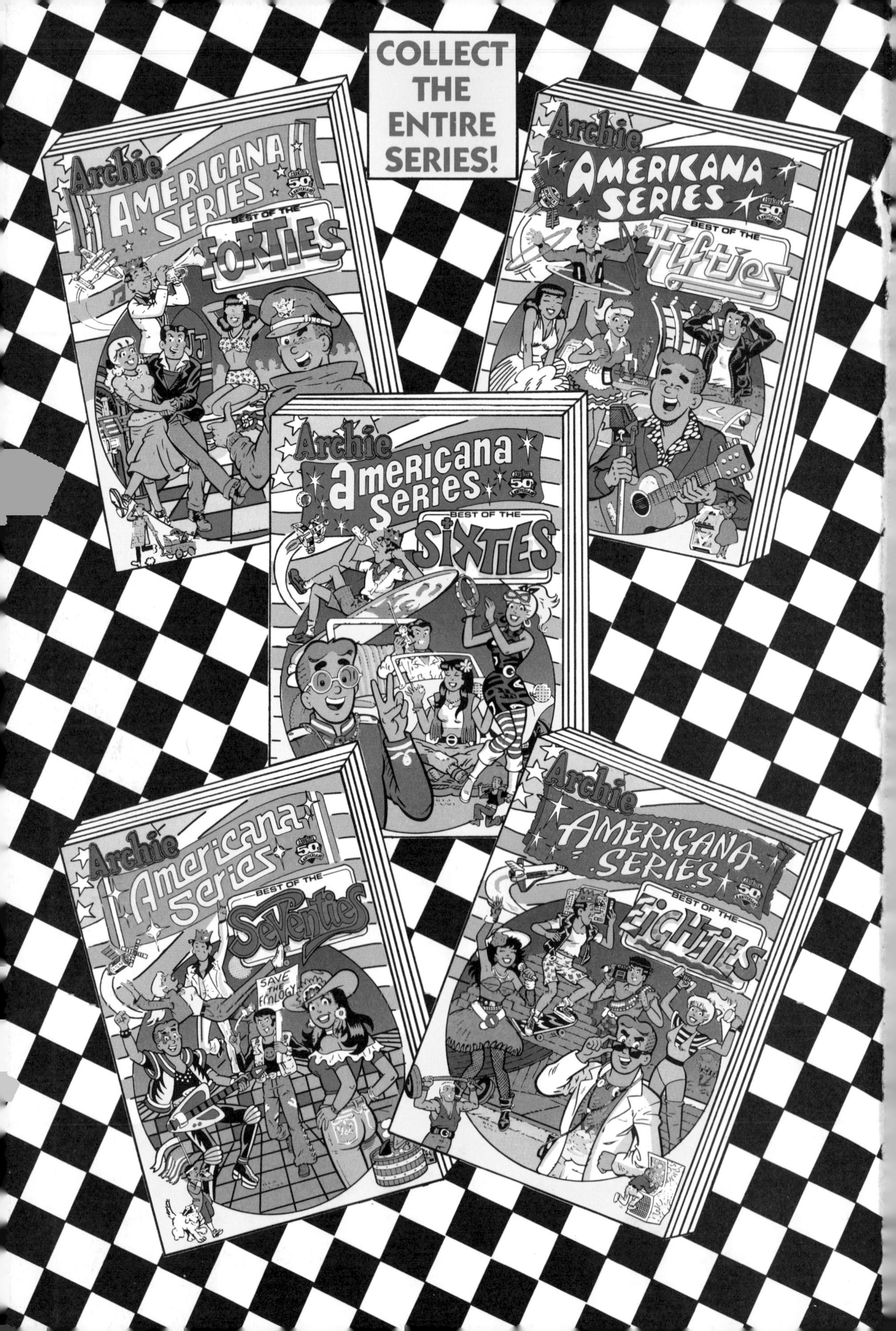

COLLECT THE ENTIRE SERIES!
Archie AMERICANA SERIES
BEST OF THE FORTIES
Archie AMERICANA SERIES
BEST OF THE Fifties
Archie americana series
BEST OF THE SIXTIES
Archie Americana Series
BEST OF THE Seventies
SAVE THE ECOLOGY
Archie AMERICANA SERIES
BEST OF THE EIGHTIES